A Ghost Hunter Novel

Linda Zimmermann

You can order the author's other books
or contact the her at:

www.ghostinvestigator.com

Dead Center
Copyright © Linda Zimmermann
Eagle Press
First Edition 2003
Second Printing 2011

10-digit ISBN: 0-9712326-3-6
13-digit ISBN: 978-0-9712326-3-1

The time has been
That when the brains were out, the man would die
And there an end; but now they rise again…

Shakespeare, *Macbeth, III, 4*

Chapter 1

It was a terrifying sight.

This was the first bathing suit that Grace Hopkins had tried on since giving birth to her 3-month-old son. It was painfully obvious that pregnancy and motherhood had not been kind to her figure or features. Wincing at her own image, Grace wondered how fitting room designers could be so heartless as to install this excruciatingly honest lighting system. The relentless beacons sought out every wrinkle on her sleep-deprived face and deepened the hue of the bags under her eyes. As if by cruel intent, the lights not only highlighted, but also seemed to magnify every ounce of extra fat and every sagging muscle.

Despite being disgusted with the image before her, she couldn't help but raise her left arm to examine the suit's tag once again. It was a good price, and Grand Opening sales would not be repeated. Perhaps if she really began those morning walks she had been planning for so long, and started actually drinking the *Slim Fast* stored in the back of the pantry, in a few weeks her shape might be a little more appealing.

On the other hand, $49.99 was still a lot for a square foot or two of material that might end up on the bottom of her closet and never again see the light of day. Turning away from the mirror, she began to unfasten the top. Unhooked, Grace hesitated. She really did need a bathing suit, and the pool party was just for relatives. Surely her cousins, aunts and uncles, and even her in-laws would understand if she was a little out of shape. Perhaps she was being too hard on herself; was it really as bad as she had imagined? And after all, it wasn't as if she would be out in public in this suit, for all the critical eyes of strangers to see.

Hooking the bathing suit top back in place, Grace closed her eyes and spun around to face the mirror. She would take one more serious, honest look. After a deep breath, Grace opened her eyes and screamed at the top of her lungs.

The image looking back at her from the other side of the glass was that of a ragged, bleeding man. An ugly gash across his forehead had sent blood flowing down his gaunt cheeks. His lips appeared black, as if covered with soot, and his tattered blue clothing was caked with mud and filth. Grace tried to move, but fear paralyzed her limbs. Despite the terror, though, she was also mesmerized by the tortured, haunted look in the man's eyes, and felt a rush of pity—until he began to move toward her.

Like a fog rising from the surface of a lake, the bleeding apparition started to pass through the mirror and into the fitting room. A horrible stench suddenly filled the air— the unmistakable odor of rotting flesh. Gagging, Grace broke free from the hypnotic spell and fumbled for the door handle. The temperature in the tiny room seemed to have dropped by forty degrees and the cold sweat on her hands made her fingers slip twice on the door lock. Finally able to twist the small knob on the handle, she shoved open the door. Grace Hopkins, clad only in the bathing suit, ran screaming through the *Sun 'n Surf* apparel store and right into the middle of the bustling crowds gathered for the *Wegman's Crossing Shopping and Recreation Center's* Grand Opening Day sale.

On the other side of the center (the term "mall" now having become passé), children poured into *Kinder Krossing*. In order to attract more busy mothers, the center's designers had the forethought to include a childcare facility that allowed women to shop in peace. The free service was already testing its limits as staff members scrambled to keep watchful eyes on the toddlers jumping, hanging, and scurrying along the surface of every amusement the facility had to offer.

Kinder Krossing's main attraction was the Ballroom, not of the dancing variety, but a large, darkened room filled with thousands of soft plastic balls. Like so many worms and ants, the little children burrowed beneath the mass of colorful balls, only occasionally popping up to take a breath or to throw one of the round projectiles at another child. As safety was the main concern at *Kinder Krossing*, and indeed throughout the Wegman's Crossing Center, only 25 children were allowed into the Ballroom at a time. This left a long line snaking from the entrance to the Ballroom, through the jungle of oversized, stuffed animals, and back to the Quiet Activity Corner (a place clearly not living up to its name).

Four-year-old Sammy Whitaker had just finished winging three balls at a little girl's head. Diving back under the surface, he began crawling to a more strategic position. It was not uncommon to encounter another little crawler in the sea of balls, but the object that he had just bumped into seemed a lot heavier than the children he had previously encountered. As the room was dimly lit, it was too dark beneath the plastic balls to see, so he pushed his hand forward to try giving the big kid a nudge.

He reached out and made contact with someone, but the person was definitely heavy enough to be an adult. Also, the person's clothing felt cold, damp, and a little bit sticky. Probing further, Sammy's little fingers plunged down to the knuckles into a sickeningly soft mass that felt like raw hamburger meat. A scream caught in his throat, and he suddenly felt as if he couldn't breathe. Tossing his head back to break free of the plastic balls that now seemed to be crushing him, Sammy gasped for air. He saw that there was a man lying just inches away from him—a man whose legs were nothing more than mangled stumps.

Sammy finally let out a high-pitched shriek as he tried to crawl backwards toward the door. The horribly wounded man turned his hollow eyes toward the child, his trembling hand reaching out as if begging for help. Despite Sammy's frantically flailing arms and legs, he found the balls slipping out from under him so that he was actually going down instead of back. As Sammy sunk deeper, balls on the surface started to roll in on top of him. The last thing he remembered was the man's hand about to grab his face.

Several other children also now saw the wounded man in the center of the Ballroom and ran for the door. Then another figure appeared as if from thin air—an older man wearing a bloodstained apron and carrying a small saw. He stood next to the wounded man for a moment, shook his head slowly and sadly several times and then turned his gaze on a group of three sisters huddled in the corner. He beckoned them with the hand that held the saw, and when they did not respond, he began to approach them. As the aproned figure moved, he did not step over the balls; he simply passed *through* them, as he also passed through the figure of the wounded man.

The eldest sister grabbed the hands of the other two girls and dragged them towards the doorway. By this time, all of the children in the Ballroom saw the two terrifying figures. As the kids trampled one another trying to escape, their screams of fear and pain pierced the din throughout the rest of the *Kinder Krossing* facility.

Outside of the Ballroom, everyone suddenly fell silent—but that was the brief calm before the real storm. Confused staff members attempted to respond to the rapidly escalating situation, but were unable to stem the ensuing stampede of panicked children.

As the hysterical children poured out into the central courtyard of Wegman's Center, pandemonium spread as rapidly as the speed of sound. People began shouting that there must be a terrorist attack, or a fire, or a bomb, or a crazed gunman, or a dozen crazed gunmen. Within seconds, thousands of people were running, pushing and shoving each other, and creating tangled masses of humanity at every exit.

This was not the type of Grand Opening excitement for which the management had hoped.

Chapter 2

Sarah Brooks was not a happy camper. A cold drizzle had started to fall and she scrambled to get protective covers over all of the expensive equipment. A stiff wind was already blowing across the isolated hilltop cemetery and the rain just made it all the more miserable on that dark, moonless Sunday night.

"I must be out of my friggin' mind," Sarah moaned to her youthful assistant, James Patrick O'Reilly. "And what does your sainted Irish mother think of her only son spending his evening on a ghost hunt?"

"I told her I was attending a Catholic study group and then spending the night with a friend," Jimmy said with a guilty shrug, but then brightened. "Which isn't really a lie! After all, this is a Catholic cemetery, and we are conducting a study, of sorts."

"I'm the wrong person to hear your confession, Jimmy" Sarah chuckled. "Well, it's almost 3am, the time this alleged ghost is supposed to make his appearance, so let's double check all the systems."

Spread out around them on various tripods and tables were an interesting array of electronic gadgets. There were audio recorders, electromagnetic field detectors, infrared non-contact thermometers, a Geiger counter, several cameras, and digital camcorders equipped with technology that could capture infrared images in total darkness. There was also a ragged little Teddy bear, named Mitty, standing on the table in case things got a little too intense. All Sarah had to do was take one look at those orange glass eyes and smiling snout and she was able to find the courage to face just about any situation. Teddy bears were not a typical piece of equipment for a ghost hunter, but Sarah Brooks was not by any means a typical ghost hunter.

"I hate this!" she declared rubbing her hands together and stamping her feet to keep warm. "I should be home in bed with a good book, or better yet a good man, instead of traipsing around in a cemetery in the middle of the night."

Even in the dim light, Sarah could see Jimmy's pale skin blush red. She hadn't meant to embarrass the impressionable, and surprisingly innocent 17-year-old, but she was frustrated with the direction life had taken her. Born in Connecticut, but raised in the suburbs of Boston, her father was an engineer, and her mother a biologist, so she had always naturally expected that she would follow a scientific career.

She did, in fact, receive a degree in chemistry and worked for several research facilities in the Boston area. However, after a decade of irritating bosses, project budget cuts, and a couple of layoffs, she decided her life was going nowhere fast. About this time, a visit to local museum had inspired Sarah to write an article on New England's inventions and advances in technology during the 19th century. Not even expecting to get a response, she nonetheless mailed it to a regional magazine, and to her surprise and delight, they published it.

For her efforts, Sarah received the whopping sum of $25, but it was like a chocolate bar to a starving man. Seeing her name in print, even in a small magazine like this, brought more satisfaction than all of her years among the test tubes. She quickly arrived at the conclusion that this was why Sarah Brooks had been placed on the planet, to write, to enlighten, and to entertain the masses. Although, granted, a circulation of six hundred was not exactly a mass, everyone had to start somewhere.

Having inherited the legendary New England trait of frugality, Sarah had saved a considerable amount of money from her years in the laboratory. She had also been lucky enough to make some wise investments in the market—and get out before it tanked—so she was in a position to actually pursue this new dream of writing on a full-time basis. Of course, the paychecks would have to be a bit higher than $25, but she could live comfortably for at least two years before reaching the desperate stage.

There was some limited success in the first year, but money flowed out a lot faster than it came in. Her parents offered to help by inviting her back to her old room in their house, but as much as she loved them both, that option would only be considered in her *very* desperate stage.

After eighteen months, Sarah began thinking that the world was not yet ready to handsomely reward someone who wrote and lectured on the history of technology, as it related to Industrial Age factories, through the Post-Internet era offices, in suburban Boston. Not that she wasn't an informed and engaging speaker, and a competent writer; it was just that the editors interested in her articles did not work for lucrative publications. The libraries, schools and historical societies that invited her to speak often could not offer more than a paltry sum of money or a "token of their appreciation" put together by the grateful staff. Sarah had to face facts—fruit baskets were not going to pay the rent.

As the prospect of moving back to her parents' house at the age of 35 began to look like an eventual necessity on her present lack-of-career path, an amazing thing happened.

It actually was a dark and stormy night. Sarah had been invited to lecture to the local Duxbridge Historical Society, which met on the second Tuesday of every month, as it had for the past one hundred and three years. While the society's holdings amounted to a hefty seven-figures, they had only offered her an honorarium of $50—and a basket of preserves left over from their holiday fundraiser. Sarah accepted, still hoping that somehow the exposure would lead to something better. And at least it wasn't fresh fruit in the basket this time.

Her lecture dealt with the history of the numerous patents held by the Wellman family who had come from England in the early 1800s, and made their fortune in a series of mills they built along the Duxbridge River. The society had received special permission to hold this month's meeting in one of the original mills, which had been converted into suites of offices. The landlord was on the Board of Trustees and he felt it would enhance his position in the society by hosting the event.

Folding chairs were set up in the spacious central hall which had an enormous 19th century cast iron drive wheel mounted against the original brick wall that remained exposed between sections of modern sheetrock. The hall was three stories high, and an interesting use of recessed lighting gave the place an eerie, cavernous appearance. The combination of the building and the weather put Sarah in an unusual mood that night.

As a footnote in the booklet she had prepared for the lecture (she had found that having some sort of printed material to sell at her lectures usually brought in more money than the honorariums), she had mentioned a strange event that had occurred in the mill in the 1860s. When she was about half way through her slideshow of gears and flywheels, she paused to mention that footnote.

"If you ladies and gentlemen will indulge me for a few minutes," Sarah said as she stepped away from the podium and switched the projector from Light to Fan, plunging the hall into almost total darkness, "I would like to tell you an interesting legend I came across in my research."

There was a moment of confused whispering in the audience, but they all fell silent a few seconds later.

"This legend involves jealousy, betrayal, murder…and a ghost," Sarah said with dramatic hesitation, wondering if she was about to sabotage what little career she had on the lecture circuit. However, the sudden hush gave her the courage to continue. "It was April of 1861, and two brothers who worked in this mill got swept up in the patriotic fervor and joined the local regiment of volunteers. Andrew and John Wilkerson had shared everything growing up, although Andrew didn't realize that this sharing extended to his fiancée, Clara."

Sarah heard at least three different "oohs" and one "ah" of anticipation in the crowd. She also felt an unusual exhilaration she had never before experienced while lecturing and continued the story with great enthusiasm.

"John had secretly been jealous of his older brother's success. In 1860, Andrew had risen to shift foreman and soon began courting the beautiful and beguiling daughter of the Wellman family's lawyer. While Andrew was not in the same social strata, everyone recognized that his talent would carry him far and Clara's father had no objections to the match.

"But young John was not without his talents, as well. Clara did not shy away from his obvious attentions and he secretly charmed his way into at least a part of his brother's fiancée's duplicitous heart. Understanding that the two brothers would most likely go off to the war that had seemed inevitable for many months, Clara played both sides of the fraternal fence. She would sort things out when, and if, they both returned.

"In July of 1861, the young and inexperienced new soldiers found themselves marching toward a railroad junction in Virginia called Manassas. Brimming with confidence at the Union Army's perceived invincibility, the brothers nonetheless declared before the members of their company that if one of them were struck a mortal blow, the other would avenge his brother's death. Then they added if that wasn't possible, the dead brother would return from the grave and seek his own revenge against the man who fired the fatal shot. Such bold and blustering talk was common that day in the hours before soldiers formed into lines to face the enemy.

"But early morning stout courage melted into burning fear as the heat of battle exploded upon them."

Sarah had no idea where the words she was speaking were coming from. She had always lectured in a completely professional manner. While she was never stuffy, she rarely embellished or deviated from the facts. Now she felt like a kid at a campfire—and loved it.

"The Wilkerson brothers fought side by side in the opening volleys, but as confusion swept through the Union lines, they became separated. John fell back to the rear, but Andrew stood his ground. Word of his heroism spread through the besieged regiment and emboldened by his acts, they began to regroup and rally.

"John's relative cowardice was accentuated by his brother's valor, and as he cautiously moved forward to the reforming lines, he saw Andrew standing at the crest of a rise, waving the men onward with total disregard to the shell and shot that was pouring in from the onrushing Confederate forces.

"While others felt a surge of courage and patriotism at the site of Andrew Wilkerson, something snapped inside John."

At this point Sarah paused, turned her back to the audience and walked over to the drive wheel to the left of the rows of chairs. Placing a hand firmly on the wheel so the sound of the contact echoed throughout the hall, she turned around to face the crowd that had instantly shifted in their seats like a school of fish.

"John's heart suddenly grew cold and hard. A lifetime of fraternal love was crushed beneath the towering jealously and resentment that now overwhelmed him. Calmly and methodically he reloaded his musket. He pushed the powder and ball forcefully and steadily down into the barrel, then slowly and deliberately seated the percussion cap. Lifting the weapon to his shoulder, he took careful aim, held his breath, and squeezed the trigger.

"Andrew Wilkerson was dead before he hit the ground. The bullet had pierced the heart that only a second before had been beating so strongly in defense of his country, the heart that had been beating with love for his fiancée…and for his only brother.

"A soldier standing a few feet behind John watched everything in stunned silence, until a rebel bullet tore through his thigh. A few others thought that the shot that felled the heroic Wilkerson had come from their own ranks, but in the confusion no one could be sure. And no one wanted to believe such a heinous act could be committed.

"The wounded soldier who had witnessed the fratricide was sent home to Duxbridge, and whispers of murder spread throughout the town. When an unsuspecting John Wilkerson arrived in town a few months later after his enlistment was up, he thought he would receive a warm homecoming. But he was shunned at the mill, and publicly snubbed by Clara. Guilt began to eat away at him. Residents of his boarding house said they could often hear him screaming in his sleep.

"Then workers began talking of a dark, shadowy figure being seen in the mill. Some claimed the figure wore a blue uniform, others said the apparition held a hand over his heart, and a few claimed to hear the name 'Manassas' being shouted over the roar of the mill's machinery.

"The people in the town came to believe that Andrew's promise was being fulfilled, that his restless spirit had returned to exact retribution from the man who had fired the piece of hot lead that had torn through his chest. John began to believe it, too, and each day that he showed up at the mill his features were a bit more haggard and his eyes darted from side to side more frequently."

Sarah paused again, and then slowly moved her hand from the wheel to the wall behind her. A clap of thunder and bright bolt of lightning punctuated her action.

"One evening, as a storm lashed against these brick walls of the Wellman mill, a dozen workers looked up to see John Wilkerson staggering backwards on the third floor balcony. They heard him shouting something about forgiveness. Some say he was begging with clasped hands. Lightning revealed another figure on that balcony—the figure of Andrew Wilkerson pointing a bloody and accusatory finger at his treacherous brother.

"John continued to back away from the ghostly figure that drifted relentlessly toward him, until he stumbled and fell over the railing. He was caught up in the machinery that stood where you are all sitting now, and his screams were quickly silenced by the grinding teeth of the massive gears."

A collective shudder went through the audience and Sarah knew that she had them hook, line and sinker.

"They say the spirit of Andrew Wilkerson finally found peace that day. But until that machinery was dismantled and carted away thirty years later, workers claimed to see a figure falling from the balcony on stormy nights, and reported hearing screams rising over the din of the grinding gears on each anniversary of the accident."

Sarah Brooks quietly walked back to her projector and turned on the light. She resumed her discussion on the various Wellman patents, but her thoughts were elsewhere. It didn't matter, however, because the thoughts of the audience were also elsewhere, specifically on a stormy night almost one hundred and forty years earlier. Instead of looking at the slides, Sarah could see the eyes of her audience moving from the third floor balcony, to the drive wheel and brick wall, then to the floor beneath their feet.

At the end of her lecture, there was the most enthusiastic applause she had ever received. She sold every one of the twenty photocopied booklets she had brought, with orders placed for fifteen more. Even though they contained twenty-eight pages of carefully researched technical information, Sarah knew she sold them all because of the one-paragraph footnote on the Wilkerson ghosts legend.

Opportunity didn't need to knock twice on Sarah Brooks' door.

"Did you hear that?" Jimmy asked, going pale again all at once. "It sounded like a knocking sound coming from his crypt."

The crypt in question was why they were out in the middle of the night in a cemetery. It was the final resting place of a man believed to have tortured and murdered twenty-three women and two men in the late 1920s and early 30s. He had been a wealthy man, a judge who was supposed to have been a pillar of society—until renovations were being made to his house after his death. Implements of torture and decomposed corpses were found in secret rooms, under floorboards and between walls. The evidence showed conclusively that the judge had been an unspeakable monster, and his character had apparently not been improved by his death.

In the seven decades since the judge had been placed in his crypt, there had been over one hundred and fifty reports of people claiming to have been "attacked" by a dark, menacing figure in the cemetery. While most were just scared by the apparition, there were at least twenty cases where an actual physical illness immediately followed these attacks—illnesses ranging from a day or two of nausea and dizziness, to several months of serious personality disorders.

About ninety percent of these reports were from women. It seemed as if the judge was still up to his old tricks, and Sarah had no intentions of actually coming into contact with his malevolent spirit.

Sarah checked the screens of the four laptops that were receiving data from the instruments placed around the cemetery. The stacked lines of a meter on one of the screens rose from green to yellow to red, indicating that loud sounds were indeed emanating from the judge's crypt, which was about fifty yards away. The lines rose and fell several times, also indicating that the pounding was intermittent.

"Unless there are tree limbs knocking together in the wind, we have one restless spirit over there," Sarah said with practiced professionalism she hoped masked her underlying fear. As many times as she did this, she could never get used to encountering the unknown. Never. "Let's just take a look…"

Flipping down the night vision goggles in front of her eyes, she wiggled the head straps into a more comfortable position and turned on the device that would let her see several hundred yards in total darkness. It was a pricey piece of equipment, state of the art, in fact, but Sarah didn't pay a penny for it. The company had given it to her in return for Sarah's endorsement. Neat gadgets for free were strong enticements to put up with midnight cemetery campaigns.

"Okay, I see the crypt area. There's no…trees…no…debris…no…Shit!"

Sarah froze, which was the only thing that kept her from running.

"What?! What is it? Do you see something? What do you see?" Jimmy whispered loudly, trying to monitor the screens as he rocked back and forth with nervous energy.

Sarah peered out from under her goggles for a second to see the smiling stitched face of Mitty, took a deep breath and then continued in what appeared to be a calm and scientific manner.

"The crypt door is wide open," she said as she adjusted some dials on the goggles. "I can see right inside, I can see the coffin."

As part of their normal procedure, they did a walk-through of the cemetery before nightfall to familiarize themselves with the layout, and to check for things like loose crypt doors that might blow open in the wind. The cemetery had been locked up tight, from top to bottom. There was no earthly reason for that crypt door to be open now.

"Jimmy, get all the cameras aimed in that direction. I think we just might-"

"Might what? Now what do you see?" Jimmy said with rising excitement, his numbed fingers fumbling with the tripod knobs.

"Remain calm, Jim. There's some kind of dark cloud flowing out of the crypt, roughly six…make that seven feet high…and about three feet wide, can you see it?" Sarah asked, stuffing her hands in her pockets so Jimmy wouldn't see them trembling.

"I've got something on camera one," he replied in a voice an octave higher than normal. "It's not clear in the rain, but I've got something."

"Okay…okay that's great. Of course, it could just be fog, and if it doesn't move or set off any of the motion detectors that's probably all it is."

The instant she finished speaking, a motion detector ten feet from the crypt started howling. At the same time, a red light on one of the display screens started blinking, accompanied by an innocent sounding beep. Sarah knew there wasn't anything innocent about it.

"Intruder alert!" Jimmy shouted and then laughed nervously. "Hey, you know I've always wanted to say that!"

"Jimmy, I'm afraid that *we* might be the intruders here. Let's just hope that the judge doesn't see it that way."

Sarah kept a steady eye on the black cloud, as it seemed to solidify and drift slowly through the headstones and grave markers. The shape of a torso and arms became clearer after it had moved ten yards closer. Jimmy ran back and forth between the video cameras, trying to capture the phantom image in both infrared and regular light. Sarah reached for a control box on the table next to her right hip, and without looking down pushed a lever that turned a curved, six-foot bank of cameras with telephoto and wide angle lenses toward their ominous visitor. Shielding the goggles with her free hand, she shouted to Jimmy.

"On five, four, three, two, one!"

Her thumb came down on a lighted red button on the side of the control box and the cameras flashed in unison, cutting through the darkness and casting disturbing shadows before them. A high-pitched hum signaled that the powerful flash units were recharging and in three seconds the red light turned back on and Sarah gave another five-count. Again, the cameras flashed into action.

Normally, all of this technology surrounding her would have been a comfort, but now it began to have the opposite effect. Another motion detector alarm went off, and a few seconds later, yet another. If Sarah had been watching the screen, she would have seen a series of red lights blinking a path directly from the crypt to their location. But she didn't need to see the string of warning beacons that indicated something big was moving toward her, because she was seeing it with her own eyes.

The dark figure solidified even more, and at thirty yards a head started to take shape. There seemed to be some features like eyes and a mouth, but the black mist continued to swirl and churn, distorting anything that could otherwise be called a face. Sarah's heart was now beating like a jackhammer and her toes and fingertips tingled from lack of oxygen. Her breathing was short and labored, but still she held her ground, snapping pictures every few seconds.

The motion alarm at twenty-five yards began screeching its warning, then the one at twenty yards went off. Temperature readings dropped and electromagnetic fields fluctuated wildly. At fifteen yards the last motion detector signaled that its perimeter had been breached.

"Jimmy, I need you to do something," Sarah said as calmly as possible. "Leave the camcorders running, grab Mitty, and run like hell back to the van."

"But I can't leave you-"

"Do it now, goddamn it! Go, RUN!"

Jimmy turned abruptly and knocked over the table of equipment upon which Mitty was standing. He managed to snatch the bear by the ear before it fell into the mud. The other equipment wasn't so lucky. Without another moment of hesitation, he sprinted for the van, twice hurtling over headstones, taking the most direct path possible.

Sarah still refused to budge as the pulsating figure floated straight toward her, passing through the sculpture of an angel and several headstones as if they didn't exist. Tenuous arms lifted above the twisting features of its head, as it was less than six yards away. Holding her breath and silently counting to five, she pushed the button one last time. The camera flashes pierced the night, but failed to penetrate the dark figure, which now was so solid, it cast its own shadow.

The apparition paused for an instant after the flash and then underwent further transformation until it had a completely solid, completely fierce expression.

"Oh…shit…" Sarah gasped as she realized that she had just seriously pissed off one of the nastiest spirits she had ever encountered.

With alarms wailing and warning lights and meters flashing in an impressive and expensive display of technology, Sarah Brooks, reluctant ghost hunter, abandoned it all and ran for the van as if her life depended upon it, which it very well could have, given the circumstances. The angry figure lunged toward her, but as it paused to wreak a little havoc with the electronics, she was already diving into the open side door of the van.

"Go, Jimmy! Get us the hell out of here!" Sarah shouted between heaving breaths.

The van's tires spun for a few seconds in the loose graveyard dirt. Finally catching hard ground, the van lurched forward. The written test Jimmy had taken for his learner's permit did not have any questions dealing with driving seventy miles per hour through rural cemeteries while being pursued by evil apparitions, but he figured turn signals weren't required.

Racing through the iron gates marking the boundary between the world of the living and the dead, he slammed on the brakes and the van spun 180 degrees to a screeching halt.

"Sarah? Are you okay?" he asked sheepishly.

"I don't know what was more terrifying," she replied, flat on her back, staring at the ceiling through the night vision goggles, "that demon from the underworld, or your driving!"

"Sorry, Sarah, but you said to get out fast," Jimmy said a little crestfallen.

Hoisting herself up to a sitting position, and flipping back the goggles, she extended a hand to her young assistant and patted him on the shoulder.

"You did good, Jimmy. Real good," she said as his features brightened considerably in the glow of dashboard lights. "If I ever decide to rob a bank, run a roadblock, or transport illegal aliens across the border, you'll be my man. Now why don't you get some sleep. It's only a couple of hours until dawn. We'll go back then and retrieve the equipment. What's left of it."

Jimmy crawled over the console between the front seats, grabbed a blanket and after a minute or two of fidgeting, was sound asleep. Sarah was amazed that after all that had just happened, the boy was able to sleep like a newborn babe.

That was one of the things she liked about her young apprentice, his ability to disengage from the stress and strains of the world. In the beginning, his relative calm under pressure helped convince her to let him tag along on a few investigations, and then his technical skill and enthusiasm elevated him to full-fledged Junior Ghost Hunter.

Sarah unfolded the other blanket and crawled into the driver's seat, but there was no way she would be able to sleep. Her mind raced with images of the terrifying ghost she had just encountered. Although she had seen it with her own goggles, as well as witnessed and filmed dozens of other apparitions in the past three years, her scientific mind still couldn't quite come to grips with what just happened. While the instruments and photos didn't lie, it wasn't easy to deal with the realization that spirits of the dead came back to haunt the living.

She also couldn't believe that people now stopped her on the street and asked if she was the "Ghost Lady." After years of trying to make ends meet by writing serious nonfiction, she was now raking in the cash on her ghost books, ghost videos and speaking engagements for which she could literally name her own price. The dead were not how she had intended to make a living.

For that matter, shivering in a van with a sleeping virgin teenager in the middle of the night at a cemetery was not how she had envisioned the state of her relations with the opposite sex as she approached the big four-o. And for all the financial success and fan appreciation, she felt embarrassed by the pseudo-scientific labels that had been placed upon her. And she swore that she would throttle the next person who called her a "Ghostbuster."

As the first rays of sunlight finally peeked over the horizon, she turned the key in the ignition, rubbed her bleary eyes and tried to pat some warmth through her cold, damp clothing.

Sarah Brooks was not a happy camper.

Chapter 3

Jets of hot water eased the cords of tension in her neck and back. Sinking a little deeper into the Jacuzzi, Sarah felt the stress of the night swirl away in a spiral of tiny bubbles. Thoughts of cemeteries and deceased murderers drifted away as sleep quickly and blissfully became inevitable. With barely opened eyes, Sarah used her last conscious energy to pull herself out of the hot tub and shuffle over to her bed. Not even bothering to towel off the water, she slipped between cozy flannel sheets and abandoned herself, naked body and soul, to unconsciousness.

Just as she sank into a deep, peaceful sleep, the telephone rang. The first two rings had no effect. The third brought about a groggy awareness of something like a distant motion detector alarm going off. At the fourth, she finally realized it was the phone, but she was too tired to care. The answering machine mercifully took over at that point, and though Sarah Brooks began to leave the world once again, she did hear a few words being left on her machine by the female caller. However, in the misty space between waking and sleeping states, words like "immediately," "urgent" and "investigation" were of little importance. And the word "Wegman" made no sense at all…

"Well, did you get a hold of this…this ghostbuster?" the paunchy man in the rumpled suit barked at his assistant. "And when are they going to fix this damn air conditioning?"

"Ms. Brooks is a paranormal investigator, and I left a message for her at 8:15 this morning," the assistant replied, her crisp linen pants suit standing out as a symbol of her efficiency. "I impressed upon her the urgency of the situation and asked that she call back as soon as possible. And they did fix the air conditioning, Mr. Fink, two days ago."

Lela Reynolds delivered her words with the slight corkscrewing of her features that always accompanied a conversation with her boss. She was not even aware that she did it, and she was equally unaware of how she subtly stressed the name "Fink" when she addressed him. But then, everyone who knew the Wegman's Center general manager pronounced his name with varying degrees of relish—especially when he was out of earshot, when the name of Fink was spoken as if it was a parasitic infestation in one's private parts.

"Well, Mrs. Reynolds, if they already fixed the air conditioning, how come I'm still sweating?"

Several reasons immediately came to mind, such as the fact that her boss could easily stand to lose fifty pounds, his obvious toupee was keeping in all the heat on the top of his large head, and he probably hadn't used an antiperspirant in several days. However, it wasn't a wise move to insult the general manager, who also happened, not coincidentally, to be the nephew of the owner. Her pay was good, and until the opening day fiasco, it looked like steady employment to help put her two kids through college. Once again, she would just have to keep quiet. For now, at least.

"I'll check with maintenance," she simply replied, her short response not giving her features time for the full twist.

"You do that. And call this ghostbuster dame back every hour on the hour until you get her. My ass is on the chopping block in the village square and I need things to happen fast!"

Lela couldn't decide which was more disturbing—the fact that Fink still used the term "dame," or the image of his butt being on public display, but she nodded and dutifully called maintenance.

The Wegman's Crossing Grand Opening Day hadn't actually been a total disaster. In fact, it might just have been the opportunity for which the owners and management had been looking. The incidents in the Ballroom and the fitting room (as well as a couple of reports of shadowy figures in the food court and several cases of malfunctions, such as the main bank of escalators refusing to operate) were blamed on the various Civil War preservation groups that had been protesting the construction of the center from the day the project began.

The center's substantial legal staff released a statement claiming that these fanatical organizations perpetrated these acts of sabotage, as well as the cruel hoaxes that frightened and injured children, publicly embarrassed the wife of a local politician, and provoked a panic in which dozens more were hurt. The statement provided enough finger pointing and diverting of responsibility that the lawsuits brought against the center by the panicked shoppers, Mrs. Hopkins, and the parents of the injured children, would probably be tied up in court until the toddlers were old enough to vote. The preservation groups all steadfastly denied any involvement.

The issues that had brought about the protests against the shopping center development were all too common in northern Virginia, as well as other parts of the country—an historic site was being obliterated in the name of progress. The Civil War groups insisted that the building site was the location of a particularly fierce and tragic battle (even by Civil War standards) in 1864, during the period when Grant was clashing with Lee from the Wilderness, to Spotsylvania, to Cold Harbor, and finally to the outskirts of Petersburg. While there was incontrovertible evidence of the battle itself, the problem was that no one knew exactly when or where the battle had taken place, and the few structures that had comprised the unofficial town of Wegman's Crossing had been covered by time and the dense Virginia forest.

Several counties claimed to be the site of the battle, and organizations representing descendents of both Confederate and Union veterans said that it had been their ancestors who had been victorious. However, as no actual participant in the battle ever filed an official report, and only scraps of information were available in soldiers' letters and diaries, the mysteries and controversies surrounding the battle literally remained buried for almost 140 years. Over the generations, the soldiers involved, and even the town itself, took on an almost mythical stature, and the discovery of Wegman's Crossing was something of a Holy Grail to Civil War historians.

One local historian believed he had found that Holy Grail right where the backhoes began breaking ground in the fall of 2000. Carl Henkel, the great-great grandson of a Union veteran, but also a third-generation Virginian, believed that he had ancestors who fought on both sides of the Battle of Wegman's Crossing, and he devoted many years to trying to pinpoint the site. He had finally gathered enough evidence to warrant a full-scale archaeological dig when the heavy equipment from the Octagon Corporation rolled into town. Legal battles ensued, but Octagon had far too much money and too many lawyers to be deterred.

The main groups that had valiantly opposed the project were the Union Preservation Association and the Sons of Dixie Heritage Alliance. In the frequent verbal confrontations that occurred over the two years of construction, Mr. Fink publicly referred to these groups as the Useless Protestation Association and the SODHA jerks. Such tactics are not generally considered to be good public relations, but Fink knew he could afford the arrogant stance for two reasons. First, his uncle had more money than any protest group could dream of, and secondly, the public was basically apathetic to the cause of historic preservation. If it came down to a choice between some crumbled foundations and a few historic markers, or 186 stores and restaurants, an indoor amusement park and an IMAX theater, the public's decision would be a no-brainer. In fact, the last thing Fink and Octagon needed was anyone in the public with any brains.

When Lela Reynolds called Sarah Brooks for the fourth time that Monday morning, the less than three hours of sleep Sarah had gotten gave her enough energy to answer the phone, but also made her irritable enough to be uncharacteristically abrupt.

"Yeah," Sarah mumbled into the phone.

"Ms. Brooks?"

"Yeah. What do you want?"

"My name is Lela Reynolds and I'm calling on behalf of the Wegman's Crossing Shopping and Recreation Center in Cullum Tavern, Virginia. We wondered if you might be able to pay us a visit sometime soon," Lela said, treading a fine line between professionalism and bubbliness, realizing full well that she had awakened Sarah Brooks and had probably been annoying her all morning with her calls.

Sarah rubbed hers eyes, stretched and yawned, as she thought for a moment. Hearing the name Wegman for a second time did ring a bell.

"Aren't you the guys who plowed over a Civil War battlefield and then had the nerve to name a shopping mall after it?"

This time it was Lela's turn to hesitate before replying.

"There were some unsubstantiated claims," she said diplomatically. "But allow me to get to the reason for my call. You see, the general manager, Martin Fink, would like you to come down and-"

"Wait a minute…" Sarah interrupted, as her mind gained more clarity. "How did you get this number? This is my private line. All requests for appearances should be emailed to me through my website."

"Oh, well, you see the center is owned by the Octagon Corporation, which is affiliated with the Showcase Publishing house, so we contacted your publisher, Bernie Ostrom, who gave us this number," Lela replied uncomfortably, still dancing the fine line.

Mental note, Sarah thought. *Send Bernie a rotten fruit basket.*

"Look, Delilah, I was up all night in a cold, wet cemetery being chased by a dead judge, and I'm not in the mood to discuss putting on a show for your shoppers."

"It's Lela, and we don't want-"

Click.

Sarah slammed down the phone and fumbled for the silencing switch.

Mental note. Next time I see Bernie, kick his ass.

When the doorbell rang at 4:30pm, Sarah was just regaining consciousness. Throwing on her favorite fuzzy robe and running her fingers through her hair as a crude comb, she finally made it to the door just as the visitor was switching from the doorbell to knocking. Peering through the peephole, she saw the smiling, eager face of her young apprentice.

"Hey, Jimmy, how's it going?" she said in a froggy voice as she leaned against the open door. "And how come you don't look anything like I feel?"

"I got two whole hours of sleep before school," he replied cheerfully, as he carried in two heavy equipment cases and a bag of photos.

"Two whole hours before school, no wonder you're fine now," Sarah said with obvious sarcasm, which nonetheless escaped him, as she headed into the kitchen to make some instant coffee. "So, what's the damage?"

Jimmy placed the cases in the middle of the living room rug and popped them open, taking a quick visual inventory.

"The stuff I knocked into the mud," he began with obvious embarrassment, "was just dirty. I cleaned everything up and it's fine."

"How about all of the laptops the judge was playing with?" Sarah shouted over the sound of water filling the kettle.

"Well," Jimmy shouted back more confidently. "All four of them had their batteries drained, but as far as I can tell the software and data are intact. The only casualty seems to be your homemade ion detector. It looks like he blew its mind."

Sarah liked designing and building her own gadgets, and the news of the D.O.A. ion detector did not upset her. It just meant she would have to build a better one.

"Okay, I guess it could have been a lot worse. Give me a minute to get dressed and then we'll review the video and photos."

For the next few hours, Sarah and Jimmy went over all of the evidence they had collected. They had successfully captured images of a dark shape moving across the cemetery, charted temperature variations and electromagnetic field fluctuations, recorded pounding noises from the crypt and sounds like whispered words, and traced the path of something with enough substance to set off, in order, motion detectors leading directly from the judge's crypt to their position.

To the believers, this would be astounding evidence and would solidify her position as one of the premier paranormal investigators in the field. To the skeptics, however, this "evidence" would still be nothing more than static, fog, condensation, wind, pollen, insects, shadows, reflections, faulty equipment, flawed procedures, and absolute nonsense that's nothing short of pure fraud.

It was the same old story, and to be honest, Sarah was sick of it. Just once, she wished for a case that could produce conclusive, undeniable evidence—something on such a large scale that even the most hardened skeptic would become a passionate believer.

Mental note. Keep dreaming.

Chapter 4

While deliveries were nothing new, they were usually left in a box on the front porch. Today, however, the deliveryman, Ted, rang the doorbell.

"Good morning, FedExTed! What's so important?" Sarah asked cheerfully, a good night's sleep having restored her easy-going nature. "Is the government after me?"

"Let's see," Ted replied with a big smile, running his scanner over the large envelope. "Nope, looks like it's from some shopping center."

"Don't tell me, Wegman's Crossing, right?" she said, dramatically placing one hand over her eyes as she took the envelope in the other.

"That's it. Maybe they want you to cut a ribbon or something."

"I almost cut my phone line yesterday because of them. Oh well, I guess it's better than being ignored. And by the way," Sarah added as she started to close the door, "Check my website tonight. I'll have some of the new investigation stuff posted."

"Oh cool, I will! You have a nice day, now, and don't let the spooks get you."

The first year that Sarah was investigating and writing about ghosts, she tried to keep a low profile in her small town, which was about thirty miles from Boston. However, being the local ghost hunter was not an easy secret to keep, and she found that most people were very enthusiastic and supportive of her work. Of course, the routine at the gas station where everyone always shouted, "who you gonna call," every time she pulled in for a fill-up was getting rather old, but as she told FedExTed, it was better than living in obscurity, scrambling to make ends meet.

Settling down in her overstuffed recliner with massaging action, (the purchase of which she felt was the first step toward acknowledging the approach of middle age), she tore the strip from along the top of the envelope and dumped the contents into her lap. There were several color brochures highlighting the Wegman's Crossing Shopping and Recreation Center's features.

Propaganda, she thought.

Pushing them aside, she picked up the single piece of fine stationery with the letterhead of the general manager. Skimming through the paragraphs, she looked for the date they wanted her to make an appearance or do a book signing. What caught her eye was something completely different, and she went back to the beginning to read every word.

Dear Ms. Brooks,

We are sorry to have disturbed you at home yesterday, but we were eager to contact you. I understand that you have heard of our fabulous new center, which celebrated its grand opening last week.

What you probably have not heard, as we are endeavoring to keep it quiet for obvious reasons, is that there were some unusual disruptions both during construction and at our recent grand opening festivities. While we at Wegman's Crossing are certain that these disruptions were perpetrated by several unscrupulous groups that have been staging protests from the onset of this project, there are disquieting rumors of a paranormal nature—rumors we are anxious to stop.

Therefore, we request that you conduct an investigation as soon as possible to prove that nothing whatsoever is going on here. We will place all of our resources at your disposal. For your valuable assistance in demonstrating that any claims of paranormal activity are baseless, we will pay any standard fees and travel expenses. In addition, we will gladly compensate you for any inconvenience such short notice has caused. We have taken the liberty to arrange for a limousine to pick you up and bring you to the airport at 7 o'clock tomorrow morning, and any equipment you might need will be flown down with you. A token of our good faith is enclosed.

Please contact my office upon receipt of this letter.

Respectfully yours,
Martin F. Fink
General Manager

The "token of good faith" stapled to the back of the letter was a check with enough zeros to catch her attention. Considering that Sarah never charged for an investigation (she only asked that she be able to publish any results), this token was an enticing inducement. Then there was the fact that the letter had said a lot without actually saying anything, which was even more intriguing. The clincher, however, was how insistent Fink had been about "nothing whatsoever" going on, and that he was willing to shell out big bucks in order for her to *not* find anything.

After going through the letter again, carefully reading all of the information between the lines this time, Sarah felt a little tingle of excitement spread throughout her body. This felt big, *very* big. Her heart beat a bit faster, her pupils dilated and her mind raced. This was the thrill of the hunt. The ultimate chase would be afoot. Could this finally be the case for which she had been hoping—the moment in history where the living actually grasped the dead? Or, she suddenly thought, would it be the other way around?

Sarah's little flight of imagination stopped there with that disquieting possibility, and she scolded herself for breaking one of her main rules—don't expect anything, and you'll never be disappointed. If she entered this investigation with visions of grandeur, she was just begging for trouble. After all, it may be just what Fink had said, a prank. She had certainly uncovered plenty of those in the last few years. What she needed to focus on right now, was gathering as much background information as she could on Wegman's Crossing, and she would once again rely on what had proved to be her best resource—her fans.

Code Red, she typed into the highlighted "ALERT" box on her website.

I need information about a new shopping center in Cullum Tavern, Virginia—Wegman's Crossing Shopping and Recreation Center.

What happened on the land before it was built? What happened during construction? What happened during the grand opening last week? Who are the main players and what are the controversies?

I need this info ASAP. I want to hear it all, from documented sources to rumor and innuendo.

Thanks to everyone in advance, and I know I can count on you!

With a few clicks of the mouse the alert was posted, which she knew meant that computers around the world were now beeping. Sarah always felt it was something like turning on the Bat Light over Gotham City, because devout members of the "Shadow Patrol," as her fans had dubbed themselves, were on constant alert, just waiting for her signal so their fingers could spring into action.

However, the Shadow Patrol did far more than just track down information on the Internet. Once, when Sarah was updating the "Current Investigations" section of her website, she wrote about a case involving sightings of a ghost ship off the coast of Rhode Island, and of a man in a brass-buttoned uniform who had been seen pacing along the beach, tearing at his red hair and crying out in some foreign language. Sarah found that a ship had indeed gone down in the area in 1856, and the captain had come from Finland. As she always tried to get as much history as she could behind the events and people potentially involved in a haunting, she mentioned that it would be nice to know more about the ill-fated captain.

A few days later as she was checking her email, she came across a priority message entitled, "Captain Juutanainen Portrait and Family History." Opening the message, she was stunned to discover that a member of the Shadow Patrol, who lived in England, had flown to Finland, tracked down the sea captain's descendants and found that they had a small oil on canvas portrait of their ancestor. He then photographed the portrait, copied down all of the available family history (including translating and transcribing some of the captain's personal letters), and then sent it all to Sarah from his laptop as he sat in the airport waiting to fly back to England.

More remarkable than the decidedly fanatical dedication of this Shadow Patrol member, was the portrait of the flame-haired Captain Juutanainen, who sat for the artist while wearing his captain's uniform with two rows of gleaming brass buttons. The prophetic last words he wrote were also remarkable. In a letter to his wife, written a few weeks before he went down with his ship off the coast of Rhode Island during a fierce nor'easter, he apologized several times for leaving her while she was pregnant. He explained that the profits he could reap from this venture far outweighed the risks of an Atlantic crossing at that time of year. He promised it would be his last voyage, and wrote that if anything did happen to him, he would never forgive himself, and never rest in peace.

This was the kind of information that could make or break a case—the kind of information that Sarah hoped would soon be flooding her email Inbox. It was plain to see from Martin Fink's letter that he would not be forthcoming with information, and the more *she* knew, the less *he* could get away with.

Sarah spent a couple of hours putting essential gear into special travel cases. Before actually packing any equipment, however, she had to go through a "preflight" check—power sources were replaced or recharged, equipment was tested, and instruments were calibrated. As electronic equipment was prone to erratic behavior (or complete failure) at haunted sites, she needed to make sure that if anything dead was causing problems, it wasn't the batteries.

By mid-afternoon, Sarah felt it was time to wade through the email that must have been pouring in over the last few hours. With great anticipation she clicked on the Alert Response Inbox and watched the download of one, two, three…three…three…

"Only three messages!" she shouted in disbelief. "Where the hell is everyone today?"

Typically, a Red Alert brought a minimum of a hundred responses in the first hour. Before opening the three measly messages, Sarah went to her website to make sure the alert had been posted properly. There it was, surrounded by a red flashing border of little animated ghosts. Such images may have been a bit juvenile, but she had a weakness for the simple animations, and barely a page on her site was without at least one.

Disappointed and somewhat baffled by the lack of response, Sarah clicked on the first message.

Hey, Sarah, it's Roger Cameron from the D.C. Herald. I'm happy to hear you'll be back this fall to speak to our group again. We're trying to book the Barlow Mansion for the meeting, which should be the perfect place for you to present your latest research—and scare the hell out of us again :-)

Anyway, here's the short scoop on the Wegman's deal. It seems like they went through a lot of construction workers as the place was being built—about five times more than normal. The average time on the job was only a couple of weeks, which delayed the project by many months. It also seems like Octagon went out of their way to bring in out-of-state laborers and guys who couldn't speak English very well.

I was doing a routine story on suburban sprawl last year and I visited the construction site. There were a handful of Civil War battlefield preservation guys picketing, but other than that it appeared to be just another huge, ugly shopping mall going up.

I interviewed management, got the usual line of company bull, and was about to leave when I overheard an argument. A couple of Hispanic guys were arguing with a foreman. They were trying to leave and he was trying to talk them into staying by raising their wages. My Spanish kind of sucks, but I picked out enough to realize they were claiming that there were evil spirits or something and they wouldn't stay for any amount of money. Then they crossed themselves and practically ran away.

Naturally, as a charter member of the Shadow Patrol, I tried to find out more, but no one would talk and I couldn't get permission to get back on the site. Then 9/11 happened and I forgot all about the place until last week.

I've attached an article about the grand opening fiasco. It ran in a small independent newspaper in northern Virginia. I wanted to go down and do a story, but my boss informed me that I had a choice: I could chase ghosts or remain employed by the Herald.

Anyway, people claim they saw ghosts of soldiers. Management claims it was the protestors pulling a hoax. A lot of things also malfunctioned, but the place is new, so that's to be expected. I really don't know what to make of this whole thing, I just don't know enough about it.

I've attached a couple of other articles and some photos, it's not much but it should give you more background. Sorry that this is all I have, but I'm sure you are swamped with info.

Sarah clicked to reply.

Seems like someone's gone and drained the swamp. Thanks for the info, Roger, it's a lot more than I had before. I'm heading down to Wegman's tomorrow; I'll keep you posted if I find anything juicy.

The second message was a two-page apology from a fan in California who was sorry he hadn't heard anything about it, but promised not to eat or sleep until he had some information for her. Sarah responded by thanking him, and insisted that it wasn't so important that he needed to neglect his body's basic functions.

The third message was from an anonymous source and simply read, "Grace Hopkins was the woman in the dressing room," and a phone number followed. Sarah wasn't sure of the significance of that enigmatic information until she read all the material Roger had sent. According to the local article, there had apparently been two major incidences on opening day—one in the Ballroom involving children, and one in the *Sun 'n Surf* dressing room with an unidentified woman. Assuming the anonymous responder had made that identification, Sarah picked up the phone and dialed Grace Hopkins' number. She always found it awkward calling someone who wasn't expecting to hear from a ghost hunter, but she felt she had a good angle on this one. And she didn't have to exactly say she was looking for ghosts…

A woman answered the phone on the third ring and positively responded to Sarah's inquiry that she was indeed Grace Hopkins. Sarah then put on her professional, yet sympathetic voice, and officially began her Wegman's Crossing Shopping and Recreation Center investigation.

"Grace, my name is Sarah Brooks, and I'm an independent investigator. The management at Wegman's has asked me to look into the details of the unfortunate incident at *Sun 'n Surf.*"

"I already told the sheriff everything, and I would rather not have to go over it all again," Grace stated, but in a hesitant tone that indicated she would actually love to rehash every detail, if given the proper sympathetic cues. After years of dealing with the dead, Sarah found the living much easier to handle.

"I can understand that. It must have been very embarrassing for you. I know I would have been mortified in that situation, and I don't know if I would have been able to handle it as well as you did," Sarah said with the ease and familiarity of a sister or best friend who already knew the entire story, even though she didn't really know what actually happened. She simply tried to put the pieces together and take a calculated gamble. "And if you don't mind, I'm going to record your story, because I don't take notes very quickly."

Without further delay, Grace Hopkins told Sarah everything she wanted to know, including some things she would have rather not heard. For instance, that the red and blue swimsuit covered all of Grace's stretch marks from her recent delivery, but it didn't enhance her bust as well as the yellow suit, and since breastfeeding had boosted her to a D-cup, she wanted to take advantage of the temporary enlargement, and so on.

The lengthy and detailed description of Grace Hopkins' post-natal anatomy caused Sarah to recall the results of a recent study that showed how willing women were to divulge very personal information to absolute strangers over the phone. At first, Sarah thought the study was complete nonsense, but Grace had proven to be worthy of a study all her own.

Once Grace finally stopped talking, Sarah had a few questions to clarify some crucial points.

"You said there was some type of mist that appeared to come out of the mirror?"

"Yes, it was like a fog. It looked like it was only a reflection at first, but then it started to fill the room. I guess they had one of those fog makers you get at party stores," Grace replied, obviously having been convinced by management that living, breathing protestors had created a hoax.

"Did they find a fog machine?"

"Well, no."

"And the air very suddenly got colder?"

"It was like opening the door to the freezer. They must have turned up the air conditioner."

"And the bad smell was there only *after* the fog and the soldier started to come into the room?"

"Yes. Maybe they put some stinky chemicals in the fog machine," Grace continued with the explanations management had spoon-fed her.

"And how do you think this man was able to appear to step out of the mirror?" Sarah asked, hoping she was able to conceal her growing annoyance with these obviously company-fabricated excuses.

"It must have been lasers or holograms, or something like that, you know?"

"Did they find any type of laser or projection equipment?"

"No, but they can do amazing things with special effects. You know, like Disney's haunted house. Have you seen it?"

"Yes, I have seen it, but is that what this man looked like?"

"Well...no...not really. He looked really...solid. He looked like a real wounded soldier. And that look in his eyes..." Grace said softly as her voice trailed away, but then became very strong, and agitated. "This *was* a prank, right?

This was one of those protestors who did this, right? I mean, I didn't actually see a real ghost, did I?"

"I don't know, Grace," Sarah said in her most soothing tone. "It's probably all just a bad joke, but that's what I'm trying to find out. Now please tell me, honestly, how did you *feel* about this man and what does your gut tell you it really was?"

"I…I…I don't know. I was so scared, and it happened so fast, but I guess what I also felt was that this man was suffering and…and needed help. I did *feel* that, deep inside. But like I said, I was so scared I just ran like hell."

"I don't blame you, and I won't bother you with anymore questions," Sarah said with genuine sympathy this time. "Whatever it was I'm very sorry you had to go through it."

Sarah gave Grace her cell phone number and told her to call in case she remembered anything else. She also said that she was flying down the next day and would like to meet with her if possible, and perhaps see if they could flesh out some kind of sketch of the man and his uniform. Grace said she would consider it, but Sarah could tell that doubt as to the nature of the event in the dressing room had now crept into her mind and she would be more reluctant to provide any additional information. While victims of a hoax usually become indignant and actively seek justice, witnesses of the paranormal often turn inward and become tight-lipped about their experience. However, Sarah had difficulty thinking of the words "tight-lipped" and "Grace Hopkins" being used in the same sentence.

When Jimmy came over after school, Sarah tried to gently break the news to him.

"Oh boy, this is great! I've never been to Virginia, and-"

"No, stop right there, Jimmy! Didn't you hear a word I just said?" Sarah laughed as she grabbed both of his ears and shook them. "I said *I* was going to Virginia tomorrow. You can't get out of school for this. You need a good education so you can get a real job and not end up like me."

"But I *want* to end up exactly like you!" he replied with that lost-little-boy voice and puppy dog eyes. With anyone else his age, this kind of behavior would be pathetic, but for Jimmy, it was just his genuine and endearing nature.

"Oh, Jimmy, Jimmy, Jimmy. What am I going to do with you?"

"Take me with you?" he said, brightening.

"You know it's not that I don't want you to come, but you have to go to school and I have been hired to do a job. I'll let you know what's happening every step of the way and I'll also let you know if there's anything you can do for me here," Sarah said as she watched his features fall further with every word.

"I have next Monday off, you know. I could come down Friday night and help you this weekend," he offered with relentless hope.

"All right. Maybe. But I really don't think I will be there more than three days. I'll probably be on my way home on Friday."

Jimmy appeared to be satisfied with the possibility of joining Sarah and cheerfully helped her finish packing the equipment. Sarah really would have liked for him to be able to go, but she also didn't want him spending too much time with her. He needed to spend more time with kids his age. High school should be a time for friends, dating, and exploring life—not a time for chasing the dead.

One week after its grand opening, the Wegman's Center's sales figures were at the very least disappointing, and at most, potentially devastating. Due to suspicion of sabotage, as well as the rumors of ghosts, curses, and evil spirits, the number of shoppers and diners was nearly fifty percent below official projections. The three anchor stores were already grumbling and many of the smaller businesses had approached management about renegotiating the terms of their leases.

Of course, it didn't help matters that disturbing occurrences continued to take place every day, and especially every night. After closing, security cameras would pick up images of shadowy figures. Guards were always dispatched to apprehend the intruders, but no one was ever found. The main bank of escalators refused to function properly, even though technicians could find no reason for the malfunctions. *Kinder Krossing* reopened, but parents were reluctant to leave their children there after the opening day nightmare. *Sun 'n Surf* was forced to keep an employee in attendance in the dressing room area, because customers refused to go back there alone.

In seven days, 109 employees had reported objects moving on their own, strange sounds, cold spots, bad odors, or the overwhelming feeling of being watched. Thirty-nine had already quit. No one wanted to be left alone to close up a store at night, and no one wanted to go alone to open up the next morning. Security personnel were being called for every little thing that happened, from a hat seemingly falling off of a shelf by itself, to a stapler being misplaced. Paranoia and near-hysteria were threatening the very life's blood of the Wegman's Center—its cash flow.

Even Martin Fink, professed skeptic, requested a security guard to escort him to his car every evening, on the pretense that he felt that the protestors might try to do him bodily harm. The truth was that on several occasions he had heard strange noises, and thought he had seen someone out of the corner of his eye. If there was something to these haunting rumors, he was not about to go alone into the underground parking lot.

Despite management's best efforts, word of the weird occurrences was slowly seeping into the neighboring communities, and beyond. By Tuesday evening, a few dozen curiosity-seekers (some with crystals and dousing rods) were seen poking around the center. Two men who were sitting in lotus position and chanting in the middle of the main courtyard had to be physically removed. One New Age spiritual healing group started handing out pamphlets in the stores and restaurants, until they were not so politely asked to leave the premises. However, these little nuisances were merely the first few drops seeping through the tenuous dam.

At least a hundred fans that had seen the red alert message on Sarah Brooks' website were planning to arrive at Wegman's Center within twenty-four hours. Many had been begging for years to be included in one of Sarah's investigations, and they felt that this was finally their chance to help. Then the rumor started that Sarah would be at the center in person on Wednesday, and hundreds more started to make plans. Of course, those hundreds of fans told hundreds of their friends about the alleged impending "group ghost hunt" led by Sarah Brooks herself, and clubs and individuals across the country suddenly set their sites on northern Virginia.

By dawn on Wednesday, unexplained activity inside Wegman's Center was reaching a fevered pitch. Lights flickered, items flew off the shelves, and moaning sounds echoed down the long corridors.

Outside, lines of cars, vans, and campers containing Sarah Brooks' fans and other ghost hunters were already pulling into the parking lots and setting up "command posts." Reporters and television trucks were also on their way, as someone had leaked bizarre stories to the press.

Like armies massing for battle, it appeared as if some powerful forces were on a collision course, and Sarah Brooks was heading straight for the dead center of it all.

Chapter 5

When the alarm went off Wednesday morning at 5am, Sarah stretched lazily and thought about the day ahead. After several weeks of tense and physically demanding ghost hunts, she was looking forward to a quiet, peaceful, and orderly investigation of Wegman's Center. Despite Grace Hopkins' compelling description, there was a chance it was all just some very clever hoax and she might quickly wrap up the whole thing, make some easy money, and be able to relax and treat the trip more like a vacation.

However, while she showered, the pleasant thoughts of some leisurely research slowly became overshadowed by a nagging feeling that she just might be about to bite off more than she could chew. But considering she was still quite a reluctant ghost hunter, when all things were considered, experiencing such doubts and fears on the day of an investigation was not uncommon. Yet, these unsettling feelings were particularly strong.

As Sarah dressed, she went back and forth to her computer to check her email. At first she didn't realize how many messages there were, and she simply glanced at the first five or six. They mostly contained rumors three or four times removed—somebody had a friend who had a cousin who knew someone who had heard, etc., etc. However, all of the rumors had the same basic premise, which meant that they either all had the same erroneous source, or there was some underlying truth.

The main rumors seemed to involve classic symptoms of very disturbing, and very widespread, haunting activity both during construction and in the opening days of the center. While she would read the messages more carefully on the trip down to Virginia, she was already compiling an extensive mental list of what had allegedly occurred, and what she was planning to do about it.

In between fastening her earrings, Sarah tapped the "Scroll Down" key to see if there were any more messages and finally realized that since the time she had gone to bed over two hundred emails had flooded her Inbox. Sitting down, she clicked and scrolled and tried to absorb the gist of the messages.

To her horror, it appeared as if her loyal and devoted fans saw her request for information about Wegman's Center as an invitation to conduct their own investigations. Quickly opening her website, she posted an emergency message asking everyone to please stay at home. She explained that this was a private investigation, that she had a professional reputation to maintain, and the last thing she needed was a circus atmosphere. But even as her plane touched down at Dulles Airport, the dog and pony shows were about to commence.

"I want these damn people off my property!" Fink yelled to a security team outside the main entrance.

The Grand Entrance (as it was referred to in the brochures) of the center was fronted by an enormous columned overhang in the style of a classic antebellum southern mansion—with rather incongruous modern touches such as bold neon signs. It was a combination you either loved or hated, something like *Gone with the Wind* meets the Las Vegas strip. And not unlike the set of the legendary movie, by the 10am opening at the Grand Entrance it looked as though there would be a cast of thousands.

Not since the opening day had such crowds gathered to get in. Normally, Fink would have been elated to see people anxiously awaiting the unlocking of the doors. However, these people did not look like typical shoppers. In fact, they didn't even look like typical people. Many were wearing T-shirts bearing the logos of their local ghost hunting clubs, and they had various unrecognizable gadgets and meters hanging over their shoulders or strapped around their waists. There was even one man who had a tin foil cap, but he was probably a crossover from an alien abduction group. While not everyone looked as though they used pocket protectors, Fink saw enough curious characters to immediately give them one of his derogatory names.

"Get these Ghoul Geeks out of here, I said," Fink yelled even louder. "None of *these* people are allowed into *my* center."

The chief of security, Dan Garrison, didn't flinch, but he was clearly uncomfortable in the face of his boss' ranting.

"Sir, unless they are creating a disturbance or in some way breaking the law, we legally have no authority to refuse them entrance," he stated in the military tone that had become part of his nature from twenty years of service.

"Well you just better find a law they're breaking if you want to keep your job!" Fink growled, clenching his fists like a little bully who wasn't getting his way.

"Look, Mr. Fink," Garrison began, pronouncing the name Fink as it if was some prime military target, "my people can keep out anyone you want, but then *you* will have to deal with the lawsuits."

Some of the ghost hunters near the front of the crowd heard the word "lawsuit" and as if on cue started chanting, "Discrimination! Discrimination!"

Fink turned purple for an instant and then rapidly faded to a ghostly white, "Lawsuits! I can't have any more lawsuits! Quickly, let them in. Let everyone in. Just keep your eyes on them and don't let them scare the shoppers. I have to call the lawyers… I have to call the sheriff…"

Martin Fink mumbled to himself as he dabbed his expansive forehead with his handkerchief and retreated back into the center.

"If this *Fink* calls me one more time…" the Sheriff of Brandon County's words trailed off as he tried to rub the tension out of his temples.

The four women who worked the day shift at the sheriff's office—one deputy, a dispatcher, and two secretaries—each silently wished she could massage the tension out of her chiseled-featured boss. Tall, blond Sheriff Beauregard Madison Davis had won two terms in landslide elections, with no small help from the fact that each time he received over ninety percent of the female vote. During the last campaign, one woman told a reporter that she was voting for Davis because his blue eyes looked like a southern dawn after a stormy night. Even though the reporter, a man, had no idea what she was talking about, he printed the story anyway—much to the dismay of Davis, whose buddies still relentlessly kid him every time it rains.

Some of the male population voted for Davis because of his long and distinguished southern lineage, although they conveniently overlooked the fact that his mother was born and raised in New Jersey. Everyone was allowed one mistake.

Then there was actually a fair amount of people who voted for the thirty-something sheriff because he had an undergraduate degree from Princeton and a law degree from Columbia, was smart as a whip, and was tough on crime. He had implemented several innovative programs throughout the county that reduced drug use, cut down on the number of repeat offenders, increased the conviction rate, and generally affirmed the popular local saying, "Hell no, ya don't mess with Beau."

For Sheriff Davis, all of this nonsense was a distraction from his work, and his future goals. In the short term, he just wanted to create the safest county possible, which was something of a personal quest since it was home to his family and friends. In the near future, the position of state attorney general didn't sound too bad. In the long run, he didn't see why Senator or Governor shouldn't be part of his title. However, despite these lofty goals, Davis was about as unassuming and unlike a politician as one could get, which was another key to his success.

After making a deep sigh that seemed to renew his strength, Sheriff Davis continued speaking to his staff.

"Now he has some damn ghostbuster from up north flying down this morning. What the hell is he thinking? We're trying to downplay all this spooky nonsense and he rolls out the red carpet to someone who writes books about this crap for a living!

"All he needs now are a bunch of guys in biohazard suits and some radiation containment squads—then he can *really* soothe the public's fears!"

As their boss ranted, the four women thought his eyes looked more like a southern dawn right before a storm. They all sighed their own little sighs.

"I had better meet this woman right off and straighten her out about this whole situation," Davis said more calmly. "And Dorothy, get Mac and head over to the center right away. It seems like there's a bit of a welcoming committee for this ghost quack. I have a feeling it's going to be one of those days when I wished to hell I had stayed buried in some cushy law office somewhere."

Deputy Dorothy Franklin snapped out of her reverie and snapped to attention at the sound of her name. While Sheriff Davis didn't go in for formality, while on duty she liked to operate in a more military mode of conduct. Being a woman in what was still very much a man's world, she felt this made her seem more professional, and that she would be taken more seriously.

"Sure thing, Beau...I mean Sheriff Davis! Right away, Sir!" she stammered like a rookie. She had a crush on Beau since junior high, and if she wasn't vigilant every time she spoke to him, these kinds of things inevitably happened. So much for her professional mode of conduct.

As Sarah's limo drew closer to Brandon County, she was already seeing some disturbing sites. Her parents had always made sure that family vacations included something educational, and visits to Civil War battlefields were often on the itinerary. Initially, Sarah was bored stiff with what she considered nothing more than dull landscapes with endless plaques and historical markers. And each place sold the same stupid souvenirs—plastic soldiers, toy muskets, and misshapen lumps of lead reputed to be bullets from the battles.

Then sometime during the sixth grade, her attitude began to shift. One of her teachers was a Civil War reenactor, and he came to class one day in full uniform. He portrayed an actual soldier from a local regiment, and, based upon the soldier's diaries and letters, told stories about the years leading up to the war, the euphoria of enlisting, the tedium of camp life, and the terror of battle. He wasn't able to talk about the end of the war, though, because the soldier had been killed at Cold Harbor, Virginia, in June of 1864.

Sarah learned a great lesson that day. Behind every statistic, plaque, and historical marker, there were living, breathing human beings who sacrificed themselves for what they believed. From that day, Sarah could not pass an historic site without wondering what the people who lived and died there had experienced. This appreciation and recognition carried over into her ghost investigations, as well. Whereas many people thought it would be "cool to have a ghost," she constantly reminded them that these ghosts were the souls of human beings, which needed to be released, not kept as entertaining pets.

Over the past few years, Sarah had personally been involved with trying to save several historic buildings and sites in Duxbridge and the surrounding area. She had also written a couple of articles about historic preservation, specifically highlighting the plight of many Civil War sites. As she now looked out the window of the limousine, she saw just how desperate the struggle for preservation had become.

Suburban sprawl was spreading ever deeper into northern Virginia. There were strip malls bearing the names of battles, streets of housing developments named after generals, and there was even a "Mosby's Camp Daycare Center." This hypocritical trend of pseudo-preservation appeared to know no bounds, as historic ground disappeared under new construction, only to be named after the very site that it destroyed! Sarah was aware that it was a difficult task balancing history and the growing demand for housing and shopping areas, but the scales had clearly tipped completely in favor of "progress" over preservation.

The closer she got to Wegman's Center, the worse the problem appeared. An access highway had been cut through the heart of formerly pristine, densely wooded land, and other businesses already dotted the length of the new road. And there seemed to be at least one enormous billboard for every store and attraction at the center—a sight that reminded Sarah of the garish casino signs every few feet on the expressway leading into Atlantic City. Obviously, the center was not willing to gamble on simple word-of-mouth advertising.

Sarah also noticed something else unusual. There was a lot of traffic along the final mile approach to the center, with an inordinately high percentage of multi-passenger vehicles and RVs. Then two sheriff's department patrol cars went speeding by with lights flashing. Thinking there must be an accident ahead tying up traffic, she went back to her laptop and notepad. As they crept and crawled along the congested highway, Sarah noticed out of the corner of her eye that a large white truck had pulled up alongside the limo. She suddenly got a sick feeling in the pit of her stomach as she realized this was no ordinary truck. Turning to get a full view, she saw it was a Fox News mobile broadcasting vehicle, and she finally comprehended what she was about to walk into.

Grabbing her cell phone, she dialed Lela Reynolds' number. The general manager's efficient assistant answered on the second ring with a cheery, "Hello" and an announcement of her name and position.

"This is Sarah Brooks. We are stuck in traffic on the highway near the center, and I have a sneaking suspicion that something is going on," Sarah said as she looked at all the dishes and antennas on the roof of the news truck.

"Well…" Lela began with hesitation, "we do seem to have a situation developing here."

"A 'situation' developing?" Sarah asked with the combination of a smile and a grimace. "Isn't that what they say in the military when they are about to be overrun?"

"That would be a fair analogy," Lela replied. "It seems that we have a lot of amateur ghost hunters on the premises, and the press has caught wind of the whole thing."

"Great. Just what I needed," Sarah said mostly to herself, but then spoke up with greater emphasis. "I hope you don't think *I* invited any of these people or the press."

"No, I know how word can spread. And this whole mess has been bottled up so long it was bound to burst open sooner or later," Lela said and then fell silent for a moment, as if regretting her last words. "But anyway, please instruct the driver to take you to the west parking garage to the area reserved for management. You won't be bothered there and you can come straight to the office."

"Okay, thanks. And maybe sometime today we could have a talk about just what has been going on?"

"Uh, I, uh, *really* don't have *anything* to tell you. *Everything* has been *carefully* documented and is in the *official* report," Lela replied like a prisoner of war trying to convey a secret message within a scripted statement.

As Sarah put away her phone, she jotted down Lela's name on her notepad, and scribbled a bold asterisk next to it. Her instincts told her that Lela was just as eager to talk as Grace Hopkins had been. If this investigation was about to become a full-fledged battle, she needed to know whom she could count on and where she could get reliable information. It was obvious from Fink's letter that management could be considered "Stonewaller's Brigade," and if she could convince a certain assistant to gather intelligence from the inside, it would make her job a lot easier.

Sarah conveyed the message about the garage to the limo driver, and then decided to have a little fun. Lowering her window, she motioned to the driver of the news truck, who was now just about even with her. The driver leaned out of his window and she asked what was going on.

"There are ghosts running all over this new mall, attacking people. Some exorcist from Boston is coming today to get rid of them," he replied enthusiastically, obviously thrilled to be part of covering something other than a political speech or some dull, Washington, D.C. event.

"Ghosts! An exorcist! You're kidding me!" Sarah said with convincing shock and amazement.

"No, seriously! This priestess exorcist lady is going to drive away all the demons—hopefully while our cameras are running!"

The lines of traffic suddenly lurched forward, and Sarah managed to yell, "Good luck!" before the two vehicles separated. As she closed the window, she used her other hand to massage her forehead. Things were deteriorating by the minute, and she hadn't even reached the center yet. What she had hoped would be a quiet and dignified scientific investigation now threatened to become a nationally televised fiasco featuring High Priestess Sarah Brooks conducting the Rites of Exorcism in between beer and fast food commercials!

The official entrance to the Wegman's Crossing Shopping and Recreation Center's property began just beyond the growing crowds of preservation protestors. Dozens of reenactors in both blue and gray held up signs asking everyone to boycott the center. Many were also chanting something amusingly derogatory about Martin Fink, but Sarah didn't catch the last line of clever limerick—although it wasn't difficult to imagine what words completed the rhyme.

Large white columns bearing the WCSRC logo (which looked more like tangled spaghetti than elegantly intertwined letters) marked the property line. Several dozen odd-looking modern sculptures stretched beyond the columns for about a hundred yards on either side of the road. Before she could ask just what these towering monstrosities represented, the driver explained that these were "interpretations of southern plantation trees" created by a Japanese artist whose only experience with anything southern was eating Kentucky Fried Chicken in a Tokyo restaurant.

But there were more assaults on the senses to come, as the Grand Entrance appeared at the crest of a massive, sloping parking lot. Typically, it was not in a retailer's best interest to make patrons walk uphill to get to stores and restaurants, but Octagon had thought that the dominating presence of the façade more than made up for the extra energy required to get there. Effect over exertion, they contended.

In reality, the vast majority of people bypassed the pseudo-mansion entrance with its blinking lights and rotating signs, and parked on one of the other sides where the exterior was more sedate, and the parking lots were level. Today, however, it appeared as if all the action was front and center, and Sarah watched as the Fox News truck headed for the section of parking lot where CNN, NBC, and some local stations were already setting up camp. She could also see a section of RVs and vans, with several flying the distinctive "ghost between the crosshairs" flag of a national ghost hunting organization. Large groups of people were congregating near the Grand Entrance, but the sheriff's cars and the center's security vehicles were parked directly in front, providing an unambiguous statement that no disturbances would be tolerated. The entire scene looked to be only moments away from complete mayhem.

Sarah breathed a sigh of relief when the limo driver turned left, away from the Grand Entrance, and followed the long curving road that encircled the entire complex. Other amorphous sculptures lined the perimeter of the property, with one particularly bizarre piece causing Sarah to muse over whether it was a Latvian's interpretation of a tobacco plant, or a Tanzanian's concept of a cotton gin.

Sarah's focus took a sudden shift, however, as they pulled into the underground parking garage. A shudder went up her spine and there was that distinctive tingling feeling she always felt when entering a "haunted zone." In fact, Sarah became so lightheaded for a moment that she was grateful to be sitting down. Something powerful was in this building—something that was not at rest, and not at all happy.

Chapter 6

Dr. Carl Henkel checked his watch for the third time in ten minutes, as he uncharacteristically squirmed in the conference room chair. The spacious room in the Dallas hotel was filled with fellow neurologists, and they were all listening to a speaker presenting the latest findings of her university's project, which involved implanting microchips in the optic nerves of blind rodents. These implants were then connected to photosensitive devices that converted simple images to electrical impulses that would stimulate the brain in a manner identical to the rods and cones of a normal rat's eyes. In layman's terms, this was groundbreaking technology that one day might enable the blind to see.

It was a fascinating lecture, but as Dr. Henkel glanced at his watch yet again, it was clear his mind was elsewhere. The speaker was already twelve minutes into the lunch break, and he needed to call home. His wife had left a message that something incredible was happening at Wegman's Center. For two weeks prior to the start of the neurological association's conference, the Henkels had been enjoying a friend's villa in Mexico, having little contact with the outside world. He then went straight to Dallas for the three-day conference, and his wife went home to Virginia. Obviously, something important had happened while they were away—perhaps evidence had been uncovered that would substantiate his claims that the center had been built directly over the site of the Battle of Wegman's Crossing?

As his thoughts drifted further from the lecture, he caught himself about five bars into humming "Three Blind Mice." Embarrassed at his rude and unprofessional conduct, he was relieved to find that no one around him seemed to notice. Finally, mercifully, the lecture ended and he bolted out of the room in as dignified a manner as possible. As soon as the door to his hotel room clicked shut, he phoned home.

Henkel had been hoping that new documents had been discovered, or that someone involved with the construction of the center had produced some crucial artifact. The last thing he could have imagined was the wild tale his wife proceeded to tell him. Ghosts, stampedes, growing crowds of protestors, paranormal investigators, and reporters! If he hadn't known better, he would have suspected that his wife had taken home some Mexican peyote as a souvenir. While he was glad the center was getting publicity that might help garner support for his cause, he was somewhat nauseous over the type of insanity producing it. How on earth could all this mumbo jumbo and mass hysteria possibly help him uncover and preserve an historic site?

The private elevator to the fourth floor offices had a one-way mirror that allowed a view of the stores on each floor of the west wing of the center. The shopping areas looked like those in any other mall—perhaps a little fancier than most—but there was one noticeable difference. There should have been customers.

Sarah counted no more than eight people on the first three floors, and two of them appeared to be security guards. A place like this should have been filled with women pushing strollers, businessmen going to lunch, older folks getting their daily exercise, and teens playing hooky. It was no wonder that management was willing to shell out big bucks to get her to debunk the stories of ghosts.

Before the thought of debunking had time to leave her mind, the elevator jerked to an abrupt stop, knocking her off balance and sending her face first into the one-way mirror. Other than leaving a distinct nose print on the glass, she was unhurt, and unconcerned. It was probably just another glitch in one of the center's new systems.

As Sarah stood waiting alone in elevator, looking at the concrete between the third and fourth floors, a little tickle ran up the back of her neck. It suddenly felt a bit cooler, too. Quickly kneeling on the floor, she popped open the latches of her briefcase. A cold, clammy air mass seemed to be seeping out of the walls, and like a gunslinger reacting to an opponent stepping out of the shadows, in one swift movement Sarah withdrew an instrument and pulled the trigger. A small panel on the back of the instrument lit up and displayed the current temperature.

"Sixty-four, fifty-seven…forty-nine," Sarah said out loud from habit, so that all readings could be recorded by the camcorders and tape recorders usually surrounding her.

Keeping the trigger depressed on the infrared non-contact thermometer, she reached back into her briefcase and pulled out another handheld instrument. It was an electromagnetic field meter (or EMF, for short), and it immediately indicated that there was some type of energy present in the elevator. Sarah slowly stood up and turned around once, allowing her instruments to scan the entire small space from top to bottom and side to side. Of course, she didn't need any instruments to tell her she was not alone—the goose bumps on her arms and her "internal sensors" were providing ample evidence of that.

"I am not here to deny your existence or drive you away," Sarah stated with calm authority, or at least the outward appearance of such. "I'm here to uncover your message and help you find peace."

The tingling up her spine intensified to a wave that raced through her limbs with a quick, sharp, shudder, and the cold air became so heavy it almost felt as though she was trying to breathe underwater. Just as Sarah felt she was going to have to let out a scream, the icy, nerve-wracking presence simply vanished. In an instant the EMF meter read zero, and the thermometer registered a comfortable seventy-two. The elevator smoothly resumed its ascent of the final half-floor, and Sarah barely had time to drop her instruments in her briefcase and stand up before the doors slid open.

Waiting outside the malfunctioning elevator was Lela Reynolds. She was a tall, athletic-looking woman, impeccably dressed in a pale green suit. Her dark skin showed no signs of aging, and her kind features also made her look years younger. Sarah never would have guessed that Lela was older than she was, with kids in college.

"Ms. Brooks, are you all right?" Lela asked with concern, "I'm Lela Reynolds. Were you hurt?"

"All in one piece, I think," Sarah said extending her hand, and she was not disappointed by the strong, honest handshake Lela returned. Although shaking hands was still predominantly a practice in the male domain, Sarah always made a point of it on an investigation or during any type of business negotiations. As her grandfather had said, "There's nothing a man can tell you about his character that isn't in his handshake."

"I'm so sorry. We've never had any problems with *this* elevator before," Lela said, motioning to a maintenance man who had just come up the stairs.

The control room on the fourth floor, just off the main atrium, was the nerve center of the entire complex, and the moment the elevator had lost power, a red light flashed on a huge map on the wall, as well as on several monitors at various maintenance and security stations. Similar maps were against each of the other three walls, representing the four sprawling floors. Red lights were commonplace since the center opened, but anything in the management office sector commanded immediate attention.

"You all right, Ma'am?" the young man asked somewhat shyly.

"Yes, I'm fine. And thank you for coming to my rescue," Sarah replied, thinking that if she tried to shake this blushing boy's hand it would confirm her suspicion that he was far more comfortable with machines than women.

"I didn't do anything, yet. It just started back up on its own. Never had no trouble with *this* one before," he said mostly to himself as he entered the elevator with his heavy toolbox.

"Please let me know what you find," Lela said over her shoulder as she led Sarah through the lobby decorated with original, and valuable, artwork. Unlike the ultramodern oddities outside, these sculptures and paintings were recognizable as real objects and people. On the surface, they all conveyed the sense of genteel southern living and hospitality, but with little effort you could also see that they really represented wealth—and lots of it. Octagon was filthy rich, and they wanted everyone to know it, but in a refined and dignified manner, of course.

A set of nine-foot-high glass doors led to the offices of upper management. As a security guard released the electronic lock to allow them to enter, Sarah was amused to see that cleverly placed panels of thin, etched glass actually disguised the thick bulletproof glass behind it. They weren't taking any chances here, although they neglected to realize that such protective measures were only effective against the living.

Lela's office was the most tastefully decorated place Sarah had yet seen, and she was not surprised to learn that the efficient administrative assistant had a hand in choosing her own artwork, colors, and fabrics.

"I guess there wasn't anything you could do about those sculptures outside?" Sarah asked with a smile.

"Completely out of my hands!" she laughed. "But a few of us have a pool going to come up with an overall best name. Jack, down in accounting, called the one across from this window 'The Bride of Finkenstein,' and no one yet has been able to beat that."

At that moment, Fink's voice barked her name, and Lela put a hand over her mouth and looked as if she feared for her job. But it was just the intercom, and she relaxed and pressed the button to respond.

"Yes, Mr. Fink?"

"Is that Brooks woman here, yet?" he asked gruffly.

"Yes, Mr. Fink, she just arrived."

"Well, she'll just have to wait. I have to make a few calls."

Sarah could see that Lela was somewhat mortified, and decided to be as gracious as possible, under the circumstances.

"I think I'll just sit here and wait for a bit then, shall I?" Sarah said as she settled into a comfortable chair in the corner.

"Perhaps you would like to look over some of the reports in the meantime," Lela said, handing her a stack of folders, all color-coded, neatly labeled and placed in chronological order.

"The green ones are the monthly progress reports during construction, blue is personnel, and red are the incident reports," she explained, pointing to the thick layer of red at the bottom. There were also quite a few red folders spaced among the green and blue, and it was these earliest incidents that interested Sarah the most, especially since it looked like trouble started the moment ground was broken.

As Sarah absorbed herself in the reports, she didn't notice when Sheriff Davis entered the office, but he definitely noticed her. The law enforcement side of him saw the finely tailored suit, designer shoes, precision Swiss watch, and pricey briefcase. As a man, he saw a great pair of legs and full, sensual lips. The suit's jacket seemed to stick out in the right places, but he couldn't swear in a court of law as to what was underneath. That would require further investigation.

In the time it had taken him to walk two steps into the office, he had gathered all this data on the woman in the chair, and had confidently concluded she must be some legal big shot from Octagon who worked hard, and more importantly, played hard. His kind of woman. He would try to get the inside scoop from Lela after he met with Fink to take care of all this ridiculous business.

"So, Lela, has this bogus ghostbuster from Boston showed up yet?" he said in what he considered his most amusing tone, and then was surprised and puzzled by the wide-eyed look of alarm on Lela's face. He also didn't understand why the woman in the chair suddenly stiffened. When she didn't look his way, he assumed she was just trying to pretend not to notice him, so he decided to really turn on the charm and humor.

"You'll be able to spot her a mile away. She's probably some burned-out hippie from the sixties in a tie-died jumpsuit wearing a 'proton pack.' I mean, can you believe someone actually makes a living ripping off suckers in these ghost scams?"

Sheriff Davis just couldn't understand why neither woman was laughing. Suddenly, he got a very sick feeling.

"Sheriff Davis," Lela began, and then had to clear her throat before continuing the unpleasant introduction, "I would like you to meet Sarah Brooks, the paranormal investigator from Massachusetts."

Keep the moral high ground, Sarah thought. *Keep your cool, and don't let this ignorant jerk get to you. This is an important job, and you need the sheriff on your side. Keep the advantage!*

These were all really good thoughts she had in the few seconds it took for her to put down the reports and stand up to face the man who had just insulted her. But when she saw his squeaky-clean, All-American good looks and that almost cartoon-like chin, something snapped.

"Look, Dudley Do-Right, unless there is some local law against having an IQ, you just stay out of my way and let me do my job," Sarah said with smoldering anger. She knew she had already said way too much, but there was something about his face and his accent that just egged her on. "But don't worry, I promise that if I see anyone rustling cattle I'll call on you and your trusty six-shooter."

Advantage lost.

The storm clouds once again gathered in his sky blue eyes, and his pale cheeks flushed red with a combination of anger and embarrassment, but the anger was clearly taking charge. Realizing his right hand was tightly gripping his holster, he let go and raised a waving finger toward the woman who had just infuriated him more in fifteen seconds than everyone else combined had during the last fifteen months of the ongoing Octagon battles.

"Now let's just get something straight here," Davis began, trying to remember all the relaxation techniques he had learned during his last campaign. "If you think I'm going to let you—"

"Well, you must be Ms. Brooks!" Martin Fink bellowed as he came out of his office and walked right past the sheriff, either unintentionally or deliberately oblivious to the argument in progress. "It's a pleasure, a real pleasure! I've heard so much about you and your fascinating work."

Fink's handshake was powerful, but uncomfortably slippery. Sarah couldn't help but be reminded once again of her grandfather's words of wisdom.

"Please, come into my office. I'm so sorry to have kept you waiting," Fink said as he escorted her past the sheriff, whose finger still pointed to where Sarah had been standing. "I see you've already had the pleasure of meeting our excellent sheriff. Come along now Davis, don't keep us waiting."

"Deep breaths, happy thoughts," Lela whispered as she gently lowered the sheriff's upraised hand and patted him on the shoulder.

Sarah and the sheriff were ushered to side-by-side chairs in front of Fink's massive chrome and glass desk. Fiber optic lighting illuminated the various odd-shaped panels of glass, and Sarah would have bet her bank account that Fink personally selected the hideously expensive desk.

Hideous is definitely the key word in this office, Sarah thought, glad that she had something to distract her at that moment. If not for her pretended interest in the questionable décor, she and Davis would undoubtedly be glowering at one another.

"I can see you have an eye for works of art," Fink said, beaming. "Not *everyone* appreciates my refined sense of taste."

His last words were squarely aimed at Davis, who now appeared torn between which one of them he would like to punch first.

"Can we just get on with this," Davis said through tightened jaw muscles, which made his fictional Mounted Policeman's chin stick out even further. Sarah had to refocus on the light show in Fink's desk to avoid snickering.

"Of course, of course," Fink said, settling down with great satisfaction into the largest leather chair Sarah had ever seen outside of a palace. "You know I'm confident you two will make a great team, both having gone to the same school, I mean."

"You went to Princeton?" Davis asked, as his mood lightened for a moment.

"Yale," Sarah stated defiantly, as their dark expressions turned toward Fink.

"Oh well, Yale, Princeton, same thing. They both have that ivy growing on their walls, don't they?" Fink said cheerfully, not realizing he was throwing gasoline on the fire. "Now, let's get down to brass tacks. Ms. Brooks, we need you to quickly set up your little gadgets, gather your photos and statistics, and write your report so we can clear up this entire matter and get back to business, hopefully by this weekend.

"Sheriff Davis, we would appreciate if your people could control this situation more effectively. There are crowds of strange individuals scaring away my customers. Put on your riot gear and knock a few heads if you have to, but keep these Ghoul Geeks away from my center!"

Twice, Sarah and Davis started to speak at the same time, and then Sarah insisted the sheriff go first, giving her a few more seconds to compose herself.

"You know I can't do anything unless someone is breaking the law. I'll keep a couple of my people on the premises, but the Brandon County Sheriff's Department is not your private police force!" Davis stated in a tone that instantly earned him some respect in Sarah's eyes. She had just assumed the sheriff was one of Fink's little toadies.

"And I can't make any guarantees about the length of my investigation," Sarah chimed in, hoping to keep Fink on the ropes. "I never fabricate evidence, nor do I cover up anything I might find. My sole purpose is to uncover the truth, and if that conflicts in any way with your agenda, I can head right back to the airport."

Sheriff Davis also decided to reevaluate the woman who had just so articulately stood up to the general manager accustomed to always getting his way. Although Davis still considered her a scam artist, she had a head on her shoulders, and a spark in her eyes.

"Please, please, you both misunderstand me!" Fink protested with doe-eyed innocence. "As you can imagine, I have been under great stress, and I merely want us all to work together to bring this matter to a swift and mutually agreeable conclusion.

"Now, Ms. Brooks, please tell me what you need from us in order to conduct a proper investigation."

"Well, I would like to get started right away," Sarah responded in a more friendly manner since Fink had taken on a more conciliatory tone, for now. "First, I want to see every square inch of this complex, and I'll need to know what has happened where. Tonight, I'll set up some equipment in a few key spots and monitor whatever is, or is not, going on. I should at least have some idea, possibly by morning, as to the situation here."

"By morning! Good. Very, very good," Fink said, gleefully rubbing his hands together. "And do you need any help from my staff, or from the sheriff?"

"I would prefer to work alone in the initial phase," she replied, although she was tempted to ask if the sheriff could be available to get her coffee. "I do request that no one be present in the areas where I will be setting up my equipment. Also, the ventilation system should be shut down, and all doors and windows be closed. It would also be helpful if the place could be swept, vacuumed, and sprayed for flying insects."

"What are you, the Martha Stewart of ghostbus-", Davis began to say and then quickly corrected himself, "of paranormal investigators?"

He meant the comment as a friendly jest, and hoped he had not just provoked another argument. Fortunately, Sarah sensed the different tone and responded without rancor.

"The goal is to try to eliminate drafts, bugs, and airborne particles which could be misinterpreted as paranormal activity. Moths and balls of dust can look rather spooky in infrared."

Sarah even managed to smile at the sheriff as she spoke, but while she was willing to forget his insults (it wasn't like she didn't hear that kind of thing all the time!), she doubted her Dudley Do-Right remark would be so easily forgotten.

"Whatever you need, Ms. Brooks," Fink said obligingly. "Just let Lela know your requirements. She will arrange to have one of the security guards escort you through the center, as soon as you've had a chance to freshen up, of course. Your hotel is just outside the main gate, and the limo will take you there, now, if you would like."

"Yes, thanks," Sarah said, rising. "I would like to change into more suitable clothing for this kind of work."

Sarah reluctantly once again shook the slippery hand Fink extended. As she turned to leave, she nodded respectfully to the sheriff, who made no motion toward offering his hand. *Still sulking*, Sarah thought. *Oh well, with any luck I won't have to ever meet this man again. Although, that chin does look kind of cute when he pouts...*

As soon as Sarah got to her hotel room, she kicked off the uncomfortable designer heels, and tossed her suit on the back of a chair. Slipping into her favorite investigation jeans and a SWAT vest, she double-checked that the many pockets held her smaller instruments, flashlights, pens, and a can of pepper spray—just in case she needed to deal with the living when she was alone in a remote location.

She had less than an hour to go through the rest of the reports before her appointment with the security guard who would show her around. It seemed that Roger's information about high employee turnover was correct. In fact, it was an understatement. Personnel files indicated that within the first six weeks after breaking ground, almost the entire construction crew turned over twice. Incident reports showed that the rate of minor accidents was forty-three percent higher than normal (Sarah checked the Internet for the national average).

On several occasions, welders burned co-workers standing nearby, and stated that the incidents had occurred because they had been "distracted." Over two dozen people were hurt by construction materials and tools falling on them, although no one was ever identified who could have dropped or knocked them down. Several dozen workers tripped over equipment they claimed wasn't there just seconds earlier, fell through planks that were supposed to have been secured, or tumbled from scaffolding on which the bolts had been loosened. Sabotage and lack of training were listed as the official causes, but Sarah had the distinct feeling that there was far more here than the reports revealed.

The most intriguing cases involved the twenty-three men dismissed for "mental instability" brought on by "fatigue, stress, or possible drug use." Symptoms of this alleged "instability" were "hearing voices, hallucinations, and acute paranoia." Apart from the striking similarity to Sarah's freshman year of college, these symptoms sounded remarkably like those she heard time and again from people who were being scared out of their senses by ghosts.

Of course, she would need to interview some of the accident victims and supposedly unstable people before she could draw any conclusions. However, that appeared to be a difficult task as no contact information was included on the reports. A line of fine print on the bottom of the forms indicated that private information would be kept confidential—in other words, under lock and key at headquarters. Still, there were names, and she would email a list to a friend who had a knack at tracking down people.

Just as she finished sending the email, there was a knock at her door. She hadn't been expecting anyone—least of all the sheriff.

"Well, Sheriff Davis! Are you here to deliver an official warning, or to plant some phony evidence so you can haul me off to jail?" Sarah said with just enough humor to outweigh the sarcasm.

"Neither. May I come in? I promise I left all the phony evidence in the car," he replied in a completely non-confrontational tone.

"Sure, why not. Have a seat," Sarah said as she moved over to the desk and discretely placed a folder over her notes and lowered her laptop screen.

"Don't worry, I'm not here to spy, either," he said with a smile.

Must work on my discrete hiding techniques, Sarah thought, and then spoke. "So just why are you here, then, Sheriff?"

"To say that the enemy of my enemy is my friend," he stated.

"Okay…and a penny saved is a penny earned, but what does that have to do with anything?"

"Fink," Davis replied as if he had just stepped in something.

"Oh, *that* enemy!"

"Exactly. As soon as you left Fink's office he told me how he wants me to keep an eye on you. It seems he doesn't trust you at all, and he's afraid you might do something to exploit the situation."

"Then why did he hire me?"

"He's desperate—no offense—and has to do something to dispel this whole ghost thing. If he doesn't resolve this soon, Octagon will find someone who will."

Sarah paced back and forth for a few moments, deep in thought. Leaning back against the desk, she folded her arms and looked directly into the sheriff's blue eyes.

"So why are you telling me this? We didn't exactly get off to a very good start, and you obviously don't approve of me."

Davis took a deep breath before continuing.

"You're right, I don't really believe in ghosts, but I wouldn't care if Wegman's was the most haunted place on earth. What I care about is keeping this county safe and secure, and getting Fink off my back. If you have any influence with all the people that have gathered here, I would personally appreciate it if you could talk to them and ask them to just go home, or at least stay out of trouble.

"You also have experience in uncovering hoaxes. If someone or some group has deliberately done all of this, maybe you can help us catch them."

"Fair enough. But like I told Fink, if something unusual is going on here, I'm not going to sweep it under the carpet. Let's just see how things go this afternoon and tonight, and I'll give you a call in the morning."

"Okay. Here's my card with my cell number. I can be reached 24-7 if you need me—even if I'm out riding across the territory on my trusty steed," Davis said with a grin as he struck a Hollywood hero pose.

"All right, all right, I apologize for that Dudley Do-Right crack. Now get going so I can strap on my proton pack and get to work."

Chapter 7

"Dan Garrison, chief of security, ma'am."

"Please, it's Sarah," she said as he reached to take the case of equipment from her hand. "And thanks, but I would like to carry this, it's not heavy."

Lela had cautioned her that their chief security officer was less than pleased with the rumors of hauntings and with all the bizarre people who had showed up. It was Lela's polite way of saying that Garrison didn't approve of Sarah, either.

"Whatever you say, ma'am," he said, clearly uncomfortable with her and the entire situation.

Sarah was determined not to alienate another valuable ally, but she didn't know how to break the ice with this man. After several minutes of polite monosyllables, she glimpsed the black ink of a tattoo as he raised his arm to unlock a door, and realized it was a golden opportunity.

"So, Dan, I see you were Airborne," Sarah said, pointing to the edge of the military insignia tattoo visible under his short sleeve. "It wasn't the 101st, by any chance?"

"Yes, ma'am, the Screaming Eagles!" Garrison said beaming, standing up a little straighter. "Those were the best years of my life! You have a husband or brother with the 101st?"

"Ex-boyfriend, actually, but we still stay in touch. He's stationed at Fort Campbell right now, but of course he could be shipped out any day."

"Well, God bless him. God bless all those lucky bastards, ma'am," Garrison said, practically misty-eyed with pride.

Sarah gave up on having him call her by her first name, but she was quite satisfied that she had scored some major brownie points with him. She didn't realize just how many, however, until another guard approached them singing the *Ghostbusters* song. Garrison gave the unsuspecting man a thorough military-style chewing out and told the guard to pass the word that he would not tolerate any disrespect toward "Investigator Brooks."

The first objective was *Kinder Krossing* on the main level of the east wing, to the right of the atrium by the grand entrance. Sarah had requested a copy of the floor plans and used color-coded marks to identify places of varying interest. Some locations had blue or yellow squares and triangles, but *Kinder Krossing* was currently a red X, as was the *Sun 'n Surf* on the second level of the west wing. As Sarah folded up her map, she wondered just how much red ink would cover it before her investigation was through.

Garrison introduced Sarah to *Kinder Krossing's* manager and staff. Fortunately, thanks to a memo and an active grapevine, he was spared the awkward task of explaining why Sarah was there—everyone had been buzzing about it all morning. Two of the younger employees even risked their manager's raised eyebrow as they requested Sarah's autograph.

"Okay, if we could get down to business, now," Sarah said while obliging the request, and then quickly engaging the manager's attention before the woman could rebuke her employees. "Were you here on opening day, and could you tell me, in your own words, exactly what happened?"

The manager basically described a scene of chaos as screaming children stumbled out of *Kinder Krossing* and spread their terror and confusion throughout the center. As she had not personally witnessed any of the costumed men in the Ballroom, she could not add any further details to the incident.

"I see. So do you know how these hoaxers were able to leave here without being spotted on any of the security cameras?" Sarah asked in a practiced neutral tone, as she waved her pen in the direction of a series of cameras mounted the length of the facility.

"Well, I...I don't know *how* they did it," she replied, clearly not so sure of herself after all. "All I know is that by the time I got to the Ballroom, there wasn't anyone there."

"Who was the first person to go into that room after the incident began?" Sarah asked, making eye contact with all of the staff as she spoke—all, except one teenaged boy who looked as if he was trying to melt into the wall behind him. "Would that have been you, Bill?"

The boy was startled by the sound of his name, apparently not realizing that his enormous, pink, bunny-shaped nametag was the source of Sarah's seemingly miraculous knowledge.

"I was just trying to help the kids get out of the Ballroom. I heard them screaming, I didn't know what was going on. I was only trying to help!"

"Bill was very helpful getting the children out," the manager spoke up, both trying to bolster the boy's confidence, and prevent him from answering any further questions. "He even carried out the little Whitaker boy who had fainted. Bill is a very valuable employee, and he didn't *see* anything."

If Bill wants to keep his job, he didn't see anything, Sarah thought as she jotted down a few notes.

"Well, I thank you all for your time, and I don't want to keep you any longer. If you don't mind, I'll just poke around for a few minutes and maybe take a few pictures. Bill, why don't you show me the Ballroom?" Sarah said as she placed a hand on the boy's arm and summarily moved him toward the back of the facility, away from the manager.

Over the years, Sarah had developed many techniques and excuses for separating witnesses for questioning. Granted, this was not her most subtle approach, but she didn't have time to finesse every one of the hundreds of witnesses and employees involved in this mess.

Bill stopped abruptly, at least ten feet from the Ballroom door, and with an unsteady finger pointed and blurted out, "There it is."

The door to the Ballroom still had remnants of yellow crime scene tape, and all of the balls had been removed during the investigation. The broken furniture and crushed toys had also been removed from the area, but Sarah could still imagine the mayhem that opening day.

"It would be helpful if you would go in with me and show me exactly where you found the Whitaker boy," Sarah said gently, but then prodded just a bit. "You aren't afraid to go in there, are you? You didn't see anything unusual that day, did you?"

The poor boy's forehead glistened with sweat, and he rubbed his hands together as if he was trying to remove something sticky.

"The manager told you I didn't see anything," he said as his wide eyes stared past Sarah and through the small window into the Ballroom.

After looking around to make sure they were not being watched, Sarah took a step closer and put a reassuring hand on his shoulder.

"Look, it's okay to be scared. Just the other night I was so scared I ran away fast enough to win a big chicken gold medal," she said softly, as the boy finally made eye contact and managed a thin smile. "Let's go inside, and you can tell me exactly what you saw, and I promise not to say a word to your boss."

Shaking his head in agreement, he nonetheless reluctantly followed Sarah as she stepped down into the large, empty Ballroom, and he didn't notice as she turned on a tiny recorder built into the surface of her equipment case. Thanks to the resourceful staff at Spygear.com, nervous witnesses like Bill never felt needlessly inhibited about their every word being recorded.

Before the boy spoke, Sarah took a few pictures, and quietly noted a couple of possible anomalies on two of the digital images. Pulling her EMF meter out of a vest pocket, she casually began walking toward the area where the odd-shaped blobs of pale light had appeared.

"So, Bill, you hear kids screaming, and see them start to run out the door. What did you do?" she said as she glanced at the meter and saw that there was indeed an elevated electromagnetic field there. Hair was standing up on the back of her neck, but she didn't move, and didn't stop smiling.

"Well, I ran over to the door and helped a few kids who had fallen. I asked what was happening, and one girl yelled that there were men inside," his voice began to trail away and he took a step back towards the doorway.

"It's okay, Bill. Just relax and tell me what you did next," Sarah said calmly, even though her own skin was crawling as she stood firmly in the midst of an unpleasant paranormal disturbance.

"I yelled for someone to call security, then a second later the doorway was clear and I jumped inside. At first, all I saw was a couple of kids a few feet in front of me, right about here. They were screaming and struggling to get to the door, but kept falling down. I grabbed their arms and pulled them back this way to the door. I lifted them out, and then I turned to see if anyone...if anyone else..."

This time words completely failed him.

"Were there any men in here, Bill? Did you see someone?" Sarah said more forcefully.

"There was a man, at least I thought it was a man. It was dark, I couldn't be sure, but he was standing, well, just about right where you are now," Bill said pointing that shaky finger again.

What a coincidence, Sarah thought as she switched off the meter and headed back toward Bill.

"Go ahead, go on. What else did you see? What did he look like?"

"It was dark, I can't be sure, but it kinda looked like he was wearing a big apron, and he had a hat."

"A soldier's type of hat?"

"Yeah, maybe."

"Was there anyone else?"

"There was something else, something long, bigger than a kid, down on top of the balls."

"Another man?"

"Coulda been."

"And what did these two men do?"

"Nothing. I only saw them for a couple of seconds, and then they weren't there anymore."

"They left?"

"No. They disappeared," Bill said in a whisper of terror—and relief that he had finally been able to tell his story.

"All right, Bill, you're doing very well. Now after the men disappeared, where did you find the boy?"

"I stood here for a couple of seconds, thinking I was out of my mind. Then I heard a kid crying, over by where I thought I saw those guys, and I kinda snapped out of it. I got over there as soon as I could and found the boy under the balls. I pulled him out and carried him out of the room. I told everyone I didn't see anything because I didn't want to lose my job. You won't tell, will you? You won't tell anyone how scared I was, or what I saw?"

"I would never say a word without your permission," Sarah assured him. "And I think you are very brave for standing your ground, and then rescuing that boy. Tell you what, here's my card if you need to get in touch with me for anything. Thank you very much, Bill, you have been extremely helpful."

"Get all you need here, ma'am?" Garrison asked as she exited *Kinder Krossing*.

"Yes, thanks. I'll be setting up some cameras and equipment here tonight, so please let everyone know to stay away from this area after closing," Sarah replied as her pulse quickened with thoughts of the night to come. She was certain this would not be any ordinary ghost hunt. Not that you could really call *any* ghost hunt ordinary, of course, but this place felt like it was built on top of a spiritual powder keg. The real question would be whether she would be able to defuse it before it blew up in her face.

"Where next?"

"Let's work our way up and over to the *Sun 'n Surf*, and let me know if we pass any points of interest," Sarah said with mounting enthusiasm. She could hardly wait to get to the dressing room where the amazing apparition passed through the mirror, but she didn't think running and making whooping sounds would help her credibility.

The two young female employees of the *Sun 'n Surf* were more than happy to let Sarah go alone into the dressing room area. Her palms were actually moist, and her breathing more rapid, as she grasped the handle to the infamous dressing room #1. Would she open the door and come face to face with a phantom soldier? Would the icy cold hit her skin like a slap in the face, and would the stench of long-dead flesh fill the air?

Taking a deep breath, she pushed open the door, but all Sarah saw was a small padded bench, a few hooks on the wall, and the same blue-green carpeting that covered the rest of the store. The mirror was bright and shiny, and didn't appear as if it was about to become a portal between the worlds of the living and the dead. The temperature was normal. She took many photos, from every conceivable angle, but nothing unusual appeared. The EMF meter held steady at zero. The only scent hanging in the air was from some cheap perfume, no doubt worn by a recent customer. There were no sounds, nothing reached out and grabbed her, and the only thing Sarah felt was damn foolish.

Sitting down on the bench, her body relaxed from full-alert status, and she playfully tapped on the mirror and said, "Helllooo, is anybody in there?"

Laughing at herself, she pulled her hand back and a finger brushed against the metal clip of a hanger left on a hook. The contact sent a sharp zap of electricity up her hand, but she was certain it was nothing more than static built up from walking on the new carpet. Still, it was sobering, and she reminded herself never to tease the dead. They could be very touchy about such things.

The rest of the second level, and the third, as well, showed little or no activity. By the time they reached the fourth level, the scent of things like fresh coffee, pizza, tacos, pretzels, and French fries from the food court dispelled all thoughts of ghosts, and the growling of demons from hell would be nothing to the sounds being produced by Sarah's stomach.

"Could I buy you some lunch, Dan?" Sarah asked, well prepared not to take no for an answer.

"No, ma'am, thanks anyway. You go ahead and eat and give me a call when you're done," Garrison said as he backed away from both Sarah and the very idea of sitting down on the job.

"It would be my honor to treat a Screaming Eagle! You could tell me all about your adventures…and I could let you in on a few of the recent stories I've heard," Sarah said, shamelessly dangling an irresistible carrot.

"Well, maybe just some coffee, for just a few minutes," he replied with a grin he couldn't hide. "Of course, I don't want to bore you…"

"Enough! No more!" Sarah finally said in protest.

"I'm sorry, have I been rambling on too long?" Garrison said after finishing his tenth or eleventh army story.

"No, not at all!" Sarah said quickly, having actually enjoyed watching the stiff security guard let down his hair—figuratively, of course, given the crew cut—and tell a series of hilarious and harrowing stories about his years jumping out of planes into all manner of situations. "I mean, enough of this food! I can't eat another bite. We must have just consumed more Greek food than they have in all of Athens."

"Oh come on, just one more little bite, " Garrison said chuckling, as he began to raise a large fork-full of food toward her. But his arm suddenly stopped, and the smile disappeared from his face.

"What's wrong?" Sarah asked with concern, hoping all her loosening-up techniques had not just backfired.

"Trouble," he replied, motioning behind her.

"Let me guess…" she said as she slowly turned in her seat to see a group of at least thirty people heading her way.

Garrison sprang to his feet and positioned himself firmly between the oncoming crowd and Sarah. She also stood up, and sidestepped just a bit to see past her self-proclaimed bodyguard. She recognized a few of the shirt-logos, and some of the equipment they carried, and knew that these were members of ghost hunting clubs. She also saw that the muscular security chief's very presence intimidated many of them more than any apparition they ever encountered.

"It's okay, Dan, they're friendlies. I hope," Sarah said, and then stepped out in front of him to put the crowd more at ease.

"You're Sarah Brooks! We've been looking all over for you! What have you found? Can we help? Wait 'til you see what we found, Sarah," about a dozen people said all at once.

Mothers with little children started packing them into strollers and hurrying away at the site of the large group of unusual-looking people, and many other shoppers turned away from the food court thinking there was some kind of fight brewing.

"Look everyone, we are creating a bit of a disturbance here," she said smiling, although feeling extremely uncomfortable and a bit embarrassed by the situation. "Dan, is there someplace around here we could all go to get out of the way?"

"Back in the corner, behind the *China Express*," he replied tensely, and then spoke a few words that she couldn't hear into his walkie-talkie, although Sarah had no doubt more guards would be arriving shortly. The situation could get very ugly.

"Okay, let's go back over there so we can talk," Sarah said, graciously signing a few books and a couple of T-shirts that were thrust her way as they walked.

Garrison let some space open up between him and Sarah, but never more than would allow a rapid response should any of her fans get out of hand. The group did appear just very friendly and enthusiastic, but there were a lot of crazy people in this world—at least thirty-two by Garrison's quick headcount.

As the group gathered behind the *China Express*—much to the dismay and consternation of the oriental girl who's platter of General Tso's chicken samples was suddenly emptied—Sarah noticed at least half a dozen guards, and two dozen more ghost hunters approaching. It was soon going to get very cramped in that access hallway.

Sarah grabbed a chair to stand on and called for everyone to settle down. She was always amazed at how crowds fell silent when she started to speak, and often felt a guilty pleasure as if she was a schoolteacher in control of a room full of obedient little kindergartners. But she also never forgot that if not for a few quirks of fate, she might easily be one of the crowd. Then there was the fact that she still couldn't take her own celebrity status seriously, which actually only fueled her popularity.

"I want to welcome everyone here today," she began, immediately turning on the charm. "I see a few familiar faces from some of my lectures. Aren't you Ricky, from the New York club?"

The burly man in front actually blushed at being acknowledged, and turned downright crimson when she went on to compliment him on his work on a recent investigation he had led. Sarah then skillfully used the opening to segue into the more pressing matter.

"Now I know you all just want to help, but I'm sure Ricky can tell you, and you all know from your own experience, that the best way to conduct a reliable investigation is with as few people and as little distractions as possible. I have been hired to do a job here, a professional job, and I know none of you want to compromise this investigation in any way," Sarah said employing all of her diplomatic tact, hoping it was enough, as she glanced back to see a V-formation of security guards behind her, with the ever-alert Dan Garrison as point man.

"But we want to help!" one woman in the back shouted. "We came all the way from Texas to be here!"

Several other people shouted out their states or the miles they traveled to get there.

"I understand, believe me, I do understand. I'll tell you what, just give me a chance tonight to be alone and do some preliminary work. If I find out I'm going to need some help, I'll put a message up on my website and we'll get together again and work out a plan. Is that fair enough?" Sarah asked with both hands raised, hoping it didn't look too much like she was pleading with them, which, of course, she was.

There was some mumbling and grumbling, but then Ricky spoke up.

"She's right," he said in a deep, booming voice. "Let Sarah do what she does best. I know *I* wouldn't want a bunch of bozos like us messin' up one of my investigations."

Thankfully, everyone laughed and more cheerfully agreed to give her some breathing room. As the crowd dispersed, Sarah stepped off the chair and shook Ricky's massive hand.

"I appreciate that, Ricky. And let me know how I can get in touch with you tomorrow to give you a personal update," she said handing him her note pad.

"Here's my cell, or you could just ask for me at this motel," he said scribbling down the information. As he handed back the pad, he glanced quickly around and then whispered. "Hey, just between you and me, there's a real shitload of activity here, ain't there?"

"I don't know if that's exactly the technical term for it," she said, unsuccessfully trying to keep a straight face, "but, yeah, Ricky, I think there's a real shitload."

"Okay, Sarah, you're okay," Ricky said with a pat on the back that almost floored her. "You give me a call anytime, we'll be there for you. You're okay!"

Chapter 8

Jimmy O'Reilly couldn't concentrate on his homework. Every three or four minutes he looked at the time, wondering why Sarah hadn't yet called. He had been hoping she would page him at school with an urgent message to get down to Virginia ASAP. When he got home, he was sure there would be a message in his email or on his answering machine. Even though she had said she would call after 4pm, by 3:59pm he couldn't stand the suspense any longer and reached for his phone.

"Hi, Jimmy, I just now walked into my hotel room," Sarah said glancing at her watch. "You just had to call, you just couldn't wait, could you?"

"To be honest, no, I couldn't! What did you find? Tell me everything."

For the next twenty minutes, Sarah told Jimmy all about the protestors, reporters, and ghost hunters converging on Wegman's Center, the feeling she had entering the parking garage, the incidents in the elevator and the Ballroom, and the lack of anything substantial in the dressing room. She described the interesting characters she had met—the slippery general manager, the efficient assistant who knew more than she let on, the strong-jawed sheriff, and the noble and fearless chief of security. Jimmy insisted on hearing every detail, and she hoped by obliging him it would curb his desire to cut classes and hop on the next shuttle to D.C.

"So, you need me, then, right?" Jimmy asked as Sarah tried to recall having that much boundless energy and enthusiasm at his age.

"It would be nice to have you here, but there are at least 300 people already here willing to help if I need it."

"But none of them are like me!" he said more like a desperate question begging to be answered.

"Of course not, Jimmy. I'm sure none of them are as brave and efficient as you. Now, don't you have homework to do?"

"All right. But you have to let me know what happens tonight as soon as you finish. Promise? I'm not going to school until I hear from you."

"Okay, I promise. Now let me take a nap so I have the strength to get through this night."

Before even attempting to rest, Sarah made sure the front desk knew to hold all of her calls. The media was hounding her for interviews, but she simply couldn't handle ghosts *and* reporters in the same day.

Dr. Carl Henkel paced back and forth as he waited for the limo to pick him up at the airport and bring him home. He had taken an earlier flight out of Dallas, but neglected to arrange for an earlier ride. He had hoped to get back in time to get to Wegman's Center before closing, but that didn't look likely now.

His calls to Fink's office had not been returned, his wife had no more news, and the sheriff's office was not releasing any information. When performing brain surgery, Henkel faced the direst situations with unflappable patience and resolve, but with this mysterious state of affairs at Wegman's, he couldn't stand the suspense.

When he finally got home, he kissed his wife, dropped his bags and went right into his study to prepare a full report. He had previously submitted reports on all his findings and conclusion to anyone who would listen, but his audience had been small. Perhaps now, the time would be right to get his evidence seen and understood.

Henkel read and reread his words out loud, to reassure himself of their accuracy, clarity, and impact. He double-checked all of the copies of letters, reports, and diary entries he had found. Three times he went over the details of the map of Wegman's Crossing in 1864 that he had drawn based upon the scraps of information he had pieced together.

Actually, it wasn't really much of a map, and he would be the first to admit it, but it just might hold the key to a lot of questions. In the northeast corner of the map was the tiny town of Cullum's Tavern, surrounded by woods and having no more than a dozen houses and businesses, including, of course, the famous tavern. There was also a creek flowing south—optimistically called the William River—named for a grandson in the Cullum family. Henkel slowly and methodically used his finger to trace the path of that little winding ribbon of ink on the page that represented the creek, as if hoping he would feel some undeniable sensation when it passed over the true location of the missing Wegman's Crossing.

The crossing itself had been no more than an infrequently used bridge with a nearby house and barn. It had been the property of Azel Wegman, who lost his wife during childbirth, lost his only son in the first year of the war, and was listed as missing and presumed dead shortly after he volunteered to fight for the Confederacy in 1863. Birth and death records existed, there were documents showing that he paid his taxes every year, and there was even a mention in a local newspaper in 1857 that Azel Wegman was the proud owner of a prize pig, but no evidence survived pinpointing exactly where Wegman's Crossing had been.

The best Henkel had to go on when his search began was that the bridge over the William River was somewhere between one and three miles to the southeast of the tavern. Unfortunately, the same dense woods and notorious underbrush that ensnared the armies during the Battle of the Wilderness grew just as thickly for many miles around Cullum's Tavern. During the 1980s, Henkel spent two or three weekends per year combing the forest and riverbanks for any signs of the bridge, house, barn, or battle. On occasion, his metal detector came across a stray Minié ball, but nothing else ever materialized.

Henkel, with his busy schedule, always thought that when he retired from his practice he would devote more time to the search. Although the search eventually transformed itself into something of a personal quest, there was no immediate sense of urgency—after all, everything had been buried for well over a century, what was another decade or so?

However, as the 1990s passed, Henkel nervously watched as housing developments and businesses stretched ever deeper into the Virginia woods. The growing sense of urgency threatened to turn to panic when plans were announced to build the country's second largest shopping center in Cullum's Tavern along the banks of the William River. The river itself would be redirected through an underground tunnel running to the western edge of the center's parking lots. The clock was ticking, and Henkel was acutely aware of every second that was being lost.

After creating a website and having letters published in several Civil War history periodicals, Henkel managed to assemble a group of volunteers to help in the search. It was a small, but diverse and talented group, and one and all were happy to use their expertise in the quest. One investment banker had his own plane, which they used for aerial mapping. A university professor arranged to borrow some ground penetrating radar equipment. High technology in many fields was employed, but even as the town board prepared to vote on Octagon's building proposal, not a shred of evidence was uncovered.

Tired, frustrated, and running out of time, Carl Henkel stood in the gathering darkness one Sunday night on the banks of the William River and suddenly thought about his grandmother. She had been a woman of strong faith, and had always told her favorite grandson that, "Sometimes you need to be lost to be found." As he had wandered far from his car that day, and literally didn't know in which direction to go at that moment, he stopped and pondered his grandmother's enigmatic words.

If ever there was a time that I was lost, and needed to do some finding, this is it, he thought as he shoved his compass into his pocket and just started walking. He didn't exactly feel his prayers had been answered, however, when after going no more than a few hundred feet he stumbled over a rock and fell. Rising to his hands and knees, he turned to get a better look at the object at which he was about to hurl a string of very creative curses. Before he let loose, however, something interesting caught his eye.

Switching on his flashlight, he noticed what appeared to be bits of some type of mortar, and the conservative, no-nonsense doctor actually felt his whole body begin to tingle with excitement. Tearing away some underbrush and scraping at the dirt with his bare hands, he saw that the large rock was actually several chiseled stones mortared together. Forgetting he had a backpack full of expensive tools, he grabbed the nearest stick and frantically dug deeper. The more he uncovered, the more disappointed he became that the angles and proportions of the stones were unlike those of a foundation.

Sitting back down where he had fallen, he pointed the strong beam of his halogen flashlight on the handful of exposed stones and ran through a short list of possibilities. It was doubtful that they had been part of a fence, as masonry walls were uncommon for a small farmhouse in this area. They didn't look like the stones usually used for wells, either. The answer eluded him until he stood up and literally shifted his focus from ground level to something higher.

"A chimney!" he shouted into the darkness. "This is the top of a goddamned chimney!"

It had become too dark to do any further investigating that night, but with great satisfaction he unfurled one of the red marking flags he had been carrying for almost twenty years, and firmly drove it into the ground near his discovery. Retracing (and counting) his steps back to the creek, he stuck another flag into the moist soil a few feet from the water. He again counted the number of paces along the creek until he found the path leading back to his car. He would take no chances losing what he had just found.

Henkel got little sleep that night, and the following morning he canceled all his appointments and arranged for two of the volunteers to meet him. He was trying not to get his hopes too high, but he had the strangest feeling he had finally found the elusive and almost mythic Wegman's Crossing. There was no explanation for the feeling, nor was there any denying it.

Thanks to his notes and the red flags, the three men had no trouble finding the few pieces of stone that had so ably caught Henkel's attention. Using them as a center point, they laid out a grid and powered up the metal detectors. Within fifteen minutes, they found eighteen Minié balls. Ten minutes later, one of the men unearthed a small, flat, round object. Carefully brushing away the dirt, the three grown men acted like children on Christmas morning when they saw it was a Confederate uniform button.

However, the most compelling, and gruesome, discovery was to be Henkel's. Working just a few yards from the chimney stones, his detector signaled a solid hit—most likely gold. Meticulously removing and sifting about 10 inches of soil, the unmistakable glint of gold shone out of a layer of dirt as black as ash. Unlike the discovery of the button, the three men were silent as Henkel slowly brushed away the last bits of dirt, and solemnly lifted out a gold tooth and fragments of a jawbone.

"Okay, that's it," Henkel said after wrapping the bits of human remains and placing them in a box. "It's time for the professionals. We have no idea how many bodies may be here, and this needs to be done right!"

The two other men agreed without question, and packed up their equipment with barely another word. Although this discovery was most likely the culmination of a life's dream, there was no joy in it. Henkel knew in his heart, and felt it in the pit of his stomach, that the ground on which he now stood was not only the site of an historic old farmhouse and a Civil War battle—it was a cemetery.

Henkel assumed that he would announce his findings, and the site would be protected, excavated, catalogued, studied, and preserved. He dared to even think that he would gain some measure of fame for the discovery, although clearly he was not in it for personal gain. He even imagined that some day there might be a museum on the site and it would become part of the National Military Parks system. Of course, first they would have to confirm it was the actual site of the battle, and then spend years studying and interpreting the artifacts, but it was never too early to start dreaming.

Unfortunately, sometimes it is too late. Just a few days before Henkel's discovery, the Octagon Corporation had closed the deal on the land purchase. The previous owner had given Henkel permission to search the property. Octagon had not. The previous owner was sympathetic to the cause of historic preservation. Octagon was not.

Rather than finding fame and glory, Octagon's legal team confiscated all of the artifacts and threatened to charge Henkel with trespassing, theft, and everything else they could think of. They publicly suggested how convenient it was that after twenty years of fruitless searches, Henkel was able to find these artifacts "just in the nick of time." They further pointed out that the artifacts weren't anything that couldn't be purchased in a hundred gift shops or online, and it wouldn't be beyond the capabilities of a physician to obtain pieces of human bone. While they stopped just short of accusing Henkel of out and out fraud, they were a mere legal hair's breadth away.

Henkel rallied support from numerous historic organizations and groups, but the battle was over before it even began. An Octagon lawyer put it best when he stated that, "No court in the land would halt a project worth hundreds of millions of dollars because of a few souvenirs and an old tooth." There was simply not enough evidence to warrant any change of plans for the massive new shopping center, and no one with any real power in the state dared speak out against a future tax revenue generator of this size.

The lawsuit filed against Octagon was swiftly dismissed, although the judge did say that he urged the developers to voluntarily come forward if they uncovered anything significant. Henkel knew better than to hold his breath.

When the alarm went off, Sarah had no clue as to where she was. All she knew was that it was another hotel, another investigation, and another time she was waking up alone. The temptation to hit the snooze button was strong, but as the mental haze lifted, the name "Wegman" wafted through her memory. That triggered a burst of adrenalin that blew away the last cobwebs of fatigue, and she literally jumped to her feet. She couldn't recall the last time she was this excited, and nervous, about an investigation, and her hand actually trembled as she ran through the equipment checklist. Before closing the last case, she gave Mitty the bear an extra tight squeeze and felt calmed by the crooked stitched smile on his tattered snout.

"Stick close to me tonight, Mitty," she said out loud, making sure his mohair coat didn't get pinched in the lid. "I think we are in for a wild time."

Sarah had requested that a rental car be delivered to the hotel parking lot, as she had wanted to be less conspicuous than traveling around in a limo. Picking up the keys at the front desk, she then wheeled her stack of equipment cases out a side door, hoping to be even less conspicuous. Checking the plastic key tag for the type of car and the plate number, Sarah hadn't gone more than a few yards out the door when a bright light blinded her. Not only couldn't she see the key tag, she never saw the curb she subsequently stumbled over. Squinting and shielding her eyes from what she thought were car headlights, she saw a rush of people heading straight for her. They had cameras and microphones, and they suddenly swarmed around her like killer bees.

"Ms. Brooks, do you really think Wegman's Center is haunted?"

"What proof have you uncovered that there are ghosts at Wegman's Center?"

"How do you respond to critics who say you are a fraud?"

"Will you be performing an exorcism tonight?"

A dozen questions were shot at her simultaneously, and the camera lights and mob of reporters blocked Sarah from getting to her car, or even having a chance of finding it.

"Please, everyone, I'm just beginning my investigation tonight," she shouted over the din. "I'll speak to you when I have something to report, but I can't do anything unless you let me go!"

Undeterred, the reporters continued to encircle her and shove microphones toward her face. Losing her grip on the handle of the luggage cart she used for the equipment cases, they were quickly knocked over and trampled by the crowd. That was the last straw. Sarah was about two seconds away from pulling the can of pepper spray out of her vest pocket, when an even brighter light blinded her.

Fortunately, this light was on a sheriff's patrol car. Deputy Dorothy Franklin quickly pushed her way through to Sarah, and ordered the reporters to back off in a voice that commanded attention. Deputy Franklin may have been small, but she carried a big stick, and her tone implied that she wouldn't hesitate to use it. None of the reporters cared to test that premise, and they collectively took a step back, finally giving Sarah a chance to catch her breath, and her balance.

"You two, pick up those cases," the deputy barked, waving her nightstick at a pair of overzealous local reporters she had busted last year for trespassing during a fatal accident investigation. Trying to be the first to get photographs, they literally crossed the line (of police tape) one too many times after being warned. Their brief jail experience had had a sobering effect.

The two men quickly loaded the cases back on the cart and wheeled them over to rental car that they, and the rest of the reporters, had been watching, ever since being tipped off that the car was going to be used by Sarah Brooks. The rental company itself had provided the information to the media, thinking that it might bring some free publicity. It seemed that everyone wanted a piece of the action.

"Beau, I mean Sheriff Davis, thought you might need a little help," Deputy Franklin said as she opened the car door and positioned herself to block the crowd so that Sarah could get in.

"Thank you *very* much," Sarah said with great sincerity. "I don't know what I would have done without you."

"We'll have a talk with the hotel management and see if we can't keep these people back on the sidewalk and out of your face."

"Again, I really appreciate this, and please thank Sheriff Davis for me."

The deputy cleared a path for the car, and then Sarah had to resist the nasty little impulse to stomp on the accelerator and take out three or four of the major networks all at the same time. It was such a relief to pull onto the open highway and leave the glaring camera lights in her rearview mirror. Several news trucks and vans pulled out after her, but they would not be able to follow her to the private parking area of the center, or so she hoped.

The last customers were just leaving as Sarah arrived, and the doors were being locked behind them. The movie theaters still had some patrons for the last shows of the evening, but they would have to exit directly into the parking lot, as the inside gates had been shut. The cleaning staff had been ordered to stay clear of the designated investigation areas and everyone had been asked to power down all nonessential equipment—especially the toy store which normally kept its talking dolls chattering throughout the night so they wouldn't have to restart them all each morning.

Dan Garrison was waiting for Sarah as she pulled into the parking garage. This time she welcomed his help with the equipment.

"This is some heavy stuff for trying to catch some wispy spooks," Dan said good-naturedly.

"I like to look at my work as paranormal special ops," Sarah replied with a wink. "But seriously, you would appreciate some of the night vision and surveillance equipment I've got. Latest generation stuff. And there's some really cool software I've had modified that-"

"Well, Ms. Brooks!" Fink bellowed as he entered the parking garage with the security guard who escorted him to his car every night. "I see you have all your little toys with you. I'm sure they won't really be necessary, but let's do whatever we can to clear up this whole thing quickly, shall we? Well, good luck, and just let Garrison know if you need anything."

Fink hurried to his car, locked the doors, and sped away. He came and went so quickly that Sarah didn't have time to do serious damage to her tongue, which she had to bite as soon as he started talking.

"That man is one serious horse's ass," Sarah said, shaking her head.

"Now, ma'am, that's doing quite a disservice to horses," Dan replied dryly.

Dan Garrison escorted Sarah to her three investigation sites to drop off equipment, and to make sure she didn't get lost. The once bright and noisy center seemed a world apart in the silent darkness. It was always remarkable how different places like schools and offices appeared when everyone went home and the lights went out. Even such benign locations seemed eerie, so it should not have come as any surprise that this cavernous center, rife with restless spirits, would be particularly unnerving after hours. Still, Sarah was unpleasantly surprised at just how unsettling it was.

Once she had her bearings, and the right cases were delivered to the right locations, Sarah shook hands with the head of security and promised for the fourth time to call him on the two-way radio he gave her if she needed anything. Even though he had been at work since early that morning, he insisted on remaining on duty throughout the night as well. This was clearly more than a job to him, and he had taken it upon himself to make Sarah his personal responsibility.

The first site was the Ballroom at *Kinder Krossing*. Sarah needed to take a deep breath before passing by the oversized stuffed animals. They appeared grotesque and menacing in the dim glow generated by the red status indicators on the emergency lighting units and security cameras spaced along the ceiling. Although she was packing enough candlepower to support a small lighthouse, she tried to keep artificial lighting to a minimum to eliminate any results that could be misinterpreted.

If she only had a dollar for every photograph or video clip fans had showed her of alleged ghosts, which upon analysis proved to have embarrassingly simple explanations. There were the parallel streaks of car headlights passing by cemeteries, the countless reflections in mirrors, windows, road signs, and even plastic slipcovers, and spirals and orbs from fellow ghost hunter's flashlights. It was also remarkable how heavy smokers always had the greatest "ectoplasm" photos, and always categorically denied that such images were the result of their own clouds of cigarette smoke.

Then there was the all-time classic—accidentally photographing your own camera strap. The effect of a camera's flash reflecting off a braided cord, just inches from the lens, produced literally hundreds of "bright twisting vortex energy" images that filled her mailbox on a regular basis. Such images were distinct and unmistakable, and Sarah always felt a bit awkward deflating someone's expectations by gently pointing out that they had not actually captured an image of a powerful spirit of the dead. Of course, it wasn't any easier explaining to them that the "shadow beings" at the edges of some photos were most likely the tips of their own fingers.

This expertise was hard won, however, because if there was a mistake to be made in the ghost hunting world, Sarah had made it, in duplicate and triplicate. She had quickly learned that searching for spirits was not like conducting an experiment in the controlled environment of a laboratory. There were few rules, and rarely was any aspect of the situation under her control. It soon became clear that the key to becoming a successful paranormal investigator was to learn from her own mistakes, and then share this knowledge and experience with others—if they were willing to listen.

The Ballroom door had been left open, and a folding table, extension cords, and power strips were in place as she had requested. However, despite the fact that it appeared as if the investigation would progress in an orderly fashion, the goose bumps on her arms were already standing at attention as she opened the first equipment case.

"Yes, yes, I know you are here, and you know that I know you're here," Sarah said out loud, not to provoke a response, but just to settle her own nerves. It didn't work.

A puff of cold air hit her for a spilt second, and was gone. Then from somewhere behind her came a loud banging noise, as if a door slammed, or something heavy fell off a shelf. Sarah's fingers tingled as she raced to get the instruments hooked up, and the cameras and sensitive sound equipment recording. Everything was connected to the laptops that were programmed to mark any change in temperature, humidity, movement, sound, light, radiation, and electromagnetic fields. This way, she did not have to sit through hours of tapes that had recorded nothing unusual. The computers would create lists of time-stamped events upon which she could then focus her attention.

Once everything was up and running, she stepped softly away, back towards the *Kinder Krossing* exit. There were never any certainties in the ghost hunting world, but she would bet a hundred fruit baskets that the Ballroom would produce some amazing sights and sounds. She was tempted to stay and observe first-hand, but there was a lot more haunted ground to cover that night.

The next objective was the expansive food court. This large area called for a ring of motion detectors set up in a pattern that would allow the calculated direction, speed, and size of anything dense enough to disrupt their beams. It had taken Sarah over a year to come up with the ideal pattern, but now it was second nature as she placed the detectors at various heights and angles on tables, garbage cans and countertops. Each wireless detector sent its data to a central unit that was connected to a laptop. She chose the silent alarm mode for this investigation, as a bunch of wailing sirens would clearly be counterproductive under the circumstances.

Three infrared camcorders with wide-angle lenses were next to be set up, outside the perimeter of the motion detectors. Then she placed a few more instruments in what she guessed to be key locations, based upon the activity reports she had read. When everything was ready, she sat for a moment to jot down some notes. As she wrote, she had the distinct feeling of being watched, and thought she might have heard something moving in the broad corridor of stores leading to the food court.

Immediately snapping into what she referred to as her "predator mode"—muscles tensing, pupils dilating, pulse quickening, ears straining for the slightest sound—she turned slowly to face the corridor. Almost immediately there was another faint sound, like the rustling of leaves. It couldn't be rationally explained, but something *felt* different about these sounds. She actually felt threatened, and quickly decided to ease her own restrictions on artificial light. Slowly and silently, Sarah pulled a hefty halogen flashlight from a belt loop, aimed it toward the corridor, and switched it on.

The powerful beam cut through the darkness and sent a bright circle of light down the center of the corridor. There were some benches and large potted plants about one hundred and fifty feet away, and Sarah put a short monocular to her eye to get a better look. One of the palm-like plants was swaying slightly from side to side, as if something had brushed by. All the other plants stood still.

"Is anyone there?" she called out in what she hoped was a fearless voice.

There was no response. Moving the beam of the flashlight down each side of the corridor, she looked for any movement or unusual shadows along the elaborate storefronts. A strange figure made her catch her breath for a moment, until she realized it was simply a cardboard cutout of a man holding a six-foot cell phone. Another minute passed and there were no more sounds, so she switched off the flashlight and made a note of the time and approximate duration, so she could later check it against the images and data she was collecting. Even though it had probably been nothing, Sarah decided to check with Dan on the radio.

"Hi, everything is okay. I just wanted to make sure none of the staff is anywhere near the food court," Sarah said, half-wishing to hear that some janitor had mistakenly wandered her way.

"No, ma'am. Everyone is accounted for and right where they should be. In fact, the cleaning staff was sent home early. Just me and a few other guards here now. Is there a problem?" he asked with concern.

"Nope, just hearing things," Sarah said with a bit of a forced laugh. "But then, that's what I'm getting paid for, isn't it?"

"Where you headed next?"

"I'm going to *Sun 'n Surf*."

"Do you want me to meet you there?" he asked in a tone that indicated he was ready to spring into action.

"No, that's okay. Everything is fine. As soon as I finish the last set up, I'll swing by your office and we'll have a cup of coffee."

"Sounds good."

Just hearing another human voice made Sarah more relaxed, but still, she avoided heading back through that fourth–floor corridor. Instead, she used the stairs down to the second floor and then made her way to the infamous bikini shop. She made a point of first opening the case that held Mitty. Even in the dim light, his orange glass eyes had a sparkle that made her smile.

"You would think I would be used to all this by now," she said to Mitty as she straightened one of his ears and tried to fluff some of his flattened mohair. "But, then again, you would think I wouldn't still be talking to stuffed bears. No offense, of course, Mitty."

The set up took a little longer than she had anticipated, as she had to take the liberty of unscrewing the hinges and removing the door from the dressing room where Grace Hopkins had the scare of her life. It had been necessary so she could get the proper camera angle on the mirror where the soldier had appeared. Just as she finished placing the last piece of equipment, there was another odd noise behind her again, somewhere in the store.

How come sounds are always behind me? she thought. *Why can't anything ever be in front of me, where I can see it?*

Removing her night vision goggles from a case on her left hip, she slipped the unit over her head. Before flipping the goggles down over her eyes, she pressed a couple of buttons and verified that all the equipment was functioning properly. Almost instantly, readings began fluctuating, and it looked as if this dressing room would prove to be a legitimate paranormal hot spot—or cold spot to be more accurate, as the temperature was steadily dropping. But another sound distracted her, something like hangars clicking together on the racks of bathing suits in the store. Switching on the goggles, the store now appeared to be bathed in a bright green light and she could see everything quite clearly.

Immediately, her attention was drawn to a rack near the front entrance. The straps of a few bikini tops were swinging back and forth. There were no drafts, no vents blowing air—something had caused them to move. As she stepped out of the dressing room into the store, there was yet another sound, but that she recognized as the rapid and rhythmic pounding of her own blood against her eardrums. Something was there with her, and it felt bad. Very bad.

Long ago she had learned to trust her intuition, and to get the hell out of a situation before it was too late. Unfortunately, by the time she decided to head for the exit, it was already too late.

A large figure sprang up from behind a display case of sunglasses, and a powerful hand clamped over her mouth before she could utter a sound. Sarah used both hands to pry and claw at the hand, but a sharp jab in her throat suddenly stopped her struggle.

"Don't make a sound, don't move," an ominous voice whispered, "or I'll cut your throat."

Sarah could already feel a trickle of warm blood running down her neck, so she knew she had no choice but to comply, and her arms dropped to her side. The man behind her with the knife pressed his body more tightly against hers, but fortunately eased the pressure of the razor sharp point.

"You see, I can't let you do this," he said in the same raspy whisper. "I've been watching you tonight. You're doing the work of the devil, and he must be stopped at all costs. The devil deceives, he appears in many forms to confuse mankind. There are no such things as ghosts, they are demons in the guise of the dead. God has chosen me to do His work, and I must stop your unholy summoning of these demons!"

Sarah could taste the pungent and salty sweat from the palm that pressed hard against her lips. She gagged, and thought she would vomit, until the man pulled his hand away.

"There, you see, the demons are already trying to flee your body because they recognize *my* power. Once I complete my work here, I will have driven the devil and all his evil helpers from this place!"

She was desperately trying to remain calm, but she was feeling light-headed, and was afraid she might pass out—which could prove fatal. Then in the bright green glow of her night vision goggles, she saw a plus-size macramé bikini hanging on a rack a few yards in front of her. Even in the midst of this perilous situation, the absurdity of such a skimpy and revealing suit for such a large woman made her think, *Now that's real horror!* The plus-size bikini was just what she needed to help clear her head and refocus on staying conscious—and alive. With her eyes fixed on that bathing suit, she found the courage to speak.

"You're mistaken, I'm only conducting a scientific investigation," Sarah dared to say between heaving breaths, hoping she wouldn't further provoke him.

"Lies!" he now shouted into her ear. "The Lord has said that the devil will send demons in the guise of spirits of the dead to deceive mankind. You invite such demons. You are filled with such demons, and must be cleansed!"

The man punctuated his last sentence with another sharp jab to Sarah's throat, and she suddenly realized just what being "cleansed" really meant. For a moment she thought she might faint again, but another glance at that macramé bikini brought her back to her senses. She tried to ease her hand up to the radio, but the man's right hip was pressing against it and she couldn't reach the call button. She was going to have to try to talk her way out of this one.

"Please, just let me know how I can help you do your work. If I have been deceived, then I want to fight the devil, too."

The point of the blade eased for a second, but then pushed deeper into her flesh. The trickle of blood increased to a steady flow.

"No! It's too late. You speak for the devil and he is trying to deceive me. I only hear the voice of the Lord!" he declared in what Sarah thought would be the last thing she would hear on this earth.

"How about *my* voice!" another man shouted as the lights snapped on. "Can you hear *me* when I tell you to drop the knife, or I'll send you to see your Lord right now!"

It was Dan Garrison. Armed, dangerous, sharp-shooting, blessed Dan Garrison. Even though the light in her night vision goggles was too much to bear, Sarah peered underneath them and squinted enough to see the head of security standing thirty feet away with a lovely semi-automatic pistol aimed at the head of her assailant. The only trouble was that her head was just inches from his.

"This is God's work!" the crazed man bellowed with every ounce of self-righteousness he possessed. "I must cut the demons from this devil-worshipping whore!"

That was all Sarah needed to hear to completely clear her head and spring into action. Call her an exorcist, call her a devil-worshipper, call her a fraud, a fake, or a charlatan. But don't you dare call her a whore.

Sarah felt the man's arm tense as he prepared to make the final plunge into her neck, but at the same moment she yanked the can of pepper spray from her vest. Turning it in the direction of her own face, she squeezed the valve as if her life depended on it. The sting was instantaneous, but the night vision goggles deflected most of the burning spray from her eyes. Her assailant, however, had his eyes wide open.

The knife dropped as the man cried out in pain, and his hands moved to wipe the fiery liquid from his face. Sarah dropped to the floor and rolled away, not knowing if bullets were about to be flying through the air. Between the pepper spray and the bright store lights in the sensitive night vision goggles, she was unable to see a thing, but what she heard was not gunfire. It was the precise and highly effective delivering of several blows that quickly rendered her assailant senseless. And Sarah also didn't need to see to know that Dan thoroughly enjoyed his work.

"My God, Sarah, are you okay," Dan said, gently taking her in his arms and pressing a handkerchief against the gash in her throat.

"Thank God the Airborne dropped in," she said removing the goggles and rubbing her eyes.

"Hold on, Sarah, we'll get you some help." Dan brought his radio to his lips and coolly and calmly ordered an ambulance, the Sheriff, and some bottled water for Sarah's eyes.

"How come you came down here?" she asked, starting to sit up, and then thinking better about it.

"Stay down, stay down! You have a nasty cut there, so you just wait for the paramedics," Dan said easing her back to the floor, and then yanking a fistful of terrycloth bathrobes off their hangers to make a pillow for her head. "I figured you wouldn't have called me if you just thought some ghosts were rattling their chains. And when I didn't hear from you for a while I thought I had better see if anything was wrong."

"What about him?" Sarah said, pointing roughly toward where she thought her assailant would be. "Shouldn't we tie him up, or something?"

"Already cuffed him. And anyway, he's most likely going to be asleep for quite a while," Dan said, unable to mask the glee in his voice.

"Well, I hope you gave him one for me," Sarah said, taking hold of his hand and giving it a grateful squeeze.

Within minutes, enough law enforcement personnel were on scene to quell a small riot. The knife-wielding zealot was identified as Reverend Henry T. Wadsworth, Jr., who had several outstanding warrants—including one for burning down his own church in South Carolina after his congregation complained about his proclivity for trying to literally beat the devil out of sinners. He was unceremoniously hauled away—still unconscious—and the knife, still wet with Sarah's blood, was bagged as evidence.

When Sheriff Davis arrived, his heavy breathing made it obvious that he had run the entire distance from his car. Except for his official jacket, he was dressed as one might expect after being wakened from a sound sleep. He had been told that Sarah Brooks was attacked by a man with a knife, and when he saw her lying on the floor covered in blood, he feared the worst.

"Oh, my God!" Davis whispered as he knelt beside her, and then was clearly relieved when she opened her eyes. "Is she going to be all right?"

"The blood loss makes the wound appear worse than it is," replied a paramedic gingerly dabbing the cut with gauze. "I think she'll be okay with a few stitches. The doctor is on his way. Of course, a fraction of an inch deeper might have given our ghost hunter here the opportunity of doing some haunting of her own."

Sarah chuckled at the man's attempt at humor, but she also felt a pang of sick fear in her gut, knowing that only a very fine line—namely the width of an artery wall—had separated her from death. Sheriff Davis regained his composure and immediately started to take charge of the situation. The first order of business would be to make sure that the demon-slaying clergyman hadn't brought any friends along, so Davis arranged with Garrison to make a complete sweep of the center.

Once her eyes were flushed and her neck stitched and bandaged, Sarah was helped to her feet. The room seemed to spin for a moment, but that was probably more the result of nerves, than blood loss. Although the doctor and the paramedics strongly recommended she go straight back to the hotel and rest, Sarah's main concern now was for her cameras and instruments. They continued to insist, and Sarah almost agreed, until a guard returned to inform her that it appeared as though much of her equipment had been trashed—courtesy of the reverend, no doubt.

"Oh no, you don't, not by yourself," Sheriff Davis said, placing a steadying hand on Sarah's arm as she hurriedly left the *Sun 'n Surf.* "You're not going anywhere in this place without me."

"No argument there," she said, as her fingers reached up to gently probe the perimeter of the bandage. The tape and heavy gauze were uncomfortable, but it didn't bother her nearly as much as the freshly stitched wound that had begun a painful throbbing as her heart rate increased. Slowing her pace, the pain eased only slightly. Apparently, the medication she had been given was not yet working.

"Are you sure you should be on your feet?" Davis asked, holding her arm tighter. "I mean, if you aren't even up for an argument…"

"I need to find out what that bastard did to my stuff," Sarah responded, leaning more heavily against the man she had initially thought would never offer her any type of support. While Sarah was a staunch advocate of standing firmly on one's own two feet, she had to admit that having the dashing sheriff to lean on wasn't half bad.

The lights had been turned on throughout the center, as well as inside *Kinder Krossing*, and Sarah was at first worried that the bright lights would damage the sensitive infrared cameras. As she approached the Ballroom, however, she realized that would be the least of her worries.

The table of equipment and computers had been overturned, the camcorders had all been knocked to the floor, and every cable and power cord had been cut. Sarah instinctively reached for her throat again when she saw the slashed wires. Fortunately, nothing appeared to have been smashed, but such delicate electronics and optics were not designed for such rough treatment. It would take hours to check everything, but that could wait. For now, she just wanted to pack up and get out of there.

The equipment in the food court had suffered a similar fate, only here most of the motion detectors had been stomped to bits, or smashed against a wall. They were relatively inexpensive, but Sarah was nonetheless angered by the wanton destruction of her precious gadgets.

At least the equipment back at the *Sun 'n Surf* was untouched, since the reverend had been too busy reaching out to touch Sarah's neck. Everything was still running, and Sheriff Davis requested the videotape for possible evidence, in case it had recorded the actual voice of the assailant threatening her life.

"Here, take it if you think it will help put this guy away for the next hundred years," Sarah said, not even stopping to think that there might be any valuable paranormal evidence on the tape.

"Thanks. You can never have enough ammunition in court these days," Davis said, and then laughed when he saw the last item Sarah was packing. "What on earth is that ratty looking thing?"

"This happens to be Mitty," Sarah said with as much dignity as a grown woman with a stuffed animal could muster. "He keeps me company and has proven to be a very valuable assistant."

"Oookay...Perhaps you should consider engaging in a more human contact," he continued with innocent humor.

"Is that a proposition, I hope?" Sarah blurted out, and then backpedaled as fast as she could. "I'm sorry. It must be the painkillers starting to kick in."

Beau Davis' cheeks flushed a charming shade of crimson, which made his blue eyes look like a patch of clear sky in the midst of a storm. Sarah felt her own skin flush, and she couldn't believe she had made such an inappropriate remark. She always tried to be completely professional and watch every word she said, but the stress and drugs had let down her guard.

"Normally, I would be flattered," he began with a serious look, "but I've always had a strict rule against dating women with fresh neck wounds."

The moment of tension ended, yet Sarah couldn't help but wonder just how many more awkward situations she and the Sheriff of Brandon County would share. If she could just keep her mouth shut, she would be fine, but this tall drink of southern water just provoked her on all kinds of levels.

There was little time to dwell on that thought, however, because when she stood up quickly with a case of equipment, the room started to spin again—only this time it didn't stop.

"Okay, that's it! And look, you're bleeding again," Davis said helping her to a chair, and then shouting out to a deputy. "Get someone to bring over one of the center's carts."

While a paramedic replaced the bandage and told her again to stay off her feet, an electric golf cart-type vehicle pulled up to the front of the *Sun 'n Surf.* With garbled protests, the Sheriff picked up the woozy ghost hunter and planted her in the passenger seat. He then asked one of his deputies to bring her to the hotel—and not to leave her side until she was safely in her room.

"But all my stuff," Sarah said with slurred speech, wondering just what potent painkillers she had ingested.

"Don't worry, I'll have someone bring it all back to you in the morning. Now just shut up and get some rest!"

Kicking off her shoes and peeling off her vest, Sarah let herself fall backwards onto the bed. Grabbing a corner of the blanket, she rolled over twice, wrapping herself up like a mummy, and ending up sideways on the bed.

Good thing I came back when I did, she thought as her drug induced stupor pulled her into sleep, *or I might have even flirted with Fink...*

Chapter 9

"Ghostbuster Attacked by Exorcist"
"Vampire Wounding Leads to Frankenstein Stitches"
"Jack the Ripper Slashing Has Ghostbuster Near Death"

Sensational headlines were splashed across the morning newspapers from coast to coast. Television and radio news broadcasts exaggerated accounts of the "Pugilistic Paratrooper" who swooped in to apprehend the "Cut-Throat Clergyman" before he could "ritually sacrifice" the "Glamorous Ghostbuster" at the haunted and cursed Wegman's Crossing "Dead Center."

"What the hell!" Dr. Carl Henkel exclaimed just before choking on his morning toast as he read the front page of the *Brandon Courier*.

"What's the matter, dear?" his wife asked, patting him on the back as she poured more orange juice.

"That ghost woman…was attacked by a religious fanatic…last night at Wegman's Center!" he said in between coughing bits of whole wheat toast out of his windpipe. "This woman…will ruin everything!"

"I doubt very much that she wanted to be attacked," she said looking over his shoulder to see the publicity photo of Sarah Brooks next to the mug shot of the bruised and swollen Reverend Wadsworth. "Now why don't you just swallow your toast, and then swallow your pride and go see this woman."

"See her? Why, she is just making a travesty out of everything!" he declared, thinking twice about the last bite of toast.

"No, Octagon has the monopoly on travesties," she said calmly. "If you really believe in your work, you should be willing to try any avenue to achieve your goal. The spotlight does seem to be on this Sarah Brooks right now, so maybe she can open some doors that have been closed to you."

The doctor said nothing, but picked up that last piece of crust and chewed it into oblivion. His wife was probably right—she *always* was—probably because she didn't look at all this as passionately as he did. Maybe this ghost woman wasn't a complete lunatic. Maybe almost getting murdered would give her enough national attention to help him. Maybe this throat slashing could work out to be just what he needed.

After letting his own thoughts rattle around in his agitated head for a few moments, he realized that maybe, just maybe, he was a little *too* passionate about it all.

Jimmy O'Reilly was frantic. He had barely slept in anticipation of Sarah's promised call to report on her investigation. At 5am, he got up to check his email and found a message from a member of the Shadow Patrol stating that Sarah Brooks had been seriously wounded by a deranged fan. Another message claimed she was already dead. After numerous unsuccessful attempts calling Sarah's cell phone, and then getting no information from the hotel desk, his first impulse was to steal his mother's car and drive to Virginia, but then he realized that if Sarah wasn't dead, she would kill him.

"Okay, what would Sarah do?" he said out loud, pacing the only patch of floor not piled with electronic junk. "She would gather as much information as she could, and if she had to, she would lie to get it!"

Encouraged by what he perceived to be a brilliant plan, he called the Brandon County Sheriff's office.

"I'm sorry, sir, but we are not making any statements about this ongoing case," a woman said as if she was reading from a script for the tenth time in the last ten minutes. Actually, it was closer to twenty times.

"But I'm James P. O'Reilly, her assistant...and fiancé!" Jimmy stated boldly, trying to sound as if he had a much higher testosterone level. "Surely you've heard of me."

"No, sir, I have not, and we can only release information to the next of kin."

"But I am just as good as next of kin. I have to know if Sarah is okay!"

The intense emotion made his voice squeak, and he thought his adolescence was now a dead giveaway, but instead he got a positive response.

"Please calm down, sir. Let me transfer you to the Sheriff."

The bleary, blue-eyed Sheriff was just walking in the door after wrapping up the search and investigation at the center. No one else was found, and security tapes indicated that Reverend Wadsworth had hidden in a men's room until after closing. They also found his car in one of the outer parking lots, and it was filled with religious pamphlets, as well as boxes of photos of Sarah Brooks. It looked like stalking could be added to the long list of charges.

"*Who* is it?" the sheriff asked as if he had heard, but not understood.

"It's Sarah Brooks' fiancé, a Mr. James O'Reilly," the woman repeated. "He wants to know her condition. Do you want me to tell him?"

"No, no, I'll take it in my office," Davis said, wondering why he cared so much that Sarah was engaged, and also wondering why he hadn't noticed a ring. "Yes, Mr. O'Reilly, can I help you?"

"Is Sarah okay? Is she alive?" Jimmy blurted out.

"She's going to be fine," the sheriff replied, increasingly suspicious of the youthful voice. "Now, you say you are Ms. Brooks fiancé?"

"Yeah, that's right. We, we were engaged just a few weeks ago. Nobody knows about it yet," Jimmy said digging himself in deeper, and then attempting to redirect the conversation. "So, is Sarah in the hospital? Who attacked her? When can I speak to her?"

"I'll just let your fiancée fill you in with all the details. She is sleeping at her hotel, so I wouldn't disturb her for at least a few hours. Will you be contacting the rest of her family?"

"Sure, I'll let them know. Thanks for all of your help, Sheriff," Jimmy replied with a calmer and, what he perceived to be, a more manly voice.

"No problem. And why don't you try to get a little sleep before you have to go to school," Sheriff Davis said, and then hung up before the startled boy could respond.

"Here's some fresh coffee," Beverly, the sheriff's secretary said, placing the steaming cup on his desk after she saw him hang up the phone. "And you probably won't be smiling for long after I tell you that Fink has been waiting on line five. He's in quite a state. Quite a state, indeed."

Dead Center | 65

"Oh no, not now! Tell him I ran away and joined the circus," Davis groaned. "Better yet, tell *him* to run away and join the circus."

"I could just *accidentally* disconnect him," she kindly offered.

"No, I should just be a man and take my Fink medicine," he replied, straightening in his chair and taking a big gulp of the hot coffee. "And Bev, thanks for the coffee, and thanks a million for coming in so early."

"Hey, it was either this, or getting my husband and kids up, fed, and clothed. Call me early any time!"

After one more gulp of coffee, Davis picked up the phone and pressed the button for line five as if it was the switch to his own electric chair.

"Good morning, Mr. Fink."

"Good morning! *Good* morning? Are you crazy? This is the worst morning of my life. I'm ruined. *Ruined!*" Fink shouted in a manner that invited a one-way ticket to a fit of apoplexy.

"Don't go poppin' an artery, Fink," Davis said, with a complete lack of sincerity. "It's not all that bad. Ms. Brooks will be just fine."

"I don't give a rat's ass about that ghostbuster. Look what she's done! She went and almost got herself murdered in my center! The media will turn this into a circus!"

Then you could run away and join it! Davis thought, fighting to keep himself from actually suggesting it. Clearing his throat and taking a deliberate sip of his coffee, he responded.

"My advice to you would be to kiss Ms. Brooks' ass as much as you can right now, and pray that she doesn't file a lawsuit against you that's bigger than the entire budget of the great Commonwealth of Virginia," Davis stated, carefully emphasizing the one word Fink feared above all others.

"Lawsuit! Oh God, not another one. I'll just pay her off, with a bonus, and send her home. I'll be nice to her, of course, I'll send her some flowers, right away. Of course, this was a terrible event, terrible, which we naturally regret, but it was clearly beyond our control."

"Your center, your problem," Davis said, as a little voice in his head told him how much fun it would be to represent Sarah Brooks in a lawsuit against Fink and the entire Octagon corporation.

"Well, it was clearly the fault of the security personnel!" Fink declared, desperately seeking any place to park the blame. "I'll fire Garrison and the whole crew!"

"May I point out that Dan Garrison was the only reason this wasn't a murder. And who knows how many other people this nut would have killed if Dan hadn't caught him. He could have murdered dozens of employees and customers. Why, he could even have been stalking you, too, Fink!" Davis said ominously.

"Me! Why would anyone want to hurt me!" Fink shouted in abject terror. "But of course, you're right, I could be in danger. There are plenty of crazy people out there. I'll have to hire more guards then, won't I? Oh, what a mess! What am I going to do?"

"Have a nice long talk with your lawyers, and make sure it's a very large bouquet of flowers you send to Ms. Brooks. Have a nice day, Mr. Fink."

Stretching back in his chair, Davis closed his eyes. From the time he received the call about the attack, he didn't have a moment to himself. In fact, since the day of the grand opening, he had worked more double shifts than he cared to remember. If only the world would just leave him alone, for just a little while.

"Hey, Chief, you've got to see this!" one of his deputies yelled as he burst unannounced into his boss' office. Only one man called him Chief, and that was Deputy Bobby Drummond. Bobby grew up just a few houses down from Davis, and when all the neighborhood kids got together to play cowboys and Indians, Bobby always played the brave warrior of Chief Beau and Arrow. Bobby had been calling Davis "Chief" for over twenty years, and despite protocol, Davis saw no reason to make him stop. Of course, it worked both ways.

"What have you got, Foxbear?" Davis asked, having long ago shortened his friend's rather elaborate play name of Running Fox with Strength of Bear.

"You have got to see this tape! It's freaking me right out!" the deputy declared with bugging eyes.

"What tape? What are we talking about?" Davis shouted down the hall as his deputy ran off, not even waiting for his boss to follow. "Beverly, do you know what Foxbear is rambling about?"

"Not a clue. But then do we ever know what Bobby is thinking?"

"Good point."

Davis calmly entered the darkened room that held much of the department's video equipment.

"Now, Foxbear, just what are you all riled up about?" Davis asked, straddling a chair and rolling toward his deputy, who was hunched over a console.

"Remember you gave me that ghostbuster's tape from the *Sun 'n Surf*, and you asked me to see if there was any audio of the attack?" he said excitedly.

"Yeah. So did she record him threatening her?"

"Well, yes, every word was recorded clear as a bell, Chief, but that's not the point!"

"Hang me if that isn't the point!"

"No! You see, at first I was just listening to the sound on the videotape, 'cause I figured I didn't need to stare at a ladies' dressing room wall for twenty minutes. But there were some strange noises I couldn't place, and when I looked at the monitor, you'll never believe what I saw!"

Deputy Drummond started playing the tape and for the first few seconds there was silence, and nothing on the screen but the greenish infrared image of the mirror and a wall of the dressing room. Suddenly there was the sound of the struggle, and Davis shuddered to think what was going through Sarah's mind as the six foot-three inch reverend grabbed her. Then came his ranting and preaching about the devil and demons, and Davis felt even sicker as he fully understood just how insane this man was—and just how lucky Sarah had been to survive.

"That's great, we have the whole thing Foxbear, but what-"

"Shhh! Here it comes!" the deputy said, increasing the volume.

There was a strange, low, moaning sound, clearly originating much closer to the microphone than the distant voices of Sarah and Wadsworth.

"What the hell?" Davis whispered as he felt the hair stand up on the back of his neck.

As the haunting moan continued softly, something bizarre started happening with the image. At first, Davis thought the camcorder had slipped out of focus, but the developing fuzzy area was centered in the mirror. If the camcorder was out of focus, than everything in the dressing room should have appeared fuzzy.

Davis used his heels to push himself closer to the monitor. The fuzzy area slowly took on the character of a rolling fog.

"Look, Chief, *look*!" his deputy said rubbing the beads of nervous sweat off his brow.

As the deputy spoke, the fog seemed to solidify and resolve itself into a shape—a distinctly human shape.

"Shit!" Davis exclaimed, straightening so suddenly that the chair rolled back several feet. Pushing himself forward again to the edge of the console, he remained transfixed as the image took on the vague appearance of a soldier, and a wisp of fog seemed to spill out of the mirror into the dressing room.

Just as more defined features began to appear in the image's face and clothing, the bright lights in the dressing room came on. The camcorder's sensitive infrared vision was overloaded, and the monitor displayed only shimmering blobs of pixels.

"Damn, what happened?" Davis demanded to know. His answer came a moment later when he heard the faint voice of Dan Garrison telling Wadsworth to drop the knife.

"If only Garrison had come a few minutes later!" the deputy lamented, then realized the implications of his wish. "But then, Ms. Brooks would probably be dead, right?"

Davis didn't even respond to that, but asked his deputy to play the tape again, and again, and again, in slow motion. His eyes were not deceiving him. There was the fuzziness, the fog, the image of a man that—God help him— looked like a soldier. It couldn't be true, it wasn't possible, but there it was in living color—or at least deathly green.

"What *is* that thing, Chief? Is this some kind of joke, or are we really seeing a freakin' ghost!"

"I don't know, Foxbear. I just don't know. It is the damnedest thing I ever saw," Davis said shaking his head. "Do me a favor, and I know this will be tough, but keep this to yourself for now. And can you make me a copy of the tape? I think I had better show this to our ghost expert."

"Sure thing. And I'll burn a couple of DVDs for us," the deputy said, visibly pale even in the dim light.

Sheriff Davis quietly went back to his office and closed the door. His hands were cold, and he was breathing more rapidly than normal. That phantom image in the mirror had burned itself into his memory, front and center. He tried to imagine every conceivable explanation, but could only draw two conclusions— either Sarah Brooks had somehow managed to perpetrate a hoax while she was having her throat cut, or he had just seen a goddamned ghost. None of it felt right, but perhaps that was because he was feeling something else—fear.

It's never a good way to start the day when your first sensation upon waking is pain. Even though Sarah still felt the sluggish aftereffects of the medications she had been given, they were no longer effective in dulling the pain.

I'll never complain about a paper cut again, she thought as she carefully rolled over to see the time. It was almost 10am, and she realized that Jimmy was probably climbing the walls. Not even waiting to check her messages, she dialed his cell phone.

Climbing the walls would have been a comparatively sedate reaction compared with the near hysteria that obviously gripped her young friend, but he immediately began to relax once Sarah assured him that she was not at death's door. Jimmy told her of some of the rumors about the attack and her condition, and as he spoke she turned on the television and saw her face on three different cable news channels. When Wadsworth's picture filled the screen, she switched it off.

"Since I assume you haven't gone to school today…" Sarah paused, giving him a chance to deny it, and then continued during the guilty silence, "would you please post a message on the website, and also send a special email to all of the subscribers?"

"Sure, I'll take care of it right away. Anything else I can do, anything I should bring down with me?"

"Nice try, Jimmy. You thought you could slip that by me in my weakened condition?" Sarah said, laughing at Jimmy's lame attempt to get her to invite him down.

"You can't blame a guy for trying," he responded, undaunted.

"I really do need you there, for now. I have to go through all the equipment and see what needs to be replaced, other than the half-dozen flattened motion detectors. I'll start on it right now and give you a call back by noon."

Jimmy had to content himself with being useful, if not present, and as soon as he got off the phone he got to work letting Sarah's fans know she was okay. Of course, he would have to throw in some dramatic touches, like emphasizing the fact that with a razor-sharp blade resting against an artery, with only seconds to live, Sarah summoned all her strength and courage and fought off the enormous assailant. The simple message quickly blossomed into something like a couple of pages out of a pulp fiction novel. He knew that once Sarah read the graphic account he would have to delete it, but for at least a few hours he would have his chance at literary glory.

After removing her bloody clothes and taking a long, hot shower, she confronted the overwhelming number of messages that filled her voicemail,

email, and the hotel's message system. Most were from reporters, and when she parted the curtains a few inches, she could see that almost every network was represented on the sidewalk. The front desk had left a message about some deliveries, and ten minutes after she called them, a dozen flower arrangements were carried into her room.

Eleven of the large, beautiful arrangements were from family members, friends, her publisher, and some fans. The twelfth, and smallest of the bunch, was from "Martin Fink and the Entire Staff of the Wegman's Shopping and Recreation Center, Get Well Soon." Maybe it was just her imagination, but those particular flowers just didn't seem to smell as good as all the others.

After utilizing all of the table and dresser space for the flowers, Sarah ended up sitting on the floor to begin testing the equipment. Mercifully, computers booted up, camcorders recorded and played back, and all but two of the instruments appeared undamaged. These two meters did function, but they had cracked housings that would need to be replaced. The cut cables and power cords, however, were another story. Every one would have to be replaced, and Sarah patiently made a list of the types and lengths, so that Jimmy could round up new ones and have them overnighted to her.

Of course, this was assuming she still had a job, which when she paused to consider it, was not at all a certainty. There had been no messages from Fink, other than the touching and heartfelt "Get Well Soon." As she pondered just how best to broach the subject to the general manager, the hotel phone rang. She had left word that only a select few should be connected, so she answered it.

"Ms. Brooks, this is the front desk. Sheriff Davis would like to know if you are well enough to meet with him," an efficient young clerk asked.

"Yes, I guess so. Where does he want to meet me?"

"He's in the lobby. Can I send him up?"

"Yes, sure," Sarah said as she looked at herself in the mirror and immediately regretted being so hasty.

Throwing off her robe, she grabbed some jeans and a sweater and ran into the bathroom. She hadn't bothered to put on any makeup or do her hair yet, so she went into her two-minute drill. If a football team could come down the field and score a touchdown in that amount of time, she reasoned, she could certainly put up her hair and apply some eyeliner and lipstick. Unfortunately, she hadn't factored in the sheriff's long strides.

"Just a minute, I'll be right there," she shouted, deciding it was better to make him wait than appear with makeup on only half her face.

"Take your time," she heard faintly through the thick hotel door. As she went to let him in, her only consolation was that the room looked worse than she did.

"Good morning, or is it afternoon?" Sarah said, motioning for the sheriff to come in and sit in the one chair not covered with equipment, files, or clothes. "I believe I do hold the record time for trashing a hotel room."

"Looks like a combination of an electronics warehouse and florist shop in here," Davis said, as he nonchalantly took a whiff of a few flowers before he sat down, hoping to catch a glimpse of some of the message cards. "Any of these from Fink?"

"I'll give you one guess," she replied, tilting her head toward the table in the corner.

"Well, I see a lamp on that table, but I can't quite make out the other things," he said, rubbing his prominent chin as if he was very puzzled. "Those little, brownish, wilted things couldn't be flowers, could they?"

"Hey, it's the thought that counts," Sarah said with mock indignation.

"Yeah, and the thought was cheap," Davis said trying to stretch his long legs out between equipment cases. "So, which flowers are from your fiancé?"

"From my *what*?" Sarah asked, wondering for a moment if the knife had also cut an auditory nerve.

"From your fiancé. He was so concerned about you, I bet he sent that big bouquet of roses there on the dresser," Davis said, avoiding eye contact so he could manage to keep a straight face.

"Okay, I know I was a bit punchy last night, but don't tell me I went and got engaged! Is it anybody I know?" Sarah said with a suspicious smile, not sure where the sheriff was going with this little joke.

"You know, my brother-in-law is Irish. The Irish make damn good husbands, but I guess you know that," Davis continued, now watching for the spark of recognition.

"What are you talking about? I really don't…Irish? Did you say Irish?" Sarah said, and then enjoyed a deep sigh of relief and amusement. "Just what did Jimmy tell you?"

"If you are referring to Mr. James O'Reilly, he said that you and he were secretly engaged just a few weeks ago. Should I not have offered him my congratulations?"

"Well, I was hoping to wait for him to graduate high school, but what does that matter when two people are so much in love?" Sarah said, putting her hands to her heart and striking a suitable silent movie pose for a moment, then dropping her hands to her hips and getting more serious. "So, just what kind of trouble has my young apprentice been getting into while I was unconscious? He said he spoke to you, but neglected to mention the impending marriage part."

"He was just trying to find out if you were okay," Davis said, finally dropping the intentionally transparent act. "But don't worry, I let him know that he really didn't get away with it."

"Oh well, I can't say as I can blame him. After all, I'm certainly not the best role model."

"Now I don't know you well enough to know if you are baiting me with that comment, so I'm going to use what little political savvy I possess and keep my mouth shut."

"Wise choice, but no, I wasn't baiting you. I wake up most days wondering how the hell I got mixed up in all this craziness. Sure, it's fun signing books and stuff like that, but when lunatics start trying to cut the demons out of you, you can't help but question whether or not you should just forget everything and do something normal," Sarah said, consciously stopping short of confessing too many revealing self-doubts.

"Well, Sarah, before you go quitting your day job, I have something here that you just might want to take a look at."

Davis pulled the digital tape from his shirt pocket and tossed it to her. Flipping it over to read the label, her curious expression turned to one of consternation.

"This is my tape from *Sun 'n Surf*," she stated coolly, clearly not amused. "If you don't mind, I'm not quite ready to relive my near-death experience."

"No, no, no. There's something more," Davis said, getting up and taking the tape out of her hand and looking at it with an odd expression. "There is something on this tape I can't explain—something I can't even believe."

"This isn't one of your little jokes, is it?" Sarah stated more than asked.

"No, Sarah, it isn't. Take a look," he said, returning the tape to her hand and curling her fingers tightly over it.

"Okay, I'll hook the camcorder up to the television right now," Sarah said, and then paused before continuing. "But first I need to know, can you hear him?"

"Yeah, we got Wadsworth's every word," Davis said quickly, and then left it at that.

He gave her a hand by turning the heavy television around so she could make the connections. Then he carried over the chair in which he had been sitting, and motioned for her to take a seat this time, while he knelt on one knee just a few feet from the screen.

"All right, here we go," Sarah said, taking a deep breath as she started the tape. "Care to tell me what I'm looking for?"

"Shhh! Listen!" Davis replied with the same mesmerized look that his deputy had when he showed the tape.

The sound of the struggle and Wadsworth's raspy voice sent a chill through her body, and her neck wound suddenly hurt more than it had all day. Sarah wanted to shut her eyes and cover her ears, but then a low, mournful groaning sound began. Suddenly, her body tensed in predator mode, and she leaned closer to the screen. When the fuzzy patch began to appear on the mirror, she straightened back up again, in much the same shocked manner as Davis had.

"What the—" Sarah whispered, and then gasped softly when the developing fog took on a human shape. In all her years of ghost hunting, and countless bizarre paranormal experiences, this was something she had never seen before. Sarah rubbed both forearms to warm up the goose bumps.

The phantom soldier seemed to solidify, and a fog-like substance actually *came out* of the mirror into the dressing room! Then the lights in the dressing room snapped on, and the image was washed off the screen.

"Damn, just a few more seconds!" Sarah said clenching her fists in frustration, then raising an eyebrow at her own stupid remark. "Strike that last statement. Dan arrived not one second too soon."

"So, what the hell is it?" Davis said, about an octave higher than his normal voice.

"What do *you* think it is?" Sarah asked with satisfaction as she leaned back in her chair. It was always such a delight to see skeptics squirm.

"How the hell should I know! This is your line of work. Is it a hoax, is it real, what in God's name am I looking at?"

Davis' level of anxiety was actually a healthy sign that he was willing to listen to any rational explanation. While Sarah couldn't exactly claim that her explanation would be rational, she would examine the facts and present her best case. A lawyer and law enforcement officer couldn't ask for more.

"Let's look at this frame by frame," Sarah said calmly, shifting gears into her analyst mode as she had done so many times before with hundreds of hours of videotape. "Now, we know the wall behind the mirror is solid, with no holes, and no one found anything like a projector on the walls or ceiling, so I think we can safely rule out that this is some kind of externally generated hoax. Now look closely at this fuzzy area in the mirror. If the camcorder was out of focus, then this whole region would appear fuzzy, but the rest of the mirror and wall are sharp."

"I noticed that, too," Davis agreed, hanging on her every word.

"Now the moaning sound could be a lot of things—creaking pipes, wind on the roof—I'll have to run that through the computer to see if it has human characteristics."

"You're a one-woman forensics lab," Davis said with genuine respect.

"Just wait!" Sarah said proudly, getting up to get the laptop she had used at *Sun 'n Surf*. "I was already getting some anomalous readings as soon as I set up, right before…right before I was so rudely interrupted.

"Let me start the tape again from the beginning, and match the time stamps of the video with the data the computer collected."

"You go girl!" Davis said, laughing, but was nonetheless impressed with the level of sophistication at which Sarah operated. Just the day before, he thought she wouldn't be using anything more technical than a dousing rod, candles, and a few crystals. As he watched Sarah's fingers fly over the keyboard, bringing up screens of graphs and charts he didn't understand, he began to realize just how demeaning it must be every time someone called her a ghostbuster. You could disagree with Sarah Brooks' beliefs, but you couldn't criticize her methods. This was a well thought out, and expertly executed scientific investigation.

Sarah patiently described what each box of data represented, and how it might relate to something paranormal. Temperature and air pressure were self-explanatory, but when she started talking about ionization and electromagnetic field fluctuations, he decided to take her word for it. However, there was one device that really fascinated him, and he wanted to know more about it—something Sarah called "The Sniffer."

"This baby here is my remote nose," she said opening a case and pointing to a simple-looking stainless steel box with a couple of vents and a control panel.

"It's similar to some units used by the EPA to monitor air quality, but I've made a few modifications.

"You see, one of the most common occurrences at a haunted site is an inexplicable scent—everything from a little old lady's perfume to something really nasty and corpse-like. I'm sure you've had your share of that smell on the job. Anyway, the question for me has always been whether these scents are just some kind of psychically triggered phenomena, or are they actually physically manifested, and therefore measurable, molecules."

"Now you're stretching it," Davis said, fully re-embracing his skepticism, which didn't bother Sarah in the least. "You're telling me that this Sniffer can *smell the dead?*"

"In a manner of speaking…yes. You establish a baseline, essentially letting the Sniffer know that these are the naturally occurring smells in that location. Then it continually samples the air for anything not on its list, or inordinately high levels of things already there. When it smells something unusual, it saves a sample for further analysis. Pretty cool, huh?"

"Sounds good on paper, but does it work?"

"In locations where natural sources could be ruled out, I've been able to isolate molecules of tobacco smoke, perfume, and compounds consistent with the breakdown of human flesh," Sarah stated without bravado.

"You certainly do sound convincing," Davis said, shaking his head. He was still unwilling to believe such an outrageous claim, but equally reluctant to believe that Sarah was just a highly skilled fraud. "But the jury is still out on this one for me."

"No, problem. I do this for a living and it still freaks me out. Let's just put it all together now and see what we've got."

Once the computer and camcorder were synchronized, the ghost hunter and the Sheriff of Brandon County watched intently to see if there was any further evidence to support the premise that the thing in the mirror was not of this world.

"See here, before anything visual occurs, the temperature is already dropping, and there is a slow, but steady buildup of some type of electromagnetic energy."

They watched as the anomalous readings intensified, and then hit a plateau just as the fuzzy patch appeared in the mirror. As the fog began to resolve itself, there were more inexplicable fluctuations in the dressing room, and when the wispy cloud spilled out of the mirror, everything went haywire. Sarah hit a few buttons to stop the tape and data right there.

"Hey, check it out," she said pointing to a flashing icon of a nose in the bottom right corner of the computer screen. Clicking on the icon, another box was superimposed over the other items, and Sarah's eyes darted through the lines of information. "Damn. It did detect something potent, but was unable to get a sample for some reason. I guess Sniffer didn't get enough time to hold its breath."

Restarting the tape and data results, they were both surprised to see that when the lights came on in the dressing room, not only did they lose the picture, but every reading instantly returned to normal baseline numbers. Sarah replayed the last frames of tape and few seconds of data again, and the changes exactly corresponded with the moment the lights came on.

"That's not a coincidence, is it?" Davis asked, although he already knew the answer.

"Afraid not. Seems like we have a bona fide paranormal event. I'm sorry if this blows your mind."

Davis was quiet for a few moments, and then looked directly at Sarah with a sparkle in his eyes.

"Do you always stir up this much trouble wherever you go?"

"I'm an international nuisance," she openly confessed.

The detective side of Davis wanted to go over everything one more time, and see if anything in the real world could explain what had happened, but his dilemma only deepened. And just as Sarah was about to shut off everything, something else caught his eye.

"Hold on, could you play back the last few frames before we lost the picture?" he asked, moving to within just a few inches of the television.

"Sure. What are you looking for?"

"Wait…there, right there. Hold it. Is that something on his hat?" Davis asked, pointing to what looked like a somewhat more defined shape within the overall foggy image.

Without speaking, Sarah went to work capturing, enlarging and enhancing that section on her computer. A single raised eyebrow signaled success.

"Good call, Sheriff, take a look," she said sending the image back to the large television screen. "Looks like a corps badge to me, maybe the cross insignia of the Union's Sixth Corps. They were in the area during the Wilderness Campaign. I'll have to clean up the image some more, of course, but this could be quite significant."

"All right, that's it. That's it! This has all gotten to be way too weird for me," Davis exclaimed, raising his hands in surrender. "And how you can calmly sit there and analyze pictures of dead people is beyond me. I have to go home and get some sleep. I'll call you later."

With that, Sheriff Davis got up and left without another word. Sarah actually did feel sorry for him, in a way. It wasn't the easiest thing to have something you have believed your entire life ripped away with a few seconds of videotape. She had seen this happen a hundred times, and knew it would be an ongoing struggle between denial and those incredible, but documented, facts. But she had high hopes for the bewildered sheriff, as she had found that intelligence and education actually increased one's ability to grasp the concepts of a world beyond.

Too bad I still have to deal with problems in this world, too, she thought as she picked up the phone to call the management offices of Wegman's Crossing Shopping and Recreation Center. Mercifully, she got Lela Reynolds.

"Oh, Ms. Brooks! How are you? I can't tell you how upset I was to learn of the attack!" Lela exclaimed on a purely personal level, abandoning the company line, for now.

Sarah obligingly satisfied her curiosity for some of the gory details, and then candidly popped the question.

"So, do I still have a job to come back to, or is Fink pulling the plug?"

"Well, I don't know. I just can't say," Lela said as she once again reluctantly began the corporate dance. "Mr. Fink is at headquarters now, no doubt discussing that issue. I'm sure he will get in touch with you very soon."

"Can you get a message to him?"

"Yes, of course."

"Normally, I'm more diplomatic, but I obviously don't have time for that now," Sarah stated like a general embarking on a vital mission. "Tell him he has trouble at the center—*big* trouble, and lots of it. And if he sends me home now, and doesn't let me continue my work, it will only get worse, and he will regret that decision for the rest of his life."

"Yes, Ms. Brooks, I'll relay that message to him word for word!" Lela said as a dutiful secretary, and then continued in a whisper. "Could you just tell me what you found, and I promise not to say anything to anyone?"

Sarah hesitated, but only for a moment. Lela was obviously on her side, and disclosing some of her findings now could only strengthen that alliance. Sarah proceeded to describe the image of the soldier in the mirror, and the anomalous readings from all the instruments.

"Oh my! This is more exciting than the Cranberry Bog Phantom, isn't it!" Lela exclaimed enthusiastically, but then fell silent when she realized she had blown her cover.

The case of the Cranberry Bog Phantom in Maine had been one of Sarah's earliest investigations, and no one but a diehard fan would remember it. Sarah suddenly realized just who had been sending her anonymous information, such as Grace Hopkins' identity.

"So, you read my first book?" Sarah asked innocently, letting Lela decide just how far out of the bag she would let the cat go.

"Oh, Ms. Brooks, I've read all your books, at least three times each!" Lela said, glad to be free of the pretense. "I'm also a member of your Shadow Patrol. I'm Mama Sherlock!"

The user name was familiar, and Sarah recalled several helpful tips the secretive Mama Sherlock had provided in the past.

"Well, Mama, a pleasure to finally meet you. Can I assume now you might have some additional stories to tell me about what has been going on at the center?"

Relieved of the burden of deception, Lela Reynolds gave Sarah an earful. The official reports were nothing compared to the real information locked up back at headquarters, Lela asserted. From the day they broke ground, Octagon must have known that they were building on the site of a Civil War battle. Rumor had it that they gathered boxes of artifacts. They also began uncovering bones, and just decided to cover them back up and pour concrete directly over those areas rather than excavate them. It made for an unusual building plan, but human remains were simply too much of a nuisance.

Construction crews were continually tormented by things that couldn't be explained. There were so many actual sightings of apparitions that the crews started giving them individual names. There had been at least six calls to 911 reporting the sounds of gunfire late at night on the construction site, but nothing was ever found. Priests were brought in to perform blessings, but nothing seemed to work. Since the building had been completed, just about every employee had seen or heard something strange, and Lela herself, had witnessed shadowy figures and heard voices on numerous occasions.

Sarah asked Lela about the historical research done on the area before Octagon moved in, and Lela told her what she knew about Dr. Henkel and his efforts. Lela still had a copy of Henkel's original report in her files, and offered to have someone drive it over to the hotel right away.

"Lela, I don't know what I would do without you!" Sarah exclaimed with complete sincerity. "I don't know how I can ever thank you for all your help."

"Well…there is one thing you could do," Lela responded slowly. Sarah would have bet anything that Lela was going to request to come along on the investigation. Everyone always asked the same thing, and Sarah always had to politely decline, or every investigation would be a mob scene. "Could you sign my copies of your books?"

"Of course! Boy, I thought for sure you were going to ask to go on a ghost hunt," Sarah said, relieved that she didn't have to disappointment someone like Lela.

"Heaven forbid!" Lela exclaimed. "I have to work with these things, I don't need to go stirring them up, thank you very much. I'm scared enough just reading about them at home in my own bed. And just one more thing…"

"Yes?"

"Are you planning to speak to the press sometime soon? They have been hounding me something awful."

"Ah yes, the press. I've been wondering how to handle them. Let me see what Henkel's report is all about, and what Fink has to say, and maybe I'll set up a press conference for this evening. Thanks again, Lela."

Sarah ordered something to eat in her room, and as the food was being delivered, the courier from Lela arrived. While Sarah ate, carefully chewing and swallowing every bite to minimize the discomfort in her stitched neck, she pored over Henkel's compelling report. What he lacked in hard facts, he certainly made up for in enthusiasm and optimism, but there was still more than sufficient evidence to have prompted a professional exploration of the site. What fascinated her most was the map he had drawn, superimposing the outline of the sprawling shopping mall over the sites of the artifacts he and his team had discovered, as well as the conjectured locations of the bridge and buildings of Wegman's Crossing in 1864.

Sarah pulled out her shopping center guide, which listed the names of all the stores and restaurants, and also provided a floor plan of each level. Holding it side by side with Henkel's outline map, she was not surprised to find that the *Sun 'n Surf* was directly over the site of the chimney Henkel believed to be from the original Wegman house. *Kinder Krossing* straddled the barn area, and the underground parking, above which stood the management offices, was in the area of the original riverbed.

A blueprint for a haunting, Sarah thought as she pushed aside the reports and leaned back to close her eyes and think. There were still too many pieces of the puzzle missing, and nothing would be resolved unless she had a credible story backed up by solid evidence—and some semi-solid ectoplasmic evidence wouldn't hurt either...

Sarah called the office number attached to Henkel's report, and was informed that the doctor was just getting out of surgery. After no small amount of coercion, she was finally connected to his voicemail, but only after she mentioned she was calling in regard to his Civil War expertise. Apparently, the staff was told to prevent patients from filling up his voicemail, but historians had been given a green light.

The message Sarah left began in a typically awkward fashion for her, as she diplomatically tried to explain who she was, and what she was doing. Even after all these years, she still felt foolish introducing herself as a paranormal investigator. But as she began to discuss his report, the words flowed effortlessly. What information did he have on any actual regiments and corps members who might have been at the battle, specifically, the Sixth Corps? Could she see the full transcripts of the original letters and documents mentioning the battle? Just how many combatants did he believe were involved, and what were the casualty numbers?

She hoped her bulleted questions were brief and precise enough to convince the doctor to respond, but just in case, she added a few more seconds to his voicemail, asking how could she aide in his efforts to bring this evidence to the public and right the wrongs Octagon committed?

As Sarah waited for the doctor to respond, another courier came to her door. It was a letter from Fink, stating that she would be allowed to continue her investigation Friday evening, on three conditions: She must have a signed note from a physician affirming that she was fit to return, she must hire a body guard to be with her at all times while she was on the premises, and she must sign the enclosed release basically stating that she would not hold the Octagon Corporation or any of its affiliates or employees legally responsible for anything that had happened or might happen in the future.

I haven't seen such blatant ass-covering since the Clinton administration, Sarah thought, as she struggled to keep from tearing the pages into little pieces. There was no doubt she wanted to continue the investigation—in fact, she *needed* to continue— but how much was she willing to compromise?

After careful consideration, Sarah wrote a response to fax directly to Fink. She said she would consult with a physician and get his authorization. She would also have no objection to having at least one *assistant* with her when she returned. And as to the last point about signing away her legal rights, Sarah composed a very thinly veiled threat that if she was prevented from continuing her investigation, she *would* file suit against Octagon and every last affiliate and employee it used to have, had now, or ever would have.

Now that's my idea of a compromise, Sarah thought with great satisfaction as she pressed the enter key to send the fax.

Whenever things began to get really complicated, which seemed to be happening with ever-greater frequency, Sarah Brooks made handwritten lists of items that needed to get done. If she was very stressed, the list would be prioritized, and the more precise the lines and margins, the higher the stress level. As Sarah prepared to begin the tasks on her latest note, with its perfectly aligned left and right margins and evenly spaced lines, she felt some small sense that the she was in control of the situation. Of course, part of her did realize it was pure denial, but at this point, any degree of false security would be welcome.

First order of business, she thought as she put a neat check mark next to item number one, and then grabbed her phone, *get some real security*.

"Hey, Ricky, it's Sarah Brooks," she said to the burly New York ghost hunter.

"Oh my God, Sarah, are you okay?"

"I'm still more freaked out than hurt, but having your throat cut's no picnic."

"We were all freaked out when we heard, and we heard all kinds of rumors that you...well, that you didn't make it. I'm really glad you called to let me know you're okay."

"That's not the only reason I called. How would you like to join me tomorrow night when I go back to Wegman's?"

Sarah fully expected Ricky to shout with enthusiasm at the offer to join one of her investigations. Instead, there was a few seconds of silence, followed by some hemming and hawing before he produced any intelligible speech.

"Oh jeez, Sarah, you know that normally I would give my right arm to be there, but...well, I'm on the Jersey Turnpike now heading home."

"You're going home? Why?"

"Spirits of the dead are one thing, you know they never scare me. But crazy guys with knives, well...my wife called, all upset...and you know, it is kind of scary," the big guy whined like a big baby. "And just about everyone else packed up and left this morning, too, so it wasn't just me. I'm sorry, Sarah. I'm really, really sorry."

"Don't worry about it Ricky, I understand, believe me. At least one of us has some sense!" Sarah said laughing. Of course, she was disappointed, but she honestly couldn't blame him for leaving.

"I just feel terrible about this. Maybe I could call my wife and convince her-"

"Go home, Ricky! Don't worry about it!"

"All right, but if there's anything I can ever do for you again, please call. Sorry, again, Sarah."

"It's okay, Ricky. Take it easy."

Sarah thought the simplest part of Fink's conditions would be getting someone to accompany her. The day before, 500 volunteers would have been knocking down her door. Funny, how a little thing like attempted murder can take the wind out of people's sails.

There were probably a considerable number of amateur ghost hunters still hanging around, but if she didn't know their level of competency, it was too big of a risk. An entire night's work could be ruined by a stupid mistake by an inexperienced investigator. Sarah knew that all too well, having done it herself more times than she cared to remember. Of course, she could always call Jimmy, and he would be there in a heartbeat, but she really hated to encourage truancy. The assistant question would have go on a back burner for now, or at least lower on the priority list.

The separate list of replacement cables, parts, and equipment had already been emailed to Jimmy, but there was another instrument Sarah was considering. It was something she had been working on for almost a year, something for very special circumstances, and she couldn't think of any place more special than Wegman's. A full-scale working model had yet to be built, so it was a long shot, but as it was item number two on the list, it was worth a call.

"Yes, I would like to speak to Electron Man about a matter of national security," Sarah said in a high-pitched, cartoonish voice when the man with the musical Indian accent answered the phone.

"Sarah Brooks! You are alive and well!" Rabindranath Krishnamurthy exclaimed with joy. Due to his extensive name, expertise in his field, and penchant for superheroes, his friends called him by his chosen alter-ego name.

Electron Man's field was basically anything that the "experts" said couldn't be done. As a consultant, he had designed everything from optics for NASA to satellite systems for the Department of Defense. His fees were extraordinary, but so was his work. However, for Sarah Brooks, he would never charge a cent.

He and Sarah had met when he first came to the United States and got a job in Boston as an engineer at the company where Sarah worked. Though very friendly, his social skills and understanding of American culture left many things to be desired, so most people just ignored him. Since Sarah was not unfamiliar with the role of misfit, she found out his birth date, and spent the night before preparing a popular Indian dessert for him called gulab jamuns. Although her version also left much to be desired, he was so touched by the gesture that he claimed she would always be his "first and best American friend."

"I guess you heard what happened last night," Sarah said, relieved that she would not have to repeat the entire story again.

"How could I not hear! Imagine my utter surprise when I turned on the television this morning and saw my first and best American friend on the news. I was utterly beside myself with distress!"

"Well, I'm sure they made it all sound worse than it was, but it wasn't anything a little burst of pepper spray couldn't handle. Hey, maybe you could design a concealed spray system, you know, something like Spiderman has,"

Sarah said, knowing full well the invocation of such a name would generate giggles of delight from her brilliant friend.

"Oh, Spiderman! Very good idea, very good!" he said with infectious laughter. "I'll design it tomorrow and apply for a patent on Monday!"

"Well, Electron Man, could you design it next week instead?" Sarah asked coyly.

"What's this? Does the famous ghost hunter have another idea?"

"You know that instrument we've been working on?"

"Yes, of course, of course."

"I know we've only tested small-scale prototypes, but do you think you could construct a big one and produce a membrane sheet for it about six feet by three feet...by tomorrow night," Sarah said, knowing full well she was practically asking the impossible, but also knowing that was what Electron Man lived for.

"Oh, Sarah Brooks, you present me with the greatest of challenges. How can I ever thank you, and where do you want it shipped?"

When Dr. Carl Henkel returned to the office after removing a particularly aggressive tumor from the brain of a nine-year-old child, during what was supposed to have been a fairly routine operation, he was not in the mood for any more surprises. So when he began to listen to his voicemail and heard Sarah Brooks introduce herself, he almost erased the message before listening to it. However, by the time the message was over, his entire attitude had changed.

"Sixth Corps!" he said out loud, rifling through his files for a copy of his original report. "How the hell does she know anything about the Sixth Corps?"

Not only did her understanding of his report and apparent level of knowledge about Civil War history surprise him, he was also startled by her specific question. Henkel's first report had been written to Octagon in general terms, and he had intentionally not included any details such as regiment and corps identifications, so as not to overwhelm the strictly-business minds in charge. As much as he hated to admit that his wife might be right, yet again, it looked as though he should meet Sarah Brooks.

No sooner had Sarah finished her conversation with Electron Man, than her cell phone rang. She assumed it was her friend calling back with another question.

"Ms. Brooks, this is Dr. Henkel's office. He would like to schedule a meeting with you in the lounge at your hotel in one hour," the woman stated, rather than asked.

"Oh, ah, yeah...Dr. Henkel, yes, of course. One hour would be fine, "Sarah said, having been caught off guard—and thankful she hadn't answered the phone in her cartoon voice. "I'll be there."

"Fine, good day."

Now she really did have to do something about her appearance. She always thought that the one thing Sun Tzu had neglected to mention in the *Art of War* was the importance of an Armani suit with a short skirt, and just the right application of make-up to appear somewhere between all-business and blatantly alluring.

Lela had told Sarah that Henkel had little tolerance for people who believed in ghosts, and he harbored particular contempt for those who "sullied sacred Civil War sites." Lela recalled him actually mentioning that it wouldn't be such a bad idea to round up all the people who led ghost tours on battlefields, and put them in front of a firing squad.

Armed with that knowledge, Sarah prepared to disarm his pre-conceived notions of what a ghost hunter must be like. The fact that he had rapidly responded to her message, and wanted to meet with her so soon, was already an encouraging indication that she had made a positive impression. However, Sarah was not beneath using her appearance to further confound the enemy.

As she made her way to the lounge, she couldn't help thinking what a great joke this would make—*A brain surgeon and a ghost hunter go into a bar…* Unfortunately, she couldn't think of a good punch line. She only hoped that Henkel wouldn't continue to view her as a bad joke, and that he would be able to see beyond his prejudices so they could work toward a common goal.

Sarah deliberately arrived fifteen minutes early and chose a comfortable chair in a corner of the lounge so she could observe everyone who entered. Unlike most doctors, Henkel (whom she recognized from a picture in a newspaper clipping about his battle with Octagon) arrived precisely on time. There were only about half a dozen women in the place, and although he looked directly at Sarah twice, he assumed the lady ghostbuster had not yet arrived, so he took a seat at the bar and ordered a scotch on the rocks.

Perfect! Sarah thought as she slowly stood up, carefully adjusted her collar to try to conceal the bandage, and headed toward the brain surgeon at the bar. *He has no clue who I am.*

"Dr. Henkel?" Sarah asked in her sweetest voice.

"Yes?" he replied, rising from the bar stool like a gentleman, and grinning like a late-middle-aged man being approached by an attractive woman in a bar.

"I'm Sarah Brooks," she said extending her hand while suppressing her own amusement at his complete look of bewilderment. After a couple of long seconds, she continued. "Your office called and asked for me to meet you here…to discuss your report…about your information on the Battle of Wegman's Crossing…"

As his neurophysiology finally responded, he accepted her hand and said politely, "Of course, Ms. Brooks. I'm sorry, I guess my mind was elsewhere. It's a pleasure to meet you, and thank you for coming on such short notice."

"I'm grateful you were able to take the time out of your busy schedule," she replied, matching politeness with politeness, for as long as it lasted. "Shall we sit at this table over here?"

"Yes, and can I buy you something to drink?"

"If that's a scotch you're having, I'll have the same," Sarah replied, happy to see that he was pleased she was also apparently a scotch drinker, but equally unhappy that she would now have to drink the vile stuff. Perhaps her senses were just unrefined, but she always thought scotch tasted like something you should be pouring on an old cabinet to remove the paint.

There were a few moments of small talk about the weather until her drink arrived, and then they both simultaneously reached for their briefcases. Sarah was a little faster on the draw, but she insisted the doctor speak first.

"Ahem..." Henkel began, intentionally clearing his throat to stall for time, and then silently stalling for more time as he sifted through some file folders. The growing tension was palpable, and Sarah began to drink her scotch in earnest. "Ms. Brooks, while I do appreciate your interest, before I begin, I feel I must be honest and say that I really don't see how a...a person who...who does...does what you do could be of any benefit in this case."

The cards were already on the table, and Sarah could fold, bluff, or show her hand.

"I see. Well, I was hoping you could overlook your opinion of me for the sake of all of those soldiers who had their final resting places cemented over by the Octagon Corporation, but if you can't sit here and listen to someone like me for ten minutes, then leave now, and no hard feelings."

She dealt her words a little more forcefully than she had intended, but there was no sense playing games with the doctor if he wasn't going to take her seriously.

Henkel was visibly torn. He was old-world enough not want to openly offend a lady, yet he believed that anyone who had anything to do with ghosts was a fraud. While her comment about the Octagon Corporation cementing over the soldiers' graves struck at the core of his emotional obsession with the men and events at Wegman's Crossing, the idea that she might claim to be in contact with the spirits of these dead men was outrageous and intolerable. When it looked like he wasn't going to be able to speak any time soon, she decided to pull her ace out of the hole.

"Do you know Tony Marchand?" she asked, as she slapped a piece of paper on the table, but left her hand covering the text.

"You mean Dr. Antoine Marchand, the historian?" Henkel asked, even further confused. "Yes, of course. Not personally, that is, but I've read all his books. I also had a chance to see him speak in Washington a couple of years ago."

"Would you agree he is the foremost authority on the Civil War?" Sarah asked, as if cross-examining a hostile witness, which wasn't too far from the truth.

"Yes...I would say he is. I would also add that he is one of the finest scholars living today. But what does he have to do with this?"

"So, you respect him?"

"Yes."

"Would you even say you admire him?"

"Yes, I would."

"And in your opinion, as a physician, does he appear to be in control of all of his faculties?"

"Of course, but what is all this about?" Henkel demanded, starting to lose patience.

Sarah slowly pulled her hand back from the paper and didn't say a word. Henkel picked it up, held it at arm's length for a moment, then reached for his reading glasses. His lips moved slightly as he started to scan the text, but then his mouth stayed partially open as if he was about to speak. His lips remained frozen in that position, without making a sound, until he had read every word. Then he carefully placed the paper back on the table, returned his glasses to his pocket and cleared his throat, twice.

"This is a rather remarkable letter, Ms. Brooks," he said as if he was swallowing his words even as he spoke them. "I don't quite know what to say."

"Well, we could give Tony a call right now, if you would like to dispute this with him personally," Sarah offered as she reached for her phone.

"No, no! That's all right. Just give me a moment here," Henkel said as he took out his glasses again and went over a few more lines of the letter signed, "With Gratitude and Affection, Tony."

A year ago, Sarah met the venerable historian at a Civil War battlefield preservation fundraising event. At first, Sarah was uncomfortable when he immediately started asking probing questions about her ghost investigations, believing that he was making fun of her. She was about to excuse herself from the conversation when he came right out and said he had just bought a place that was haunted, and he was at his wit's end as to what to do about it. Realizing he was dead serious, she accepted his invitation to spend the weekend at his house and see if she could uncover any evidence of paranormal activity.

Actually, it wasn't just a house. It was an ante-bellum mansion that still retained its grandeur from its days as one of Louisiana's most prominent plantations. And actually, it wasn't just a haunting. It turned out to be one of the nastiest poltergeists to ever torment the world of the living. The weekend stretched into a week, and her investigation turned into a struggle against objects flying across the room, physical attacks, and general chaos in just about every room in the expansive mansion.

Based upon the evidence she gathered, along with historical records of the plantation, Sarah believed the unhappy entity was a former owner—a woman who had led a most unsavory life, and who went out of her way to inflict misery upon everyone within her sphere of influence. Old habits were hard to break, even after death, and acting upon the premise that the trouble was being caused by this woman, Sarah devised a series of actions to send her spirit packing.

For example, as the majority of the violent activity occurred in and around the room that contained a portrait of this former mistress of the mansion, Sarah recommended that the painting be removed from the house. Then a secret underground passage leading to a room where the mistress would mete out her unique forms of discipline was filled in and sealed. These steps and other such actions appeared to block all of the physical manifestations of the haunting. However, Sarah's instincts, along with a few of her meters, indicated that the evil woman had not yet left the building.

The final step was the direct confrontation, the part Sarah dreaded the most. While it wasn't anything like an official exorcism, it could get very ugly. The technique was simple—she and Marchand identified the spirit by name, read out her life's history, and then emphasized the day and manner of her death. It was essential that they made it absolutely clear that she was dead and needed to be gone. Marchand concluded forcefully that it was now a new time, he was the new owner, and she no longer had the power to display her temper tantrums in *his* home.

The letter that now lay on the table before a bewildered Dr. Henkel was recently written by Marchand to Sarah, thanking her profusely once again for her efforts in helping him rid his home of the nasty spirit. He stated that a full year had passed without so much as footsteps in the night or a single cold spot. And he also stated, and restated twice more, that she was always welcome in his home at any time, and he would always be at her service if she ever needed anything.

"Do you need to go lie down, you're looking a bit pale," Sarah commented with more than a hint of gloating, knocking back the rest of her drink with great satisfaction, and then motioning to the bartender for another round. She now assumed they would be there for a while.

"I…I just don't know how to react to this. I mean, Dr. Marchand, of all people! His *Drumbeat to Glory* was the first book I ever read on the Civil War. *He* is the reason I became interested in history," Henkel declared, then finished the rest of his own drink, and motioned to the bartender for two more of the same. Either he hadn't noticed that Sarah had just placed another order, or he was now planning on being there for a very long time.

"Look, I don't expect you to undergo a spiritual rebirth and run off to join a commune, but I should hope that now you will at least listen to what I have to say with more of an open mind. Unless you are ready to certify that Dr. Antoine Marchand has lost his marbles, I think you can at least suspend your disbelief temporarily."

Henkel didn't respond, but Sarah could see by his expression that his mind had entered into a kind of plastic state—the perfect time to leave another positive impression.

"Look, here's your map of Wegman's Crossing in 1864, with the outline of the shopping center over it. I've added these colored marks that correspond with the reports of activity, and the results I have collected so far."

For the next few minutes, Henkel sat quietly, sipping his two drinks, while Sarah explained that the most active paranormal hotspots matched the approximate locations of the river, the Wegman house, and the barn. She went on to say that during a battle, these would likely be the areas of the most intense fighting, and after the battle, the buildings would have seen the greatest suffering, as they usually became field hospitals. Henkel registered no outward changes throughout Sarah's presentation, but he became visibly agitated when she produced a copy of the image in the mirror.

"What is this?" he demanded.

"This is a frame from the infrared video taken last night in *Sun n Surf*," she explained, and then quickly added. "Sheriff Davis brought it to my attention this morning."

"Beau? Beau Davis saw this?" Henkel asked, wondering whether the entire world had gone mad.

"Yes, and then he picked this out," she continued, placing a copy of the close-up of the head and hat area before him.

With a little sharpening, and beefing up the contrast, Sarah had coaxed more detail out of the fuzzy image. Although it was something akin to taking a photo of someone at night, with Vaseline on the lens, it still looked for all the world like a Civil War soldier with a Sixth Corps insignia on his kepi style hat.

"If this is some kind of trick, I swear-"

"It isn't, and I swear! Now I know Sedgwick's Sixth Corps was nearby at the Battle of the Wilderness in 1864. Do you have any evidence linking any of their soldiers to the Battle of Wegman's Crossing?"

"All right, Ms. Brooks, in the one chance in a billion this isn't a complete load of horse shit, here's my report on who may have been there," he said tossing her a file folder as he stood up. "I need to leave now."

That would be two men running out on her in the same day—a record even for Sarah.

"Thank you. And do I have your permission to talk about your findings with the press?" she said to his back as he began to stride away.

Stopping, Henkel turned with a threatening finger pointed toward her.

"Respectfully!" he insisted in no uncertain terms. "Only if you speak about my work and those soldiers with *respect!*"

Sarah's devilish side prodded her to start singing "R-E-S-P-E-C-T," but fortunately her better half kept her mouth shut and she simply nodded in agreement.

Chapter 10

The most discrete and efficient members of the Shadow Patrol had been offered a mission. Posted on a special secure site, accessible only by a password that Sarah changed on a monthly basis, the details of their mission were spelled out. The last lines of the message strongly emphasized that no information was to be obtained through any illegal means, and that the rights and privacy of every individual, organization, and business were to be strictly preserved.

To the most shadowy members of the Shadow Patrol, they knew this was Sarah Brooks' way of telling them she didn't care what they had to do to get the information, and to be sure to forward their reports by untraceable means. To this elite group, who included computer specialists, a former intelligence operative, a private detective, and even a sweet-looking old grandmother with a rap sheet the length of her knitting needles, this was the type of call to action they lived for.

Roger Cameron was stewing. Even though Sarah Brooks had offered him an exclusive interview, his new editor at the *D.C. Herald* ordered him to cover a story about a budget meeting on a newly proposed sewer system. The editor argued that maybe a ghostbuster getting her throat slashed was the type of story people *wanted* to read, but the *Herald* was only interested in stories people *should* read.

Roger's only consolation was that since this editor had taken over, circulation was going down the toilet, so Roger would know exactly through which pipes the editor would be traveling when management finally flushed him out of his job.

Having had a chance to catch a few more hours of sleep, Sheriff Beau Davis was back on the job and preparing for the evening's joint press conference with Sarah Brooks at her hotel. When Sarah's offer to Roger at the *Herald* was turned down, she realized the best way to deal with all of the media was to do it en masse. Since the Sheriff's office was already planning a press conference, they decided to combine them and save the stress and expense of holding two. Davis and Sarah agreed that she would field any questions pertaining to the paranormal, so that the Sheriff's office would not lose any credibility. Fink declined to take part in the news conference, instead submitting a carefully worded statement expressing their shock and sympathy over the attack, while also categorically denying any legal responsibility. It was, of course, wishful thinking, but it looked good on paper.

The largest conference room of the hotel was bursting at the seams with reporters from the major networks, cable, newspaper, radio, and even a few online webzines. The story had something for everyone—violence, mystery, and the bizarre. There was even a sex angle—thanks to some allegations from several of Wadsworth's underage parishioners. Sarah felt sorry for any reporters trying to find a sex scandal in *her* past.

I should be so lucky, she mused as she waited in her room for the press conference to begin. *The only skeletons in my closet are real skeletons!*

As she entered the conference room, escorted by Deputy "Foxbear" Drummond, the glaring camera lights reminded her how much she disliked these things. It was always more than just asking questions. There were always reporters who, at the least, challenged her integrity, and at most, questioned her sanity. It was like they actually expected some dramatic, Hollywood courtroom-type confession, where she would admit to being a fraud and throw herself on the mercy of the press. There was one reporter in particular, Joe Bavesy of the *Skeptical Eye,* who harassed her every chance he got. Quickly scanning the faces in the crowd, she was relieved not to see his.

Sheriff Davis began by reading a prepared statement relating to the pertinent facts about the "alleged" crime, the history of the "alleged" perpetrator, and an approximate timeline of upcoming legal proceedings. There was no mention of ghosts, and Sarah was simply referred to as someone hired to investigate "alleged" activity at the center. While she understood that these things needed to be said in this manner, if she heard much more of it, Sarah felt that she would let out an alleged scream.

The instant the Sheriff finished, a man who looked vaguely familiar jumped up from the middle of the room and shouted out a question.

"Jerry Bavesy of the *Skeptical Eye*," he began, as Sarah realized that this must be Joe's younger brother, recognizing those unmistakable Bavesy bloodhound-like features. *Joe must be out making the world safe for close-minded people*, she thought before Jerry continued, bracing herself for the verbal assault. "My question is for Ms. Brooks. Isn't it true that you have paid people to fabricate this entire haunted story nonsense at Wegman's Center, and that you directly provoked Reverend Wadsworth into attacking you in order to generate material for another bestseller?"

Sarah was not angry by the question, just disappointed. Joe would have essentially made the same accusations, but he would have done it so eloquently as to be almost inoffensive. His inexperienced sibling had a lot to learn about annoying people. As Sarah rose to respond, Sheriff Davis motioned for her to remain seated.

"Mr. Bah-vase-eee, is it," the sheriff began, using his best southern accent to butcher the man's name. "There's an old saying that there's no such thing as a stupid question, but I do believe you might have just single-handedly disproved that time-honored adage. Now if you'll just sit back down, I'll take questions regarding the criminal investigation. Then, as is listed in the press conference schedule you all received, Ms. Brooks will make a short statement and then answer any *rational* questions you would all like to ask."

Jerry Bavesy of the *Skeptical Eye* sank about as low into his chair as he could compress himself. On his first big assignment, he had visions of glory that Sarah Brooks would crack beneath the strain of his withering question and confess to the entire world that she was a fraud. Now, his foolishness would provide juicy sound bites on the eleven o'clock news and on the morning talk shows. He was certain his big brother would demote him back to the janitorial staff at *Skeptical's* headquarters.

Sarah tried not to grin too widely, especially when Davis glanced back and gave her a quick wink. Although she was more than capable of fighting her own fights—she certainly had to do it often enough—it was nice to have someone stick up for her for a change. *What do you know*, she thought to herself, *you really don't mess with Beau.*

The other reporters proceeded to respectfully question the Sheriff about Wadsworth's past, his outstanding warrants, and whether or not he would be extradited to the other states where he was wanted. The lawyer in Davis handled each question in a professional and concise manner, and made it clear that Wadsworth wasn't going anywhere with a charge of attempted murder in the Commonwealth of Virginia.

Throughout the quarter-hour of Q&A, Davis appeared very much to be literally and figuratively the man in charge with all the answers. This was not purely by accident, as he was perfectly aware that making a good impression on the national stage might help him someday realize his secret political dreams. One of the best impressions he made, also not coincidentally, was when he knew the right time to stop talking and turn the spotlight over to Sarah Brooks.

Her statement was short and to the point, describing the details of how she was first contacted by Fink, when she arrived at Wegman's Crossing, and the timeline of events that led up to the attack. While her ordeal had been terrifying—she was not ashamed to admit it—she was determined to continue her investigation. Not wanting to reveal any information about her findings so far, she emphasized the quick destruction and disruption of her equipment the night of the attack, so as to leave the impression that there wasn't any time to collect any data or images. Until she was sure what was going on, she was not about to tip her hand.

The last part of her brief statement had been the most difficult to compose, as it concerned the reputation of Dr. Henkel, and was potentially damning to the Octagon Corporation, who was paying for her investigation. It was a diplomatic dance on a tightrope, but something had to be said.

"And finally, I would like to urge you to read the excellent report produced by a local physician and historian, Dr. Carl Henkel. He believes that he has found evidence supporting the idea that the actual Battle of Wegman's Crossing was fought on the ground upon which this shopping center was built. While he in no way agrees with my work, we are seeking the same thing—the truth.

"If those brave soldiers' graves were disturbed, it may help explain the unusual activity that has been reported here. However, even if you feel all of that is pure bunk, the fact remains that if this is an important historic site, it should be acknowledged, studied, and above all, treated with *respect*," Sarah concluded, taking a page from Henkel's own book.

The questions immediately came raining down upon her like the shot and shell of a frontal assault. Again and again she was asked if she believed Wegman's Center was really haunted, and each time she repeated the statement that she felt there were enough credible eyewitness accounts to justify an investigation. On about the fourteenth or fifteenth rewording of the same question, she finally replied, while taking hold of the bandage on her throat, "Would I still be here after all this if I didn't feel that something was going on?"

That point finally settled, there was the grilling about Octagon's possible destruction of an historic site. Since the best way to shut down her investigation in a heartbeat would be to hang Octagon out to dry on national television, she decided to simply throw out some rope and let them decide if they wanted to hang themselves later.

"The Octagon Corporation is paying for this investigation, and it wouldn't be logical for them to do that if they had anything to hide. I'm sure once all of the facts come to light, they would wish to do the right thing, whatever that may be," Sarah stated, knowing full well that logic and doing the right thing had not been part of Octagon's plan. Fink had blown it—big time—by inviting Sarah to come down and investigate, in the belief that she could be persuaded to say that nothing unusual was happening. Of course, he couldn't have known the attack would happen, and that it would draw national attention, but nonetheless, he had set a chain of events into motion that no one would now be able to stop.

Long after the official press conference had ended, reporters continued to envelop Sarah Brooks trying to pump her for details. Her publisher, Bernie, always told her that even a minute of publicity could result in a year's worth of sales. But her energy finally gave out and she reached a point where she didn't care if her books fell completely off Amazon.com's charts. As her heart fluttered and her hands began to shake, she realized she had not given herself any time to relax and deal with the emotional effects of her near-death assault. As the crowd pushed in on her, she felt like she was going to lose it.

"Deputy Drummond!" she called out over the crush of reporters, "Please get me out of here!"

The deputy, who had been ordered not to lose sight of her, quickly cleared a path and led her into the hallway where the relative calm and silence helped her keep it together a little longer. When she got to her room, she dropped the Armani suit on the bathroom floor and went straight into a hot shower, forgetting all about the bandage on her neck. After yanking back the shower curtain, she pulled off the soggy gauze. As she turned to toss it into the garbage, she saw her own reflection in the large bathroom mirror. The sight of the black stitches over the ugly red wound was the last straw.

Sarah Brooks curled up on the floor of the shower and began to cry. She cried over the terror of the attack, but she also cried over the countless stories of tragic deaths, unrequited loves, suicides, regrets, and remorse she dealt with every day. Then she cried because she was lonely. For all her relative fame and fortune, Sarah Brooks was a lonely woman who was tired of always having to appear so strong and independent. She was equally tired of appearing resilient and impervious to all the harsh criticism. But most of all, she cried because when it came right down to it, she couldn't imagine ever giving it all up.

When she awoke the next morning, her throat felt better, but her eyes were red and swollen. She had once read an article about the composition of tears, and how tears of joy had completely different chemicals than those shed in sorrow. Some scientists theorized that crying helped purge unhealthy and "unhappy" chemicals from the body. It all seemed to make sense now, because Sarah felt like a great weight had been lifted. As much as she shied away from doing "girly" things, there apparently was something to simply having a good cry.

There was also something to having an adequate blood sugar level, so before she even got out of bed, she ordered a large breakfast from room service. When asked about having coffee, she thought for a moment and then opted for chamomile tea—caffeine was probably not the smartest thing for her system at the moment.

Not until there wasn't a morsel of food left on her plate did she begin to sift through all the email messages that piled up overnight. One priority message from Bernie congratulated her on the predominantly positive publicity that had already spurred a nice bump in online sales of her books and videos.

"That's great, Bernie," Sarah typed in response, "So I guess that means you'll be giving me a nice bump in my next advance, right?"

It would be very surprising if she received a reply to that.

It was also quite a surprise when Sarah saw a message from Dr. Henkel. She hesitated to open it, but it turned out to be both brief and positive. He actually thanked her for the tactful way she handled the press conference. As a result, the website containing his Wegman's Crossing research and reports had received more hits in the last twelve hours than it had in the previous twelve months, and he had over two dozen offers for interviews and lectures. While he still couldn't resist stating that he was unable to accept the nature of her work, he did now believe it was possible for them to "establish a meaningful and productive professional relationship in regards to the factual analysis of the Wegman's Crossing site." It wasn't quite a white flag, but it would qualify as a temporary truce. At the very least, she would probably be able to drop the pretense of enjoying scotch.

There were two main items on her daily to-do list, which she had written in a much more casual style than that of the previous day's—get a note from a doctor and find someone to help her with the investigation. She had to go on the assumption that Fink would allow her to continue, because if she simply waited for him to say something, she might lose yet another day.

Sarah called the office of the doctor who had treated her, and was informed that he would see her any time of the day at her convenience. That certainly wasn't typical when trying to make an appointment with any other physician, but then most doctors don't end up on the national news for stitching up a patient's neck. Sarah didn't care how much publicity he would get out of all this, just as long as she didn't have to sit for hours in a waiting room.

She arranged to meet him at the hospital right away, and then managed to get to her car before the reporters could reach her. It was good to hear that there were no signs of infection, and that the wound was healing nicely. If she behaved herself and continued to follow his instructions, the stitches could be removed in about a week. The sooner she didn't have to look at those knotted sutures sticking out of her skin, the better, so she promised not to do anything stupid—at least in regards to her wound. All bets were off concerning the rest of her life.

After putting his signature on a clean bill of health, the doctor applied a fresh bandage and gave Sarah a small mountain of gauze, tape, and antibiotic ointment. By the looks of it all, even after she healed there would be enough bandages left over for a respectable mummy costume. Thanking the overzealous doctor, she rose to leave.

"Wait, please, there's something else," the doctor said with a hesitant, serious tone that caused her to be concerned that there was more to her condition than he had admitted.

"What's wrong?" she asked, scanning her memory for similar situations on television medical dramas, hoping that one would not be written about her case some day.

"Well…it's just that I promised some friends a few autographed pictures," he said in a sudden shift from competent, life-and-death-decision-making physician, to shy, self-conscious fan.

"Oh…of course," Sarah said with relief. "But I don't have any photos with me. You'll have to give me an address-"

"I have my digital camera right here, and I could make some prints in a couple of minutes…if you wouldn't mind…please?"

Sarah dumped the bandage supplies on the examination table and obligingly stood next to the doctor after he placed the camera on a cabinet and set the self-timer. The doctor gingerly put his arm around her waist and grinned like a schoolboy as the flash went off. He wanted to take several more shots just to make sure, and each successive pose brought a tighter embrace.

It wasn't offensive, just amusing. Sarah was always amazed how complete strangers felt it was their right to grab her in a bear hug for a photograph. Even if she never saw these people before, and never would again, her fans felt that they knew her intimately through her books and television shows. On the one hand, it was good that her words were capable of establishing that sense of familiarity. On the other hand, some of these people needed a shower. Fortunately, the good doctor had good hygiene—although his taste in cologne could use some improvement.

"Great! Just let me get a few shots of you alone, then I'll do some cropping and printing and be right back!"

About ten minutes later he returned with a stack of pictures for her to sign. It seemed as though every doctor and nurse in the hospital wanted one. Just when she thought she was done, the administrator poked his head in the room and asked for a picture with an inscription essentially declaring him the best administrator the world of medicine had ever seen. In return, he presented her with a couple of sets of scrubs bearing the hospital's logo.

"They're very comfortable, and would be great to wear on your next investigation!" he suggested hopefully, thinking that somehow they might bring some favorable publicity.

"Thanks…thanks so much," Sarah said gracefully, "but I really do have to get going now."

More people had gathered outside the exam room, and while clutching the scrubs and packages of gauze and rolls of tape and tubes of ointment, she still managed to hold a pen and scribble her name on a few more photos and scraps of paper. When Sarah finally extracted herself, she made a wrong turn in her haste to leave and ended up wandering through a few patient wards looking for a way out. Both staff and patients eyed her suspiciously as she tried to navigate the maze of corridors carrying armfuls of hospital supplies. Finally, she found the emergency room and nonchalantly attempted to leave through the large sliding doors, until a firm hand on her shoulder stopped her at the threshold.

"Ma'am, I don't believe you have authorization to leave the premises with this hospital property," a stern voice stated, as the grip on her shoulder emphasized the point that this was not a friendly observation.

Even though she was completely innocent, Sarah immediately got that cold, sick feeling of being caught red-handed. It was some weird guilt thing she always experienced every time she passed a speed trap, or even when she had to go to the municipal center in Duxbridge to renew her license or registration. Just being near courts and law enforcement officers made her nervous. Apart from habitually exceeding the speed limits, and occasionally trespassing during investigations, she never broke the law, but nonetheless there were always those gnawing pangs of paranoia. And since her nerves were rather raw at the moment, the current pangs were particularly acute.

"Look, please just call the administrator-" Sarah began to explain as she turned to face the security guard who was stopping her. To her immediate relief and then complete aggravation it was not a security guard. It was Sheriff Davis, with one enormous, self-satisfied grin. "You son of a bitch!"

Her sudden, loud exclamation only brought greater amusement to the practical-joking sheriff.

"Now ma'am, that type of language won't help your case. Verbal abuse of a law enforcement officer is a serious offense in these parts."

"Oh, that's nothing," Sarah said with a devilish smile. "I've got some verbal abuse that would peel the paint off your patrol car."

"My, my. They still don't teach you Yankee girls manners, do they?" Davis continued, knowing the North-South jab would further provoke her.

"Well apparently, your vaunted southern manners are another myth of the Lost Cause fantasy," Sarah shot back, motioning with her head to the unwieldy burden in her arms.

"All right, I'll give you a hand," Davis said, pulling out one of the shirts from the pile and holding it by the ends so Sarah could dump everything into the center and bundle it together. "Just as long as you promise you aren't committing a crime."

"Don't ask, don't tell," she replied equivocally, wondering if parking her car in the staff parking lot was technically breaking any law. "So, what is the Sheriff of Brandon County doing at the hospital? Did your horse kick you?"

"No, not today, at least," he replied, clearly delighted by the stinging repartee. Most women were sugary sweet when they spoke to him. A little pepper was refreshing. "There's a guy here who was in an accident last night who we suspect is wanted down in Texas. How about you, are you okay?"

"Yeah, just had to get a signed note for Fink, stating that I was fit to return to active duty," Sarah said as she mentally checked off item one of her list, and then got an idea about item number two. "By the way, would you possibly have any interest in a little firsthand ghost hunting?"

"Such as?" Davis asked with suspicion.

"Well, Fink won't allow me to go back to the center alone tonight, and I thought you might want to get a crack at that *Sun 'n Surf* dressing room."

"Uh, I, uh, I'm not sure about tonight…"

"Of course, if you're afraid…" Sarah said aiming straight for the ego.

"No, it's not that! I'm just very busy," he protested, and then realized she was reading him like a large-print book. "Okay, I am afraid. Just a little. But this really is very strange stuff, so you can't blame me."

"I know, it's all pretty intense, but aren't you at least curious? Don't you want to find out what's going on?"

"Of course, I do. In fact, I was thinking of asking you if I could join you tonight, but I didn't want to interfere, or make you think I was keeping an eye on you. And I am a little afraid. But just a little."

"Okay, here's the deal," Sarah said, shifting the bundle under one arm so she could extend a hand. "You protect me from the living, and I'll protect you from the dead."

"Sounds like a plan," Davis agreed, shaking the offered hand to seal the bargain. "Now go get that rental car of yours out of the staff parking lot before I haul your Yankee ass off to jail."

Caught, red-handed, Sarah thought as she quickly retreated toward her car. But for some reason, this time it wasn't paranoia she was feeling.

Martin Fink's ass was in a sling. Not literally, thank heaven, but he was in deep trouble with the Octagon big shots. Even his uncle was threatening to pack him off to one of their South American banana plantations.

Thanks to his harebrained scheme of hiring a ghostbuster, Octagon's dirty laundry was now flapping in the breeze. The publicity was so negative that even the politicians in their pockets were bailing out. Everyone was calling for investigations, and everyone wanted to find out what Octagon knew, and when they knew it. It was going to take some serious spin to pull them out of this one.

Dismissing Sarah Brooks, or trying to discredit her, were the first options on the table, but due to the attack she was now a sympathetic figure, even to those who did not believe in ghosts. And removing her still wouldn't solve the problem of Henkel's report. Knowingly desecrating the burial site of American soldiers wouldn't exactly play well in the media these days.

Since there didn't appear to be any way to fight or deny the situation, they would somehow have to appear supportive. Octagon would set its best minds on formulating a plan to turn the entire mess to their benefit. They would welcome Sarah Brooks back with open arms, and set up a commission to aid Dr. Henkel's research. They would have to find a way to turn this public relations' nightmare around, so that Octagon would come out smelling like honeysuckle on a summer's evening. And then they'd send Fink to South America.

"I told you. Didn't I tell you?" Mrs. Henkel asked for the fourth time that morning.

"Yes, dear, you did tell me," Henkel replied like a defeated man, as he adjusted the knot of his tie and then slipped the ends into his suit jacket.

"I told you Sarah Brooks could help," she continued, refusing to accept the concession and enjoy the victory. "I just knew she would be able to help you. But you're always so stubborn, you always know all the answers. If you would just keep an open mind like I do, you would be a lot better off."

I would be a lot better off if you didn't keep such an open mouth, the doctor thought, wisely keeping that to himself.

"Yes, dear."

"You take my advice and go on one of her ghost hunts and maybe you'll learn even more!"

"Now *that* I will not do!" he declared, reclaiming his manhood. "I will not take part in any such nonsense!"

"I just don't see how a man like you, who deals with death every day, can just dismiss the entire spiritual world!" she replied, unfazed by his outburst. After twenty-five years, she was as used to his stubbornness as he was of her unique character traits. "You have seen things with your patients that can't possibly be explained by any of your textbooks and journals. There are deeper meanings and plans beyond this world, and you know it!"

"It's because I deal with death every day that I know there's nothing beyond. How could there be any greater meaning or plan when innocent children die of horrible diseases, and older people completely lose their precious memories, and their dignity. There's no meaning after death, for God's sake, because there's damn little meaning in life!"

"Okay, Dr. Cynical, have it your way," Mrs. Henkel said in a sing-song voice, waving her hands to signal that she would give up trying, which both of them knew she would never do. "Have a good day at work, and remember you have those interviews this evening."

As Henkel drove off, he couldn't get his wife's grating words out of his mind. Although he invariably resisted her incessant advice, he had to admit—strictly to himself—that she was always right. Always. And it was damn annoying. Yet, how could he, a man of science, a man who often held the power of life and death in his own hands, even begin to consider the idea of disembodied spirits seeking things they didn't find in life?

"Ridiculous! Absurd!" he declared, cranking up the volume on his car's stereo to drown out all the other thoughts that wanted to be heard.

Chapter 11

It looked like Christmas in Sarah Brooks' hotel room, or perhaps, moving day. Stacks of boxes had been delivered, and combined with the equipment she already had, there wasn't much space left to get around. One of the two double beds would have to be used as a staging area where she could unpack and test everything Jimmy had sent. It wasn't that she mistrusted her efficient assistant, it was the gorillas in the shipping business that forced her to have to be so thorough.

One of her most memorable examples of man's inhumanity to packages was the delicate automated analyzer that arrived with two gaping forklift holes rammed clean through it. And the shipping company had still tried to deliver it as if nothing had happened!

"Oh, *those* forklift holes," the customer service rep had actually said, when Sarah filed her insurance claim.

Fortunately, none of the these boxes looked as if they had been props for a magician's sword trick, but they were a bit battered around the edges. Sarah wasn't so concerned for the cables and housings Jimmy had shipped. However, with her new baby that Electron Man had constructed and delivered with superhero speed, careful handling was crucial.

Sliding the tube assembly out of the longest box, Sarah found a detailed set of instructions taped to the far end. His diagrams and notes were as concise as always, and Sarah admired the elegance and simplicity of his design. However, as good as it would look when she put it together, there was that nagging little disclaimer in red italics on the cover page of the instructions which read: "This instrument has been constructed according to your specifications. However, as magnificent a piece of engineering as this is, Electron Man can make no guarantees that it will actually work. Good luck and happy hunting."

At least he was honest!

As she checked the other boxes to make sure all of the parts were there, she came across a metal container with a three-wheeled locking system similar to those on briefcases. The part number on the box didn't appear on the inventory list, and there was a "Top Secret" label attached. At first, Sarah thought that her friend must have packed the container accidentally, and that this secret component was from one of his government projects. However, as she was about to email him a message to let him know that the container was safe with her, she had a sneaking suspicion...

Electron Man never makes mistakes like this, she thought as she went over the inventory list more carefully. It was odd that the parts were not simply labeled 1,2,3, etc., and as her finger slid up and down the column of numbers, Sarah finally recognized that they followed a clever mathematical sequence. However, there was one number absent from that sequence, and it just happened to have three digits. Dialing those numbers into the lock, she pressed the latch button and the container lid popped open. Inside was a note.

"You have not disappointed me, my first and best American friend! I hope you will be able to use my special component to make your new instrument more cost effective."

Unwrapping the object inside, Sarah discovered it was an old video game coin slot. It had a label reading, "25 Cents Per Play. Insert Quarters or Tokens Here."

When Sarah stopped laughing, she couldn't decide which was scarier—that she thought like Electron Man, or that he thought like her. To create the mystery of the secret container, he had to know that her curiosity would grow into suspicion. To solve the puzzle of the lock, it would take an analytical mind adept with numbers. And last, but certainly not least, the key ingredient to the prank was a sense of humor. It was very comforting to realize that there was at least one person in the world who knew her that well.

Of course, before Sarah got back to real work, she had to affix the coin slot to the space provided on the front panel of the sophisticated control unit for the new instrument. Then she had to take a digital photo to email to Electron Man, and write the full details of what had gone through her mind from the time she discovered the container. After all, the fun was in the details. To be sure, it was a frivolous pursuit—for both of them—but the day she stopped taking time out to have fun was the day she would be as dead as the ghosts she pursued.

Once playtime was over, Sarah ordered a late lunch from room service and settled down with Henkel's hefty comprehensive report. She quickly discovered that he tended to go off on tangents. For example, when describing the Confederate button they discovered, Henkel gradually digressed from the details of the North Carolina regiment it most likely came from, to a lengthy discussion of the manufacturing process of mid-19th century buttons. In her notes, Sarah condensed those several pages to: "Confederate button-North Carolina."

For the rest of the afternoon, she went through page after page of the report, culling the essential material. A fascinating story emerged. Sometime between the battles of the Wilderness and Spotsylvania in May of 1864, soldiers from both North and South who had been wounded and lost in the dense woods, sought to rejoin their armies. A group of as many as 100 of these convalescing Union soldiers collided with roughly an equal number of their Confederate counterparts at Wegman's Crossing. There was fierce fighting, and when it was over, almost all of the combatants lay dead or dying.

Only three soldiers where known to have escaped to tell the tale. One badly wounded Confederate private scribbled a letter home with a few words describing the battle. He said that he would tell the full story another time. There never was another letter, and the soldier was later presumed dead, when he failed to return home after the war ended.

A Union private made it back to his own lines and reported the battle to a captain, who briefly mentioned it in a dispatch to headquarters. Of course, given the circumstances, a skirmish of a couple of hundred men was of little concern. A few days later, both the private and the captain were killed near Spotsylvania.

Finally, a Union sergeant told the story of the Battle of Wegman's Crossing to many of his comrades in the weeks that followed. Unfortunately, he didn't write down a word himself, but about a dozen of his fellow soldiers did make mention of this desperate struggle between wounded men. It was usually nothing more than a remark in a diary or letter such as "but our sergeant said what we been through ain't nothin to the fightin he seen at a place called Wegman's Crossing." It wasn't much, but it was something. And considering that the sergeant was killed at Petersburg, historians were grateful for even these secondhand references.

As to who else was actually at Wegman's Crossing, it was impossible to know from the evidence that existed. Thousands of men went missing during the relentless fighting during that bloody May of 1864. The wounded Confederate who briefly survived was from A.P Hill's Third Corps. The Union private had been in Hancock's Second Corps. Of greatest interest to Sarah was the sergeant, who had said he had fought at Wegman's Crossing with other members from Sedgwick's Sixth Corps. The Sixth Corps that had for its insignia the St. Andrew's cross—the same insignia that appeared in the image of the phantom soldier in the mirror.

When Sarah finally finished going through the entire report, she let it drop with a thud onto the floor. Rubbing her tired eyes, she wished she could reach inside her skull and also massage the tension out of her tired and troubled brain. The full impact of the situation was just now hitting her.

My God, she thought, as her fingers slid back across her scalp, *there could be 200 bodies buried under that shopping mall!*

Just then the phone rang, but the gravity of the situation kept her from answering it until the fifth ring.

"Hey, Sarah, it's Beau Davis. Are you okay?"

"Yes, I'm okay…Beau," Sarah replied, conscious of the shift from the formal title of Sheriff. "I was just going over Dr. Henkel's full report."

"Well, that's enough to make anyone depressed. I just couldn't get through that tangled mess of minutiae. I sure hope he's a better surgeon than he is a writer."

"I know, it wasn't the lightest reading. But what really got to me was the possibility that Octagon built that damn center over the remains of 200 men."

"They claim they only found some animal bones and a few unidentifiable scraps of metal. I know they're all a bunch of scheming liars, but would they have lied to that extent? About something like this?"

"If Fink is any indication, I would venture to say yes."

"Good point. So what's the story for tonight? I have my junior ghost busting outfit ready to go."

"Great. Can't wait to see that. The plan is to concentrate on the *Sun 'n Surf* tonight. I have a cool new gadget I want to try out. How about I meet you in the parking garage about 10pm?"

"Sounds good. Do I need to bring anything?"

"Just make sure you have your proton pack and a beanie cap with a propeller."

"Roger that. See you then."

After Sarah hung up, she thought for a moment whether she should have invited Beau out to dinner first. She could have presented the offer as a type of business meeting, but there was already enough chemistry between them that the approach would most likely be construed as a thinly veiled cover for a date. Not that she would actually mind going on a real date with the witty and handsome sheriff—God knows she could use a real date with just about anyone at this point—but she had discovered that romance and ghost hunting didn't quite mix. The interesting combination had led to some decidedly corporeal videos on more than one occasion.

Sarah arrived at Wegman's Center about fifteen minutes early so she could unload all her stuff. As she pulled into the private parking area, she saw Dan Garrison waiting for her. They had exchanged several phone messages over the last two days, but hadn't actually spoken since the almost fatal night. She wasn't quite sure how he would react to seeing her again, and wondered if now that the crisis had passed, he would be back to his strictly-business manner.

"Sarah, how are you?" he asked, lifting her off her feet in a welcome bear hug. "You doing okay?"

"Yes, thanks to you!" Sarah said, gladly hugging back. "And just what does one say to the hero who saved your life?"

Dan set her down and went all aw-shucks kind of embarrassed.

"Just doing what I was trained to do," he replied humbly.

"Speaking of that…" Sarah began with some hesitancy. "I've been thinking…If you had taken a shot when Wadsworth was holding me, what were the chances you would have hit him, and not me?"

The humble expression was rapidly overspread by a sharp look in his eyes and a supreme air of confidence.

"I am one hundred percent certain that I would have saved Brandon County the expense of bringing that bastard to trial."

"That's what I thought, but I just wanted to make sure," Sarah said, glad that a man like Dan Garrison was on her side. "I'll sleep better now."

"So, can I give you a hand tonight?" he asked with eagerness, even though the lines on his face spoke to his obvious lack of sleep over the last few days.

"Thanks, but Sheriff Davis will be here tonight. You should go home and get some sleep. I spoke to Lela this evening and she said you've been here almost constantly."

"There's just been so much to do to tighten security around here. The attack happened on my watch, and I am going to make damn sure nothing like that ever happens again," Dan stated like a man on a mission, but then softened his tone considerably. "But if Beau is going to be here to look after you tonight, then I wouldn't mind going home and catching a little shut-eye, if you don't mind."

"Go home, Dan. Sleep. Eat. Relax. I'll be okay," Sarah said, as she put her arm around him and marched him toward his car.

As Sheriff Davis drove into the parking garage, he saw Sarah with her arm around Dan Garrison. It looked innocent enough, but he still felt a twinge. It was a slight twinge, but it was a clear sign that he was coming down with a case of jealousy.

Uh oh, watch yourself, Beau, he thought as he pulled into the spot next to Sarah's car. It wasn't that he didn't find Sarah attractive and provocative—especially provocative—but he knew better than to get involved with someone in an active case. That had happened early in his career, and if the woman hadn't been so discreet, it might have also been the end of his career.

Before Dan left, he and Beau talked about fishing, getting together to have a beer, and other male pleasantries. They had really only seen each other when they were both on the clock, but they got along well, and each appreciated the professionalism and honesty of the other.

"Have you had your daily dose of male bonding?" Sarah asked smiling.

"That should just about do it for today," he replied, hefting several heavy cases of equipment. "Shall we go hunt some ghosts?"

"After you," Sarah said, as she began wheeling the rest of the equipment on a portable hand truck. Even though she knew the way herself, she wanted Beau to go first so she could check out the rear view of the sheriff out of uniform and in jeans. It was quite scenic.

"So, I guess Fink gave you the okay?" Beau said, still managing to open the door for Sarah even though his arms were full.

"Well, yes and no. He gave the okay, but the spineless weasel had Lela call to tell me. She said that Octagon is pissed at Fink and incensed by the entire situation, but they are going to try to spin everything in their direction."

"There's a real shocker. And can I assume they will not be successful in spinning you their way?" Glancing back, he saw the nails-for-breakfast look in her eyes. "Stupid question. Not even if hell froze over."

"You got it. I find what I find, no more, no less. And if they think I'm going to keep my mouth shut-"

"I'll tell them that's a physical impossibility," Beau offered cheerfully.

"Thanks. I knew I'd be able to count on you. And will I also be able to count on you tonight, in case it gets a bit...intense?"

"You just keep that stuffed bear handy and I'll make it through. After all, ghosts can't hurt you." When Sarah didn't reply right away, Beau hurriedly continued, "They can't hurt you, can they? I mean, we aren't in any *real* danger, are we?"

"No, I don't think we are in any danger. These spirits are aggressive, but they don't seem the type to actually hurt someone," Sarah said thoughtfully, not realizing the change of expression Beau's face was undergoing as she spoke.

"Then they *can* hurt you!? But I read on this website that they couldn't," he said stopping in his tracks, looking genuinely fearful.

"It's rare, very rare. But it has happened...on occasion," Sarah said, automatically glancing down at the inch-long scar on the palm of her right hand. But that was another story, and one that the apprehensive sheriff did not need to hear at the moment. "Oh come on, you big baby. If these ghosts wanted to hurt anybody, they would have nailed Fink's ass a long time ago."

"Well, that's a comforting thought... I guess."

When Sarah and Beau exited the elevator at level two, a pair of security guards was there to escort them to the *Sun 'n Surf*. Beau noticed teams of security personnel moving systematically from store to store, making sure everything was locked. Dan Garrison was going to make sure that no one like Wadsworth would ever get another chance to hide in the center after hours, for whatever reason.

The guards began to position themselves at the entrance to *Sun 'n Surf*, but Beau suggested that their time would be better spent escorting the store's lone, frightened cashier to her car. She had reluctantly stayed behind to make sure there wasn't anything Sarah needed before she left.

"We're fine, you can go home now, thanks," Sarah said smiling, trying not to look nervous about returning to the scene of the crime.

"Okay then," the girl said, grabbing her purse from behind the counter and hurrying toward the door. "And good luck. There's been all kinds of weird noises in here tonight. As soon as I find another job I'm quitting!"

The brave Sheriff of Brandon County looked as though he wanted to follow the girl back out the door, but he managed an unconvincing smile and said, "Great, let's get to work."

Fortunately, no one had bothered to reattach the dressing room door that Sarah had previously removed. It wasn't like the store needed that dressing room anyway, or any of the dressing rooms, for that matter. Saying that business there was dead would be an understatement.

Beau helped remove various instruments from their cases, but for the most part he just stayed out of Sarah's way. The last thing he wanted to do was break something. One piece of equipment he did insist on setting up, however, was the Sniffer. Sarah explained that she had adjusted the sampling rate, so as to capture even a fleeting scent, but all Beau cared about was that it was a cool gadget, like something out of *Star Trek*.

"Wait till you see *this*," Sarah said, pulling the new set of tubes out of the box. "This baby will blow your mind. Assuming it works, of course."

"What is it, a hammock?"

"Naturally, a hammock would be an excellent ghost hunting tool, " Sarah deadpanned, playing along, "but this is a wee bit more sophisticated."

"What does it do?"

"You'll see. I hope. If you could just read me these instructions, it would help," Sarah said, as she handed Beau the long sheet of paper. At that moment, there was a noise from back inside the store, as if things had fallen off a shelf. Sarah's heart skipped a beat. "Oh crap, here we go again!"

Beau dropped the paper and swiftly pulled an imposing revolver out from under his jacket. "Stay here," he whispered.

Sarah clutched her container of pepper spray and concentrated on breathing. After what seemed an eternity, Beau said it was all clear and asked her to come into the store. Cautiously, she peeked around the entrance of the dressing room and saw Beau standing beside a pile of canvas beach totes. There were no knife-wielding maniacs in sight, so she continued on.

"What happened?" she asked, quickly counting eleven bags on the floor, and noticing one with some colorful appliqué tropical fish that would be great for her next trip to the beach. Suppressing her feminine shopping instincts, she continued, "I take it that these were up on that shelf, and that you didn't knock them down?"

"It wasn't me," Beau said shaking his head, not quite believing what he was seeing. He walked out of the store and shouted to a security guard standing by the railing across the atrium on the other side of level two. "You see anyone come in here?"

"No, sir. And I've been here since you went in. Is there a problem, sir?"

"No, we're okay. I'm just going to close these doors and lock them while we are inside."

"Yes, sir."

Beau pulled the heavy sliding glass doors together and turned the deadbolt until it clicked into position. Then he gave the doors a tug just to make sure they were secure. When he went back to Sarah, he found that she was taking some photos of the fallen tote bags and speaking into a small digital recorder.

"...and a guard confirmed that no one else had entered the store," she concluded, looking up at Beau who nodded his affirmation. "Will you give me a hand putting these back on the shelf?"

Sarah purposely handed him the tropical fish bag first, so it would be in the back of the pile. It was the oldest shopping trick in the book—hiding the merchandise so no one else would buy it. Of course, she could probably just take it, and leave a note and some money on the register, but where would be the sport in that? As they had just finished placing the last tote on the shelf, there was a sharp banging sound in the dressing room.

"This isn't funny anymore," Beau said as he withdrew his revolver again and jogged over to the dressing room doorway. Sarah watched as he carefully entered and then squatted down to look under the two lines of partitions. Even though he didn't see anyone, he still moved slowly from door to door, pushing each back until every room was confirmed empty.

"All right, what the hell is going on here?" he asked with considerable agitation.

"Welcome to my world," she stated without emotion. "We had better get all this stuff up and running, ASAP."

As she started switching on the instruments, there was the same sound of dropping tote bags inside the store. Beau started to reach for his gun yet again, but Sarah grabbed his hand. "Forget about it. They're playing us. Let's just concentrate on what *we* are doing."

"I don't know about this, Sarah. I don't know if I can handle this!"

"Hang in there, Beau," she said, giving his hand a tight squeeze before she released it. "Now let's get this hammock up and running."

There were several other strange sounds as they set up the new instrument, but they both acted as if they didn't hear a thing. Sarah had several recorders running, so she didn't need to focus on these extraneous matters, if you could call something of this extreme paranormal nature extraneous. In a few minutes, they had assembled the rectangular tube structure, which was a little under seven feet high and three feet wide—just the perfect size for a doorway, or in this case, a mirror.

Placing the frame less than an inch from the front of the mirror, she then began affixing a series of wires and cables to the center of the tubes on each side. Beau watched with great interest as Sarah ran the top and left wires to a five-foot tripod that had some kind of junction box on top. The wires on the bottom and right, connected to a similar box on a tripod on the other side. Then a single cable went from each junction box to a main control unit and screen. Even though he didn't have a clue as to what it was, he was very impressed with the entire setup—until he took a closer look at the control unit.

"Twenty-five cents per play?" he asked, wondering if this was all some kind of bad joke.

"The man who built this for me shares a similar sense of humor," she replied, shrugging.

"Poor man," Beau said with great sympathy, bracing himself for the inevitable dirty look. He wasn't disappointed, even though Sarah had to agree with him. "So what is this, some kind of oversized bug zapper for ghosts?"

"More like...flypaper," Sarah said as she opened a yard-long box and pulled out a roll of some wet, rubbery looking paper. She placed one end of the strange material at the top of the tube frame and attached it with several long, flat metal clips. Slowly, she unrolled it, carefully affixing clips along the sides and the bottom of the sheet, making sure it was stretched tightly across the frame. "This membrane is the secret to the entire unit. Did you ever hear of electrophoresis?"

"Isn't that how women remove unwanted hair?" Beau replied playing dumb, to gloss over the fact that he really didn't know.

"Very amusing. But let's just see if you're still laughing at the end of the night," Sarah replied. "Electrophoresis uses electrical current to push molecules of different sizes across some liquid medium like a gel, or specially treated papers. It's commonly used for things like DNA."

"So... you're looking to separate some kind of molecules?" Beau asked, trying to follow the train of thought.

"No, electrophoresis equipment just gave me the idea for this. You see, entities seem to create certain electrical fields, and I think they are also drawn to similar strength fields. What this instrument does, is send an electric current—set to a level that might attract an entity—across this gel-coated membrane."

"You're trying to trap a ghost?" Beau asked with wide eyes.

"Not trap it, just attract it, and measure it. If some energy makes contact with this membrane, it will disrupt the flow of current and its strength and size will register on the screen. If there really is something trying to pass through this mirror, we might just be able to record a rough shape of its energy field," Sarah said like a kid with a new toy. "Nothing like this has ever been tried, and it's a long shot, I know, but if this thing works..."

Sarah's words trailed away as she sat down and powered up the control unit, then checked and double-checked all of the settings against Electron Man's reference guide. Of course, all the recommended settings were nothing more than educated guesses, as this was about as uncharted a territory as any living person could imagine. She was making some final adjustments before initiating the flow of current, when a dressing room door at the end of the row suddenly slammed shut.

"Goddamn it!" Beau yelled, after having practically jumped out of his skin. Sarah barely acknowledged the sound. "How can you stand this?"

"If I ran every time a spirit slammed a door I would have been on the unemployment line a long time ago. I won't say you ever get used to it, but in some way it's kind of like a soldier who's terrified the first time someone shoots at him, then after a while he learns to sleep through an artillery bombardment. I guess you can get desensitized to almost anything."

"But how can you *not* be scared? A goddamned ghost just slammed a goddamned door!"

"I didn't say I wasn't scared," Sarah said, sticking out her right hand to show him the slight but noticeable trembling. "I just deal with it."

"Well pardon me if I'm just plain scared out of my wits right now!" Davis declared, showing her both of his shaking hands.

Sarah stood up and tenderly took hold of them.

"Look, Beau, it was unfair of me to ask you here tonight. I'll be fine on my own. Why don't you go outside with the guards, and I'll call you if I need anything."

Sarah's touch felt good, and despite how frightened Beau was, fear was no longer his ruling emotion. However, when an eerie creaking sound echoed over their heads, fear became a very close second.

"All right, if you can stand it, then so can I," Beau's male ego asserted, as he realized that if a man expects to have any chance with a woman, he can't act like a complete weenie.

"Atta' boy," Sarah said grinning, knowing full well that he would run in a heartbeat if she wasn't there. "Now let's get the lights off and get this show on the road!"

Beau cautiously moved through the store to the front light panel switch, and one by one plunged himself into deeper darkness. Sarah left the dressing room lights on until he had returned, and was safely seated in a folding chair a few feet behind her. He would be able to see what was going on from where he sat, but Sarah didn't need the nervous Sheriff getting in her way.

The camcorders were all turned on and set to infrared, Sniffer was smelling the air, and panels of instruments silently recorded their data and sent it to the row of laptops on the long folding table in the hall between the rows of dressing rooms. The new instrument's control unit was on a smaller table right in front of the dismantled dressing room, and Sarah rolled her chair between equipment stations for a few minutes to make sure everything was running smoothly.

"Okay, Beau, I'm going to power up 'The Hammock' and see what happens." As she slowly turned on the current, she heard the distinct sounds of the rubber feet of his chair being jerked across the carpet as he tried to surreptitiously inch closer to the screen. "Never try to sneak around behind a ghost hunter! Come on, pull up your chair. Just don't touch anything."

As Beau eagerly scooted forward to get a better view, his left elbow inadvertently hit her squarely in the chest.

"Oh, I'm so sorry!" he said with some embarrassment.

"When I said don't touch anything, I was referring to the instruments, but that also applies to body parts, too!" she said laughing. "Now if you're finished groping me, watch this panel here and let me know if you see any kind of little blips on that grid. That's where any interruptions in current will register."

"This is exciting! It's terrifying, but it's exciting!" Beau said as he glued his eyes to the rectangular green grid that represented the flow of current across the membrane.

Sarah took her time bringing the current up to the range where she hoped she might obtain some results. Within a few minutes, the ghost hunter and the sheriff were working like a seasoned team, making adjustments, calling out readings, and fine-tuning the system. Current flow was soon consistent and stable, and everything was working exactly according to plan. Except for the fact that even after surpassing the upper limits of the calculated paranormal range, absolutely nothing had happened.

"Not even a single blip?" she asked after almost thirty minutes.

"We are totally blipless," Beau replied with obvious disappointment. Even the noises had stopped. He had rapidly passed from terror to boredom, and he was beginning to doubt what he had already experienced. "Maybe nothing is here after all."

"Excuse me, weren't you the one ready to soil himself a short time ago?"

"I was experiencing some physiological discomfort," Beau sheepishly admitted. "But whatever was here before, seems to be gone now."

"Don't be too sure of that," Sarah said as she reviewed all of the settings. "Maybe I'm just missing something. Maybe the current isn't right. Maybe this whole idea is a waste of time."

"I thought you had already figured it out?"

"I wish. It's all just a shot in the dark, so to speak."

"So, then what would happen if you just cranked this sucker all the way up?"

"That would be way out of the calculated range," she said a little too dismissively.

"Well, excuse me, but you certainly couldn't get any *less* results, could you?" he countered with the appropriate sarcasm.

"Okay, okay, you're right. Obnoxious, but right. What do we have to lose?" she said as she grabbed the current control dial and spun it to its limit. "But if this thing suddenly opens up a portal for all the demons in hell, don't come crying to me!"

Beau assumed, and prayed, that was just a little ghost hunter's joke and managed to force a smile. A minute or two passed with still no results, and then Sniffer quietly began blinking some of his lights.

"Sarah, what's that mean?" Beau whispered, tugging on her sleeve and pointing to the little stainless steel bloodhound.

"He smells something!" Sarah whispered back, making sure the instrument was saving samples at the rate she had programmed. "Do you smell anything?"

"Yeah, yeah I do! It smells like something burning. Is it the hammock? Are we frying it?" Beau asked with rising excitement.

"No, the hammock is fine. Kind of smells like…spent gunpowder…doesn't it?"

"Yes, it definitely does, but where is it coming from? I don't—Sarah, a blip! There was just a blip! Look, there's another one!"

Sarah and Beau watched in fascination as a dozen little specks of light glowed for a split second and then vanished. She ran a quick diagnostic to make sure the blips weren't the result of any malfunction, and then realized that she must have been holding her breath for the last thirty seconds. Letting it out slowly and then drawing a deep breath to steady her nerves, she checked the numerical readouts and confirmed that the energy *causing* the disruptions in the membrane's electrical field *was* right near the center of her calculated range.

"This is amazing," she whispered, grasping Beau's arm. "This is it, this is the real thing!"

"I can't believe my eyes," Beau whispered back. "You mean to tell me that something dead is touching that thing right now!"

"Yes! And look here, every one of those blips is being caused by something on the side of the membrane *next* to the mirror!"

"Holy shit, then this is real!"

Sarah was about to respond with even more picturesque profanity, but something started happening to the grid, and it was a lot more than little blips.

"Oh…my…God…" she said, staring in disbelief.

The tiny, fleeting blips began to transform into larger, sparkling blobs of light at a few separate locations on the grid. Slowly, however, the blobs began to grow and coalesce. They grew brighter, larger, and more distinct, until they formed a swaying, pulsating, solid figure—in a human form. Sarah gasped. Beau couldn't make a sound if his life depended on it.

The burned gunpowder scent faded as a much nastier smell filled the air. It was the smell of death, and it was as strong and certain as if a corpse was lying at their feet. The odor was nauseating, the scintillating image of the glowing form on the screen was hypnotizing, and the tortured moan that then arose from behind the hammock was almost too much for their senses to bear.

"Let's go, let's get out of here!" Beau shouted, jumping to his feet.

"No! Not now, look!"

In the dim light from the instruments, Sarah could see that the long membrane sheet was vibrating.

"What the-" Beau couldn't even finish his words as he stepped back until he was against the wall and could retreat no further.

"Look, its energy is so intense it's making the membrane move!" Sarah said as her voice raised an octave.

Carefully sidestepping the cables and equipment, Sarah entered the dressing room.

"Don't go in there!" Beau shouted, realizing the time for whispering had passed.

"Stay back!" she said, motioning with her arm behind her, but not taking her eyes off the quivering membrane.

Switching on a small red flashlight, she inched closer. The vibrations intensified, and suddenly the membrane appeared to start rippling and bubbling as marble-sized bumps flexed outward for a second, and then went flat again. It was like hail bouncing off a canopy, and the air certainly felt as cold as ice.

"Sarah, *please* get away from that thing!" Beau pleaded without effect.

"I have never seen anything like this in my entire life!" Sarah said, moving to within inches of the membrane.

Just then, the area of the gel-coated sheet directly in front of her face began bulging outward, like something was pushing hard against it, trying to break through. She was completely transfixed as this unseen force beat against the electrically charged membrane that had drawn it out from another world. Sarah knew she shouldn't, but she was compelled to reach out and touch it…

As her fingers were about to make contact, the oval-shaped bulge suddenly resolved itself into the tortured features of a human face. The features contorted and writhed like a man with a rubber sheet pulled tightly across his face, as if gasping for breath, as if in agony. Sarah couldn't move, and the face stretched out closer and closer until it pressed against her cheek. It felt cold and clammy against her skin, and then a jolt of electricity shot through her body. She stood frozen in place like someone whose muscles were paralyzed by a strong current. Images raced through her brain and a flood of emotions swept her out of her body to a distant time and place.

Beau lunged forward to pull Sarah away, thinking that she was being electrocuted. His feet caught on the tangle of cables, and when he tried to break free, he knocked into one the tripods that held a heavy junction box. It started falling forward toward the hammock, and Sarah's head. Grabbing hold of her arm, he yanked her away a split second before the junction box struck the grotesque face protruding from the membrane. It tore a gaping hole, split the rest of the sheet down the middle, and then the unit fell on top of Sniffer, smashing its sampling bottles. The face was gone. The room felt warm again and the odor of rotting flesh instantly disappeared.

"Sarah, Sarah, are you all right?" he asked, shaking her by the shoulders and anxiously waiting for any response. Her body was rigid and hardly moved. Her head tilted back slowly until her eyes met his, but her expression was blank, and she had a hollow stare that was frightening. "Sarah, are you hurt? Can you hear me? Say something!"

Sarah blinked her eyes mechanically several times until they opened and closed more naturally. Then her stiff muscles finally relaxed to the point where Beau had to hold her upright. He eased her into a chair and tried to rub some warmth back into her icy hands.

"Beau…you…"

Her voice was faint and weak, and trailed away before she could finish.

"Yes, it's me Sarah, it's Beau. What is it? What are you trying to tell me?"

"Beau…you…broke…my fucking membrane!"

The Sheriff of Brandon County didn't know whether to laugh or cry as he picked her up in his arms and almost squeezed out whatever breath was left in her.

"You are *the* biggest pain in the ass I have ever met! But thank God you're okay."

He let her rest for a few minutes to fully regain her senses while he powered down all of the equipment and turned on the lights. He had decided that in order for him to function after witnessing that horrible face attacking Sarah, he would simply have to go into complete denial. It was either that, or run screaming from the place.

"I think we've had enough of this for one night, don't you?" he said as he held her wrist to check her pulse again. "Are you sure you don't want to go to the hospital? You were almost electrocuted."

"No, that wasn't it," Sarah replied, shaking her head both to disagree, and to get more of the cobwebs out. "The hammock doesn't have enough voltage to hurt a fly."

"But I saw you, you were being shocked."

"Ohhh, I was being shocked all right, but it wasn't the current from the hammock. It was Edward," Sarah said as if stating the obvious, and then looking quickly to the left and right as if to find out who just said that.

"Edward? Did you say…Edward?" Beau said slowly, clearly ambivalent about wanting to know any more.

"Oh, God, I did," she said pressing her eyes closed and covering her face with her hands. "I remember now, I *saw* everything. I *felt* everything."

"Come on, Sarah, you're rambling. We need to get you to a doctor."

He put his hand on her shoulder to move her toward the door, but she grabbed it, held tight and wouldn't budge. It was an unnatural strength, and when she looked at him it was with an expression that made his blood run cold.

"*Don't you understand*," she said emphasizing every word. Her voice was deep, resonant, insistent. "I saw it *all*. The battle, the terrible, terrible fighting. He was wounded…the awful pain…but still, he tried to take care of his men. His friend was badly hurt…the house…the fire…but he wouldn't leave his friend. He would never leave him. The smoke, the flames…the darkness…"

Beau stared at her for a moment with his eyes bulging and his mouth hanging open. It was time for another dose of denial.

"Okay, Sarah," he said, gently prying her hand off of his. "This is one of the reasons why you don't have a steady boyfriend."

"Beau, I'm serious," she replied with a weak smile, fortunately taking a healthy step back from the entire possession scene. "Edward died right here, and I *saw* the whole thing."

"Now listen to yourself," Beau said, shaking her again, hoping he wasn't going to have to make a habit of it. "Isn't it just possible that the electricity scrambled your brain, that all of this is from your imagination?"

"Did my imagination pull that damn face out of the membrane?" Sarah asked with her nails-for-breakfast attitude fully restored.

"I *don't* want to talk about *that* right now," Beau said waving his hands. "Let's just pack up and get the hell out of here. I have had enough."

They barely said a word as they dismantled everything and loaded it back on the carts. As they were leaving the *Sun 'n Surf,* a jovial and skeptical guard across the atrium shouted a facetious question.

"Catch any spooks tonight, Ms. Brooks?"

"No, but one caught me," she replied enigmatically, as the grin rapidly faded from the guard's face.

"Are you serious? Was there really something in there?" the guard said, running along the opposite railing to keep parallel with the famous ghost hunter.

"We have no further comment," Beau stated in his official tone.

The guard stopped in his tracks and watched the two until the elevator doors closed. Then he cautiously looked back over his shoulder to the innocent looking storefront of the *Sun 'n Surf.* A shudder raced up his spine. He hadn't believed all this nonsense before. Now, he was seriously going to consider sending out his résumé.

Sarah and Beau didn't speak again until they reached the parking garage. The sound of footsteps a few rows over from where they were parked snapped Beau out of his silent contemplation, and further rubbed his raw nerves.

"How can you stand this?" he said, pacing back and forth, wringing his hands. "I mean, I'm not a coward. You know, I've been shot at, for God's sake, more than once!"

"I can understand why," Sarah replied with good-natured sarcasm, but then got serious. "Not that having someone trying to kill you is easy, I can personally attest to that, but this is different. In this business you never know what you're up against. This is another world, and we can never hope to fully understand it. I know what you saw tonight was terrifying and almost impossible to believe, but you are just going to have to work it all out in your own mind. It is a reality. Ultimately, you can not deny it."

"Oh yeah, just watch me. In high school I was voted Most Likely to be in Denial," Beau quipped nervously.

"I don't believe that for a second. You were class president and Most Likely to Succeed, weren't you?" she said, trying to prop up his ego.

"Well…yes," he humbly admitted.

"And captain of the football team?"

"Yeah, that too," he said, less humbly.

"And, no doubt, king of the senior prom?"

"Yup, that was me," he declared, ego fully re-inflated.

"You know, I really hated guys like you in high school!" Sarah said smiling, happy to see that she had finally gotten him to laugh and loosen up. "Now go home, get a good night's sleep, and forget all about what happened tonight."

"Forget! How can I forget seeing the rubber coated face of a dead guy?" Beau said, tensing up again. "How can I possibly ever think of anything else, ever again! That's it, they might as well lock me up and throw away the key. I will never, *ever* be able to think of anything but that face!"

Clearly, this situation called for more drastic measures, so before he could continue to rant, Sarah stood up on her toes and firmly planted a kiss on his lips. Stepping back, she saw that he looked more stunned than when he had seen a ghost.

"There. Now you have something else to think about," Sarah said calmly as she got into her car and drove off. In her rearview mirror, she saw the sheriff still standing there, and wondered how long it would be until he moved. She also wondered if she had kissed him just for his sake, or for hers.

Chapter 12

The most shadowy members of the Shadow Patrol had been busy. They had located four construction workers willing to talk. Although these men lived in different states and had no contact between them, each relayed the same story—human remains had been uncovered at the construction site, and had quickly been covered back up, by Octagon's orders.

One of the elite Patrol members had also managed to hack into Octagon's computer system, where he downloaded a document alluding to the "unexpected problems in the ground" during excavation, and stating "no discovery was to delay the construction timetable." Any "trouble spots" were to be immediately covered over with concrete, and the design plans would be modified accordingly. The wording was shrouded in enough mystery so it would be difficult to substantiate anything in court, but it was obvious that Octagon had gone out of its way to hide a dirty little secret. And if the time ever came that this dark secret was exposed to the light of day, upper management could not plead ignorance, as this document had been signed by Octagon's head honcho, Alexander Chivington—Martin Fink's uncle.

The sweet grandmother with the rap sheet had also done her part. She had located a lawyer who had been a key member of the original team that had bullied their way through the land purchase and building approval process. At first, he refused to speak with her, but when she pulled a thick dossier of his indiscretions out of her knitting bag, he was more forthcoming. Octagon had apparently broken enough laws and bribed enough officials to fill a made-for-TV miniseries, and the lawyer would spill the goods on them, lest Granny spill the goods on him. Blackmail had been one of her specialties in the good old days, and it felt great to be back in the extortion saddle again.

All of these reports were encrypted and routed to Sarah Brooks' email through a maze of accounts that could not be traced back to their real source. It was probably being overcautious, but Sarah might need plausible deniability if anything ever hit the fan. Maintaining the anonymity of the informants also helped maintain their effectiveness, and helped keep them out of jail, as well.

Jimmy had been busy, too. He had taken every scrap of data and every image Sarah had sent and had compiled reports cross-referencing everything he could think of. It was actually somewhat of a waste of time doing it before the investigation was complete, but he had to do something or he would go crazy.

Not being there with Sarah was worse than any horror the spirit world could throw at him. But he also knew that if he went to Wegman's Crossing without her consent, he wouldn't be able to bear her disapproval. So either way, he was bound to be miserable.

It wasn't until about 2am that he was finally able to doze off. He had been waiting expectantly for Sarah to call with details of the night's investigation—even though she expressly stated that he should not wait up, that she would phone him in the morning. Ever hopeful, however, he had set up his computer to sound an alarm if it received an email from her. As the not-so-subtle electronic howl roused him from sleep less than ten minutes later, it was nonetheless like sweet music to his ears.

Leaping out of bed and vaulting over the back of the chair, he landed on the seat and double-clicked the mouse all in the same motion. The message for which he had been praying instantly appeared on his monitor.

"Hey, Jimmy, you planning on lounging around there all weekend? You know there's work to be done down here. So why don't you get your lazy butt out of bed and hop the next shuttle to D.C. And bring The Eyes. And remember, they are worth more than your college fund, so be careful!

P.S. I've got a story for you that will blow your mind.

P.S.S. Don't try to sneak your Boy Scout knife on the plane this time!"

The "Eyes" to which Sarah had referred was probably her priciest piece of equipment—a thermal imaging camera that could "see" heat differences in objects at long distances. Police and fire departments utilized this technology to track suspects and identify the locations of victims, but Sarah had found that the device was excellent in spotting paranormal energies across a wide expanse. Naturally, her camera had been custom made for her unique purposes, and had been presented to her on "extended loan"—in exchange for her endorsement. Otherwise, she would not even dream of asking a teenaged boy to put a $40,000 camera in his backpack and bring it to a shopping mall in Virginia.

Jimmy could have waited until morning and then asked his mother to drive him to Sarah's house to pick up The Eyes, but he was so excited he immediately got on his bicycle and rode the five miles in the dark. Besides, it made him feel very special, and very mature, whenever he used his personal key to enter Sarah's house by himself. She had also given him a credit card for equipment purchases—and sudden travel expenses—and he was thrilled by the responsibility and trust she had placed in him. Of course, she probably wouldn't be too thrilled that he was going to transport an expensive and delicate camera over dark country roads on his bicycle, but if she didn't ask, he wouldn't have to tell her.

He also didn't feel it was necessary to wake up his mother to tell her he was flying to Virginia for the weekend. Instead, he left a note on the kitchen table with a few flowers he had picked from Sarah's front yard. He knew that starting a note with "Dearest Mother" and ending with "Your Loving Son" enabled him to get away with just about anything in between. Not that he ever got into any real trouble, but he did sidestep the entire notion of parental control on more occasions than he could count.

By the time Jimmy was cycling home, Sarah had set other wheels in motion. Like a general marshalling his forces for a major offensive, she drew up a battle plan and then determined what she needed to win. This campaign would require some heavy artillery, and she counted on friends and connections to supply all the necessary firepower. There was no longer any doubt. This was war—war between Octagon and the truth, between the present and past, between the living and the dead.

When she finally turned out the lights and crawled into bed, she wasn't surprised that the moment she closed her eyes the face in the membrane appeared in her mind. Rather than try to block out the image and fight the upswell of feelings that accompanied it, she surrendered to the memories that were not hers. Sarah slowly recalled the scenes and sensations that had shot through her like a bolt of lightning in the dressing room. It was not the result of her imagination, and these weren't illusions. These were genuine memories of sights, sounds, smells, and above all emotions, of the last hours of a life lived and lost almost a century and a half ago. It made no rational sense, but Sarah Brooks would stake her own life on the fact that she had glimpsed something from the other side.

By the time she was asleep, Jimmy was already on his way to Logan Airport, thanks to a car service he had charged on Sarah's credit card. He had booked himself a seat on a United Airlines flight leaving at 6:15am, which arrived in Washington, D.C. at 7:47am. There was an earlier flight on Delta, which left at 5:40am, but it stopped in Cincinnati and didn't arrive in D.C. until 10:05am. Departing thirty-five minutes earlier, and arriving over two hours later!

And people think what I do doesn't make any sense! Jimmy had thought as he checked the schedules.

As he was boarding his flight, Ricky from the New York ghost hunter's club was loading his equipment back into his van. He had a long, late-night conversation with Sarah, and despite his wife's vehement protests, there was nothing on earth that was going to keep him from going back to Wegman's Crossing now. Three other club members were going to meet him and they would all drive down together, while discussing and debating what had happened—and what was about to happen.

Dr. Carl Henkel barely slept after Sarah's call late Friday night. Her plan seemed impossible, but if he had learned one thing through all this, it was to never underestimate Sarah Brooks again. He didn't know how she had gotten the new information she had presented to him, he didn't know where or how she was going to apply the necessary pressure to force such an extraordinary undertaking, and quite frankly, he didn't give a damn. If she could pull this off, he would shelve his skepticism and become her biggest fan—at least of her abilities, if not for her bizarre beliefs.

Tony Marchand had been tickled pink by Sarah's call. He loved to ruffle feathers, and her plan afforded him the opportunity to do a whole mess of ruffling.

"I always knew you were a rebel at heart, darlin'," Tony said to her after listening to her plan.

The eminent historian had the most wheels to set in motion, as he had the highest connections and personally knew more people than were in the average town's white pages. But he didn't even consider making any early morning calls. He would wait until a more civilized hour—after he had a proper breakfast and a sit on the porch.

Lela Reynolds was up at the crack of dawn drinking strong coffee so she could finish her report and email it to Sarah. There were some very juicy bits of information in the report that were important for Sarah to know, but ultimately she would probably not reveal any of it. It was simply too compromising—for Lela. If these facts came out now, it would be obvious where the breach in corporate security had occurred, and Sarah was not about to jeopardize Lela's job.

Sheriff Beau Davis tossed, turned, and stared at the ceiling for hours before he finally fell asleep from sheer exhaustion. The horrible apparition protruding from the membrane had been the most frightening thing he had ever experienced, but that pesky little Yankee woman had indeed given him something else to think about. Yet, for all his dead of night deliberating, he never did come to any conclusion as to whether he should be more worried about the ghost, or the ghost hunter.

At Wegman's Crossing Shopping and Recreation Center, there were some things that never slept. Thanks to Sarah's stirring of the paranormal pot, activity was reaching a fevered pitch. Security guards reported more strange sounds, more shadowy figures, and more bone-chilling pockets of air than during any previous night. Surveillance cameras displayed fields of static for various periods of time for no discernable reason. At one point, all of the telephones rang in the food court, stopping abruptly after just two rings. A kiddie ride shaped like a rocket ship started up by itself, blinking its lights and roaring its engines. Stores throughout the center had boxes, clothing, and even glassware pushed off shelves and racks. Numerous patrons in the movie theaters complained about someone—or something—brushing against them in the dark.

Fortunately, things began to quiet down around dawn, but the psychological damage had been done. When Dan Garrison arrived for work early Saturday morning, there were three more resignations on his desk. These were good people he couldn't afford to lose, and he knew they would not have quit unless something very serious had happened to them. However, while it was difficult to conceive of these people being so spooked they couldn't take it anymore, it was completely inconceivable that there were bona fide spooks running around the center.

In his search for answers, Dan had been able to rule out the hoax theory and any involvement by the preservation groups. Since the episode with the knife-wielding reverend, security was tighter than a drum. After hours, no one entered the center that was not on his personally approved list, and movement throughout the center was monitored at all times. He had also consulted with electricians, plumbers, mechanics, and architects to see if there were any identifiable reasons for the sounds, malfunctions, or "shifting of merchandise," as the frequent occurrences of shelves that emptied themselves came to be known. The experts had no answers.

Dan could only conclude that what was happening was the result of some as of yet unknown natural phenomena, coupled with a potent form of mass hysteria. Although he had seen and heard many things he couldn't explain, he believed himself immune to this delusional epidemic, and he would continue to stick to what he perceived as the rational high ground. There were no such things as ghosts. Therefore, ghosts could not be causing these problems.

There was one fly, or ladybug as the case may be, in Dan's mental ointment—Sarah Brooks. He liked her, and he never really liked anyone who held a set of beliefs that significantly departed from his. Sarah was intelligent and honest, yet she chased spirits for a living. She was down to earth and had a great sense of humor, yet she had no doubt in her mind that the dead walked among the living. It was beginning to look as though he would either have to start believing in ghosts, or stop liking Sarah Brooks. Since neither option was appealing or probable, he would withhold final judgment until a third choice manifested.

While Dan set aside his personal dilemma to focus on the business of minimizing disturbances in the center, a phone call was being placed from Louisiana to Washington, D.C. that would lead to things being turned upside down—literally. After Tony Marchand had his last sip of tea on the veranda, he dialed the private number of one of his closest personal friends. When their conversation concluded, his friend made a few calls of his own.

"Mr. Chivington, this is J. Buxton Crandall. Do you know who I am?"

"Uh, why yes, *Senator* Crandall! It's an honor, sir."

"Well, we'll just see how honored you feel when I've finished speaking my peace. Now Mr. Chivington, did you know that the Crandalls have been fighting for this country even before it was the U.S. of A.?"

"I am aware that you come from a very distinguished military family, but, of course, I don't know all the details," Chivington replied with no clue as to where this was going. Nor did he know why one of the most powerful senators in the country had called him in the first place.

"Well, just let me give you some of those details. Crandalls have fought and died in countries around the world for over two hundred years, but no matter where they fall, we always bring our boys back home and give them a *proper burial*," the senator stressed, wondering when the light would dawn.

Chivington was indeed starting to see the light, and he began to squirm in his chair. It was something he hadn't done since prep school, but he was beginning to feel very much like a guilty schoolboy in the principal's office. When he made no response, the senator continued.

"And when my nephew was killed and those bastards were dragging his body through the streets, you know we got him out of there and brought him back. No one desecrates the body of an American soldier and gets away with it. *No one.*"

Chivington stopped fidgeting and decided it was time to play innocent and demand to know what the senator was implying. Senator J. Buxton Crandall the Fourth never gave him the chance.

"So now that you are clear on where I stand, let's cut to the chase. My sources inform me that when you built that shopping mall over there in Virginia, you knowingly did so over the remains of soldiers from the Civil War."

"But, sir, I-"

"You just listen to me until I'm finished, because I want this to be crystal clear. Unless you rectify this disgraceful situation to my complete satisfaction, I will have the FBI, the CIA, the IRS, and every other three-letter organization I can find give you a royal four-letter going over. By the time they are done with you, if you're not in jail, you'll be lucky to be able to get a job as assistant stock boy at a Piggly Wiggly. And make no mistake, Mr. Chivington, this is a threat, plain and simple."

"Senator Crandall, this is outrageous-"

"Yes, it is, Mr. Chivington. Yes it is. And believe me, I find it very distasteful having to sully my hands in this manner. But if it gets you and your bastard company to do the right thing, then hell, it's worth my trouble. You should be receiving a packet of information from a Miss Brooks any time now, and you just follow that lady's suggestions, and everything will be just fine."

"But, but-"

"I have already spoken with my dear friend, the Governor of Virginia, and he is on board one hundred percent. I am also going to be playing golf with the Vice President this afternoon, and I hope I won't have to trouble him with this matter, will I, Mr. Chivington?"

"The Vice President! No, of course we plan to fully cooperate and rectify any unintended -"

"Mr. Chivington, I am a busy man, so you just save up all your ripest bullshit for the reporters. Just do the right thing, and I won't be needing to make any more phone calls."

With that, the senator hung up, leaving the head of one of the country's most powerful corporations shaking in his loafers. And before he even had time to begin a plan to destroy documents, bribe employees, and weasel out of any personal liability, one of his servants was knocking on the door to his study, announcing that a special courier had arrived and would only make delivery directly to him. The timing was uncanny, and even more unnerving, but what Chivington didn't know was that the courier had been parked at the end of the driveway for the last hour, waiting for the call to make delivery.

Inside the generic cardboard box were just two file folders and a letter. The red file folder was labeled "What We Know" and the green folder read "The

Plan." Before opening either, Chivington read the letter, which had been personally signed by Sarah Brooks.

If you are reading this letter, it means that you have just had a rather interesting conversation with a man who possesses the power to make things happen.

As you no doubt know by now, I am the paranormal investigator that was hired by your nephew, Martin Fink, and what I have found at Wegman's Center has been startling in its intensity. While you may try to dismiss my evidence, consider the research of Dr. Carl Henkel, the numerous reports from construction workers, the confession from one of your former lawyers, and your own internal documentation, and I'm certain that you will see it all provides conclusive proof of what you and Octagon have done.

A synopsis of this evidence is in the red folder. Of greater importance is what is contained in the green folder—what you must do about it. In anticipation of your full cooperation, teams of professionals are being assembled at this moment, and will be prepared to act within 48 hours. Think about it, but don't think about it too long. The situation at Wegman's Center is escalating.

I fully understand what this plan will involve in money and time, but quite frankly, it doesn't matter. What does matter is that there are dozens of souls who will not find peace until their remains are treated with respect, and their memories are preserved.

After reading the contents of the red folder, Chivington knew he was beaten. It was not a feeling he had experienced very often, and not one he expected to let linger. After reading Sarah's plan in the green folder, his initial anger slowly turned itself in another direction. Alexander Chivington did not get where he was today by wallowing in defeat. Before he had even put the folders down, he was formulating a plan that would not only eliminate all of his problems, but make his precious shopping center more profitable than he had ever dreamed.

Sarah Brooks was dreaming of a certain handsome sheriff when the phone rang.

"Ahhh, it was just getting to the good part of the dream," she grumbled out loud as she reached toward the nightstand. "This better be awfully damned important."

Clearing her throat, she tried to sound like she hadn't just woken up when she answered the phone.

"Ms. Brooks, this is the front desk, I'm sorry to wake you, but we have a James O'Reilly here to see you."

At first, Sarah couldn't understand how he had gotten there so fast. Then she looked at the clock and realized she had slept most of morning.

"Thanks. You can send him right up. Oh, and I left a message that I wanted to have him stay in the room across the hall, if it's available?"

"Yes, that room will be available in a couple of hours. We will have the key sent up to your room when it's ready. Sorry again for waking you."

Sarah rolled out of bed and slipped into a bathrobe. Once again, she went through her two-minute drill to try and look decent. While a lot of men would appreciate the tousled hair, just-out-of-bed look, it was not an image she wanted to present too often to a seventeen-year-old boy. She also thought it best to try to prop up the collar of her robe to hide the bandage on her neck. No sense agitating her impressionable assistant any further.

"Sarah, oh my God, let me see!" Jimmy said, almost tackling her as she opened the door. Yanking on the collar of her bathrobe, he gasped as he saw the long, thick strip of gauze angled across her slender neck. "Are you sure you're going to be okay? I've been sick I've been so worried!"

"I'll be fine," she replied trying to step back and get some distance between them. But in the innocent emotion of the moment, he took her in his arms and locked her in a powerful embrace.

It was then that the Sheriff of Brandon County stepped into the room.

"Oh jeez, I'm sorry!" Beau said with embarrassment, as he turned his back to the embracing couple. However, as the initial shock passed of seeing a scantily clad Sarah apparently being passionately held by another man, extreme annoyance took over. "The door was open…and for God's sake, couldn't you be a little more discreet!"

Jimmy jumped away from Sarah as if her skin was molten lava, and Sarah scrambled to close the robe over her flimsy nightie. When Beau saw the youthful age of her alleged paramour, and the cases of equipment standing in the hall, he immediately realized that this was simply her exuberant assistant, but that wasn't going to stop him from having some fun.

"Wait just a minute. How old are you, boy? You know we have laws against this kind of thing down here," Beau said in his deepest southern accent.

Sarah picked up on his game, but poor Jimmy was thunderstruck.

"But I didn't…I wasn't…I wouldn't!" Jimmy stammered as he looked desperately to Sarah to explain the situation.

"It's okay, Sheriff," Sarah said, slipping an arm around her panicked assistant. "This is my fiancé."

Jimmy jumped back again, looking twice as horrified, until he realized he had just been hoisted on his own petard. With a great sigh of relief, he sat down on the bed, but instantly thought better of that and stumbled over some boxes to get to a chair.

"You must be the famous James O'Reilly," Beau said smiling, extended his hand for a friendly man-to-man shake. "It's nice to meet you. Sarah has said nothing but good things about you."

"I guess you must be Sheriff Davis," Jimmy said with a remnant of sheepishness, but clearly already warming up to the man he thought was about to arrest him just moments earlier.

"You can call me Beau," he replied graciously, as Sarah continued to admire how he handled people and situations—except where she and ghosts were involved.

"Jimmy, why don't you bring in the equipment and then go get yourself some lunch downstairs, while I see to what we owe the honor of the sheriff's visit," Sarah said with a slightly raised eyebrow, which Jimmy knew meant he should scram. Under the circumstances, he was more than happy to go.

Once the door had closed, Sarah turned to Beau with a faintest hint of a devilish grin, and asked, "So, did you sleep well?"

"No, damn you. How about you?"

"Oh, I slept well enough, although I could have used just a few more minutes," she replied with an air of mystery.

Beau eyed her suspiciously, and decided not to ask what she meant. He had more pressing questions.

"Look, Sarah, about last night..." he began and then trailed off, hoping she would jump in, but saw that she was content to make him squirm. "Come on, you know what I'm talking about."

"Yes, I do. So what about it?" she asked, appearing to play it cool and aloof, but actually feeling surprisingly uncomfortable and not knowing what else to say.

"What about it? You kissed me!" he replied with growing frustration.

"I am aware of that," she said with her own agitation level rising. What had seemed to be a cute thing to do at the time was now looking to be a big mistake.

"Well, what I want to know is if you kissed me just because I was upset, or because you *wanted* to kiss me," Beau demanded, practically shouting.

"Both! Or maybe neither! I don't know right now!" Sarah said, yelling back.

"Fine. That's just fine," Beau said storming toward the door, then hesitating for a few moments before storming back toward the most infuriating woman he had ever met. "Then maybe *I* should just give *you* something to think about!"

Taking her in his arms, he literally lifted her off her feet and delivered one of the kisses that had practically made him a legend in several counties in Virginia. When he finally lowered the weak-kneed ghost hunter back to the floor, he knew he could add at least one county in the state of Massachusetts to that list.

Sarah took a deep breath as if she had just had the wind knocked out of her. As she began to hope that Jimmy was going to have a very long lunch, Beau stepped back toward the door.

"Wait, where are you going?" she asked, incredulous.

"You have a nice day, Sarah. And sleep well tonight," Beau replied as cool as a cucumber—a cucumber that was internally reaching boiling point.

Ninety-nine percent of him wanted to stay and kiss her again. And again. But that one percent told him to run for the hills. This was not the time, and certainly not the place, to start anything. Too much was going on, and the last thing he needed was to get involved and have his picture splashed all over the tabloids with a ghost hunter. He needed to run. Fast.

When Jimmy returned from lunch, Sarah had just finished taking a long, cold shower.

"I'm not in any real trouble with the sheriff, am I?" he asked with some trepidation.

"No, you're not, Jimmy. But I am."

"What do you mean? He doesn't think that you and I-"

"No, of course not. I was just kidding. Everything's okay. But just remember that if you ever plan on dishing it out, just make sure you can take it. Now, shall we dispense with the small talk and get down to some serious ghost business?"

"Tell me everything! Twice!"

Sarah and Jimmy spent the next hour going over all the video and readings from the previous night. The boy was speechless as he watched the face appear in the membrane, and there were tears in his eyes when Sarah told him what she saw and felt when the apparition's cheek pressed against hers. He was visibly shaken by the time they were finished.

"Sarah, don't you realize what you've done? This is a way to communicate with the dead! You've created a portal between worlds!" Jimmy said with uncharacteristic fear.

"Oh portal, schmortal," Sarah said waving off his dramatic pronouncement, hoping her young assistant wasn't losing his nerve. "The line of communication was already there. I just boosted the signal, so to speak."

"What did Electron Man have to say about this?"

"You know him. He took it all in stride, as usual. And he wasn't even upset that the membrane was shredded, since he already has plans for a new and improved Hammock. He was just thrilled that the whole thing worked, but I don't think he really appreciates what that means."

"I certainly appreciate it," Jimmy said with the puppy dog expression that had to be seen to be believed.

"I know you do, Jimmy. That's why you're my right-hand man," Sarah said and then laughed when he automatically straightened up and puffed out his chest at the thought of being a man. A moment later there was a knock at her door. "Must be the key to your room."

However, when she answered the door, it was a uniformed man, but definitely not from the hotel.

"I'm from the Mercury Messenger Service," the burly man said in a thick Bronx accent, obviously embarrassed by the silver jumpsuit he was wearing, not to mention the little silver wings protruding from the ankles of his boots. The writer in Sarah knew there was an interesting story here, but she was too embarrassed to pursue it. "Are you Brooks?"

"Yeah, I'm Brooks. What d'ya got for me?" Sarah replied in her best New York accent.

"I got dis here package you gotta sign for."

Sarah signed on the appropriate spot on the clipboard, and reached into her pocket to get some money for a tip. She did all of this without making further eye contact, lest she start snickering at the unlikely Greek god before her.

"Gee, thanks, that's real generous of ya. Ya know, a lotta people don't think to tip the delivery guy, even though we bust our butts gettin' things to people faster than anyone else. That's why they call us Mercury, ya know, cause we're so swift."

Sarah was not particularly pleased that her new friend felt like sharing. Seeing that the envelope was from Alexander Chivington, she was anxious to open it.

"Well, thanks. Have a nice-"

"And ya know this is just a temporary gig for me. I mean, runnin' around in a freakin silver jumpsuit is not my long-term career goal. Ya see, I was out a work back in New York, and my brother-in-law says 'Hey, Charlie—my name is Charlie—come down to Virginia, I'll give you a job in transportation and pay you a really good salary.' So I think I'm gonna be drivin' a truck, or maybe some fancy limo, and the bastard sticks me in this fairy suit. Ya see, I figure he's just tryin' ta humiliate me cause I said he weren't no good enough ta marry my sister, but I ain't lettin' it get to me cause I just drive around all day delivering these little packages and the money comes outta his pocket for me to be doin' this.

So I ask ya, if I ain't lettin' it bother me and he's shellin' out the dough, who's the real winner here?"

"Clearly you are, Charlie," Sarah said quickly, happy to get in a word edgewise and break the mind-numbing monologue. "Now if you'll excuse me, this is rather important business. Thanks again."

"Oh, yeah, sure, I understand, lady. See, that's what I do all day, bring important stuff to people," Charlie said, looking as if he was prepared to continue, but finally took the hint when the door closed.

"You know, there's something good to be said about being dead," Sarah said to Jimmy, who had been on the verge of busting a seam the entire time. "Go ahead, laugh it up, but just remember I might get us some uniforms to wear. In fact, I think you would look quite handsome in a metallic jumpsuit."

"That's not even funny! Although, that's the way most people expect us to show up, in some kind of weird ghostbuster outfit."

"Maybe we will have to try it some time, but only with a ghost who has a sense of humor. Now, let's see if Chivington has a sense of humor."

Tearing open the envelope, Sarah pulled out a single sheet of fine quality stationery. Taking a deep breath, she began to read at loud.

"Dear Ms. Brooks, It was a great pleasure to receive your packet of information this morning—yeah, I bet it was," she added, rolling her eyes before continuing. "On behalf of myself, and the entire Octagon family, we are grateful that you have taken the time and effort to bring this matter to our attention."

"This guy is good!" Jimmy said after a whistle. Even a seventeen-year-old knew high caliber bullshit when he heard it.

"Maybe a little too good," Sarah replied, wondering just what this Chief Executive Weasel had up his sleeve. "Now, where was I...here we are—this matter to our attention. I will immediately be issuing a directive to my entire staff to fully cooperate in the implementation of your comprehensive and well thought out plan. Thank you again, and please contact the management at Wegman's Crossing Center to schedule the necessary tasks and get this important work underway as soon as possible. Sincerely, Alexander Chivington."

"Is he for real?" Jimmy asked, shaking his head.

"I can guarantee that he is planning to somehow capitalize on all of this. We'll be dancing with the devil, but hopefully the end will justify all the crazy means."

Despite her fully justified skepticism, Sarah was excited by the prospect of what was about to happen. It was all a gamble—an enormous, life or death gamble—but she knew in her heart it had to be done. After bringing Jimmy up to speed, they both hit the phones. Sarah's first call was to Dr. Henkel.

"Get your shovel, Dr. Henkel, we are going in!" Sarah announced to the incredulous doctor.

"You can't be serious! However did you pull this off? I can't believe it!" he replied like a giddy schoolboy who had just been told that school had been canceled—forever.

"Threats and blackmail, plain and simple. Works every time," Sarah said proudly.

"When do we begin?" the doctor asked, scarcely able to contain himself.

"The sooner the better. Maybe Monday, if the teams are in place. And remember, secrecy is the key word here. There's been enough trouble stirred up without word of this getting out."

"Sarah, I assure you that we will all be extremely discreet."

"Okay, Carl," Sarah said matching the first name shift. "Let's plan on all meeting first thing tomorrow and see where we stand."

"Great. Oh, and Sarah, I really don't know how to thank you for all this. This means so much to me," he said with genuine and deep sincerity.

"Thanks, but it means a whole lot more to those men buried under the center, and they are the ones who we are doing this for."

"Of course. Of course it is. Thanks again."

Sarah made several more phone calls, emphasizing to each person that the plans were to be kept under wraps. She had thought up a suitable cover story about electrical line replacement so that this delicate operation would not be under the glare of another circus spotlight as the work crews moved in.

"Uhhh, Sarah, I think you had better come here," Jimmy said, pushing the button on the television remote that raised the volume.

"What now, another infomercial that promises to enlarge your—what the hell?" Sarah's jaw dropped as she saw Alexander Chivington's smiling face on the screen.

"...of course, in lieu of this startling new evidence," he said, nonchalantly adjusting the knot of his red, white, and blue tie, "we feel it is our duty as citizens of the United States, as well as decent, civilized human beings, to immediately begin excavating underneath Wegman's Crossing Center to uncover any possible remains and give these men the dignified burials they so justly deserve."

"That son of a—" Sarah began, but swallowed her words as the reporter's interview continued.

"This is a remarkable step, Mr. Chivington," the local newscaster said, pleased as punch to be getting the exclusive interview that would give him national coverage. "You mean to tell us you are going to tear down your own shopping center?"

"Well, not exactly, Frank," Chivington said with a chuckle, as if he had known this reporter for twenty years. In actuality, they met just two minutes before airtime. "Wegman's Crossing Shopping and Recreation Center will be open and fully operational throughout this entire process, and we invite the public to stop by and view our special multi-media display that will contain up-to-the-minute information about the status of our project."

"When will all this begin?" the reporter asked.

"Almost immediately," Chivington stated with conviction. "We are assembling the appropriate teams even as we speak. I also just had the pleasure of speaking on the phone with the head of the National Parks system, and we will be working very closely with them every step of the way. Our goal is to donate portions of the center's property for a park and cemetery. It will really be unlike anything else in the country—a shopping center that incorporates one of our nation's important historic legacies."

"Thank you, Mr. Chivington, for having the extraordinary courage to undertake such a bold and remarkable-"

"Turn it off!" Sarah shouted. "Turn off that conniving son of a bitch before I throw this chair through the television."

Jimmy nervously fumbled with the remote until Chivington's obnoxious grin faded to black.

"His extraordinary courage!" Sarah continued shouting. "His plan! His duty as a citizen, my ass!"

Jimmy had never seen Sarah so angry, and he wasn't sure whether to start ranting along with her, keep his mouth shut tight, or simply crawl under the sofa and hide. Fortunately, the phone saved him from making a decision. It was Carl Henkel, and it was clear from the ensuing conversation that he was equally outraged—perhaps even more so, as Sarah soon eased up on her own tirade to try to calm him down.

So here it was. After all the years of lies and deceit, and fighting against what was right every step of the way, Chivington was now presenting himself and Octagon as crusaders for truth, justice, and the American way. Chivington had announced Sarah's plan as his own—to break through the layers of concrete under Wegman's Center, exhume the remains of any soldiers buried there, and study the evidence and artifacts to finally try to understand just what took place at the mysterious battle so many years ago.

"No, Carl, I don't think a lobotomy would improve Chivington's personality," Sarah said laughing, as her anger finally loosened its grip, albeit slightly. "Look, let's try to keep our cool and view this in a positive light. Twenty-four hours ago we were facing an almost impossible task. Now, the head of Octagon himself has pledged the full support of his corporation—and the Parks system—on national television! Let's just do the right thing and get the job done. Then you can lobotomize him."

The phone continued to ring and Sarah continued to commiserate with other team members for most of the afternoon. Finally she switched off her phone and asked Jimmy if he wanted to go get something to eat—a foolish question for a teenaged boy.

"Where would you like to go?" she asked.

"Well, I would kind of like to actually see the center, if you don't mind?"

"Of course, I'm sorry! In all this confusion I completely forgot that you haven't been there yet. Let's go eat ourselves silly in the food court, and then I'll show you around. I also need to pick up a few more things to wear, as it looks like I'll be here a bit longer than I anticipated."

Sarah neglected to say that there was also a certain tropical fish bag she had to buy, but that was strictly on a need to know basis, and Jimmy didn't need to know all of her weaknesses.

Chapter 13

The multi-media display center was already under construction in the center's atrium as reporters began filtering in looking for more dirt on the upcoming exhumations. Martin Fink was conspicuous by his absence, and the task of official liaison for this project fell upon Lela Reynolds. Headquarters wanted someone in that position who faithfully towed the company line, and believed that in Lela they had chosen the perfect lackey who would follow orders without question. But then again, they had thought that Fink would be a competent manager.

Lela's first act had been to call Sarah Brooks and tell her everything. The suits at Octagon were running scared. The prime directive was to lie through your teeth as you were smiling. Whatever incriminating evidence existed was to be shredded, anything potentially negative was to be spun in as positive a light as possible, and any employee who so much as made a peep was to be exiled to a branch in some third world nation where cannibalism was still practiced.

Lela's official instructions contained the not-so-subtle suggestion that Sarah Brooks should be sent packing as soon as possible. Of course, it had to be done delicately, as she obviously had some extremely powerful friends. The key would be to get her to want to leave, and various options were floated—everything from creating a bogus haunting story in some foreign country and anonymously sending her an airline ticket and cash, to pressuring her publisher into making her drop the case under threat of termination of contract. As the jury was still out on which underhanded method to attempt, Lela was instructed to "use all possible discretion when dealing with that troublesome ghostbuster."

Apart from that single derogatory reference, what was curiously absent from Octagon's plan was any mention of ghosts. The fact that hundreds of people had experienced paranormal activity was not even obliquely referred to. The company line of misinformation Lela was expected to tow was that this project was being undertaken now, because historians had recently uncovered evidence to place the scene of the battle squarely under the shopping center. Furthermore, some construction workers had only just come forward to say that they might have come across something resembling human bones, but neglected to report it at the time. It was a story full of holes—holes just big enough for rats to wriggle through—but not so large as to sink the carefully crafted deception.

Then there was that infamous box of artifacts. The large box contained various buttons, buckles, Minié balls, and other bits of metal found during construction. There was also the jawbone that Henkel had discovered, all securely locked away in the corporate vault. This valuable material was immediately released to the National Parks historians for analysis. The cover story for why this had not been turned over sooner was simply that the box had been mislabeled, documents had been misfiled and it was all just a big, innocent mistake.

Of course, the media wasn't so much interested in the dry details of the historical research of the site, and why the decision to implement the plan had come about—they just wanted to see some dead bodies, or at least bones. There would be those reporters who would inevitably ask whether or not the ghost sightings really led to this drastic step to tear up sections of a newly constructed shopping center, but a suitable response had already been formulated. Whoever was being questioned was to turn the tables and put the reporters on the defensive by asking—by a show of hands—who among all the professional journalists really believed in the existence of ghosts? Peer pressure should quickly silence that line of questioning.

As for those who would question what Octagon knew, and when they knew it, the strategy was denial. Chivington had already countered one reporter's accusation that they knew about the graves all along by asking, "Why would I spend millions building something, only to then spend millions more digging it up again? I am a business man, and that does not make for good business."

As Senator Crandall and others involved did not care to publicize their threats, the entire Octagon façade of innocence and nobility was not going to receive any serious challenges from people in authority. Sarah and Dr. Henkel could raise a stink, but it would only smell like sour grapes. However, truth had a way of eventually trickling out, and Sarah was confident it would all come to light someday—and if not, she would write about it and make sure that it did.

A conference room at the hotel was to be used as a kind of a "paranormal war room" for the planning and analysis of the new phase of the investigation Sarah had planned. There were two main areas where human remains were known to exist, and these areas had been covered only by a layer of concrete, with doorless and windowless voids constructed above them. These empty spaces would be the first areas to excavate, but Sarah knew there must be other locations, due to the widespread haunting activity in the center. She needed to identify every potential hotspot—places where activity might correspond with an actual corpse in the ground below—so that not a single man was left behind.

One such location was without doubt the underground parking garage. Another was most likely beneath the food court. Three floors below that at ground level, was a highly automated loading dock, but that, too, would probably have to submit to the jackhammers. Sarah had a sneaking suspicion that Chivington thought he would be able to get away with breaking up a few bits of concrete in a couple of unused rooms. It would be interesting to see if he could maintain his unctuous smile when reality finally hit home.

By 7pm, some of the best ghost hunters in the country had gathered in the conference room. Ricky from New York City was there with three of his most competent researchers. A team from San Francisco was also there. They had done some first class work at Alcatraz, and Sarah assumed that if they could handle the angry spirits of some of history's worst criminals, they should be able to stand their ground here. There were also another half dozen people from across the country who Sarah personally knew and trusted.

Another face at the conference table that Sarah was glad to see was that of Lela Reynolds—ostensibly there as official Octagon liaison, but that was just a cover. She was Mama Sherlock in her heart, and although she didn't have the nerve to actually participate in the ghost hunt, she was more than willing to offer the benefit of her extensive knowledge of the center and all that had transpired.

For the first thirty minutes or so, Sarah gave an overview of the current situation, and presented some of the evidence she had found. By design, she reserved the highlights of the *Sun 'n Surf* videotapes for last, knowing that all semblance of order would go out the window when those two pieces of footage hit the screen. If there were gasps when she played the scenes of the shadowy soldier in the mirror from the first night's investigation, there was outright shouting and screaming (predominantly, but not exclusively from Lela) when the face protruded from the membrane.

Her astonished fellow ghost hunters requested that she replay that section of video over and over again, frame by frame, explaining what she had experienced at each moment. When almost twenty minutes had transpired reviewing the few seconds of tape, she declared that enough was enough. There was some grumbling, but she promised copies to each and every one of them if they would all sit down and get back to work.

Copies of the center's floor plans, containing the color-coded symbols for the various paranormal activities catalogued thus far, were passed around the long table. Aware that certain groups and individuals had particular strengths and weaknesses, Sarah presented the objectives and let the team members decided which areas they would like to tackle. For example, Margaret from Baton Rouge was an audio expert, but she was as claustrophobic as one could be and still manage to live with a roof over her head. Her natural choice was the expansive food court.

Two places not on the night's schedule were the *Sun 'n Surf* and *Kinder Krossing*. Those locations were paranormal slam-dunks, and besides, at ground level beneath each place was one of the enclosed voids already scheduled for excavation.

"Our goal is to leave no spirit unaccounted for," Sarah said as the meeting was about to conclude, and the group prepared to head to the center with their night's assignments. "This task obviously will not be completed in a single night.

I plan to remain on-site continuing the investigation for as long as it takes—or until Octagon succeeds in kicking me out. I know some of you have other commitments next week, but let's see what we can accomplish tonight and tomorrow, and just take it from there.

"And besides, I have one of those funny feelings that the whole ballgame is going to change the moment those concrete tombs are breached and the bones start surfacing."

That was something no one else in the room had considered before. This was already one of the most robust hauntings on record—once the actual remains were unearthed, would the activity subside, or multiply in intensity?

"That's just great!" Ricky said sarcastically. "Let me just warn you all now, if I see a face pushing through concrete, I'm outta here!"

Everyone chuckled as the big man made the exaggerated, slow motion movements of running in panic and pretending to push people out of his way. It eased the tension in the room, but only slightly. They all were acutely aware that this was a haunting on a scale that no one had ever encountered—or even dreamed of in their worst nightmares. It also didn't help that, except for Sarah, no one there had ever taken part in the actual exhumation of a set of human remains—let alone possibly over one hundred of them. This was one jittery bunch of ghost hunters, but Sarah hoped that once they were setting up their instruments and getting down to business, the excitement of the investigation would overcome the fear.

She delivered a brief pep talk to close the meeting, and as they began to file out of the conference room, she couldn't resist a parting comment.

"Fasten your equipment belts," she said paraphrasing the famous old movie line in her best Bette Davis impersonation, "there's going to be a lot of things going bump in the night."

Even though it was a Saturday night, many of the stores at Wegman's Center had closed early, and by the official 10pm closing time only a few curiosity seekers still wandered the near-empty corridors. Once the big news had broken earlier in the day, even those diehard shoppers who had chosen to ignore the reports of ghosts now got cold feet when they realized they would be walking over graves. Picking out a new shade of lipstick or sipping a cappuccino was not too appealing when you were doing it on top of dead bodies.

Several storeowners had even told their employees not to return to work until further notice, as there was no sense paying salaries when no sales were being generated. In lieu of this, many of the center's tenants planned to meet at a local restaurant after hours to discuss their next step—which was most likely to retain legal council for the purpose of renegotiating or terminating their lease contracts. By Octagon's own admission, there were a hell of a lot of skeletons in the closet, and their existence had not been disclosed to all those tenants who shelled out big bucks for what had been billed as "the most desirable retail space in the country."

Octagon knew they would have to make some concessions, but their legal teams would push to settle for rebates. They would do just about anything to avoid a mass exodus of stores and restaurants. The huge corporation had debts of its own to pay, and vacancies never helped the bottom line.

As for the adjacent conference center, there had only been one cancellation, as meetings and conventions were usually planned far in advance, making them difficult to reschedule or relocate on short notice. Fortunately, a national meeting of morticians was scheduled for the upcoming week, and the conference center management was confident that this group should be the last bunch of people to get squeamish over a matter as trivial as scores of dead people around them.

However, except for that one bright spot in the financial picture, the outlook for Wegman's Crossing Shopping and Recreation Center was grim, for the short term at least. Sarah had hoped that the center would close down for a couple of weeks, which would make her work much easier, but she had not wanted to insist upon that in the plan delivered to Chivington, fearing it might be a deal breaker. However, if tenants continued to mutiny, the center might shut itself down.

As darkness fell on the lovely warm spring day in Virginia, it turned raw and stormy. When Sarah left the meeting and went back to her room to get her equipment together, she paused by the window to watch some distant flashes of lightning. She imagined that was how artillery fire looked at night, and the rumbles of thunder only added to the warlike impression.

Images from the face in the membrane seeped back into her conscious mind, filling it with vivid scenes of battle and suffering. Closing her eyes, Sarah was so deep in thought that she was unaware when she leaned closer to the window and pressed her cheek against the cool glass. It was like she was face to face with the soldier once again, in a trance that put her into another time—a desperate time with a desperate struggle between life and death. The soldier knew—she knew—that the struggle would be lost, but the memory should not. He must make sure these men's stories were told. She must make sure these stories were told. *They* would make sure...

"Hey, Sarah?" Jimmy asked with some concern, as he had entered her room and found her with her face against the window, oblivious to his presence. "Sarah, do you feel okay?"

"Sure, I'm fine, no problem," she said, dazed and a bit embarrassed, straightening up from what must have looked like a bizarre position. "Just lost in thoughts. You know how I get."

Jimmy laughed and replied that he had long ago stopped asking where she went off to in her little flights. He never stopped wondering, he just stopped asking.

They ran through the pre-investigation instrument checklist like seasoned fighter pilots. This time, however, there was one very special extra piece of equipment.

"Is it still in one piece?" she asked, purposely hesitating before opening the case that contained the expensive thermal imaging camera.

"Of course! It's fine! If there's anything wrong with it, I didn't do it intentionally!" Jimmy exclaimed in an odd way to protest his innocence. Sarah chalked it up to the Catholic Guilt Syndrome.

"I'm only kidding, Jimmy," Sarah said, carefully peeking into the case, now half expecting to see bits of broken glass.

Fortunately, this precious piece of equipment she called "The Eyes" was without a scratch, and everything checked out okay—no worse for the long bicycle ride to which Jimmy was on the verge of confessing, until he saw there was no need. *Spare the confession and save the contrition*, he had lately made his motto. In his case, it would save a lot of time.

Massive drops of cold rain pelted them as they hurried back and forth to the car, loading the cases of equipment. Actually, it was less equipment than they normally brought, as there would be several other teams on the job that night. Sarah and Jimmy would mostly be using The Eyes to scan large sections of the center trying to pinpoint areas of activity, as well as further rule out those places that had not previously had any reports of the paranormal problems afflicting the rest of the center.

The ever-faithful Dan Garrison was once again waiting in the parking garage for Sarah's arrival. She introduced Jimmy, who was delighted when Dan said, "A pleasure to meet you, *Mr. O'Reilly.*" Jimmy then did his manly best to conceal the grimace as Dan shook hands with his trademark, vise-like grip.

"So, I have to ask," Sarah said with some hesitation, hoping her friend was not angry. "How are you taking the news about them busting up the center? Are you okay with it?"

"Me? Are you kidding?" Dan said with an unusual, but impressive combination of a scowl and a smile. "If I knew there were American soldiers under this place I would have already torn it apart with my bare hands. Even now I have to restrain myself from setting a few well-placed charges of C4 and bringing down the whole rotten place."

Sarah had no doubt that he would be the man who could do it, too.

"I don't know how you did it, Sarah," Dan continued, "but I salute you!"

Her cheeks flushed as she proudly returned the salute, but she knew there was a long road ahead before anyone could start waving flags. The other teams soon arrived, and Dan called several guards to escort them to their assigned locations. Rather than merely acting out of a sense of duty, the chief of security now seemed eager to take part in the investigation, although Sarah wouldn't get her hopes up that he was actually coming around to her way of thinking. As long as Dan now had a solid reason to be on her side, it was good enough for her.

Ricky and the New York City team remained in the parking garage, claiming they chose that location because they had the most experience with pavement. Actually, they had developed an effective grid system for isolating paranormal activity in a large warehouse, and that technique should be equally effective in the vast, underground parking area.

As the management offices were located above this garage, Ricky had managed to persuade Lela into sitting in her office with a walkie-talkie and reporting anything unusual. Initially, she was terrified at the mere thought of having any part in a ghost hunt, but Ricky convinced her that it wouldn't be any different than any of the other nights she worked late by herself. Of course, he might have failed to mention that he and his team would be intentionally trying to provoke the spirits in order to gather evidence on them.

Sarah made the rounds of the center to make sure everyone was in place and had everything they needed. She tried not to appear too dictatorial, but this night's work was critical. Even with people she trusted, she never really trusted them one hundred percent when it came to an investigation. It was a science and an art, and unless she was personally present, she could never rest easy that the right disciplines were being applied in the right proportions. But these were top-notch people with first-class equipment, so she managed to play it cool and mask her anxiety.

When Sarah returned to the fourth floor where she had left Jimmy and the equipment, she found that he had rigged one of the center's electric carts into a mobile ghost hunting command center. As they would be covering several hundred acres of space along the expansive corridors on four floors, he thought it would save hours setting up, breaking down, moving a few hundred feet, and setting up again. It was a very clever idea, but as Jimmy prepared to get behind the wheel of his creation, Sarah decided that wasn't very smart.

"Oh no, you don't!" she said waving him back as she recalled his last driving escapade in the cemetery. "You manage the instruments, and I'll drive."

"Don't you trust me?" he asked, a bit hurt, but fully aware of his propensity to put the pedal to the metal.

"I would just prefer not to see just how many pieces of equipment—and bones—we could break by driving a golf cart at top speed through a storefront. No offense, but I'm getting a little tired of being carried out of here."

"Okay, go ahead, you can drive," Jimmy said pouting, as he tossed her the keys, but brightened when she complimented him on his technical wizardry in converting the cart into a ghostmobile. Instruments and laptops were strapped to the back seats, and the flat screen monitor for The Eyes was hanging down between them like a giant rearview mirror.

"Does Dan know what you did to his cart?" Sarah asked as they took off.

"He helped me," Jimmy said beaming. "And he thought it was a great idea, too. When this is all over, he's thinking of turning one the carts into a mobile security and surveillance vehicle."

"Hey, maybe we can get Electron Man in on it to provide some satellite uplinks and laser-guided weaponry and really make this a kick-ass golf cart!" she said in a completely serious tone that made Jimmy think for a second.

"You know, someday that attitude of yours is going to get you in trouble," Jimmy said, as if he was scolding a child.

Even though Sarah laughed, she knew he was absolutely right, except that "someday" was now. A prime example of her attitude in action was with the

Sheriff of Brandon County. She had most likely irreparably botched the whole thing, when all she really wanted was—

"Sarah, look out!" Jimmy yelled, just as she was about to ram the cart into an elaborate display of potted honeysuckles.

Swerving at the last second, she missed the brass planters, but they both got a face-full of honeysuckle branches. As she slammed on the brakes, fragrant blossoms rained down all over the equipment.

"Jesus, Sarah, what the hell were you doing?" Jimmy shouted as he frantically tried to brush away the tiny fragments of flowers and leaves before they worked their way into the keyboards and instrument panels.

"I was not paying attention," Sarah freely admitted. "I'm really sorry, are you okay?"

"Yeah, sure, I'm all right," he replied much more subdued. "And I'm sorry I kind of hollered at you."

"Oh please, holler away. I have no excuse. Here, you can drive, and I'll handle the instruments and maybe my mind won't wander," she said getting out of the cart and brushing off the white blossoms that clung to her clothing.

"You know, Sarah, I'm getting worried about you," Jimmy said with genuine concern. "You just don't seem to be yourself. Maybe all this has been too much for you."

Jimmy pointed at the bandage on her neck, and her hand automatically moved up to press on the tender neck wound. The physical cut was the least of it. The attack had deeply affected her, and made her feel more vulnerable than at any time in her life. The emotional roller coaster ride with Beau certainly didn't help, either, and the psychic bonding with the dead soldier hadn't exactly been a stabilizing force. Maybe Jimmy was right, maybe this was all too much for her...

As she slid into the passenger seat, she saw a pale blue wisp float across the monitor connected to The Eyes. The sensitive thermal imaging camera was mounted on the dashboard, but Sarah gently lifted it off the bracket with her right hand, while motioning with her left hand for Jimmy to look at the screen. The hunt was on, and all her troubles and self-doubts vanished like an apparition in a spotlight.

Stepping carefully back out of the cart, Sarah lifted The Eyes up to her own eyes, made a few slight adjustments and held her breath. Another thin, blue wisp appeared in the camera's field, about ten yards in front of them. The bluish color indicated a cooler temperature than the surrounding area—and just might also indicate the presence of a wandering spirit.

Using hand signals, Jimmy and Sarah silently communicated EMF and ion readings, temperatures, and positions. Jimmy pulled the infrared camcorder from the floor of the cart, and as it was already attached to the tripod, he had it up and running in a matter of seconds. All of the cart's equipment was now directed at one spot, but that one spot multiplied.

Another diaphanous filament of blue light appeared next to the first, then a third, and a fourth. Although they swirled and swayed gently, they did not move from the roughly ten-foot diameter circle they hovered above. Unlike many phenomena that come and go in the blink of an eye, these cool slips of air hung in place for a solid two minutes.

"What does it mean?" Jimmy whispered. "What is it?"

"An invitation," Sarah said confidently. Placing The Eyes back on the bracket, but keeping it aimed at the visitors, Sarah reached into her vest pockets for the walkie-talkie, and her global positioning unit. Still whispering, she held the walkie-talkie to her lips, "Andy, it's Sarah."

A few seconds passed until the whispered reply came from the lead member of the San Francisco team. "Hey, what's up?"

"I'm about to give you some coordinates. I think you're somewhere nearby, check it out," Sarah said as she slowly moved toward the spot where the blue lights waited. Although she couldn't see any colors or lights without the cameras, the hair rising on the back of her neck and arms signaled she was headed in the right direction.

Jimmy stared in amazement at The Eyes' monitor as the deep reds and whites of Sarah's body approached the blue wisps. When she was within six feet, the tightly bunched group slowly separated in four different directions. Jimmy was about to tell her they were leaving, but they stopped after just a few feet, became more diffuse, and formed a circle of pale blue light that Sarah was about to step into.

"A few more feet," Jimmy said softly, then added, "They're waiting for you."

While she appreciated the information, it really wasn't necessary. The invisible barrier of cold air penetrated through to her soul as she stepped between worlds. Shaking off the chill, she pressed the transmit button on the walkie-talkie, and carefully and deliberately read and repeated the coordinates from her GPS unit. She knew the San Francisco team was in the basement somewhere four floors below her, but she had no idea how close they were.

"Shit, Sarah, that's right where I'm standing!" Andy said, feeling like something of a blind pawn in an enormous multi-level chess game. "How did you know that?"

"I didn't," she replied as the air temperature began to rise and the goose bumps receded. "They did."

Jimmy watched as the pale blue wisps resolved back into separate entities, and drifted slowly to the floor. They lingered around Sarah for a moment, then disappeared into the floor beneath her feet.

"They're gone!" Jimmy announced. "Went right through the floor!"

"That's what I hoped for," Sarah said, abandoning the whisper. Hitting the transmit button she sent a quick message. "Hang on, Andy, things are about to get interesting down there."

Andy began to reply, but then two of his team members started shouting, and Sarah could hear all kinds of instrument alarms going off. The transmission ended, but Sarah knew the fun was just beginning for the boys from the west coast.

"Do you think they're okay? Should we go and help them?" Jimmy asked between short breaths, still slightly shell shocked by the seemingly choreographed paranormal display.

"No, they'll be fine. Those guys live for this stuff."

"Yeah, I guess you're right. And Sarah, I really have to apologize for saying this was all too much for you. I mean, that was incredible what you just did—you just walked right into those things!"

"Well, I guess ghost hunters do rush in where even fools fear to tread," she laughed as she tried to rub some warmth back into her chilled arms. Even she surprised herself sometimes, but after dancing cheek to cheek with a dead soldier, a few frosty friends were nothing. "Come, James, back to our chariot. We have a lot more ground to cover."

The remainder of the fourth floor corridors had no more surprises. While they were taking the cart down the service elevator to the third floor, Ricky called in to say things were starting to pop in the garage, although fortunately for Lela, it was quiet upstairs in the offices. The other teams also checked in with generally positive results, except for the San Francisco group who apparently still had their hands full and didn't have time for a call.

The third floor was also wisp-free. However, just as they were being lulled into complacency, the second floor slammed them back to reality—at least a ghost hunter's version of reality. As Jimmy was cruising along the north railing of the atrium, the cart jerked spasmodically several times.

"Come on Jimmy, don't fool around," Sarah said, preoccupied with The Eyes' monitor, so she wasn't able to notice that the erratic motion wasn't the result of anything he had done. Before he could reply, the monitor blinked off and on, flashed brightly with a screen full of glistening multi-colored pixels, then went dark. A second later the cart lost all power and rolled to a stop. "Can I assume you are not playing games?"

"Not me," he said, turning the key several times, and finally punching the dashboard in the time-honored tradition of all great repairmen. "Nothing. How's The Eyes?"

"Well, the monitor blinked out, but the camera seems to—Whoa! What was that?"

An icy gust blew past them with such force that the remaining honeysuckle blossoms were swept out of the cart and over the edge into the open expanse of the atrium. However, before they had a chance to float down to the first floor, another gust blew by in the opposite direction. That one blacked out most of the equipment in the back seat.

"This one doesn't feel very good, Sarah," Jimmy said, clutching his arms in front of him and looking as though he was about to curl up into a fetal position.

"Get out of the cart, Jimmy. Right now," Sarah ordered, as a third icy blast hit, rattling everything in the cart that wasn't strapped down. They both stepped back about ten feet on either side of the powerless cart, Jimmy in the front, and Sarah behind. "This one isn't like all of the others. This one is pissed. *Really* pissed."

As the cart continued to shake, the screens and instruments blinked on and off several times. The walkie-talkie was on the dashboard, and while its transmit and receive lights flashed, loud, garbled voices and sounds sporadically burst out, as if someone was rapidly spinning the dial of a radio with the volume cranked up. Without any instruments or cameras, Sarah felt helpless. Her intuition wasn't of much help either, as all she sensed was anger and hatred—directed at them, or at least their equipment.

As the light and sound show continued, Sarah was about to suggest that they move back even further, but she never got the chance. Suddenly, the cart's high beams turned on, and Jimmy raised his hands to shield his eyes. Sarah got a sick feeling in the pit of her stomach, and before she could shout a warning, the cart's motor turned on to full power, and the half-ton vehicle lurched forward, straight toward Jimmy.

Fortunately, he also had experienced a sense of imminent danger, and had begun to take a step to his right. The move was just enough to get most of his body behind a sturdy metal garbage receptacle. The cart sideswiped the yard-high container, grazed Jimmy's left leg with enough force to knock him to the floor, and continued on thirty feet more until it slammed into the overstuffed belly of a giant Teddy bear standing outside the *Make a Cuddly Friend* craft store.

Sarah couldn't see how badly Jimmy had been hit. She only knew he was on the ground and she screamed his name and ran to him.

"I'm okay! I'm okay!" he said springing back to his feet, both to alleviate Sarah's anxiety—and be prepared to run if the cart came back at them.

As soon as she was sure he was all right, Sarah ran over to the cart, which was now idling quietly, two feet into the bear's stomach. She pulled out the keys, lifted the hood and yanked out a couple of wires running to the battery. The vehicle went dark and silent, and looked as innocuous as any golf cart on a tranquil putting green. Of course, there were some marked differences—it was full of ghost hunting equipment, it was sticking out of the gut of an eight-foot Teddy bear, and it had just tried to kill her assistant.

Then out in the darkness to her right, Sarah could hear what sounded like several men running toward her. *Oh please, please let these be living men,* Sarah thought as she hurried back to Jimmy, who had wedged himself even further behind the garbage receptacle.

"Sarah, Jimmy, you okay?" shouted the chief of security, as his powerful flashlight cut through the darkness and illuminated the two ghost hunters, who he was pleased to see where both on their feet.

"We're okay, Dan. Nobody was hurt," Sarah replied, looking to see if his gun was drawn this time, but Dan and two of his guards were only carrying flashlights.

"Our security cameras on this area went blank for a minute," Dan explained as he aimed the beam of his flashlight to the spot where the cart had originally stopped. "When they came back on, all we saw were a pair of bright headlights and someone going down."

"Well, hopefully that won't happen again," Sarah said, handing one of the guards the torn out wires.

"I can't understand it," Dan said as they all walked toward the cart, with Jimmy very much bringing up the rear. "This has never happened before. It should only be able to move when someone is depressing the accelerator."

"Maybe someone was," Sarah said enigmatically.

"Come on, don't tell me demons drove the cart," Dan said, but with a decided lack of his usual certainty.

"I'm not going to tell you a thing," Sarah replied nonchalantly. "I'm going to wait until your experts tell me there's nothing wrong with the cart, that it was impossible for it to move on its own and try to run down Jimmy. Then I'll let *you* tell *me* what happened."

Even in the dim light, Sarah could see that the two guards were terrified, and didn't want to go near the cart. She assured them both that whatever it was, had gone, but they still kept a healthy distance from it. She and Jimmy began to unload the equipment, but Dan said not to bother, as they could pull the cart out of the Teddy bear's stomach and roll it into the service elevator. The guards didn't budge.

"That was not a suggestion, gentlemen," the chief stated with authority, as the two men immediately decided they would rather face a rampaging devil cart, than an angry boss. The cart rolled harmlessly backward, and with Sarah steering, it was a simple task to get it into the elevator and bring it down to the parking garage.

As they approached the area where Ricky and his team were working, they heard some odd hissing noises, and it took a moment before they realized it was the sound made by spray paint cans.

"You know these New Yorkers," Sarah said in response to Dan's questioning look. "They can't stand clean concrete, they have to cover it with graffiti."

In truth, she knew that they were marking the stanchions and pavement to indicate the areas of the most intense activity. Ricky waved them over as he turned on a bank of bright work lights. Sarah had expected to see a few spots of paint here and there and was stunned to find that an enormous section of the garage was beginning to look like a Claude Monet canvas.

"No way!" Jimmy exclaimed after a long whistle of amazement.

"Does every spot of color mean there's a ghost there!" one of the terrified guards asked as he froze in his tracks.

"No, just areas of measurable paranormal activity," Ricky replied, as the guard eased his rigid posture. "Although it very well could be a separate entity responsible for each anomaly."

The guard was not pleased by the remainder of the response and decided to go back and take his chances with the cart. While the color spot/anomaly discussion continued, Sarah slowly circled the area they had spray painted, which was roughly one hundred and fifty feet long, but less than half that in width. In fact, there was one narrow stretch in the middle that was barely twenty feet.

Something else was odd. The greatest concentrations of fluorescent paint markings were at either end of this narrow strip, forming a shape reminiscent of old-fashioned round barbells. There was something about this bizarre pattern that seemed to make sense, but Sarah just couldn't put her finger on the answer.

"I see you noticed the two nodes," Ricky said from behind Sarah, startling her for a second. "Sorry, didn't mean to scare you."

"Oh, you'll have to do a lot more than that to scare me tonight," Sarah said, shaking her head.

"Yeah, I heard you had a little car trouble."

"Something like that. You guys run into anything nasty?"

"Fortunately, no. All the activity seems to be aimed at just getting our attention. Nothing threatening at all."

As he was finishing his sentence, a muffled banging noise echoed through the cavernous garage. The three other New York team members all immediately raised an arm and gave the thumbs-down signal, which was their way of indicating that they weren't the ones who caused the sound. The other guard quickly hurried back to stand by his friend near the cart. Dan stated that the noise could have been anything, but he was sounding less convincing with each pronouncement.

"So, as you were saying, about these nodes," Sarah continued.

"Yeah, it's kind of weird," Ricky said, pulling out his note pad. "We haven't taken all the measurements yet, but here's some rough numbers. I'll get all this plotted tonight an email you a copy."

Sarah looked at the measurements and "spot counts" and then walked back and forth between the nodes, following the thin strip of colored activity markings. Her cheek—the one had made the extraordinary contact—began to feel cold, and shadows of memories drifted over her mind's eye.

"This is roughly aligned from west to east, right?" she asked closing her eyes and trying to imagine the landscape almost a century and a half earlier.

Ricky consulted his compass and confirmed the directions. Sarah tried to remember Henkel's crude map of Wegman's Crossing in 1864, and recalled that this garage used to be where the course of the William River originally ran, before Octagon diverted it farther to the west. Her cheek started tingling, the clouded images dissipated, and light began to dawn.

Grabbing Ricky's arm, she pulled him over to the area between the two nodes. The other team members could see that something was up, so they put down their paint cans and hurried over, with Jimmy and Dan right behind them. Even the two guards decided to go where the action was, rather than being left completely by themselves.

"Does she get like this often?" Dan whispered to Jimmy, when he saw the excited, almost crazed expression on Sarah's face.

"You don't know the half of it!" Jimmy whispered back "I've got stories…"

"Okay, picture this," Sarah said, turning herself and Ricky to face east. "It's 1864, there are a couple of hundred soldiers in the area who are lost and wounded. One group, I don't know if they're Union or Confederate troops, are up ahead of us, just recently having occupied the Wegman house and grounds."

Everyone found himself closing his eyes and trying to picture the scene.

"Now, the other band of soldiers is looking for food and medical help, so they figure they will follow the river, and hope that they will eventually find the right army. Just about when they reach the area behind us, where the outer wall of the parking garage now stands, they see a bridge. Not a very big bridge, maybe twenty feet wide, but they assume that there's a good reason for this bridge to be there, and it must lead to something. Moving forward, they have no idea they are on a collision course with destiny."

Sarah was definitely on a roll—"in the zone" as she called it when she delivered one of her mesmerizing lectures. Only this time it was something even more than her usual storytelling ability. This time it was almost as if she was speaking from personal memory.

"They send out a couple of scouts, who start to cross the bridge—that narrow strip spanning the river, exactly where we now stand. But before they get half way across, probably right at this very point, they realize the enemy is over on the other side. They hope to go undetected, because their ragtag band of soldiers is in no shape for a fight. But it's too late. They draw fire from enemy guards, return fire, and try to fall back.

"Neither side is prepared for a battle. They're sick, they're wounded, starving, exhausted. But the shooting has started, and each side knows they can't run—but they don't know that the other side is as banged up as they are. Both the Union and Confederate soldiers decide they are going to have to slug it out right here and now. It is a fight nobody wants, but it's a fight they can't avoid."

As Sarah spoke, the air around them somehow felt heavier and closer, as if they were standing amidst a crowd of people. But Sarah didn't notice. She was feeling the hot sun of a cloudless spring day in 1864, and smelling the gunpowder smoke of a battle that had suddenly erupted.

"The soldiers occupying the Wegman house—they're probably Union soldiers—yes, they're the Union soldiers up there ahead of us—they form a line perpendicular to the road. The Confederate troops on this side of the bridge form into groups and try to storm across. Many of them are cut down as they try to get onto the bridge, more fall on the planks of the bridge itself, the old, dry wood quickly soaking up the spilled blood. Those who do cross pause to return fire, creating some cover for the men coming up behind us. The casualties begin to mount on the eastern side of the bridge, too.

"Despite the heavy losses, step-by-step, the Confederate forces are beginning to push back the Union troops, many of them already have awful wounds from previous battles that haven't had time to heal. They fall back to the house and barn, where the terrible fighting continues. A few men from both sides run off into the woods, but everyone who remains continues fighting until every man is mortally wounded, or dead. Those who cling to life for a few desperate hours try to help one another, regardless of whether they're wearing blue or gray, because the pools of blood are all the same color.

"There's little hope. Then the fires begin…"

Sarah's voice trailed off into silence. No one moved, except to wipe away a tear, and they all stood transfixed within the vision of the past that Sarah had painted with her words and emotions. The only sound to be heard was from the rolling thunder, as even the mysterious banging and tapping had ceased while she spoke.

"She got all that from these colored spots on the floor?" one guard tried to quietly ask the other guard, not intending for his voice to carry so far.

"Shut up, you idiot," the other guard replied in an even louder voice. "She's in a trance or something, communicating with the dead like that guy on TV does."

Sarah took a deep breath and slowly opened her eyes.

"No, it's okay. I'm just theorizing," she said, nonetheless rubbing her cheek to try to stop the tingling sensation. "And I'm done now."

"That was one hell of a damn theory," Dan piped in as he cleared away the mist from his own eyes. "I don't mind telling you it sent a chill up my spine."

"And I don't mind telling you that you freaked me right out!" Ricky exclaimed, pulling a handkerchief out of his back pocket and giving his nose a hefty blow. "Listening to you, it was like I was there. I think you are absolutely right, this is where the Wegman's Crossing bridge stood, and men died in bunches at each end, and right here in the middle, too."

"It is one possible scenario, given the evidence," Sarah stated calmly, not wanting to bury the science of ghost hunting beneath too much art.

"You nailed it and you know it," Jimmy asserted with complete conviction. "I know you want it all to be neatly arranged in graphs and charts, but you have something more than any instrument or computer. You can see it…you can *feel* it…"

Afraid that he was saying too much, especially in front of strangers, he fell silent and took a step back. His pale cheeks flushed almost as brightly as one of the shades of spray paint and he wished he had kept his mouth shut. However, support for his assertions immediately followed, and from an unlikely source.

"The kid's right, Sarah," Dan admitted. "You know that I thought on day one that you were as phony as a Clinton affidavit, but I've seen you work. I see how you connect with all this, how you look at something and see things nobody else does. I know you have all those fancy, high-tech gadgets, but hell, that's all just worthless data without you to understand what it all really means. It's the damnedest thing, but you honestly do seem to have some ability to see what has happened in the past!"

"Well, yeah, maybe, a little bit," Sarah stammered, a bit overcome by the chief of security's speech. "But regardless, let's not lose sight of why we are here. No matter how we find the answers, the important thing is that we find them."

That was something with which they could all agree.

The New York team got back to work with even greater enthusiasm, now that they had a solid theory upon which to focus their efforts. Lela even found the courage to come down and join them, although she made sure she was never more than a few feet away from Ricky at all times. Dan and the guards headed back to the security office so they could keep an eye on the other ghost hunters spread out across the center.

While Jimmy started to remove the equipment from the cart, Sarah decided to go check on the San Francisco team. She found them in a general state of disarray—as if several entities had suddenly descended upon them and made their equipment go haywire. Not one of them was complaining, however. In fact, they had that euphoric look in their eyes of thrill-seekers exiting a four-g roller coaster ride. Only this ride had been wilder than anything an amusement park could offer.

Sarah was impressed by the data the team had managed to collect as they stood by their instruments despite the frantic excitement. She was equally pleased by the restrained use of spray paint, as only a few small red circles marked the concrete floor of this basement corridor and adjacent storeroom. Still, Octagon would not be pleased that yet another excavation site had been added to the list.

Calling the other teams on the walkie-talkie, Sarah made sure that everything was okay. She was particularly concerned because of the cart attack, and she was relieved to hear that everyone was safe and sound. As she started to head back to the parking garage, she hesitated, and called Jimmy to say that she would be just a few more minutes. Then she went to the nearest elevator and returned to the second floor.

Standing by the railing on the south side of the atrium, she looked across the wide open space to the area where the angry entity had stalled their cart and tried to hurt Jimmy. Nothing unusual had been reported in that area before on the second floor, or any of the other floors for that matter. It was just an open floor space, a roughly two hundred foot-long walkway that joined the two halves of the massive complex. Stores were on either end, but the only thing behind it was the towering wall of glass that stretched from ground level to the peak of the fourth floor.

Pulling out her map of the center, she studied the layout of the basement level in that area. There were a few storerooms and a couple of maintenance areas—none of which had reported so much as a peep at any point during construction or since the center opened. Of course, this wasn't like a game of Pin the Tail on the Ghost. There was not necessarily a direct correlation to the site of paranormal activity with an unhappy corpse—although it was usually somewhere within the confines of the original property.

In the case of the Wegman farm, that area was substantial, but it is likely that only a few acres were probably cultivated or otherwise utilized by the family. During a battle, however, there were seldom boundaries. The rampaging spirit could be originating from just about anywhere inside or outside of the center. That wasn't good. However, as she walked along the railing approaching the north side, her attention was drawn more to the expansive window than the spot where they had felt the wrath of the undead.

Leaning with her back against the railing, at the exact spot where the encounter first began, she left all her instruments in her pockets and just watched and listened. The temperature remained steady and the air stayed still. There were no feelings of dread or imminent danger. But that didn't mean that Sarah felt she was alone for one second.

Who are you, and what story do you have to tell? She thought to herself, and waited patiently for some type of reply. There was nothing. After a few minutes she started to leave, but her attention was drawn back to that window yet again. There was something there, something outside, something very angry. But whatever it was had no intention of revealing itself again that night.

I have time, she thought as she turned her back to the window and started to walk away. *I have time, and you're not going anywhere. We will meet again.*

Chapter 14

Sunday brunch! One of the more civilized customs, Sarah thought as she settled behind a corner table with a plate piled high with food.

Jimmy had slipped a note under her door telling her that he had gotten up early and was going to walk over to the center to look around. She had slept until the alarm went off at 10:30am, and then spent about half an hour going over the reports from the teams. They had done good work, and she looked forward to getting together with them at their afternoon meeting.

Directly following, there would be the all-important joint meeting with representatives from the previously opposing factions, who would now be working together during the demolition and excavation. That meeting promised to be a memorable event. Sarah made a mental note to bring her pepper spray.

Wearing some old sweatpants, an oversized T-shirt and dark glasses, with her hair bunched on top of her head with some haphazardly placed pink plastic barrettes, Sarah entered the hotel's large dining room through a side door. Her goal was to go unrecognized, relax, and eat enough for a family of four. She was not in the mood for reporters, fans, or anyone else for that matter. The late hours, infrequent meals, and high stress levels were beginning to take a physical toll, as well, and she needed to get her strength back. Unlike Jimmy, who could sleep for two hours, grab a candy bar and be good to go for the day, she was finding that while over forty wasn't exactly over the hill, the steepness of the grade had increased significantly.

Pushing aside all unpleasant thoughts, Sarah turned her attention to the crispy hash browns at the two o'clock position on her plate, which were in danger of getting soggy from the adjacent lasagna. The great thing about brunch was that you could start with breakfast items and transition right into lunch. What a timesaver!

Now if they could only invent a combination of all three meals—something like "*brunchner,*" she mused, discovering that hash browns *with* lasagna wasn't such a bad combination after all.

"Trying to give yourself an ulcer?"

The deep voice and long shadow cast across her table were unmistakable. Part of her wanted to be sweet and charming, but that attitude of hers stepped right in.

"Well, if it isn't the Sheriff of Virginiaham, come to darken my brunch," Sarah said without looking up, as her appetite suddenly ebbed.

"Yes, and I've come to steal from the rich," Beau said as he grabbed a cinnamon toast stick off her plate and invited himself to sit at her table. "But don't worry, unfair maiden, I'm not here just to torment you."

"Then pray tell, why are you here?" she asked, looking up long enough to snatch the cinnamon stick out of his hand just as he was about to take a bite.

"Lela asked me to attend the meetings, so I thought I would have something to eat first. The food is good here, and the clientele is unparalleled," he said, raising an eyebrow and looking her up and down. "So tell me, what did you do, mug a homeless man for that outfit?"

As she raised her head to counter the snide remark, his hand shot forward, grabbed the contentious cinnamon stick once again and shoved it quickly into his mouth before she had time to get it back. The self-satisfied grin spreading across his face as he chewed was just too much.

"Owww!" Beau whined after Sarah whacked him on the knuckles with her large soupspoon. "You meant that to hurt! At least you could have used your little teaspoon."

"So arrest me," she replied, meticulously wiping the spoon with her napkin as if it had just touched something unclean. "Or maybe you should just kiss me and get the punishment over with more quickly."

"My, oh my, I can see that someone is not in a mood to socialize," Beau said rising, and then pushing his chair firmly back under the table. "If you will excuse me, madam, I think I will get some food and then sit down on the *other* side of the dining room."

Sarah didn't say a word as the handsome sheriff walked away, leaving her to feel like whacking herself with a spoon for being so stupid. Socializing was exactly what she needed right now. Beau might be irritating, but it was a very attractive sort of irritation, if that made any sense—just the type of thing she needed to get her mind off of death and destruction for a while.

The breakfast burrito suffered the consequences of her ensuing ire, as she repeatedly stabbed it with a fork while fighting with her conflicting emotions. She liked Beau. In fact, she *really* liked Beau, but there was so much going on right now, and she was under so much pressure and scrutiny, that it would be foolish to even attempt to get involved with someone. Still, *tempus fugit*, and maybe it would be more foolish *not* to have some fun while she had the chance.

With renewed appetite, she made short work of the remaining contents of her plate. Then she decided to saunter back up to the buffet, get a few dessert items and casually sit down at Beau's table as if nothing had happened. It was a good plan, but as she glanced over the pastry platters stacked three-high, she saw that not one, but two women had seized the rare opportunity to have brunch with the Sheriff of Brandon County. Recognizing that using a spoon to beat the women away from the table would make her appear too desperate, she abandoned her dessert plate and went back to her room.

Just a few minutes before the first meeting, Jimmy arrived at her door, flushed and glistening from his brisk jog back from Wegman's Center.

"Hey, Sarah, you look really good. Are those new?" he asked, getting a hand towel from her bathroom to wipe off the sweat.

The new mint green silk blouse and pastel floral print wraparound skirt really set off the color of her hair and eyes, and they didn't hurt her figure, either.

"What, these old things?" she replied nonchalantly, but quickly scanned her outfit to make sure she had pulled off all the price tags. "The meeting this afternoon is very important. We don't want to look like we're homeless people, now, do we?"

Jimmy looked down at his own rumpled, sweaty clothing and took the hint.

"I'll jump in the shower, get changed and meet you in the conference room in a few minutes," he said, attempting to give the towel back to Sarah.

"No, that's okay, you keep it," she said waving him away.

"Okay. And oh, I forgot to mention, there's like no one at the center. Half the stores aren't even open. Everyone is really pissed."

"Great. That's good to know. I'm really looking forward to that joint meeting now."

Sarah rubbed her agitated stomach. It was probably just the breakfast burrito, but maybe she actually was getting an ulcer.

The ghost hunters from across the country had gathered in the conference room and were enthusiastically sharing stories of their night's adventures. Many had stayed at the center until dawn, and though their eyes were puffy from lack of sleep, they still had a sparkle of excitement. None of them had ever encountered anything of this magnitude, and they knew they were part of paranormal history.

When Sheriff Davis arrived, he thought he would be given the cold shoulder since he was an outsider, and represented the law. To his surprise, however, he was greeted as something of a celebrity. He had been there to witness the face appearing in the membrane. He had pulled Sarah Brooks away from the psychic grasp of the entity. He had trashed one of the most sophisticated and expensive pieces of ghost hunting equipment ever made. In the ghost hunting world, it didn't get any better than that.

As Beau was just finishing the second dramatic rendition of his account of that memorable night in the *Sun 'n Surf* dressing room, Sarah arrived. She looked stunning, and his train of thought was not only lost, but completely derailed as he watched her enter and move across the room with those confident and self-assured strides he so admired. In that outfit, there was also a lot more to admire, and not an inch of it escaped his attention.

The teams again broke up into groups to give a final look at the material they were about to present, and Beau wandered over to where Sarah sat at the head of the table.

"Quite a transformation from brunch," he said as a compliment to her appearance, but then looked concerned as he continued. "Has the attitude also improved?"

"I have no idea what you mean, Sheriff," Sarah replied with a disarming smile.

"Then I guess I must be mistaken. I thought for sure you were the derelict who assaulted me in the dining room."

"Ahh, that must have been my evil twin. She gets out once in a while, but I have her locked up again. I do hope she wasn't too much trouble?"

"Oh no, nothing I'm not used to. Although I wish she had stuck around a bit longer. It would have spared me the company of the Muffin Twins."

"If you are referring to the two women seated with you at brunch, I don't think I want to hear *that* story," Sarah said, implying that something risqué was to follow.

"Oh no, nothing like that," Beau laughed. "They got those nicknames because every time one of them targets a potential new husband, they always send the poor guy a basket of their homemade muffins and pies. The way to a man's heart, you know. Sounds silly, but it's worked for them a total of five times."

"And you're target number six?"

"I would be most surprised if there wasn't an assortment of baked goods on my desk tomorrow morning."

Jimmy came bounding into the room, apologized for being two minutes late and announced that the meeting could now commence. Lela actually began the proceedings by reluctantly reading a statement from headquarters. In essence, Octagon declared their *intention* to cooperate fully, but cleverly worded a few potential loopholes citing some nonsense about safety concerns and integrity of historic sites, just in case they felt the need to pull the plug at some point. There was a general grumbling around the room, as everyone easily saw through the flimsy pretense.

Rather than disheartening the group, however, the statement redoubled their determination to ensure that the job would be done right, and followed to completion. They set to work on the large basement floor plan spread out across the table, carefully mapping out the regions to be excavated. There were four sites of high priority: the parking garage, the areas under the *Sun 'n Surf* and *Kinder Krossing* (including the nearby section under the food court) and the area of the basement where the San Francisco team had their hands full. There were probably other smaller areas that might require attention, but they decided to let the work commence and see what transpired.

The floor plan map was completed just a few minutes before the joint meeting was to commence in another conference room down the hall. Lela had already gone on ahead, as she was the official representative for Wegman's Center. Or so she thought. As the eager ghost hunters, and the sheriff, prepared to move en masse down the hall, Lela returned and put up her hand to stop them at the door.

"I'm sorry, everyone, please sit down again," she said slowly, clearly weighed down with bad news. She waited a minute until they had returned to their seats. "I was just informed that the meeting format has been changed. Only Sarah will be allowed to attend. And that's not all—the rest of you are requested to return home."

Bracing herself for the backlash, she was nonetheless overwhelmed by the storm of protests.

"Hang on, let her speak!" Beau ordered in a manner that always commanded compliance.

"Look, I had nothing to do with this!" Lela said in her own more forceful style, once the crowd was subdued. "They are saying that due to state and local regulations, as well as insurance requirements, they will not be letting any of you be present at any of the excavation sites. That goes for Sarah, too. They said that from here on, it's up to the construction people, professional historians, and archaeologists."

Sarah felt that breakfast burrito doing handsprings in her stomach. However, as much as she wanted to rant and rave, she needed to keep her cool and calmly present her case. Octagon was probably counting on the fact that she would just get mad and go away.

"All right, give me the floor plan and I'll see what I can do," she said, straightening her skirt and smoothing back her hair. Despite the attention to her appearance, there was a look of steely determination in her eyes. "If they want a fight, I'll give it to them."

"Sarah, wait," Ricky said, hurrying forward and putting a hand on her shoulder. "Most of the people here have to leave tonight, anyway, right?"

There was a quick show of hands, and brief polling of the others who indicated they would be leaving in a day or two. Ricky then continued.

"So you see, if you are going to fight, fight for yourself. Don't worry about us."

"But it's not fair—" Sarah began to argue.

"Of course it's not fair," Ricky cut in. "But who the hell expected these bastards to be fair? Look, we were all here, and we got a chance to be part of something incredible. We are all grateful to you for that, and the last thing any of us wants to do is jeopardize your chance to stay!"

As convincing and confident as he sounded, Ricky still glanced back over his shoulder to make sure the rest of the ghost hunters agreed with him. Fortunately, they all chimed in with a consensus opinion—they would go, Sarah *must* stay.

"I appreciate this, I really do. But don't give up yet," Sarah said, putting the rolled up floor plan under her arm and striding out the door.

"You gonna give 'em hell?" Beau asked, catching up to her with just a few of his long strides.

"We'll see if my evil twin will have to make an appearance," she replied, holding her hair in a bunch on top of her head for a moment, and arching one brow to create a suitable evil eye.

"Uh oh! This could get ugly," Beau said over his shoulder to Lela, who was far behind, practically dragging her feet toward the dreaded meeting.

The first person Sarah saw in the other conference room was Dr. Carl Henkel—an uncharacteristically beaming Dr. Henkel. He also uncharacteristically gave Sarah a hug and profusely thanked her for all her extraordinary efforts. Dan Garrison then joined them, and as they spoke, Sarah quickly scanned the room to assess the players. The National Parks people were easy to spot—thanks to the uniforms—and they looked at her with curiosity, but no malice. The construction representatives were also identifiable—by the look of dollar signs in their eyes.

Then there were "the suits"—two men from Octagon who looked upon her with no curiosity, just malice. They also had dollar signs in their eyes, but they were strictly red ones from the enormous sums of money they would have to shell out for this project. And there was but one person to blame for the hit to their bottom line—Sarah Brooks.

After Henkel was finished with his lavish greeting, Sarah strode past the parks and construction people, making a beeline to the Octagon men. Beau wasn't sure if he should tackle her now, or wait until she roughed them up a bit before he pried her off of them. Lela held her breath and grimaced as she was certain things were about to get very ugly. When Sarah got within a few feet of the suits, she began to raise her right arm, and both men secretly feared she was going to try to physically wipe the smirks from their faces.

"Gentlemen!" Sarah said, extending her hand in alleged friendship, turning her charm on up to the hilt. "I'm Sarah Brooks. It's a pleasure to meet you both. I'm so glad you could make it."

"Has she snapped?" Beau whispered to Lela.

"No, I bet she's going to use the same tactic she did in the Rosary Academy case back in '98," Lela whispered, unaware that only a devoted fan would have any clue about how Sarah managed to coerce certain obstinate church officials.

However, Beau didn't need to know the specifics, he could already see the results of the "Brooks Maneuver." The puzzled men were clearly caught off guard, and stammered their names and titles in an awkward introduction.

"Mr. Dunning, Mr. Morton. Again, a pleasure to have you here to take part in this historic event. You must be highly regarded to be entrusted with such a venture," Sarah continued, in so convincing a manner that if Beau didn't know her better he would think this was a genuine display.

The two men continued to have very few intelligent things to say. They had prepared for two scenarios—an argument, or a capitulation. Sarah Brooks was not playing by the rules, but then, she never did.

"You know, I was just saying to Mrs. Reynolds, when she told me that I was not to be allowed at the excavation sites, that I was certain it was a misunderstanding. In fact, several reporters from cable TV and the networks were just asking me this morning if I thought you people at Octagon would try to cover up any results of the excavation by excluding independent observers. You know, I don't think they trust you. Of course, I told them that you *wanted* me there every step of the way, because who else could they find who would be more unbiased than me? I told them you were sincere about this project, and that they should only get suspicious about your motives if I *wasn't* allowed in."

The eyes of everyone in the room were on Dunning and Morton, and they could feel the heat of scrutiny. As Dunning thought about how they should have used his idea of the phony haunting and airline ticket to get her out of the way, Morton tried to remember who it was who had talked him out of his idea of having Sarah's publisher threaten her. The clever, but exasperating ghostbuster had painted them into a corner, and they could not afford to call her bluff.

"Naturally, Ms. Brooks, our directive did not apply to you," Dunning finally said as if the words themselves tasted bad as he spoke them. "However, we do insist that none of your other colleagues be present. There are safety and liability concerns, you know."

Dunning and Morton cringed, preparing for Sarah's next barrage of coercion, but they were surprised once again.

"Of course, I understand completely," Sarah said like a mother who anticipates her child's every desire. "I already told them all to go home. And if things really do start getting dangerous again once you start digging, I'm sure I could get one or two of them to return in a week or so."

"Dangerous? What does she mean by that? Are my men in any danger here?" the construction supervisor, Atkins, demanded to know.

"No, certainly not, Mr. Atkins," Morton responded immediately, then shot a nasty look Sarah's way. "I'm sure I don't know to what she's referring."

Sarah opened her briefcase, removed a single sheet of paper and pushed it across the shiny surface of the table toward the construction boss.

"Not to worry," Sarah continued. "As you can see by this compilation of incident reports from the initial construction, no one was actually *killed*. And maybe those *dozens* of *serious* accidents were simply just accidents, and not the result of any strange powers acting beyond anyone's control. But I'm sure *you* were aware of these reports before."

"No, I damn sure wasn't," Atkins replied angrily.

The National Parks people leaned across the table to see the report, as they were also completely unaware that something dangerous could be lurking in the ground. No one wanted to admit that he or she was superstitious, but each and every one of them would never dream of walking under a ladder, either.

"I think what Ms. Brooks is saying," Sheriff Davis offered, "is that tensions may be running a bit high throughout this process, and it would certainly help if some professionals were on hand to determine what the nature of any unforeseen occurrences might be."

"Ms. Brooks, do you and your people have the ability to keep my men safe?" Atkins asked point blank.

"Don't ever underestimate Sarah's abilities," Dr. Henkel stated in a solid show of support, for which Sarah was grateful.

"We would be your best chance of monitoring the situation and avoiding certain potential danger spots," Sarah replied. "But it's too late, I've already told them all to go home."

"Can't you two convince her to get some of those people to stay?" Atkins asked the Octagon boys. "'Cause if my men won't be safe, we can forget the whole thing right now. You know, I thought it was kind of strange that you didn't hire the same people who built this place."

It was Morton's turn to endure the awful taste of swallowing one's pride and surrendering to the enemy.

"Ms. Brooks, on behalf of Octagon," Morton began and then paused to take a drink of water to clear his palate, "we would appreciate if you would consult with a few of your most trusted colleagues and try to persuade them to remain in case we require their services."

"Well, I'll certainly give it my best shot, although I'll be rather embarrassed asking them, since I just told them to go away," Sarah said, effortlessly continuing the lie.

The men from Octagon clearly took some solace in her apparent discomfort, so at least they didn't look upon the situation as a complete defeat.

"You could trick a snake right out its skin," Beau whispered to Sarah as she took her seat.

"I think I just did," she replied, trying to suppress a self-satisfied grin.

Sarah then surreptitiously held her cell phone under the conference table and sent a brief text message to Jimmy: *Some can stay. Octagon pissed. Too bad.*

There was some lingering tension in the air during the ensuing meeting, but for the most part it was cordial and productive. Octagon had feared that demands would be made to tear up the entire basement level, and the two representatives were actually pleased by the obvious restraint and careful consideration that went into identifying just four well-defined areas. Granted, in their opinion it was four too many, but it was still a mere fraction of what they had braced themselves for.

Henkel and the parks people got along famously, and their excitement was contagious. As the meeting progressed, Atkins and his men began to see the project as more than just a lucrative job; it was a patriotic endeavor that could put them on the national scene. Beau and Dan once again presented themselves as being competent and efficient, answering any and all questions about security concerns. Over and above any uneasiness about restless spirits, the knife-wielding reverend was still very much on everyone's mind, and all personnel involved needed to know that their backs—and their necks—were being covered.

Lela Reynolds had very little to say. Actually, in truth, she had a lot she wanted to say, but she essentially had been told to be seen and not heard at this meeting. If not for the bleak employment outlook and the need to put her kids through college, she would have walked right then and there. However, if she was going to stay and put up with this nonsense, she wanted to maintain the appearance of the staunch company supporter who could handle tricky situations. As Fink had seriously dropped the ball and had been "unavailable for comment" for several days, his position could shortly be up for grabs. It was a long shot, but she knew she could run that center better than anyone, and if she played her cards right throughout this crisis, she just might be the right person in the right place at the right time.

After her initial presentation of the paranormal roadmap for excavation, Sarah shifted gears away from the ghosts. Fortunately, she had legitimate credentials as an historian and preservationist, and her knowledge and insight about the Civil War and archeological undertakings quickly earned her the respect of the National Parks delegation. It was actually refreshing for her to get into the straight historical aspects, as in that field you never had to wonder who in the room was thinking that you were nuts.

It was decided that three crews would bring in the heavy equipment and begin demolition bright and early Monday morning. While one crew would work on the relatively easy task of tearing up the blacktop and removing some columns from the parking garage, the other two groups would be knocking down the reinforced concrete walls of the empty, enclosed spaces under the *Sun 'n Surf* and *Kinder Krossing*. The plan was to have the construction crews remove the pavement and concrete—making sure the structural integrity was not compromised—and set up high-intensity lighting systems, then turn the exposed dirt areas over to the historians and archaeologists.

This was yet another of those times that Sarah wished she had a couple of clones of herself. She was hoping they might approach this project one site at a time, but Octagon was clearly anxious to get all this over and done with. She would have to divide her time between the sites, but there would be no question as to where she would be first—the void under the *Sun 'n Surf* where she had no doubts that an "old friend" was buried.

As the meeting ended and everyone stood up and started to leave, Sarah took a deep breath and asked Beau out to dinner. She immediately regretted doing so when she saw his awkward expression.

"Um, uh, that would have been really nice, but—"

"But you don't want to be seen in public with a crazy ghostbuster," she said, cutting him off and walking away.

"No, no it's not that," Beau said grabbing her by the arm to stop her retreat. "Well, it is a little of that, but I already have a date tonight."

Sarah wasn't quite sure that information made her feel better, but it did provide her the opportunity to make him feel more uncomfortable.

"I see. And just how big is your appetite—will it be one or both of the Muffin Twins?"

"Neither, thank you very much. She's really just a friend, but we arranged this a couple of weeks ago, but I suppose I could cancel," Beau waffled in a genuine dilemma.

That did make Sarah feel better, to at least know he would like to go out with her.

"No, please don't cancel. It's just as well anyway. I haven't been getting much sleep, and I have to get up very early tomorrow," she said to make him feel less guilty, but then realized she did need the rest. "I'll probably take a long hot bath with some of those absurdly expensive aromatherapy candles and go right to bed."

"Well now, if you had suggested *that* instead of dinner, I would have had a very different answer," Beau said with a wink that made her heart flutter. Now she felt much better, but wouldn't let him know that.

"Does that kind of line really work with the women around here?" Sarah asked, shaking her head.

"Generally, yes," Beau replied, rubbing his prominent chin as if deep in thought, trying to calculate the actual numbers.

"Have a good time tonight, Sheriff Davis," Sarah said with a platonic handshake. She then turned and walked away, making sure she put a little extra zip into her hips.

Jimmy was practically bouncing off the walls waiting to hear the full results of the meeting. However, he had not sat idly by waiting. He had called the principal of his school and explained that he had the opportunity to take part in an historic project of national importance. Employing his full command of the blarney embedded deeply into his genetic code, Jimmy persuaded the principal to arrange for his class lessons to be emailed to him each day, and he would in turn submit all required homework in the same manner. To top it all off, he even convinced the man to offer some substantial extra credit for giving a presentation on the project to the entire school when he returned.

Jimmy knew Sarah was going to try to persuade him to go home and go back to school, but with this tidy little arrangement, she wouldn't have a leg to stand on. He had learned a lot about the power of persuasion from her—when to use preemptive strikes, when to hold back and let the enemy make the first move and commit himself, how to anticipate someone's actions and stay a step ahead. There was more to learn from Sarah than her ghost hunting tricks, and it was now time for him to use some of those same tactics against his wily mentor.

When Ricky heard the news that some of the ghost hunters could stay, he immediately got on the phone with his wife and told her he *might* not be back on Tuesday, but that he would *definitely* be home by Wednesday night. He explained the situation by elaborating—and exaggerating—about how the National Parks people, Octagon officials, the construction boss, the Brandon County Sheriff's Department, and the center's chief of security all specifically requested that he and his team remain to safeguard all the personnel involved in the project.

He knew she would get a kick out of telling everyone in the neighborhood that her husband was on a very important assignment, so he played up that aspect, while also voicing his alleged reluctance to be away from her any longer than necessary. Hinting that even some of the big boys in Washington, D.C. had their finger on the pulse of this case (he had no idea how right he was with that one!) really put him over the top. By the time he was finished, not only did he have her blessing to remain for the entire week, but there was a good chance he could stretch his absence well beyond that.

The other three New York team members also arranged to stay, as did Andy from San Francisco. Everyone else who was not catching a plane that night did their best to extend their time there. It would have been best to have full teams in place at every site, but at least a few warm bodies would be there to measure the cold spots.

Jimmy had left the door to his room open so that he could catch Sarah the second she returned. As usual, she had to recount everything that went on. She was overly obliging in her details this time, as she was about to deliver a request that she knew would upset him. After going on for some time about the importance of a good education, and how he would appreciate and understand that when he got older, she asked Jimmy to go home and go back to school. Only after she had finished her eloquent presentation, did he tell her about his arrangement with the principal.

"So I can do both—stay here and help you, *and* do all of my schoolwork!" he concluded proudly.

Sarah still could have insisted he go back, that this was not the type of situation for someone his age, etc., but she knew when she had been outmaneuvered—and she could respect that.

"Don't you know you're supposed to do as I say, not as I do?" Sarah said, nonetheless smiling proudly at her cunning protégé. "I've created a monster, haven't I?"

"I'm still Mrs. O'Reilly's dear sweet boy," he said putting a finger to his chin and striking an angelic pose.

"Saints preserve us!" Sarah laughed.

"So, you having dinner with the sheriff?" Jimmy asked with the devil in his angelic eyes.

"No, I'm not, Mr. Smarty Pants," Sarah responded, and then decided not to reveal the real reason why she wasn't. "For your information, I'm going to relax and go to bed early tonight. Can you fend for yourself this evening?"

"I've already arranged to go out with Ricky and the others, 'cause we figured you would be busy," Jimmy replied. "Are you sure you don't want to go out with us? We're going to an all-you-can-eat barbeque place."

Sarah automatically put a hand to her stomach, where the breakfast burrito was still making its presence known. She declined the offer of a spicy dinner, but did accept the 6am breakfast date where all the remaining ghost hunters would get together before heading over to the center for the big day.

The hotel room's tub was slightly oversized with a couple of water jets, but it was nothing like her Jacuzzi at home. In fact, at the risk of sounding like Dorothy, there was no place like home. She had put a lot of time, effort, and money into creating an eclectic and comfortable living space. The only problem was that she was hardly ever there to enjoy it. It would be nice if she could spend most of her time there, get a dog, develop a social life; normal things like that. Of course, she also understood herself well enough to know that such a sedentary lifestyle would quickly have her climbing the walls. However, she was determined to make a compromise—whenever this case was over, she would take at least a month off and enjoy the beautiful New England spring in her own backyard.

Of course, the way things looked, it might be more like the beautiful New England summer by the time the work here was completed. But all such thoughts soon began to fade as the hot water and lemongrass-sage candles began to take effect. There was a momentary relapse when her hand brushed across the bandage on her neck, but she was not going to let anything bother her tonight. The Do Not Disturb sign was on her door, her phones were off, the computers were unplugged, and she would revel in these few precious hours of anonymity and oblivion.

When the alarm went off at 5am, Sarah didn't feel grumpy, anxious, or groggy. It was something else, something unusual—she felt rested! *What a concept*, she thought as she calmly prepared for perhaps the biggest day of her life. Plugging back into the outside world, she was pleased to find that there were no frantic emails or alarming voice messages.

"The calm before the storm?" she said out loud, drawing back the curtains to see what side Mother Nature was going to take that day. A few faint stars still twinkled, so it appeared as though it would be another glorious day in northern Virginia. Although she was a Yankee through and through, there was something to be said for the warmth and blooming flowers. Perhaps she would be able to find some reason to visit this area every once in a while?

As Jimmy was trying to push a crumbled slip of paper under her door—with limited success—Sarah opened it.

"Oh, hey, you're up!" Jimmy said as he came bounding into the room and plopped down onto her bed. "I was just leaving a note to tell you I was up early. You really missed a great time last night. You should have seen Ricky! He ate more ribs than I've ever seen anyone eat, although Dan really packed them away, too."

"Dan? Dan Garrison went out to dinner with ghost hunters?" Sarah asked, incredulous.

"No, we just saw him and his wife there and invited them over. After a bunch of beers and some shots we even got him to tell us the story of how he beat the crap out of that crazy guy who attacked you," Jimmy said, mimicking a few martial arts moves, obviously having the time of his young life. "Everyone was pretty drunk by the end of the night."

"Gee, sorry I missed that. I hope everyone will be in shape this morning after this booze and barbeque bash. And I trust that you weren't doing any drinking?" Sarah asked, aware she was treading a line that might make her sound too much like his mother.

"Naw, they wouldn't let me," Jimmy said with chagrin. "So, you ready yet, I'm starved!"

"Ready, willing, and not hung over," Sarah declared, hoping she would find the others in the same state.

One look at the motley crew in the breakfast room instantly dashed those hopes. A few were wearing sunglasses to protect their bloodshot eyes from the pale dawn light, and everyone was clutching large cups of coffee. Although Sarah was angry she decided not to yell at them, but that didn't mean she wasn't going speak very loudly.

"So, how's everyone this morning!" she said as if speaking to a room filled with a hundred people. The sensitive group cringed en masse at the noise.

"Please, we all ate too much last night," Ricky said in a whisper that still appeared to cause pain.

"Oh, come on, since when did a few ribs ever hurt anyone," she said slapping him on the back. It was a dangerous move, as the barbeque could have made an unwelcome reappearance. "But then, it must have been the food, because I know that no self-respecting ghost hunters would dream of getting trashed the night before the biggest day of their paranormal careers!"

"All right, so maybe we celebrated a bit too much," Andy confessed. "It was a very, very stupid thing to do. I certainly know that now. But we have another hour and plenty of coffee, so I'm sure we'll all be fine."

It was a good thing she hadn't woken up grumpy, or she really would have blasted them. As it was, she tried to remain calm, eat her breakfast, and focus on the day ahead. Ricky's team would remain in the parking garage, she and Jimmy would be under the *Sun 'n Surf*, and Andy and three others would be at the basement area under *Kinder Krossing*—if they weren't in the bathrooms getting sick, that is.

Demolition wasn't scheduled to begin until 8am, but the crews would have arrived by 6am to prepare. The ghost hunting teams had arranged to be in place by 7am to scan the areas and make sure there were not any significant levels of unusual activity. Sarah was both anxious about the preparations, and annoyed at the teams, so as soon as she finished eating she decided to go over to the center. Jimmy was going to go with her, but as he still had a mound of food on his plate, she told him to stay and just come over with the rest of the group.

On the short drive to the center, Sarah practiced some breathing techniques designed to help her relax. They were beginning to work until she pulled into the parking garage and saw three or four men running to their cars and then speeding away. That dizzy feeling she had when she first arrived at the center the week before hit her again, and she knew something was very wrong.

"Who's in charge here?" she demanded as she jumped out of her car and approached a group of people who had tried to persuade the fleeing men to stay.

"That would be me, lady," a short, weathered, older man replied, clearly not in the mood for an aggressive woman at the moment. "What are you, a reporter? You're not supposed to be in here. Get lost."

"I'm Sarah Brooks," she said in a much more subdued manner. "My teams were supposed to monitor the sites, *before* you started. What just happened here?"

"So, you're that ghostbuster," he continued with a sardonic smile, as Sarah smiled back through gritted teeth. "I don't know what the hell is going on, you probably got everyone spooked with your mumbo jumbo. Those guys were just busting through a wall and they started screaming like little girls and took off. But who knows, maybe we really do need your help. You got your ectoplasm vacuum to suck up all the nasty ghosties and stuff 'em into containers?"

"What wall were they taking down?" Sarah asked, ignoring the little man's big insults, and resisting the temptation to tell him exactly what he could stuff and where he could stuff it.

"Let's see, they were here at Site #2," he said, pointing to a map that had already managed to become grimy and wrinkled. Even with the details obscured, Sarah knew that he had indicated the site under the *Sun 'n Surf.*

"You were supposed to wait for me!" she said shaking her head, as she grabbed a case from her car and headed out, double quick.

"Yeah, well, the Tooth Fairy showed up so we started early," the foreman yelled, waving a couple of feet of his tape measure like a magic wand, as his men broke out into a good belly laugh. "Hey, lady, careful you don't get slimed!"

It took all of her self-restraint to not turn back and rip his ignorant, underdeveloped brain out of his puny skull, but she could always do that later. She could also call the head honcho, Atkins, and have him address the lack of respect issue with his foreman, which would certainly be less messy for her.

Sprinting down the basement corridors and throwing herself against several heavy metal doors to open them more quickly, she was at Site #2 in less than a minute. The bright construction lights blinded her for a second, but then she saw the three-foot high hole punched through the center of a wall, with nothing but blackness behind it.

Putting down her case and pulling on a headband flashlight, she cautiously approached the opening. EMF readings were wildly fluctuating, and she didn't need a thermometer to tell her it was as cold as the grave. When she was a yard from the gaping hole, a noise behind her caused her to spin faster than one of her rapid heartbeats.

"Who is it? Who's there?" she demanded, half-expecting to see a Civil War soldier march up to her. A figure did move among the shadows, and Sarah took a short breath with a forced exhale, as if she was about to attempt a clean and jerk with a few hundred pounds. But as the figure emerged into the light, she saw that it was one very alive, and very scared, young man.

"It's just me, J…Joe. I'm supposed to b…be working here," he stammered, staring at the hole in the wall as if it was a gateway to hell.

Sarah purposely moved to block his view of the opening, turned off her headlamp, and spoke very softly.

"Joe, my name is Sarah, I kind of work here, too. Are you hurt?"

"N…No, I'm okay, just real cold," he replied as his teeth chattered.

"Okay, let's just go back out into the other corridor and you can tell me what just happened," she said, keeping her body between him and the hole in the wall as they moved to the door. Once on the other side, blood seemed to return to the boy's face and hands. "So, Joe, how old are you?"

"Nineteen, and this is just a summer job. I go to college in the fall," he offered with no speech impediments.

"Good for you. What's your major?" Sarah asked, trying to get him to settle down before she asked the tough questions.

"I want to be a defense attorney, like my uncle. He has his own firm in Richmond, and he says there's a job waiting for me when I graduate," the boy said, improving by the minute.

"A lawyer! Well, I certainly know some *very* interesting people who are lawyers," Sarah said with a voice of experience. "The best of luck to you."

"Thanks!"

"So, were did all the other guys go who were working here?" she asked, as the terrified expression returned to his face as suddenly as if turning on a switch.

"I…I don't know. They were starting to work on that wall, and they were all kidding me that the Boogey Man was going to jump out and get me," he said, and then managed a short, nervous laugh. "I was checking some hoses, so my back was turned when they knocked out that section…"

His account stopped there for a moment, but he rubbed his eyes, took a few breaths and continued.

"There was the weirdest sound, like someone moaning or something, and all the lights went out for a couple of seconds. I thought the guys were yanking my chain, but when the lights came back on, two of them were on the floor, and the other two were running for the door. Then the guys on the floor started yelling, got up and ran, too. I heard this place was supposed to be haunted, but do you think that's for real, or where they just playing a joke on me? Did you see them on your way here, are they coming back?"

"I think it's safe to say they you won't be seeing them any time soon," Sarah said, as she put a reassuring arm around the boy's shoulders and started walking him further away from the site. "Why don't you go back to your foreman and ask him what you should do."

"Okay, but aren't you coming? You're not going to stay here alone, are you?"

"Don't worry about me. You just go ahead and tell your boss all about what happened." As soon as the boy was through the next door, Sarah reached for her cell phone. "Jimmy, I need everyone here ASAP. One crew has already run off. Wait for me in the garage, I'll meet you there in fifteen."

Sarah got some small satisfaction thinking about the hung-over ghost hunters leaping up from the table and scrambling for their gear, regretting every drink with each head-pounding step. Hopefully, the adrenaline rush would help dispel the results of overindulgence, and she was sure there would also be handfuls of aspirin being consumed just in case.

As the teams sprang into action at the hotel, Sarah calmly pulled on the headlamp and returned to the hole in the concrete. The edges of the opening were jagged and dusty, and some pieces of rebar were sticking out, but there would be enough room for her to squeeze through. Placing her hands on either side of the opening, she leaned forward to get a glimpse of the floor on the other side, to make sure she wasn't about to take both a figurative and literal plunge. The bottom of the empty room looked to be level with the floor outside, so she climbed onto the edge of the hole and prepared to jump.

Although it was only a few down to the floor, Sarah felt as if she was diving off a cliff into an abyss. A life flashed before her eyes in that split second, a life not her own. The scenes of a fierce battle, of terrible wounds, of final moments, replayed again in her mind. So gripping, so irresistible and detailed where these visions and emotions, she thought she might never emerge back into her own life. Then her boots hit the concrete.

The first thing Sarah looked at was her watch, just to make sure she hadn't lost an hour—or a day—during the flashback. It would have been amazing to find that she was floating in limbo for hours. But as the time was essentially unchanged, it was even more remarkable to realize that everything she had just experienced had transpired in the few thousandths of a second it had taken for her to drop from the edge of the hole to the floor.

Adjusting the headlamp for a wide field of illumination, she then took a hefty halogen flashlight out of her vest to provide a bright, focused beam. The room looked smaller than she had imagined, but it was certainly large enough to encompass the footprint of an old farmhouse. Sarah took a few readings and several photos, but then she just wanted to walk quietly around the perimeter of the empty concrete room.

With help from her imagination, the concrete beneath her feet became transparent, and she "saw" through it to the layers of dirt, debris—and human remains. This was the place; she had no doubt. This was where Azel Wegman had built his home and raised his family. When that family was gone, this abandoned house became the site of a Civil War battle, and then a shelter for the wounded and dying afterwards.

Feeling herself being swept away again, she turned off the flashlights, got down on her hands and knees and lowered her cheek to the floor. The cold concrete greeted her like the touch of an old friend. Then she thought she heard a sound from deep within the ground, a strange, hissing type of noise. Pressing her ear against the floor, she strained to hear it as it grew, and transformed into something almost human, like attempts at words coming from a parched throat. The sound rose up from the depths, strengthened, until finally it became clear and unmistakable.

"Sa-rah!" the desperate, rasping voice whispered just beneath her ear.

Never before had she jumped to her feet more rapidly. Rubbing her ear as if something had burrowed inside, she stumbled backward toward the opening, but never took her eyes from the spot in the concrete where the disembodied voice had risen up to speak from the grave. The bright work lights outside the room cast a thin path that she continued to follow walking backwards, still in a considerable state of shock.

When her feet encountered the pile of rubble below the opening, her hands reached back to find the edge of the hole. Another hand was reaching in at the moment, and cool fingertips brushed against the back of her neck as a voice spoke.

"Sarah?"

The seasoned ghost hunter, who had faced the worst the world of the dead had to offer, let out a piercing scream as she spun around. The figure on the other side of the opening also screamed, and at an impressively higher pitch.

"Shit, Jimmy, you scared the crap out of me!" Sarah yelled, putting a hand to her heaving chest.

"Damn it, you scared the crap out of me, too!" Jimmy yelled back, dropping to his knees to wait for the wooziness to pass.

Sarah climbed through the hole and joined him on the floor. Once they had caught their breath, they both laughed, and then Sarah pretended to strangle him.

"Don't you ever do that again!"

"I'm sorry, I thought maybe you were in trouble."

As she explained why she had been so tense, Jimmy's eyes grew wide and he fixed them on the hole, wondering out loud if she needed him to go in there now.

"No, I think we have enough to go on. There's nothing threatening here— just anxious. The tough part will be in convincing the work crews. Where's everyone else?"

"Ricky drove me right over, and he stayed in the parking garage. The others will be here in a few minutes."

"Good, let's go back to the garage and see what's up."

A crowd had gathered in the center of the parking garage. The crew at Site #3 under *Kinder Krossing* had heard about their co-workers running off, and they left their site, too, albeit by walking, to join up with the garage crew in assailing the foreman. The angry and frightened men were demanding to know what was going on.

Atkins arrived, expecting to find a smoothly running operation, and instead found a third of the workers already gone and the rest in a state of mutiny. Everybody was shouting, and the foreman wasn't helping matters by yelling and cursing at everyone and everything. However, at the sight of the big boss storming toward them, silence suddenly descended upon the group.

"What the hell is happening here?" Atkins bellowed.

At that moment, Sarah and Jimmy entered the garage.

"It's all her fault!" the foreman shouted, pointing a finger that looked to have been broken at least twice.

Sarah actually turned to look behind her, and then realized that the foreman was trying to place the entire blame on her. However, before she could respond, a timid voice spoke up on her behalf.

"T…That lady had nothin' to do with it," Joe said, speaking up to protect the innocent, even if it cost him his job. "She wasn't even there when those guys took off."

"Is that true? Did you start without Sarah and her teams? Did you fail to properly brief these men about what they might encounter?" Atkins asked the startled foreman. The man had not counted on his boss being on a first name basis with Sarah, and also didn't anticipate Joe speaking up against him.

"So what if I did?" he replied boldly, and completely unrepentant. "My men get a bonus if we finish ahead of schedule, so you think I'm going to waste time waiting for this ridiculous ghostbuster?"

"No, what I think is that you totally disregarded my explicit orders. Why don't you take an early lunch right now and don't bother coming back," Atkins said, using his thumb to indicate the nearest exit. The irate foreman shot one last nasty look at Sarah, then got in his pickup truck and sped away, tires squealing. "Now, does anybody have any idea what is going in here? You, were you there?"

"My name is Joe, sir. I was there."

As Joe described in detail the bizarre events, the rest of the construction crews looked like they wanted to run, too. Atkins could see the fear in their eyes and asked Sarah to say a few words. She began by assuring them that nothing at the three sites was harmful. (She specifically didn't say that *nothing* in the entire center was harmful—as was evidenced by the cart incident.)

"However, even if you don't believe in ghosts, these are the remains of men we are endeavoring to retrieve—soldiers who deserve your respect," Sarah continued. "I suggest you do not make light of the situation, that you do not try to scare your co-workers, and that you go about your business with the solemnity of a funeral."

At that point, three cars pulled into the garage with the other team members.

"The people who just arrived will be joining Ricky, Jimmy, and I to insure your safety. There may be some energies here that can create sounds and sensations, and we will be monitoring those energies. Occasionally, we might request that you step away for a few minutes, just as a precaution. As I said, nothing at these sites will harm you, although they can sure scare the hell out of you. But, hey, if I can stand it, certainly all of you big, strong men can take it!" Sarah concluded, using the ultimate weapon—the challenge to the male ego.

There was some conversation among the crews, and a healthy dose of bluster and bravado. The general consensus was that they wouldn't run off because of a few weird noises. The only disagreement among the men was which site got to have Sarah to protect them.

Atkins got on the phone to see about getting replacements for the runaways, and found that the situation would be remedied in a few hours. In the meantime, he chose a man from each of the other two crews to join Joe, so work could continue. He allowed his men to mingle with the ghost hunters for a few minutes to ask questions, get acquainted, and generally feel more at ease about the situation. When he felt there had been enough socializing, he barked the order for everyone to get back to work.

Sarah reluctantly donned a hardhat, which was one of the rules she agreed to in order to be allowed at the sites. In addition to being just one more thing to weigh her down, she knew it would do very unflattering things to her hair. Concrete dust, dirt, and sweat wouldn't help, either, so she was prepared to look like hell by the end of the day.

A ghost just whispered in my ear and I'm still worried about my hair, Sarah mused, as she tossed a bright yellow hardhat to Jimmy, who was equally unhappy about the dress code.

"Aw, c'mon, do I have to?" he moaned.

"Put it on now, or I'll draw a smile face on it and then make you wear it."

"Sarah, sometimes you're just plain cruel," Jimmy complained, but nonetheless put on his hardhat as quickly as possible.

Before heading back to Site #2, Sarah pulled aside Ricky and Andy and told them of her experiences, and the voice calling her name. She wanted them to let the others know what they might expect, but it wouldn't be wise for word of it to get to the construction men. They were spooked enough.

Thanks to Jimmy's efficiency, it looked like most of the monitoring instruments were already in place by the time Sarah arrived. As she was about to compliment him, she realized that he had only set up equipment in the corridor, and not a single thing inside the empty room. The cart incident had rattled the boy, and while she was certain he would regain his courage, there was no reason to push him if he wasn't ready.

"Jimmy, while you're finishing up out here, why don't I take care everything inside the room?" she offered in a matter-of-fact way that would not arouse any suspicion, as Jimmy had often insisted that she never, ever coddle him.

"Sure, okay, that's great. I mean, I was going to do it, 'cause I'm not scared to go in there or anything, but if you don't mind…"

As much as Jimmy had learned from Sarah, he still hadn't mastered the art of saying what you don't mean.

With the sun climbing higher in the clear blue eastern skies over Wegman's Center, paranormal activity began to decrease. There were still a few tense moments when the wall at Site #3 was breached, and the first section of blacktop was removed from the parking garage, but by late morning, the new crew had arrived and work was progressing at a rapid pace.

When it was time to break for lunch, Sarah slipped Jimmy a few folded bills and suggested he ask Joe out to eat. She had noticed that the two were getting along well, with each fascinated by the other's job and equipment. She hated to act like his mother again, but she always encouraged Jimmy to spend more time with kids his age, especially with someone like Joe who was looking forward to going to college. Not that she wanted her assistant to become a lawyer—heaven forbid!—but she insisted that he pursue some degree.

Lela had invited Sarah to lunch, ostensibly to receive a report on the morning's progress, but actually to get all the dirt. The flow of dirt went both ways, as Lela told of the very latest Octagon rumblings. Fink was still MIA, with the official line being that due to sudden health concerns, he had gone to rest in a private health resort in Arizona. Chivington was also feeling some heat from major stockholders and the "money men" who helped finance the center.

"Who knows, if the pressure gets too much for Chivington, maybe he and Fink can get a family rate at the sanitarium," Lela quipped, feeling better about her position with every passing hour.

By the end of the workday, the results were impressive. Much of the pavement had already been removed from the parking garage. It had been decided that the archaeologists could begin the next day on the exposed ground, while the remainder of the site was being cleared. At Site #2, the two walls that adjoined the corridor had been removed, and a small section of the floor had been broken into pieces. It was a similar situation at Site #3, and it would most likely take another two days to adequately prepare those sites for the archaeologists, historians, and preservation specialists.

When the order was given for quitting time, Sarah tried to brush some of the filth out of her clothing, and inadvertently sent a cloud of dust into Joe's face.

"I'm sorry, Joe."

"That's okay, Ms. Brooks. A little more dirt won't make much difference. Ms. Brooks, would it be okay if Jimmy came over to my house for a while? It's just about half an hour from here, and I promise not to bring him back late, since we all have to get up early tomorrow."

Oh god, I have become a mother! a little voice screamed in Sarah's head. However, she played it cool. "Please, it's Sarah. And it's fine with me. I'll see you guys tomorrow. Have fun."

As she entered the parking garage, she remembered she was still wearing the hardhat. Leaning forward, she removed the hat and pulled out her hairclip. When her hair fell to its full length, she used both hands to fluff it and shake out the grit. Then with one movement, she retrieved the hardhat from the floor and stood up quickly, tossing her hair back behind her. It was only then that she realized she had an audience.

About a dozen men stood behind the construction barricades, and they were all looking her way. She had no idea who they were, and felt extremely self-conscious until a familiar voice called out.

"Sarah, it's Carl. Do you have a minute?"

She was dirty, grimy, and tired, and after the hair performance she just put on, she wanted nothing more than to crawl into a dark corner, but she put on a big smile and tried to forget that she looked like a tunnel rat.

"Carl, good to see you again! Did you get an update on the progress?"

"Yes, I just spoke with Lela, and isn't she a breath of fresh air after Fink?" he replied, as Sarah caught a whiff of herself and decided to remain on her side of the barricade. "I want you to meet these gentleman. They represent various organizations of the descendants of Civil War veterans. They were all supposed to be at the meeting yesterday, until that was changed at the last minute."

The introductions went on down the line, and no one hesitated to shake her hand, even if it was covered in powdered concrete.

"It's a pleasure to meet you all, but I'm afraid the sites are off-limits to anyone else," she stated, hoping that they would not insist on gaining access, throwing yet another wrench into the plan.

"That's not what they are here for," Dr. Henkel said quickly. "Sam, it was your idea, why don't you tell her."

Sam was a tall, stately man with bushy red facial hair over gaunt cheeks—the perfect Civil War reenactor.

"You see, Ms. Brooks, it's like this," the Confederate descendant said in a smooth, dignified southern accent that made Sarah want to get in a hoop skirt and sip mint juleps. "We all got together and decided that these men buried under here are long overdue for the honors they deserve. Don't you agree?"

"Yes, of course," she replied, unsure of where this was heading.

"Well, me and the boys here were thinking that we would like to be on hand when any remains are uncovered."

"I'm sorry, as I said before-"

"No, no, let me finish, Ma'am. We would like to provide two color guard units representing both the Confederacy and the Union. We would stay out by the entrance to the garage and simply dip our flags in respect as the remains passed by."

Arrangements had been made for each set of remains to be brought to a local university facility to be examined, before eventually being re-interred at a proposed new cemetery on the center's property. While there would be elaborate ceremonies at the dedication of the cemetery, no type of formal observance had been otherwise planned.

"I can't think of a finer way to honor these soldiers," Sarah said, a bit choked up. "But why ask me? I don't have the authority to approve it."

"Well, Carl seems to think you're the woman in charge," Sam stated, then realized he might have said too much. Sarah avoided eye contact with her former antagonist to save him the embarrassment.

"I guess the pressure is on me, then," Sarah said reaching for her phone. After brief conversations with Lela and Atkins, it appeared that Sarah *was* the woman in charge. "They both think it's a great idea, and don't see any problem, as long as you do not enter the excavation sites."

Sam reached for Sarah's hand, and she assumed he wanted to shake it again. Instead, he lifted it to his lips and tenderly kissed it.

"Ma'am, on behalf of the Sons of Dixie Heritage Alliance, the other noble organizations represented here today, and all of the brave soldiers who died here, we express our heartfelt gratitude."

Tears running across the dirt on her face would really have completed her un-pretty picture, so before she lost it, she briefly thanked him, excused herself and hurried to her car. When she got back to the hotel room and looked in the mirror, she gasped at the filthy image, and even rubbed the surface of the mirror with her sleeve to make sure the dirt was actually all on her and not on the glass. Standing in the bathtub, she peeled off her clothes and dropped them right into a plastic bag. As her dirty clothing had been piling up for almost a week, she decided that dinner and a Laundromat would be in order for the evening.

First, however, came the much-needed shower. It was amazing to see the pile of concrete gravel that gathered around the drain, and she didn't even want to think of where the little pieces had all managed to stick to her. As she was toweling off, the phone rang.

"This is the sheriff, are you harboring any minors in your hotel room?"

"No, but I am expecting a major at any minute."

"Hmm, I see. Then I guess you don't want to have dinner with me tonight."

"Well, I suppose I could tell the major to get lost, if you know of a restaurant near a Laundromat."

"That's a first—dinner and a good spin cycle! I'm sure I could find…sorry…wait a sec…sorry, can I put you on hold?"

Sarah was almost finished dressing by the time he returned.

"I'm sorry, Sarah. There's a hostage situation at the industrial park. Don't bother waiting for me."

"No problem. Good luck."

Why is it that I only get to spend quality time with dead men? she thought as she kicked off her slinky skirt and grabbed her old sweat pants.

Work resumed the next morning with everyone on time, and not hung over. Throughout the day, the dirt floors in the two rooms were slowly but surely being exposed. The last of the pavement in the excavation zone in the parking garage was removed and hauled away. The first team of archaeologists had mapped out a grid and had already begun removing and sifting dirt. It was not the usual slow, meticulous operation—orders had been to dig everything up and get it out of there as quickly as possible. There would be plenty of time to study everything at the university.

It wasn't long before they hit something solid. Excitement rose, but as they carefully brushed away the dirt, it was found to be rock, not bone. The disappointment abated, however, as a rectangular stone and masonry shape was further revealed. There was a quick conference amongst the historians and scientists. They could not be certain at this early stage, but it could have been a support base for one corner of a bridge. Dr. Henkel was promptly paged, as per his request, and he promptly canceled all of his appointments until further notice, and then raced to the center.

Ricky alerted Sarah, and as things were quiet at her site, she decided to go have a look. Jimmy was content to remain behind—he wasn't interested until bones turned up. He should have gone with Sarah.

About twenty minutes later, as Sarah and Carl Henkel watched the team quickly remove layers of soft dirt, a small speck of white appeared in the dark earth. Sarah's spine and limbs tingled, and Carl grabbed her hand and squeezed it until it almost hurt. The ghost hunters gathered at the edge of the grid and it looked as if no one was breathing.

It seemed to take an eternity as the woman on her hands and knees carefully brushed first one side of the white spot, then the other. It had a definite curved shape, and Sarah felt as if she would burst until the woman announced, "It's a skull! It's a human skull!"

No one needed to look at the instruments to know that there was a sudden spike in paranormal energy in the parking garage. The sight of the first human remains to be uncovered was more than enough to send a chill through everyone, and no one was immune to the dizzying effects of the discovery.

Word went out to the other sites, and to Lela and Dan, and soon a crowd formed along the perimeter of the barricades and yellow tape ringing the site. Atkins was also there, and didn't even think to complain that his crews were taking an extended break. He even asked one of his men to invite Sam and the other members of the color guards to join them.

Normally, it might have taken days before such a find was carefully removed, but with the clock ticking and video cameras running, the entire set of remains was exposed in under half an hour. And there would be no mystery about the cause of death of this unfortunate man—a shattered pelvis, splintered ribs, and a gaping hole in the side of the skull revealed that this soldier had been shot numerous times. The horrific wounds were most likely all received in the same deadly volley of fire, as any one of the shots would have dropped him instantly. At least he never knew what hit him.

Several detectors indicated that encrusted lumps in and around the skeleton contained metal. Even though these amorphous blobs meant nothing to the untrained eye, the experts felt confident in identifying several of the lumps as buttons, a belt buckle, and the mechanism of a musket. However, as per their agreement with Octagon, there was no time for a close examination, and both human remains and artifacts were scooped up and placed in a plastic box and tagged *Site One- Remains One.*

Dr. Henkel, Dan, Atkins, and Ricky helped as the box was carefully lifted over the barricade. As they carried it to the transport van, one of the men from the Union's color guard lifted his bugle and began playing taps. The soulful sounds echoed throughout the garage, and by the time the last note drifted away, there wasn't a dry eye in the place.

At that moment, there was a tremendous shift at Wegman's Center, from the basement to the fourth floor, and from the movie theaters to the food court, to the central atrium. As if on cue, everyone from sales clerks to kids playing video games to women having their nails done stopped what they were doing for a moment. There were no outward sounds, no cold blasts of air, no filaments of light. But there was something everybody sensed, and it seemed to come from the floors and out of the walls and from the escalators, cash registers, and clothing racks. It was as if everything solid moved as one, in a great sigh of relief.

The sudden vibration was gone as quickly as it manifested. Kids went back to their video games. Clerks and shoppers resumed their business. No one took much notice that the sunlight streaming through the skylights seemed a bit brighter, the advertising banners hanging from the ceilings looked more colorful, and the air throughout the center smelled fresher.

For professional ghost hunter Sarah Brooks, the vibration washed over her like a warm ocean wave. The band of tension that tightened around her every time she stepped into the center suddenly eased by several notches. The other ghost hunters experienced similar feelings, and knowing glances were exchanged amongst them in silence.

This was the first step toward relieving almost a century and a half of anguish. It was a small step, but the first one that went in a positive direction. It was the first time that something else hung in the air besides despair—there was now hope.

"Sarah, if you don't stop crying, I'm not going to be able to stop," Jimmy whispered as he surreptitiously elbowed her in the side.

"Well, I can't stop crying until those guys in the color guard stop," she replied, digging out a few more tissues from her vest and handing them out.

Gradually, the powerful emotions of the moment turned toward jubilation at the early success of the project. Dr. Carl Henkel was particularly overjoyed, as he now felt vindicated after so many years of fighting for what he believed in. Tears of sorrow in the crowd became tears of joy, but that joy was short-lived.

"I've got another one!" a voice shouted, as all others fell silent. "Oh God, there's a lot more of them!"

A graduate student from the university sat in the soft sediment of the former river's edge, which now lay in the center of the excavation site. His expression was a mixture of horror and disbelief, as he pointed to what he had just uncovered at the base of another stone bridge support. It wasn't a single skeleton, neatly and cleanly laid out. This was a tangled mound of bones—femurs, tibias, ulnae, vertebrae, ribs—all sticking out of the earth like some grotesque garden. It was impossible to tell how deep this mound of remains was, or how many men's shattered bodies it took to create it, but the sorrows, the joys, the relief of the last hour were all pushed aside. There was serious work still to be done, and there was no time for sentimentality.

Dan Garrison was the first to find his voice to speak.

"Okay, I think it's time everyone got back to work and let these people do their jobs."

"That's right, everyone back to work!" Atkins barked, but more like a poodle than in his usual Doberman style.

Sarah put her arm around Jimmy's shoulder and turned him away from the gruesome sight. This was more than a young boy should see. All of this was more than someone his age should ever have to witness.

"Jimmy, why don't you go back to the hotel and get some rest. I can finish monitoring our site."

Rather than pull away from her and protest that she was coddling him, he drew closer and felt very much like a frightened little boy.

"I don't understand, there's so many. How did they all get piled up like that? Why would someone do that?" he asked softly.

"Ugly things happen in war. Maybe the casualties were all placed in one spot, maybe a flood washed them all to the base of the bridge, I don't know. It won't be easy, but try to put it out of your mind. Why don't go back to your room and watch some TV, or maybe give your mother a call."

Jimmy was about to acquiesce, until he saw Joe donning his hardhat and heading back to work. Straightening up and wiping his eyes, he told Sarah that he was fine, and wanted to go back to the site and do his job.

Maybe he doesn't need a mother right now, Sarah thought as Jimmy jogged on ahead to catch up with Joe. *Maybe a big brother will do the trick.*

The mood back at Site #2 was somber, to say the least, but there was little time for reflection as jackhammers pounded the concrete floor into manageable chunks. The pieces were then lifted onto small trailers and towed to the nearest loading ramp to be dumped into trucks. It was backbreaking work, and it didn't give you the time or energy for thinking about your troubles, so Sarah readily agreed to let Jimmy help for the last couple of hours of the shift. It was painfully obvious that he was not accustomed to manual labor, but she felt a certain pride in seeing that he was too stubborn to give up. She figured that was due in part to his Irish heritage, and in part from her sometimes less than sterling examples of pigheadedness.

Sarah offered to take the boys out to dinner and a movie, but neither felt hungry or in the mood for any shallow entertainment. There had been too much reality for their young minds that day. When they reached the parking garage, Sarah asked Joe if he would drive Jimmy back to the hotel, because she wanted to check on the progress of Site #1. There were no objections, and neither of the boys showed any interest in seeing for themselves how the excavation of the bone pile was progressing.

As she approached the site, there were no signs that either Ricky and his team, or archaeologists and historians were quitting for the day. She soon discovered why. The tangle of human remains had been excavated to a depth of almost six feet. The scene reminded Sarah of the catacombs in Europe where grinning skulls and grasping fingers protruded from the walls.

"There's at least a dozen men in there. Maybe fifteen, maybe twenty," Ricky told her as he shook his head, his normally ruddy complexion now looking anemic. "I just wasn't prepared for this."

"None of us were," Sarah admitted. "When are they stopping?"

"They brought in a few extra volunteers, and more are on the way. They pretty much think they might work right through the night. We'll stick with them, though," Ricky said, haggard, but determined.

"How about I run upstairs and grab a bite to eat, then I'll stay here while you all go back to the hotel, have dinner and catch a few hours of sleep," Sarah offered. "Then two of you could come back, and then switch out again."

"Well, there isn't much in the way of paranormal activity, but this is our site, and we should be here," he stated, but without much conviction.

"And you will be here, after you guys take a break. Don't worry, I don't plan to be here all night!" Sarah said, suspecting that was most likely a lie.

Sarah had no clue that the sun was beginning to rise outside Wegman's Center that Wednesday morning. She had spent most of the night in the pit, lending a hand wherever it was needed—filing buckets with dirt, holding measuring sticks against the remains as they were being photographed, and lifting box after box of human bones with remnants of fabric, pieces of leather, and encrusted metal. The deeper into the pile they went, the more well preserved were the artifacts, as if the very density of the bodies helped shield those below.

One piece in particular was practically in museum quality condition, having been sandwiched between a rock and a crushed skull. It was an oval belt buckle that clearly read "CSA"—Confederate States of America. In addition to being a valuable key to unraveling the mystery of the Battle of Wegman's Crossing, it also spoke to the ferocity of the fighting, as a Minié ball was still firmly implanted in the middle of the buckle, saving the owner from certain death. But obviously, it was merely a temporary reprieve.

Carl Henkel had also rolled up his sleeves and spent the night in the disturbingly fragrant soil of the pit. Although the soldiers' flesh had long ago rotted and been consumed by worms, there was still the unmistakable smell of death, even if there were no organic reasons for it.

Sarah and Carl took turns grabbing a few twenty-minute catnaps here and there. Different members of the ghost hunting team swapped in and out. Two rotations of archaeologists came and went, and it was only when the third shift arrived that Sarah realized she had actually been working for almost twenty-four hours.

Jimmy arrived at 6am, and it was his turn to play mother, scolding her for staying out all night and not taking care of herself.

"And I hate to say it, Sarah, but you really stink, too!" Jimmy added for good measure, trying to waft the foul stench away from him.

"Hey, you try spending the night in a mass grave and see if you come out smelling like roses," Sarah replied, pulling clumps of filth off her knees and elbows. "Maybe I should take a few minutes and go back to the hotel and change my clothes before we get to work at our site."

"Maybe you should do a lot more than that. How about a shower? Or two? Get a few hours of sleep, I can handle the site for now."

"They'll start digging today. I have to be here for that," Sarah protested.

"That won't be until at least after lunch. Please, Sarah, for all our sakes, get out of here for a while!"

"He's right," Carl said, approaching them and then stopping to yawn, as if he didn't have the energy to walk and yawn at the same time. "Your brain needs a few hours of downtime. Not to mention that if you even smell half as bad as I do we should both be arrested for endangering public safety."

"Okay, I give up. I'll go, but don't you hesitate to call me for anything!"

Taking a couple of yards of plastic sheeting from dig site, she covered the driver's seat of the car. It was a rental, after all, and she didn't want to have to pay for new upholstery.

Once again, she stripped down in the bathtub so the majority of the muck would be contained. Her clothes went into a plastic bag, although she would have thrown them directly into an incinerator if one had been available. The shower felt good, but it wasn't quite enough for her dirty, exhausted, aching body. Redirecting the flow, she began filling the tub with very hot water, and didn't shut it off until it was right up to the level of the bandage on her neck.

Not even the most horrible scenes of worms crawling through empty eye sockets or spines splintered into a hundred pieces could keep her awake as the hot water drew the last bits of grime out of her pores. Sinking into a deep peaceful sleep, her only dreams came hours later. She dreamt that she was alone and wounded on a battlefield. She couldn't move, and it was cold, so cold…

When her cell phone rang from the top of toilet just a few feet from her head, Sarah had no idea where she was, what was happening, or even what century she was in. All she knew was that she was freezing. Another ring, and she realized she was in a tub of cold water, and by the third ring she realized that she must have fallen asleep in what was once a soothing, hot bath. Now she was in the early stages of hypothermia.

Pulling herself out of the water, she reached for her phone with one hand, while grabbing a towel with the other.

"Hel…lo," she answered through chattering teeth.

"It's Jimmy. Trouble at Site #3. One of the guys may be hurt."

"On my way."

Sarah ran to her car in her socks, with her shirt unbuttoned. With the car's heat blasting to return some warmth to her thoroughly chilled flesh, she tried to jam on her boots while she drove dangerously fast. As she entered the parking garage, there was a host of flashing lights from sheriff's patrol cars and an ambulance. Jimmy was waiting for her, and his expression was grim.

"Talk to me," Sarah said, hitting the ground running.

"Andy's team started getting some bizarre readings," Jimmy shouted over his shoulder, running a step ahead. "They were telling the construction guys that they should stop for a while, and then some guy with a torch flips out and starts threatening everyone. He might have hurt his legs, he's delirious or something, and he won't let anyone near him."

Sarah's shirt was more or less buttoned and one boot was tied when they arrived at Site #3, which stretched from the loading dock to the void under *Kinder Krossing*. Andy immediately pulled her aside and told her what had transpired just before the incident.

"It was like a volcano getting ready to burst," he explained, wringing his hands. "We told everyone to leave, all the meters were off the scale. Most of the guys came out of the room and into the corridor, but one was in the back corner using an acetylene torch. He couldn't hear us. Before we could reach him he was on the ground waving his torch, screaming at everyone to stay back. He's yelling something about his legs. We tried to warn him, Sarah. We tried!"

"Hang in there, Andy, I know you did your best. What are the readings now?"

"Uh…let's see…they've calmed down for the most part. A few spikes here and there. But whatever happened, it was big. And it was just as that guy started going nuts."

"Okay, thanks. Keep me posted."

Sarah hurried over to the edge of the site, where a wall once separated the corridor from the empty void. Only a few of the bright work lights were functioning, and none of them were in the back left corner were the construction worker was waving his fiery torch, and screaming at the top of his lungs.

Dan, Beau, and Deputy Drummond were conferring with Atkins and the shift supervisor, and all five men stood on the freshly exposed earth. Paramedics were standing close by, but no one was even attempting to go near the crazed man with the torch. Sarah had other ideas.

"I'm going in and talking to him," she stated as if there was no need for approval.

"Oh, no you don't," Dan and Beau said simultaneously, as both men turned to block her path.

"This is strictly a matter for my men and the sheriff's. This has nothing to do with you," Dan said more like a protective father than the head of security giving an order.

"You don't understand-" Sarah began to say, but then stopped when the raving man starting screaming again.

"No, no stay back! Don't take my legs! No! No! Get away from me!"

The voice sent shivers through her, and she already had plenty of her own from the ice bath.

"This guy is out of his mind, and he's dangerous, and you are not going in there," Beau said, in no uncertain terms. "He tried to fry a guard and two of the paramedics. This is not your field of expertise."

"I'm afraid it is," Sarah said in manner that indicated she was dead serious.

"What do you mean by that?" Beau asked, putting a finger under his collar, as it suddenly felt too tight.

"Gentleman, not to make light of the situation, but I think this is what we in the business like to call 'illegal possession.' I have to speak to him," she said, pausing while the full weight of her statement had a chance to settle in.

"You mean some ghost has taken over that guy?" Atkins said, not sure whether to laugh or start running.

"I mean there's a good possibility that his mind is being influenced by thoughts that are not his. And it wouldn't be the first time that's happened around here," Sarah said, specifically directing her last line to Beau.

"Look, Sarah, this is just too much-" Dan began, before Beau cut him off.

"Let her try," Beau said, much to everyone's surprise. "God knows I've seen enough things around this godforsaken place that I'll never be able to explain, even if I live to be a hundred."

"Thank you, I will be careful," Sarah said, picking up a flashlight.

"You'll need more than that," Beau replied, firmly placing a stun gun in the palm of her hand. "If you get close enough, and he threatens you, *do not* hesitate to zap him with this. Am I clear?"

"Yes, sir. Loud and clear."

The shift supervisor filled her in about the man's background. There wasn't much to say—family man, steady worker, never any problems. Andy gave Sarah one of his walkie-talkies and told her he would let her know if the activity started to increase. Dan showed her a few quick self-defense moves. Finally, Jimmy asked if she was sure she knew what she was doing.

"Hell no, I haven't been sure of a damn thing since I started ghost hunting," she whispered back to him, not wanting the crowd to know that she had no plan, and little confidence.

There was about a hundred feet of uneven ground with small chunks of concrete to traverse before she reached the dark corner lit only by the white-hot torch. She was about thirty feet from the man before he first noticed her.

"Stay back! I'm warning you! No one is taking my legs!"

"Al? Is that you?" Sarah asked, turning the bright beam of the flashlight toward him for a few seconds. "Are you hurt, Al?"

There was a man huddled in the corner, with his right leg sticking out straight. His right hand appeared to be trying to stop the flow of blood from his thigh. In his left hand he waved the deadly torch like a sword. His expression was one of abject fear.

"Get back, you can't trick me! My name isn't Al!"

"I thought for sure you were Allan R. Johnson," Sarah said, inching slowly forward. "Don't you live right over here in Cullum's Tavern, with your wife Becky, and your two kids?"

"Becky? No, no, you're trying to confuse me. That man wants to cut off my legs!"

"What man, Al? Do you see him right now?"

Sarah recalled the statements of the children who had been in *Kinder Krossing* on opening day. The horribly wounded man with no legs, the man with the apron and the saw—she knew the reports had not just been the ravings of hysterical kids.

"No, I don't see him right now. But you know him, he'll cut me, He'll take my legs."

"He's just the surgeon, he's only trying to help," Sarah said, adjusting her tack now that she could see Al wasn't the one in charge. "You've been wounded, he at least needs to examine you."

"I...I...have been wounded. It was a rebel ball, got me in both legs. Please, don't let them take my legs!" he pleaded with her, lowering the torch to a less threatening position.

Sarah was now only six feet from the man, and by the glow of the torchlight, she could see that a piece of rebar was sticking about eight inches out of his thigh. He must have tripped, or something startled him, and he fell back onto the metal rod. She was deciding on whether or not to make a lunge for the torch, when her walkie-talkie started beeping.

"What's that?" the man shouted, raising the torch again and waving it at her. "It's a trick!"

"It's only headquarters," Sarah said, really ad-libbing. "I'm going to try to find out what our orders are…Andy, what's going on?"

"The readings are skyrocketing again, Sarah. Are you okay? Beau told me to tell you to zap him the first chance you get."

"I'm okay. And the man has a piece of rebar in his leg so I don't think I should zap-"

The man started screaming again.

"There he is, there he is! Keep him away!"

If there was one moment in her life that Sarah really didn't want to see an apparition, this was it.

Okay, Sarah Brooks. This is what you do, she said to herself. *This is who you are.*

Closing her eyes and holding her breath, she spun around and counted to three. When she opened her eyes, she had to clamp her hand over her mouth to stifle a scream. There was a pale, misty shape of a man drawing closer. It was like an image being projected into a fog, and it rippled and wavered, then slowly began to take on more defined features. The wounded man in the corner screamed as if Death himself was coming to take him.

Removing her hand from her mouth and taking a deep breath, Sarah managed to shuffle her leaden legs a few steps to her right, to block the path of the apparition to the man. The figure brightened, and the white apron it wore almost glowed with red streaks and stains. The bone saw by his side also glistened with ethereal blood.

"Doctor!" she called out. "This soldier doesn't need your help. There are others who are much more badly wounded."

The transparent figure stopped for a moment, his deep-set eyes gazing at her with a look of understanding. But then the man in the corner started screaming, and the figure raised his saw and began to move forward again. Sarah wasn't sure if she was going to wet herself, throw up, faint, or all of the above. When the phantom doctor was only ten feet away from her, she dropped to her knees, put both hands on the ground started doing some of her own pleading.

"Edward! Edward, I need your help, *now!*"

She tried to envision the soldier who had touched her face, and her soul. She tried to connect with him, to somehow let him know that she needed him; she needed him to stop the doctor who was only one step away from walking right through her. Shutting her eyes, clenching her teeth, she braced for the inevitably icy, shocking impact with a spirit of the dead…

A second passed. Two seconds…five. There was nothing. Slowly opening one eye, there was nothing but an empty room before her. And there was silence, blessed, scream-free silence. Jumping to her feet, she turned on the flashlight and aimed it at the wounded man. He appeared confused, and in great pain, but his expression had lost its look of terror.

"Al, is that you?" Sarah asked, going back to where she had started.

"Yeah, it's me. I'm hurt bad. I need help. I...I don't know what happened."

"It's okay, the paramedics are here. We just need for you to turn off the torch. Can you do that, Al?"

"Yeah, sure, okay," he replied, moving his blood soaked right hand to turn off the valve on the handle.

The instant the flame was extinguished, Sarah shouted into the walkie-talkie.

"All clear! Get them in here, *now*!"

What sounded like a stampeding herd immediately headed her way, but it was actually an organized and efficient response team. In less than five minutes, they had Allan Johnson—complete with the section of rebar that had skewered his leg—on the stretcher, with an IV in his arm. The man had no clue how he had been hurt, and no recollection of anything that occurred since the accident, least of all, ghosts of doctors or threatening anyone with an acetylene torch.

After a paramedic made sure Sarah was all right, she backed away from the crowd, crouched down against the wall and put her head in her hands. Beau found her there a few minutes later.

"Want to talk about it?"

"Nope."

"You okay?"

"Been better."

"Anything I can do?"

"Just give me some time."

Atkins spotted Sarah and was coming over to thank her when Beau waved him off. He seemed to understand, and headed back over to his man who was being carried out.

"Okay, you just let me know if you need anything...And Sarah, I don't know what you did, and to be honest, I don't think I care to know...but you did good. Real good."

Sarah looked up and managed a smile, before returning her head to her hands. She needed some serious decompression time to clear her head. However, two minutes after Beau left, Jimmy came running over.

"Are you okay? Did he burn you?"

"I'm fine, Jimmy, just a bit freaked out," she replied without looking up.

"What happened? Tell me what happened!"

"Later."

It had taken over a year, but Jimmy had finally come to learn that later definitely meant *not* now.

"Okay, sure. I'll be in the corridor if you need me."

When everyone had left the room, Sarah got up and started pacing back and forth, mumbling to herself.

"So what if I just encountered a possessed construction worker and a dead doctor with a saw...no biggie...I've seen worse...I can handle it. And so what if spirits are whispering in my ear, touching my face...been there, done that. Oh

yeah, and then there's the guy who tried to kill me. So what, could happen to any
body…"

Picking up a grapefruit-sized chuck of concrete, she hurled it against the
wall.

"Just how much more of this shit am I supposed to take!"

Stomping on a few small bits of concrete until they were dust, she decided
that throwing things was much more satisfying. Jimmy and a few of the other
ghost hunters working near the entrance could hear that Sarah was having
something of a tantrum, but they all pretended not to notice. No one understood
the pressures of the job like they did, and every one of them had experience with
unique ways of letting off steam. In fact, a few were tempted to join her.

After a couple of minutes the ranting and raving ceased, and the sounds of
smashing concrete were no more. Sarah calmly emerged back into the corridor,
casually pushing a few wisps of hair back into place.

"Would anyone care to join me for lunch and a couple of drinks? My treat,"
Sarah said as if she hadn't a care in the world.

Eyes darted, and no one seemed to want to speak up. Finally, Jimmy glanced
at his watch and spoke.

"It's only 9:45am."

"Oh, is it? I forgot my watch. Okay, then how about breakfast and one
drink?" she said grinning, as if she was already three sheets to the wind.

"No thanks, we're all good," Andy replied for his team, as they desperately
looked to him to get them out of sitting through a meal with someone they
considered to be just a wee bit unstable at the moment. "We have work to do."

"Too bad, I had quite a story to tell," Sarah said as she walked away. "Quite
a story!"

Everyone looked to Andy again with a completely different expression, and
he immediately changed his tune.

"Wait, Sarah, that would be great. They aren't starting up again until this
afternoon anyway."

"No, don't worry about it. I'll just sit in a restaurant all alone and talk to
myself," Sarah said, bugging out her eyes and wagging her tongue as if she was
insane.

Those who didn't know her that well were taken aback, but Jimmy breathed
a sigh of relief.

"Now *that's* the Sarah I'm used to," he assured the others.

Site #1 already had three times the number of workers than had been called
for in the original plan. Octagon had intentionally skimped on the personnel,
fearing they would have to pay their salaries, but volunteers were pouring in
from around the country. However, these were not just people with good
intentions and a shovel, these were professionals with international credentials.
Hands that had that dug into the soil of Troy, the cities of the Incas, and the
sands of Egypt, now delved into the rich Virginia earth.

Their efforts were concentrated on the two nodes that Ricky and his team had marked out, which indeed corresponded with the two ends of the bridge once known as Wegman's Crossing. No one seemed to care that they were following plans laid out by ghost hunters, because they were getting positive results—which unfortunately translated into human remains. The color guards were being kept very busy.

The multi-media display center in the atrium was quietly dismantled and carted away. While in theory it sounded like a great idea to let people know about the up-to-the-minute details of the scientific and patriotic project, in practice it was rapidly becoming a high-tech tote board for the rising body count. In its place, there was a small sign with a vague statement about an ongoing project, and a three-inch American flag.

By 1pm, the "dirt people"—as they had been dubbed, to differentiate them from the construction workers and ghost hunters—were ready to begin on Site #2. Sarah was there, and raring to go. She was feeling much better, not from the one Bloody Mary she had at breakfast, but due to the cathartic experience of telling her story to the other ghost hunters. Just having one sympathetic ear to share the burden of these paranormal nightmares helped, so a group of like-mined people was all the medicine she needed. Of course, those who heard the tale of the saw-wielding surgeon and possessed man would have trouble sleeping for weeks, but it was always better to know what you might be up against.

Sarah was once again impressed by the efficiency and professionalism of the dirt people. Although most of them had never met, they meshed together and worked like a well-oiled machine. Granted, some of the grad students fresh out of libraries and classrooms were not accustomed to actually getting their hands dirty, and a few had turned green on occasion at Site #1 (especially when uncovering skulls), but they learned quickly and got the job done.

No one was sure what to expect at Site #2. Would there be tangled masses of bones like Site #1? Would there be anything at all? Would the ground be soft and pliable, or would they strike a vein of that legendary Virginia muck that used to swallow wagon wheels and soldiers' boots?

Dr. Henkel—cleaned up and rested—held a brief meeting with the dirt people to discuss what he had found years earlier. It had been decided to first try to locate the old chimney and work out from there. Although conditions weren't ideal, they brought in some ground penetrating radar equipment that would give a fairly accurate outline of any solid structures below them. At lower frequencies, the equipment could provide substantial detail on objects just a few feet below the surface. Higher frequencies could penetrate as much as sixty feet down, with substantially less detail, but no one wanted to even consider digging to that kind of depth. As parts of the Wegman's Crossing area were known to have seasonal floods that left heavy deposits of silt, the hope was that most the structure might actually be intact, buried, and preserved under generations of deposits—and not too far under the surface.

"No, the house burned down after the battle," Sarah plainly stated, as if reading from a travel brochure.

Everyone looked at her, then glanced at their notes to see if there was something they had missed, and Sarah suddenly felt rather self-conscious about blurting out knowledge a dead man had imparted to her.

"Sarah, why do you say that?" Henkel asked, curious, but not judgmental. "We did find the jawbone in very dark soil, which could have contained ash, but after all, it was near the chimney."

"Trust me on this one," she said, avoiding eye contact with the others, many of whom were no doubt rolling their eyes as she spoke. "I think it burned down after the battle, and there were a lot of wounded men packed inside at the time. You're going to have to go deep for this one. You're going to have to go deep to get them all."

There were a few audible snickers from a group of graduate students who had just arrived on the scene, but silence quickly descended when Dr. Carl Henkel glared at them with the look that even made HMO administrators tremble.

"Might I take a moment to remind everyone here that none of this would be happening if it was not for the extraordinary efforts of Ms. Brooks," Henkel began, with fire in his eyes that appeared more dangerous than an acetylene torch. "All of those men recovered from Site #1 would still be laying underneath SUVs and minivans, and probably would have remained there for eternity. And just this morning, she risked her life to help an injured worker, so I suggest you show her proper respect or *get the hell out of here!*"

The withering rebuke had the desired sobering effect, and even resulted in several apologies being offered. Sarah was outwardly gracious about the whole thing, but she still would have enjoyed kicking a few of them in the shins with her steel-toed work boots. When the crowd dispersed, Sarah quietly thanked Carl for his eloquent defense.

"Don't mention it. Anyway, some of those kids remind me of those damned med students who waltz into the hospital and think they know everything. And by the way, do I want to know *why* you think Wegman's house burned down?"

"No, you do not. And you also do not want to know about the barn burning, trapping the doctor and more wounded men," she said with a wink.

"I must admit that part of me would still take pleasure in finding that you're wrong, but you have taught me this past week to keep my mouth shut before I stick my foot too deeply into it."

"Why thank you, Doctor, that's one of the nicest things anyone's ever said to me."

While the survey team walked slowly back and forth with the ground penetrating radar, Sarah checked on the other sites. Fortunately, no more large piles of bones had been uncovered at Site#1, but there were still plenty of remains and artifacts scattered in and around the nodes. The accident investigation continued into the afternoon at Site #3, but no one was too upset to learn that work would not resume until the following morning. It had been an unsettling incident to say the least, and time away from the site was welcome by one and all.

Of course, nobody even thought about going home, and construction workers, ghost hunters, and dirt people offered to pitch in wherever they were needed at the other sites. Sarah was more than happy to be relieved of monitoring duty, so she could get her hands in the soil. This was so much more than a job. This was personal.

Preliminary results of the radar revealed a roughly rectangular structure—possibly the foundation of the house. There were many other smaller objects inside the rectangle, but the results were not definitive, and no one was prepared to go on record that these were human remains.

Octagon's bulldozers had done some site preparation here prior to construction, which essentially translated into several feet of dirt to level the area. This meant they had to remove an enormous volume of soil just to reach the original ground level where Henkel found the chimney. To facilitate this process, they brought in small earthmovers that just made it through the corridors. Sarah thought the mini-movers looked like one of those Japanese scale models out of a Godzilla movie, but when these mighty midgets started to work they instantly gained her respect.

Even with this mechanized division, it was labor-intensive work, and noisy, as well. All of the dirt needed to be sifted before being dumped into trucks, and experts had to constantly inspect the ground for any indication that it was time to work by hand. In the late afternoon the din suddenly ceased, as someone announced he found something.

There was a flurry of activity near the center of the large room, and after what seemed to be an eternity, there came an announcement.

"It's the chimney!"

Dr. Henkel was visibly misty-eyed. After so many years he was finally back where he had started—only this time everything was different. This time, they would uncover the truth.

The earthmovers were pulled back to the perimeter of the room, and the dirt people concentrated in the middle. The stones were rapidly being exposed, and it was soon discovered that this was not the top of a two-story chimney. Part of it had apparently collapsed at some point, and while they could not say how many feet had fallen, this was very good news. It meant the foundation was closer to the surface, perhaps as many as ten feet closer than they had expected. That also meant that if any of the first floor of the house existed, they should begin to see signs very soon.

Sarah had taken a break from her stint with the dirt people to sit with Jimmy for a while. The monitoring equipment was very quiet.

"This is awfully suspicious, don't you think?" Jimmy asked.

"Oh, I don't know. Maybe the fireworks are over. I'm prepared to be optimistic at this point. Those men wanted our attention so they could be found, and we are certainly getting close," Sarah replied, finally allowing herself the luxury of picturing light at the end of the tunnel.

"You mean that's it? The fun is over?" he said with obvious disappointment.

"Fun? Is that what we've been having? How come no one told me?" she said as if she hadn't a clue what he meant, although knowing full well that there was always some feeling of a letdown after an exciting case. A "post-paranormal depression" as she called it. "Look, if you're bored, you can always go back to school. Or I could arrange to have a cart run over you."

"No thank you, and I never said I was bored," Jimmy said as if that was the end of the discussion.

Sarah was considering finding a cozy corner somewhere to curl up for a quick nap, but she heard her name being called from inside the room. A few seconds later, Carl stuck his head into the corridor, caught sight of her and said one word.

"Ash!"

"What did he call you?" Jimmy laughed, as he followed Sarah to see what all the excitement was about.

The leaders of the dirt people were leaning over a folding table scattered with plastic sample bags. They straightened up when Sarah walked over, and Dr. Jacobs, from the university, unceremoniously tossed one of the bags to her. Catching it, she held it up toward a bright work light and saw that the contents were almost black.

"At first we thought this charred material was simply from the chimney, but we now see it is quite pervasive across the site," Dr. Jacobs said, clearly irritated that the evidence pointed to a fire. Although he wasn't one of the people who had snickered, he clearly was not one of her fans, either. "Any other voodoo predictions for us, Ms. Brooks?"

Henkel was about to speak when Sarah grabbed his arm and shook her head.

"It's a good thing you smiled when you said that, Dr. Jacobs, or I would have been tempted to call upon some of my demon helpers to teach you a lesson," Sarah said, with absolutely no hint of a smile. The professor sort of chuckled, but he was not completely sure it was a joke.

"You promised you wouldn't do that anymore," Jimmy said in a loud whisper, making sure everyone heard.

"What's the matter, Jacobs, you're looking a little pale—but maybe that's just the contrast between you and all this black ash from the fire that brought down the Wegman house," Sarah said, delivering the *coup de grâce*.

It was Henkel's turn to snicker.

Stakes were set up to roughly mark the suspected foundation line, and dozens of workers with brushes and hand tools descended inside the perimeter. Very quickly, pieces of old windowpanes began surfacing. There were also various latches and hinges that the metal detectors located, some with fragments of charred wood still attached.

Within minutes, every one of the dirt people—of whom Sarah was one—had blackened hands, smudges on their faces and filthy clothes. Being in actual contact with the remnants of a fire that took so many lives was something of a psychic overload for Sarah, but it was also like an addictive substance. She needed to be there, she had to be there. She must reconnect with these men...

"Ms. Brooks, isn't that...isn't that a hand?" one of the grad students working just a few feet from her asked, as he looked up to see her slowly running her fingertips back and forth over several skeletal digits protruding from the black earth. "Shouldn't you tell someone?"

Sarah looked at the young man with a puzzled expression, and couldn't understand what he was talking about. Then she looked down and saw that she was stroking a bony hand as if comforting a dying friend. She had no recollection of uncovering the remains, and no idea how long she had been caressing the fleshless fingers.

"I...I was just trying to clean them off a little more...uh, to be certain of what they were," she stammered, pulling her hand back and rubbing some warmth into it. "Over here! I found something over here!"

Henkel and Dr. Jacobs rushed over, and the circle of dirt people contracted around the find.

"Looks like you've found the first one, Sarah," Henkel said, helping her to her feet.

"But certainly not the last," she replied, not caring if anyone thought it was a voodoo prediction.

"I'm sure you're right," Dr. Jacobs said to everyone's surprise, until he added, "We've been analyzing more of the radar data. Looks like there *were* a lot of men in here. A *lot* of men."

"Well then, I had better step aside and let the professionals do their work," Sarah said, as everyone presumed she was being gracious by acknowledging Jacob's staff's expertise.

In reality, Sarah was considerably shaken by the bone-caressing episode. As hard as she tried, she could not remember uncovering the remains, and had no idea where her mind had been until the student spoke to her. This had gone beyond personal, it was obsessive—bordering on possession—and she needed to step away.

Part of her wanted to leave, to run to some clean, white sandy beach, or a cold, fresh mountain lake. But she knew she had to stay close to this blackened graveyard, this seemingly endless pit of death and despair. So many soldiers had died on this spot...so much pain...so much suffering...

"You look like hell," Sheriff Davis said as Sarah unlocked her car.

"Thanks so much for noticing," Sarah replied, glancing at her reflection in the side view mirror to find that she resembled something out of a minstrel show of the damned.

"Just dropped by to let you know that Allan Johnson will be okay."

"Well, that's one piece of good news."

"He still doesn't remember falling, or threatening anyone with a torch. The doctors are chalking it up to shock."

"Yeah, there's a lot of that going around. Well, at least it will save time filling out the 'Possessed by Spirits' forms for the insurance company," Sarah quipped, feeling better just talking to Beau. "Now if you will excuse me, this ghost hunter needs to go off duty for a while."

Sarah got into her car and put down the windows so she would be able to get as much fresh air into her lungs as she could. To her surprise, as she leaned out to say goodbye, Beau leaned down and kissed her softly on the lips.

"Take care of yourself, Sarah," he said, and only then thought to look to see if anyone was watching. Fortunately, no one had noticed the brief, tender moment between the sheriff and the ghost hunter.

Beyond any underlying passion, it was just so comforting to feel the touch of the living again. Still feeling the need to reconnect with life, when Sarah got back to her room, she decided to call her parents. There's nothing that can ever match the reality check of speaking to your mother—for better or for worse! But it was good to talk to people who cared about her, and despite all the hoopla and coverage on the national news, still wanted to know if she was eating right, taking her vitamins, and making sure she wasn't straining her eyes with all those computer screens.

She then made her daily call to the eminent and irreverent Dr. Tony Marchand, who wanted to be kept abreast of everything that happened, both archaeologically and paranormally. He in turn, kept Senator Crandall apprised of the situation. The senator then spoke to the Governor of Virginia.

As Sarah knew her words would travel down the information pipeline, she made sure to give credit where it was due. That usually resulted in praising the merits of the highly competent and savvy Sheriff of Brandon County. When Lela gave her the skinny on Beau, she mentioned his political aspirations, so it wouldn't hurt for the governor to know that there was a talented civil servant ready, willing, and able to work for the greater good of the Commonwealth of Virginia, and further his own career in the process.

She also returned a call from Roger Cameron at the *D.C. Herald*, who had finally convinced his editor that this was a story bigger than the sewers. She had promised him an exclusive, and she delivered, although reserving the juiciest details for the book she would write. It was good to go over her experiences to put everything in perspective. Ten days ago she barely knew anything about Wegman's Crossing. Since then, the events had been so overwhelming, she had begun to feel as if this was her entire life, but it wasn't much more than a week. And in another week, it might all be behind her.

At 6pm, she crawled into bed, curled up into the fetal position and hoped to put everything behind her, for at least a few blessed, unconscious hours.

Chapter 15

Lela Reynolds had become the de facto manager of Wegman's Crossing Shopping and Recreation Center. Although previously, anyone who wanted something done would go to her over Fink anyway, now she sat in the big chair in the big office. As long as she kept the fiber optics inside the desk turned off, it wasn't such a bad arrangement. Of course, if she did get the chance to move in permanently, anything that Fink ever touched would have to be removed, including the paisley carpeting that made her dizzy every time she looked down.

However, before she ordered new business cards, there were a few hurdles to overcome first. For instance, the fate of the entire center was in question. Would storeowners pull out as they had threatened? Would shoppers ever return? Would lawsuits bury everything under debt thicker than concrete?

As dark as the outlook appeared, Lela chose to ride the new wave of optimism that flowed through the center. Even though sales figures were so low that ground penetrating radar would have trouble finding them, she believed that the recovery of the human remains was such a positive and noble endeavor that those involved would be rewarded. Of course, at this point she would be happy to settle for simply not being punished any longer for concealing the truth.

At 6am on Thursday morning, digging began at Site #3. It was not long before they encountered a blackened layer similar to that at Site #2. There had clearly been a fire, and the rusted and charred farm implements and tools found by the metal detectors indicated that it was indeed a barn that had burned. There were also a few more disturbing metallic finds—objects too small and delicate to be farm tools. Though badly degraded, one of the experts pronounced these pieces to be surgeon's instruments. There was a general feeling of queasiness among the workers when they heard the news. This would be an ugly recovery scene.

Site #2 had recovered approximately two dozen sets of remains during the night. The hand that Sarah had uncovered was just the tip of a boneyard nightmare. Almost every square foot of the area within the foundation lines contained some piece of a human body, as if that floor of the house was literally filled wall to wall with people when it burned.

The find did not contradict known history. After a battle, nearby houses became temporary field hospitals, and the wounded would cover every bed, table, sofa, and chair. When the furniture was filled, helpless men would be lined up in the hallways and on any available section of floor. There were accounts of homeowners complaining that every inch of their carpeting and wood flooring was stained with blood.

At Site #2, the blood was gone, but the skeletons remained. As work progressed, someone commented that it would be impossible the walk across the site without stepping on a bone. Equally disturbing, was the condition of the bones. Many were splintered from gunshots. Several skulls had remnants of burned hair still stuck to them. Foot and hand bones were blackened by fire. As the horrible scene was slowly revealed, the thought of these wounded men lying there, unable to move as the fire consumed them, was too much for a few of the diggers, and they asked to be reassigned to a support team.

Site #1 had the remains and artifacts cleared from the majority of its exposed surface. They were going to have to tear up more blacktop on either end of the nodes, as a few sets of remains extended farther out than the original perimeter. Due to the tangle of bones at the base of one of the bridge supports, an exact number had yet to be determined, but the total count for the site was also over twenty lost lives.

A fourth site was scheduled for excavation—the spot where Andy's team had encountered the wispy blue spirits. Though it was only a small section of a corridor that would be torn up, it would create a big problem with people and equipment trying to pass by. It was decided to punch a hole in an adjacent wall to create a bypass. Lela had approved the idea. After all, what were a few more holes at this point?

Sarah woke up and looked at the bold red numbers on the clock. They read "6:08", and it was hard to believe she had only been asleep for eight minutes. Then she noticed the "AM," and was stunned to realize that she had slept for twelve hours and eight minutes. It was like waking up on the wrong side of a time warp, and she immediately reached for her cell phone to find out what she had missed.

"Jimmy, why the hell did you let me sleep so long? Is everything okay?"

"Everyone agreed to leave you alone so you could get some rest. Everything's under control, don't worry, we can handle it."

"Where are you?"

"I'm at our site and there's no problems. Take your time getting here, okay?"

Her natural inclination was to jump into her clothes and rush to the center, but her stomach had other plans. Taking the time for a hefty breakfast, she did not regret paying attention to her body for a change. She even spent a few minutes updating her website to keep her anxious fans satisfied, for the moment. One man had actually suggested she wear a wireless webcam on her head so they could have live streaming video of her every move at the center, so she knew any satisfaction in this case would be short-lived.

"Well, you're looking human again!" Ricky said, greeting her as she pulled into the parking garage.

He gave her a full report on his site, and let her know that the work at Site #4 would be commencing. The two ghost hunters stood on the edge of the enormous hole in the pavement as he explained in detail what had been found and where.

On the paranormal end, there had been a few tense moments—chilling air masses, a few reports of people feeling as if they had been touched—but the dirt people and construction workers were beginning to take it all in stride. A few people needed to take extended breaks, and one woman screamed, twice, but they all knew the importance of what they were doing and stuck to their trowels.

Sarah's breath caught in her throat when she entered the room for Site #2. When she left, there had been a few finger bones sticking out of the black dirt. Now there was a sea of white. Skulls, arms, legs, all scattered the length and breadth of the pit like some grotesque game of pick-up-sticks.

"They're everywhere," Jimmy said, stating the obvious, but then adding, "and they think that's only the first layer."

Dr. Jacobs approached her, although she didn't recognize him until he spoke. His face was as black as a coal miner's, and he had clearly not slept—or washed—since she had left.

"Ms. Brooks, it looks as though this was the second floor of the house. It most likely collapsed onto the first floor during the fire, and we believe there may be another layer of remains under this," he informed her without any snide remarks. He was too overwhelmed and way too tired to be combative. Although he wasn't tired enough to openly concede that she had been absolutely correct, the knowledge of it also made him somewhat more accepting of her and her unique methods.

"When you reach the cellar, I need to be there, please," Sarah said, hoping she would not need to explain further.

"Sure, okay, but that's going to take a while," he replied, lifting his glasses so he could rub his bloodshot eyes. "I'll let my people know. I need to leave for a while now."

The thousand-yard stare and shuffling footsteps Dr. Jacobs exhibited were becoming all too familiar sights at Wegman's Center. Even the people with reputedly tough skins were seen wiping away tears and getting choked up as they tried to speak. There was no way for any human being to stand in the midst of this scene of pain and death and not be moved.

The most poignant moment came about noon, when a distinguished professor of archaeology emerged from the pit openly weeping. She held something tightly between her hands and walked over to the table where remains and artifacts were given a cursory examination, logged in, boxed and labeled.

"What do you have, Agnes, remains or an artifact?" one of the men seated at the table gently asked her, as everyone within earshot fell silent.

"Both," she replied between sobs, but then straightened up and spoke clearly and succinctly. "From grid B3. There are phalanges and metacarpals…and a dag, possibly spouse."

In layman's terms, Agnes had found the bones of a man's hand still holding a daguerreotype—an early photograph on metal—of his wife or sweetheart, which he had been clutching as he died. No one spoke as Agnes carefully placed the little bones and the picture case on the table. A conservator wearing gloves took up the leather-bound case that had hardened in the earth, protecting the precious image inside. Slowly opening it, she gasped at the sharp image of the pretty young woman who looked back at her from across a century and a half of time.

The woman in the photograph, no doubt posing in her finest dress with its wide skirt, with ribbons in her hair, and with the faintest blush of hand-applied pink coloring to her cheeks, never knew the fate of the man she loved. While he breathed his last holding her picture, she was at home wondering when she would next hear news of him. The weeks and months passed, the war was over, and still there was no word. How long did she live with that secret pain? Had that pretty young face grown aged and wrinkled with grief, and had the thick locks of dark hair turned thin and white as time passed? How many years, how many decades did she go on, not knowing what fate had befallen him?

Work stopped at Site #2, as everyone came to look at the photograph. It was like a funeral procession passing by the table. The picture of the smiling woman lying next to the hand and finger bones was too much to bear for many of them. The supervisor of the site immediately announced a mandatory lunch break. No exceptions.

"Go outside, sit in the sunshine, have an ice cream sundae," he added over the loud speaker as people began filing out. "And don't come back until you're sure you're ready."

Sarah was still full from the substantial breakfast, so she went to see how things were going at Site #4. As she approached the corridor from a side hallway, she was surprised that there weren't the deafening sounds of jackhammers and men shouting. Turning the corner, she found that there were a handful of construction workers standing together about fifteen feet from the cordoned off section. Only a few square yards of concrete had been removed. Andy stood next to the men trying to explain something using expressive hand gestures.

"Hey, Sarah, I'm glad you're here," Andy said, waving her over. "Tell these guys it's okay. Yeah, we just heard a few bizarre sounds before, but I'm trying to tell them there's probably only four bodies here, and when their spirits appeared to us, none of them were threatening."

Sarah recognized a couple of the men from Site #3, who had been there when their co-worker was injured, and then threatened to kill them. They were evidently not happy about the prospect of stirring up any more trouble for themselves, and it wasn't helping matters that Andy was explaining all about the four wispy entities and the flurry of paranormal activity he had encountered.

"I heard that Al is doing just fine," Sarah began her end-around run as the men all expressed their relief and good wishes. "It was kind of weird what happened to him, but hell, if I had a foot of rebar sticking out of my leg, I would go crazy, too."

"So…it wasn't a ghost that hurt him?" one of the men asked sheepishly.

"It was not a ghost that hurt him," Sarah stated with confidence. Of course, she was not about to complete the statement by adding that it was only after he was hurt that she believed he was possessed by the spirit of the wounded soldier and then saw the apparition of the doctor who wanted to cut off his legs. That much information might be just be a bit counterproductive.

"So, none of these spooks here are angry at us?" another man asked, already feeling foolish about their reluctance to work because of a few strange noises.

"I'll tell you what I think," Sarah said, intentionally drawing closer, as if about to disclose a secret. "I think all the unusual things that have gone on in this place happened because these soldiers *wanted* to be found. They were pissed at Octagon for putting a damn shopping center on top of them. I think the only thing that would get them upset now, is if they *weren't* discovered and dug up."

"So, like you mean, they could get mad at us if for just standing around here, not working?" a third man said, as light dawned.

"What do you think?" Sarah asked, sidestepping to let the decision come from them.

"I think we had better do our jobs," the first man declared, as the others heartily agreed.

As the jackhammers roared into action, Sarah pulled Andy aside.

"Do you want me to stay with them," she asked. "It's not fair that you keep getting the tough assignments."

"No, I'm fine. I guess these guys are just a little jumpier than I thought," Andy replied. Of course, he was still considerably jumpy from the accident, and did not want a repeat of the incident on his watch, but he still had the brains and grit to see it through.

"Good enough. Just give me a buzz when our four friends are uncovered."

After lunch, every member of the Site #2 team came back on schedule and ready to work. It was a great credit to their professionalism, and yet another affirmation of the healing powers of sunlight and ice cream. By the end of the day shift, the first layer of remains had been removed, and the grisly second harvest was coming to light.

The first floor of farmer Wegman's house had also been filled wall to wall with wounded men. As both Union and Confederate artifacts were turning up, it looked as if despite having just tried to kill one another in battle, they lay side by side once the fighting was over. And side by side, they died.

Jimmy and a mixed group of ghost hunters, construction workers, and dirt people had decided to go to the infamous all-you-can-eat barbeque place again— with promises not to get drunk this time—but Sarah felt the need to stick by the center. Site #3 was continuing to have problems, with sporadic spikes in paranormal activity preceding each event. Fortunately, there were no more serious injuries, but there was just enough going on to make everyone uncomfortable, and unproductive.

Lights flickered, equipment failed, voices were heard, and several people swore that someone had brushed against them. Others complained of sudden and severe pains in their arms, legs, and abdomens. A few had to be helped out of the room, and when they left the site, they felt fine. These pains were being explained away as muscle cramps from dehydration and fatigue, but Sarah knew this wasn't something that Gatorade would fix.

Consulting with the three ghost hunters on duty, they decided to clear the site for a more thorough investigation. As soon as all the workers left, the lights and equipment were turned off and the place became as dark and silent as the grave. While Sarah used The Eyes, the others employed their full repertoire of instruments to try to isolate any pockets of particularly strong activity.

The general feeling inside the room was most unsettling. It was a combination of fear and despair that was so potent it was difficult to concentrate. The four ghost hunters were repeatedly drawn to two specific sites, both by their instruments and their intuition. At one of the spots near the back wall, The Eyes revealed a swirl of faint shimmering points of light. Sarah had never seen anything quite like it before. It was reminiscent of shaking a snow globe filled with sparkles. This spot was also icy cold and within an eight-foot radius it produced a nauseating feeling. All indications were that many restless souls were concentrated there, but it did not make sense that so many would be in such a relatively small area.

The other targeted spot was near the center of the room. This area was shaped roughly like a ten-foot square, and just passing through it made one woozy. One of the ghost hunters had a panic attack at that spot, and he had to hand his instruments to his friend and run outside. Whatever was here was extremely agitated, and needed to be dealt with quickly.

"The two of you feel like getting your hands dirty?" Sarah asked the man and woman who remained. With some reluctance, they agreed. Sarah then contacted the supervisor for the site and asked if she would return with half a dozen volunteers. "It's going to be very intense, make sure they know that."

A few minutes later, the supervisor returned with four men and two women, all of whom looked scared, but determined. As the lights were turned on just in the center of the room, Sarah tried to explain the situation.

"We need to work fast. There is a heavy residue of emotions here, so it's not going to be easy. You're going to feel all kinds of things, but whatever you experience, just keep telling yourself it's not *your* thoughts and feelings. It's like picking up a TV broadcast in your head. If you have to leave, okay, but let's try to stick together and stick it out."

"What are we looking for?" the supervisor asked. "Why is this place so different?"

"I'm not exactly sure, but I have my suspicions," Sarah said, weighing the option of full disclosure, then deciding the crew was freaked out enough. "Let's just say this spot may hold the key to the activity in this area of the center."

Three camcorders were set up on tripods around the spot, and one was attached to a pipe on the ceiling to produce a visual record of their work. Sarah had a feeling that what was about to happen would not make for an enjoyable home movie.

The group of ten archaeologists, students, and ghost hunters spread out along the perimeter of the square, got down on their hands and knees and started digging with trowels. Almost immediately, one of the female grad students stopped to look behind her.

"What's wrong?" the supervisor asked.

"I thought someone tapped me on the back," she replied wide-eyed.

"There's no one there, is there? It's just your imagination, so keep digging," the supervisor replied curtly, with the added authority of being the girl's graduate program advisor.

Sarah's skin was crawling, there were shooting pains throughout her body, and she could "hear" screaming in her head. She glanced at the other's faces, and it was obvious they were all experiencing something similarly unpleasant.

"Got something!" the professor across from her declared.

A hint of white appeared in the black earth, and digging intensified, as did the feelings. The girl who had been tapped threw down her trowel and started digging frantically with her hands. The man next to her did the same thing.

"It helps, using your hands helps," the man yelled, sweating profusely and panting.

As Sarah felt as though she was about to do some of her own screaming, she decided to toss her trowel and claw at the ground with her fingernails. In a way it eased the pains wracking her body, but it also increased the feelings of desperation and anxiety. Soon all ten adult professionals were scraping at the dirt with their bare hands in a frenzy akin to the panic of discovering you had just been buried alive.

Terrible scenes raced through Sarah's mind, scenes of blood and gore, and excruciating torture. The pain was unbearable, and there was nowhere to run, people were holding her down on a table...the pain...the pain...the awful pain...

"It's a femur. Oh God, it's only *part* of a femur!" the professor exclaimed in horror, as he pushed away the last bits of dirt to reveal the leg bone that had been cleanly cut a few inches above where it should have joined the knee.

Two people got up to vomit, but came right back and began digging again. More bones surfaced, but it was a confusing tangle of ribs, as if two sets of remains were pressed together. There were fragments of burned wooden beams, two skulls, bits of fabric.

"Oh crap, look at this," the supervisor said, scraping dirt from between the jaws of one of the skulls. She pulled out a crushed lead bullet, still bearing the clear impressions of the teeth that had clenched down on it as the man's leg was being sawed off—without anesthesia.

The female grad student fainted head first onto the exposed rib cages. Two men lifted her up and set her down a few feet away and hurried back to their digging. Sarah and the fellow ghost hunter next to her were exposing another leg; only this one was complete—in a manner of speaking. The bones around the knee joint were shattered, and the femur showed the same signs of being cut, only the job hadn't been completed. The bone had only been half-sawed.

"Damn. Goddamn it!" Sarah yelled, tears in her eyes, using every fiber of nerve to hold her ground. "Where's the saw? Where's the goddamned saw? It has to be here somewhere!"

Everyone stopped for a moment and stared at her as if she had lost her mind. It was not hard to believe, because everybody was feeling the effects of the maelstrom of paranormal activity. It was as if insanity had suddenly descended upon them all. One of the male grad students jumped up, screamed, and ran from the room.

The supervisor pawed at the sweat and grime on her face and in her eyes and shouted, "What are you talking about? What the hell are you talking about?"

"I need the goddamned saw, can't you see?" Sarah yelled in a rage she could barely contain. "Are you all blind? The operation was never finished! These two sets of remains together here, this is the doctor on top of a soldier. He was cutting his leg off when the barn collapsed from the fire. Find that fucking saw so I can finish the operation, goddamn it!"

There was a second that seemed like an eternity as their half-crazed minds tried to process their feelings, the sight of the mass of bones, the shouted command to find the saw, to try to make any sense out of anything at all. But ultimately it didn't matter, it was something they had to do, and they had to do it now to stop the pain!

"I've got something, something metal," one of the women screamed, as three other diggers practically knocked her over to claw at the buried object.

"Hurry, hurry, faster!" Sarah yelled, unsure if she could retain consciousness long enough to complete the one hundred and forty-year-old operation.

Several hands yanked a badly corroded saw blade with a bent handle out of the dirt and tossed it to Sarah.

"Do it! Do it now! Cut him!" the supervisor screamed like a mad woman.

Sarah clasped the useless blade in her fist and pounded at the half-sawed femur. Her hand started bleeding, but she kept pounding at it with all her strength until a sickening crack signaled that the leg had finally been amputated.

Someone grabbed one of the lower leg bones and threw it as far as he could, shouting, "There, it's done. See, it's over! Now leave us alone. For God's sake, leave us alone…"

The man sank to his knees sobbing. Nobody else moved, except for the heaving motions created by their own breathing.

Sarah felt as though she had just awakened from a nightmare. Looking down, she saw her own blood running along the blade of the saw that had been wet with the blood of a hundred men. It was like some final bonding, a symbolic gesture that irrevocably linked her to the men who fought and died at Wegman's Crossing in 1864. In a way, she felt honored. In a way, she was now one of them.

"Is it over?" came a thin voice in the darkness. "What happened?"

The female grad student had regained consciousness and walked on shaky legs to the site of the former operating table.

The supervisor, embarrassed by her behavior, tried to casually readjust the clumps of hair that had fallen out from under her hat, and then she spoke calmly, "Yes, I believe it's over, now. Isn't it, Ms. Brooks?"

"God, I hope so," Sarah said, smiling through her tears. "You all did good, damn good. Of course, I don't think any of us will win any historic preservation awards, but I believe it served its purpose."

A few managed to laugh, but it was like the nervous laughter of people who had just survived a plane crash.

"Can we leave now?" someone asked, as all eyes turned hopefully to Sarah.

"There's another spot…but not like this one," she quickly added.

"Aw, hell, let's go for it," the female grad student said, retrieving her trowel. "Point the way."

"What is it this time?" the supervisor asked with a blank expression, still suffering the effects of the ordeal. "More soldiers being operated on?"

"No, not quite," Sarah said, deciding to come clean this time. "I think it's the aftermath of the operations."

As the nine remaining members of the archaeological SWAT team descended on the second spot, it quickly became evident what she meant. They soon uncovered a pile of hands, feet, arms and legs, all cleanly cut with the surgeon's saw. This was the amputated limb pile, where the buckets filled with the freshly cut pieces of soldiers were dumped out a window of the barn until the grisly stack reached the level of the window.

"I bet the soldier's other leg is here," the man who had tossed the bone said softly. He had retrieved that bone, and then made a silent promise to find the other leg so that the soldier could be buried again as a complete man.

When it appeared as if the tormenting spirits had at least granted them a temporary respite, the supervisor called for the rest of the Site #3 crew to return. But first, the ten demon diggers of the surgery site all agreed to tell the basic story of what they had just experienced, but would leave out the details that could be used to certify them as temporarily insane. Sarah also agreed to take the videotapes for now and "misplace" them, at least until the project was completed. There was no sense fueling already overactive imaginations, or any realistic fears.

As Sarah was getting back to the hotel, Jimmy was just being dropped off from the barbeque dinner.

"Hey, Sarah, you hungry? I brought some leftovers," he said pointing to a bulging doggy bag.

"No thanks!" she replied, holding up both hands. "I've had enough ribs for one night."

"You did? Wait a minute…there's a story here, isn't there? Did I miss something?"

"Well, remember when I said I thought the fireworks might be over?"

"Yeah? What happened?"

"Something went boom."

All four sites were blessedly quiet on Friday. While remains continued to be uncovered at Sites #2, 3 and 4 (where only four soldiers appeared to have died—no surprise), the parking garage appeared to have yielded its last victims. No one was disappointed. There were still plenty of Minié balls and various artifacts, but the lack of bones was perfectly acceptable. Twenty-seven sets of human remains were more than enough.

Everyone had been working around the clock, as it was the general understanding that Octagon wanted to put the pavement and concrete back and return things to normal as soon as possible. Then word began circulating that Chivington had other ideas. His plan was to build a replica of the Wegman's Crossing bridge right there in the garage, on its original site, and turn it into a tourist attraction.

Although it wasn't a bad idea, it was the motive that sparked the press to begin crucifying the allegedly noble CEO. He had claimed that the excavation project was being undertaken because "it was the right thing to do." In reality, it was now obvious that it was because it would ultimately be the profitable thing to do. His plans also extended to the site of the house and barn, although full reconstructions would not be possible, as that would entail knocking out part of the first floor. At these sites, just the foundations and some of the artifacts would be displayed. Then, of course, there was the proposed National Cemetery, conveniently located adjacent to the Wegman's Center parking lot.

There was some grumbling about commercialism, and exploitation of American soldiers, but as Chivington had asked the National Parks system to operate the sites and retain any profits, there were no real objections. It was clear he was hoping that everyone who came for the history would stay for the shopping and dining, but it was better than the alternative of burying everything again.

There were other plans in the works. However, these had nothing to do with profit or tourism. Families who believed that their ancestors might have died at the Battle of Wegman's Crossing were coming forward demanding that DNA testing be performed on the remains. Such testing would be time consuming, and expensive, and no one was stepping up to the plate to offer that kind of funding. As thousands of men from both the north and south had been lost during the campaigns throughout this area, it would be impossible to locate and test descendants of all of them. They needed some way to narrow the field, but how could they find any clue as to the identities of the men who died here?

At Site #2 on Saturday morning, the last remains from the first floor of the house had been recovered. Test holes were being dug into what they assumed was the basement level, but nothing but a few old bottles and household items were found. Sarah was growing impatient, pacing back and forth along the edge of the pit. Edward was still down there, with at least one other man, why couldn't they find him? Could her mind have been playing tricks on her? Were all the vivid memories she had experienced been part of some type of stress-induced hallucination?

"Ms. Brooks, there doesn't seem to be anything else down there," Dr. Jacobs informed her, with the slightest hint of a smirk, hoping she was dead wrong about this one. "We keep hitting rocks, which must be the floor of the cellar."

"Please, keep digging," Sarah asked humbly.

"We have the rest of this room to work on, and I don't see any reason to continue to waste manpower on an empty cellar," he declared, almost giddy in his triumph.

"Excuse me, Dr. Jacobs," Gary, one of the male grad students began, "but I've been examining the stonework at the different sites."

"So?" Jacobs replied with obvious irritation.

"Well, based on the dimensions of the bridge supports, the barn foundation, and the chimney of this house, it looks like Wegman believed in heavy-duty stonework," the young man continued, not self-assured enough to look the site director in the eye as he was about to contradict him, and not daring to look at Sarah as he was one of the people who had openly laughed at her the first day.

"So, what's your point, Gary?" Jacobs asked, his short fuse already approaching the end.

"From what I can see of the foundation of this house, it just doesn't add up. I mean, it's too small, and you think he would make his house the sturdiest thing," he stated with growing confidence.

"Then you think the stones there are not from the floor of the cellar?" Sarah asked, brightening with renewed hope.

"No, ma'am. Houses from this time period in this area usually had dirt floor cellars. I think what we are looking at is the upper parts of the foundation which collapsed inward," he concluded as if completing his dissertation.

Henkel and two other archaeologists overheard the last part of the conversation and came over to discuss the possibility. Jacobs was forced to douse his fuse in the presence of distinguished colleagues, and finally agreed that it was a plausible scenario. Reluctantly, he gave the order to start removing some of the stones.

Several brawny construction workers were called in to pry the stones loose and heft them out of the pit. Sarah grew increasingly anxious with each rock that was removed, as nothing but dirt seemed to be underneath.

Come on, Edward, I know you're here, she said to herself. *Where are you? For God's sake where are you?*

When about half of the exposed stones had been removed from the center and nothing was found, Jacobs announced that he was pulling the plug on the operation. Sarah closed her eyes and tried to recall the scenes that the face in the membrane had thrust into her mind. It was a cellar, he was with at least one other man, his friend. He had dragged his friend inside through some kind of storm door, down a few steps.

"The back of the house!" Sarah suddenly said out loud, jumping into the pit. "Where's the back of the house? Did you find any stairs?"

"Over here!" Gary replied, also jumping down, and hurrying over to a bulge in the foundation where a rough stone staircase might have existed.

The construction workers didn't even look to Jacobs for instructions to go ahead, they just started pulling up stones and tossing them aside. When the third stone was pried loose, the man lifted it and prepared to heave it behind him, when he suddenly froze. There were the points of several vertebrae were sticking out of the ground.

"Edward! Thank God, we found you," Sarah exclaimed, not caring who heard her.

More stones were pulled away, and pieces of a second set of remains were discovered.

"All right, get in there and start digging," Jacobs finally yelled to his team.

Sarah let the others do the digging; it would have been too much for her to pull clumps of dirt out of his spine and eye sockets. But she stayed close, still feeling anxious…about something…very important…

"There's a box!" someone exclaimed. "He was laying over a metal box as if to protect it, and it looks intact!"

Jacobs jumped into the pit and rushed over to take charge of the potentially significant find. However, a little mutiny was brewing. The man who dug out the box wouldn't hand it over.

"No, Sarah Brooks should be the first one to look inside!" he declared.

Jacobs began to insist, but everyone in the pit rallied around the ghost hunter who had made all of this possible, and stuck to her guns so that no man would be left behind. The rest of the team in the room caught wind of what was going on, and they, too, cast their votes for Sarah. Jacobs crossed his arms, knitted his brow, swore in Latin a few times, and finally relented.

Sarah took the box in her hands as gently as if it was a newborn babe. Several people helped her out of the pit and the crowd followed her to the conservator's table. Slipping on a pair of gloves, she began to carefully work the lid off the box that had been closed the day of the battle, and shielded from the elements by its owner's body, and a stone tomb.

Using her sleeve to dab the corners of her eyes, she then gave a finally tug on lid and it came loose. Inside, there were papers, a diary, and a photograph case, all looking almost as new as the day they were made. Picking up the case, she opened it to find a tintype of a happy couple, on their wedding day. The blushing bride was only in her teens, smiling with all the confidence of invincibility felt by a youth who knew nothing of the world.

The groom was dressed in a Union officer's uniform, and his kind, yet troubled, features spoke volumes about what he had so far experienced in his young life. Sarah knew all about his hopes, his dreams, the nightmares of battles he had witnessed. She also knew his face. This was the face that had reached across the boundaries of death to touch her.

"Edward and Emma Cabot, Boston, February 1864," Sarah said, reading the inscription from the inside cover, but speaking the words as if from memory.

Then as if in a trance, Sarah picked up the diary. The first page had the signature of Captain Edward Cabot, and he had drawn a little St. Andrew's Cross to signify that he was a member of the Sixth Corps. Gently turning the pages, she found that the last entry was dated the morning of May 11, 1864.

"That's today!" Jacobs blurted out. "Today is the eleventh of May! What are the chances?"

Sarah didn't even acknowledge him as she began to read the words written on this spot, on the morning of the battle.

Last night we came upon an abandoned farmhouse. A local boy said it was Azel Wegman's place. No livestock, no food, but at least there's a roof over the heads of these poor souls. Many could not have gone any further. We pray for their recovery in this peaceful place, away from the roar and carnage of war. Billy Stanton grows weaker from the fever, but remains in good spirits.

The entry ended there. No one spoke as Sarah put down the diary and unfolded three sheets of wrinkled, bloodstained paper and continued to read.

The rebs found us this morning and a bloody fight erupted. Every man who could stand fell into line of battle. We repulsed their first attempt to cross the bridge, but on their second charge we had to fall back to the house. I watched as sick and wounded men fought like tigers, fighting hand to hand when the ammunition ran out. It was madness, nothing but complete madness as men spent their last breaths trying to take the lives of others.

I was wounded three times, grazing shots on head and neck, and a ball that went clean through my shoulder. When no one had the strength left to fight, those of us who could, helped the others into the house and barn. Dr. Maddox is doing his best to help the worst of them, but by god, there are so many.

Billy was gut shot. There's no hope. He told me to let his mother know that he faced the enemy to the end, and even though he wasn't always the best son or solider, he did his duty when it counted.

The next page was covered front and back with a list of names and regiments. At the top of one side was scribbled "To Whom it May Concern: Wegman's Crossing, May 11, 1864: U.S." and then a list of 73 names. On the back the "Rebs" numbered 64. Henkel, who had been leaning so closely over Sarah's shoulder that she could feel his breath, suddenly exclaimed, "The soldier's names! My God, he wrote down all the names of the men who fought here so that they would be remembered!"

It was an extraordinary find, arguably the most historically important one uncovered. But as much excitement as the list evoked, there was still one piece of paper left unread. Sarah motioned for quiet, and with trembling hands she prepared to read the words that had been ringing in her ears for days.

The handwriting was terrible, and it was obvious that Edward had written this page under great stress. It took a moment for her to familiarize herself with the agitated pencil strokes, but then she began.

A lamp got knocked over in the barn, and it lit up the place like a torch. A few of us who could still walk tried to get the wounded men out, but it was no use. Oh God, the screams. As long as I live I will never forget those screams. The doctor was one of our men lost in the blaze, but many brave souls perished.

I am now by Billy's side, darkness has fallen, and his breathing gets slower and slower. Some cinders from the barn blew onto the roof of the house and there was a small fire, but the boys think it's under control. Please Lord, no more death. No more screams of the dying.

There was a blank section on the page, and Sarah took a moment to wipe her eyes. The writing that followed was now scribbled in a frantic hand.

I smell smoke, there are men yelling fire upstairs. Something is blocking the cellar door, I pounded on it but it won't budge. Oh Lord, oh Lord, forgive my sins and watch over my dear sweet Emma. Let her know the comfort of your blessings, and teach her that there is good in mankind, and she should never lose faith, or hope.

Carefully folding the papers, Sarah placed them back in the box with the photograph and diary. Then she rested her head on her arm and cried as if she had just read about the death of her closest friend. Henkel knelt down and put a comforting arm around her, and used the other hand to wipe away his own tears. Even Jacobs was blubbering like a baby.

"I'm sorry, Edward," Sarah whispered. "I'm so, so sorry. But we found you, and now you can go home to Emma."

Chapter 16

After Sunday morning brunch, Sarah helped Jimmy load cases of equipment into the limo that was taking him to the airport.

"I could stay another week, you know," he said with the look of a lost puppy that almost made Sarah relent. "It's okay with my mother and the principal."

"Well, it's not okay with me," Sarah said pretending to be annoyed, and intentionally doing it badly. "You're just too smart and too clever and you're making me look bad!"

"You're just going to have to learn to live with that because when I get back to school I'm going to get so much smarter it's gonna make you sick."

"I look forward to becoming violently ill."

"Okay, but you're sure-"

"I'm sure I can handle it from here. Now get out of my sight and have a safe trip," she said, giving him a big hug and then pushing him into the car. She spoke to the driver in a voice loud enough for Jimmy to hear. "Don't let him convince you he left something at the hotel and has to come back for it. He's a compulsive liar and I don't know where he gets that from."

Ricky and the New York team were also loading up their van, and the other ghost hunters were in various stages of preparations to leave. There hadn't been so much as a blip on any instrument for days, and no reports of paranormal activity anywhere in the center. It looked as though their work was finally over.

The preliminary tally from the sites was staggering: Site #1 yielded twenty-seven sets of remains, #2 had sixty, #3 had thirty-three, and there were four at Site #4. That was a total of 124, and Captain Edward Cabot had listed the names of 137 men. It was known that at least three soldiers survived and got back to their armies. A few more may have lived, and others could have died just about anywhere on the Wegman property or surrounding woods. There was simply no way to account for everyone on the list, and it was also not certain that Edward was able to get the names of everyone who lay wounded, and dead, after the battle.

It would have been ideal to recover every soldier, but Sarah had to consider that the lightning fast recovery effort was a resounding success, honestly beyond her highest expectations. Of course, there would still be months or even years of studying the remains and artifacts, but now that they had been discovered and removed, the terrible, pervasive haunting activity was over.

Still, there was the cart incident, and no bodies had been linked to that paranormal event. She decided to drop in on Lela, who had been working twelve to sixteen hours every day since taking the helm of the center.

"Sarah, I'm so glad you're here. I was just thinking that maybe you could make some kind of appearance, and make a statement about all the ghosts being gone. You know, like a second grand opening," Lela said, hoping she wasn't pushing their friendship too far.

"And maybe cut a ribbon?" Sarah said, smiling at her own inside joke.

"Sure, maybe a blue and gray ribbon. And Dr. Henkel could be there, and the archaeologists and historians, and the Civil War organizations," Lela said as the wheels were turning.

"Sounds like a great photo op, but could we hold off a little while longer?" Sarah asked, settling into the chair in which she sat when she first arrived at the center and met with Fink and Beau. It seemed like a lifetime ago.

"Why, is there still a problem? I thought everything was back to normal," she said with a look of panic.

"Remember when the cart tried to run over Jimmy? I haven't found a suitable explanation for that. It still bugs me, and when something bugs me like that I can't let it go."

"What do you want to do, tear up the atrium!" she asked in alarm.

"No, I don't think it's in the building," Sarah said, happy to see that Lela began breathing normally again. "What do you know about the area outside that big atrium window? Anything go on there during construction, or since the center opened?"

"Nothing I can think of," Lela said slowly, trying to remember anything unusual.

"Were plans changed at any point, anything redesigned or altered?"

"I'm just not sure. I wasn't on site until the offices were almost completed."

Sarah tried to picture the view out of the atrium window. It was really a spectacular view of the woods and hills, except for those hideous modern sculptures that ringed the perimeter.

"I don't know, maybe I'm on the wrong track. It could have just been activity from one of the soldiers we recovered, but this was so different. This one was so much more angry and violent. Maybe it's just the view of those sculptures that gives me the creeps there," Sarah said laughing, rising to leave.

"Oh, I know what you mean. And they originally weren't even supposed to be there, Lela said, shaking her head.

"What do you mean? Where were they supposed to be?" Sarah asked, immediately sitting back down, feeling that little tickle on her neck.

"There was supposed to be a park and sculpture garden off the eastern parking lot, to be built this summer, and all the sculptures were in storage. Then about two weeks before the opening they started putting them around the parking lot," Lela replied, now wondering why there had been such a sudden change. "The sculpture garden was Chivington's idea. That was his baby. Why would he change it? It wasn't as if they couldn't afford it."

"Which was the first sculpture put up?" Sarah asked, eagerly anticipating the answer.

"Well, I guess it was the one you can see from the *atrium window*," Lela said with emphasis. "There must be more soldiers under there! Let's knock it down and dig it up!"

"Now is that any way for the acting manager of Wegman's Center to talk," Sarah exclaimed, appreciating the bravado, if not the prudence. "I don't have enough evidence, in fact, I don't have any evidence to warrant that. I haven't even been over there."

"Well, you're a ghost hunter aren't you? Get your instruments and meet me there in half an hour."

"Yes, Ma'am!" Sarah said, rising and saluting. "Should we also ask Dan to bring a chunk of C4 to blast the statue to bits?"

"Don't tempt me…"

Sarah was surprised to see Dan standing by the statue with Lela when she returned with some instruments. They were both circling the twelve-foot bronze as if looking at it from all sides a few dozen times might reveal some clue as to what it was supposed to represent. It looked something like an elongated onion with thin, concentric sections spiraling upward to a point.

"I give up," Sarah said getting out of the car. "What is it?"

"The plaque says, 'Children of Africa Yearning to be Free'," Lela said with an arched eyebrow. "Oh yeah, well none of *my* kids ever looked like this!"

"Beauty is in the eye of the beholder," Dan said shrugging, "You should have let me bring the C4. So, Sarah, Lela says you think there's more soldiers buried under here."

"I don't know. Ever since the night the cart tried to run over Jimmy, I've felt like there's something out here. Then Lela told me about the change of plans with the sculptures, and it just didn't smell right."

"Well, take a look over here at this one," Dan said walking toward the next sculpture over. "The base of this one is completely different."

The base of the other statue was perfectly square, carefully poured concrete, with a decorative brick border. They walked to a few more statues and the bases were all the same. However, the big onion's base was a crude, uneven slab of concrete with no border. There were even a couple of shoe impressions.

"Looks like someone was in a rush, and didn't quite know what they were doing," Lela said, the Mama Sherlock in her coming to the surface.

Sarah took out her instruments and began taking readings. There were a few fleeting abnormalities, but nothing to warrant an excavation. Still, she did sense some remnant of the anger from the night of the rampaging cart.

"I'll need to come back tonight and do a thorough investigation," she began. "There's just not enough to go on-"

"Let's do it now!" Lela exclaimed.

"Yeah, before most of the construction guys and all their heavy equipment leave tomorrow," Dan chimed in.

"Are you serious? *Right* now?" Sarah asked, not sure if they were pulling her leg. "Isn't this just a bit premature?"

"According to that list you found, there were at least 137 men here. Maybe this is where the missing ones are," Dan said.

"But why would they have even been digging here, especially once the center was done? The statue is twenty feet away from the pavement on the dirt, it doesn't make sense," Sarah said, not quite believing that she was arguing against the idea.

"Oh no, the day Sarah Brooks starts worrying about things making sense we are all in trouble!" Lela said laughing.

"Point well taken. Hey, it's your center and your sculpture, let's mess it up!" Sarah said, rolling up her sleeves.

A few of the large crates in which the statues had been shipped were still at the center, so one was brought out and placed over the big onion. A crew of about a dozen men used ropes and a backhoe to tip the statue on its side and lower it to the ground. Before the jackhammers roared into action, Lela gave a final order.

"Leave those footprints intact, they may be evidence!" she said with a dramatic flair.

The flimsy layer of concrete crumbled like stale cake, and the construction crew agreed that this was the worst job of pouring concrete they had ever seen. As they were lifting away the chunks, and angry, icy wind blew past the site.

"What the hell was that?" one of the men said, straightening up and looking at the tranquil blue sky and the tops of the trees that didn't even flutter from the slightest breeze.

Sarah's instruments were starting to fluctuate, and she warned the men to be on guard. The backhoe suddenly turned itself on and lurched forward, and three men had to jump out of the way. Dan leaped onto the machine as if jumping out of an airplane, slammed on the brake and pulled out the key. The backhoe stopped just short of going down an embankment.

"Not this again!" Dan said, jumping down and tossing Sarah the keys. "Need any more proof?"

"Hell no. Let's start digging," Sarah said, grabbing a shovel.

There was about a one-foot layer of gravel under the concrete. Once that was cleared the bare earth was exposed, and so was a terrible odor.

"Is this what you meant by something not smelling good about this place?" Dan asked, putting a handkerchief up to his nose. "This is no Civil War era gravesite."

Dan Garrison knew what death smelled like—recent death. He got on his phone to the sheriff's department and suggested that they may want to come by the center. He then ordered the crew to stop digging.

"What's wrong, what do you think is under there?" Lela asked, as the horrible odor caused her to gag.

"I'm just being cautious," Dan said calmly. "Maybe it's just a deer under there, but it certainly isn't something that died over a hundred years ago."

Sarah kept quiet and monitored her instruments. She also knew what dead bodies smelled like, as she had several opportunities to find out firsthand during

investigations. It was all beginning to make sense. This was why this particular
spirit was so different, so vengeful and potent.

Deputies "Foxbear" Drummond and Dorothy Franklin were on the scene
within minutes. They spoke quietly with Dan, then the order to resume
digging—carefully—was given.

About two feet down, one of the men uncovered a piece of heavy plastic
sheeting. The smell was nauseating, and they had to put on masks to continue.
After exposing a few more feet of plastic, Foxbear bent down and shined a
bright light on the object inside.

"We have a body," he tried to say calmly. "And it's a fresh one."

"Okay, this is now a crime scene," Deputy Franklin said, motioning
everyone away from the site and back onto the parking lot. "We had better call
Beau, I mean Sheriff Davis."

Beau Davis was taking a well-deserved day off, and after a morning of
fishing with his dad, was enjoying a pleasant lunch with his family. When his
phone rang, he was so relaxed he was tempted to throw it in the pool.

"Sheriff Davis," he answered reluctantly.

"It's Foxbear. We got ourselves a real body at the center," he said excitedly.

"Oh for God's sake, you called me for that? We found over a hundred
bodies," he replied angrily, about to hang up.

"No, Chief, it's no Civil War soldier. It's a real smelly corpse wrapped in
plastic. It's murder!"

"What? Who is it, where did you find it?" Beau asked, already on his way to
his car.

Foxbear filled him in on all the details as Beau drove toward the center.
Despite the serious nature of the situation, he couldn't resist calling Sarah's cell
phone.

"Hello, Sarah Brooks."

"Why is it wherever you go dead people turn up? You know, this was a very
peaceful county until you came along"

"Hey, if the sheriff of this jerk-water town had been doing his job, I
wouldn't *need* to be finding all these bodies."

"Oh, one these days, Ms. Brooks. One of these days!"

"Promises, promises."

By nightfall the body of a young male had been removed from the site and
sent to the coroner's office. Evidence was being collected from the crime scene,
and Lela was praised for having the insight to save the shoe prints in the
concrete. As proud as she was of her role in this discovery, she now had to
inform headquarters that on top of everything else, there was now an active
murder investigation underway at Wegman's Center.

The press was just eating it up, and Monday morning's headlines read "Dead
Center Claims Another Victim." As Sarah sat in bed reading the newspaper, she
learned that a green card found on the body identified the man as an immigrant
from Guatemala who had worked at various odd jobs throughout the northeast.
The cause of death was a broken neck, but there were also significant internal

injuries and other broken bones. Several employees at Wegman's Center remembered seeing the man working with the clean up crews a few weeks before the grand opening, but when he failed to show up for work one day, everyone just assumed he had moved on. There were no suspects.

What the paper didn't say is that Chivington had to approve of the sculptures being hastily erected around the parking lot—and therefore over the corpse of the murdered immigrant—and Fink must have had some knowledge, as well. If Sarah knew anything about Beau, she was certain he would already have their feet to the fire. She had suggested to Beau the possibility that the man had been killed in the atrium, perhaps near where the cart had gone wild. As she read the descriptions of the man's injuries, an actual fall from one of the balconies would have been sufficient to cause the broken bones and internal bleeding. The author in her even imagined the entire scenario of an intentional murder, or perhaps just an accident, being covered up by Fink and Chivington to avoid any more bad publicity.

But that was for the crime investigators to determine, not a ghost investigator. And if her final sweep of the center that night still showed no signs of paranormal activity, she would pack up and go home on Wednesday after the second grand opening ceremony. As she thought about leaving, that "post-paranormal depression" started to creep over her. From the moment she arrived, her experiences had been intense, terrifying, heartbreaking, and completely and utterly overwhelming, and she was going to miss it.

That was why Sarah Brooks was a ghost hunter.

There was also something else she was going to miss—a certain blue-eyed sheriff. With all the insanity of the last couple of weeks, she and Beau never had a chance to get together, and with the ongoing murder investigation, it looked as if they would never find the time now. That just made Sarah all the more depressed.

That night, she made a full sweep of the entire center, the four sites, and even the statue area. Nothing. Not a drop of a single degree in temperature, not the slightest fluctuation in electromagnetic fields, not a spec of light in infrared, and not a single hair stood up on the back of her neck—which was now happily free of stitches. She should have been proud of herself, but instead, she just felt very lonely.

Sarah spent all day Tuesday packing equipment to be shipped home. She had a call from Beau, and they almost were able to make a date for dinner, but at the last minute he had to conduct the interrogation of some suspects. She ended up having a nice dinner with Dr. Henkel and his wife, but it wasn't quite the same.

On Wednesday morning, Sarah got dressed in her lovely new coral suit and matching shoes—which she had bought at the center at a considerable discount—in preparation for the Wegman's Crossing Shopping, Recreation, and Historical Center's Second Grand Opening Day celebration.

There was a surprisingly large crowd in attendance when Sarah cut the blue and gray ribbon. She made a short speech, beginning with a joke about the only spirits remaining in the place being of the eighty-proof variety in the bars on the fourth floor. There was about an hour of signing autographs, then her driver arrived to say it was time to head to the airport.

There were hugs and kisses all around as she said her farewells to Henkel, Lela, and Dan. It was actually very sad to leave the people with whom she had gone through so much. It was even sadder that Sheriff Davis wasn't able to be there to say goodbye.

Before getting into the limo, Sarah turned and looked at the garish, mammoth shopping mall one last time. What had happened there would change her life forever. It would be quite an undertaking to write about it all, to adequately convey within the pages of a book all the thoughts and feelings that swept through her during the most incredible investigation of her career.

As they drove away, she already started jotting down some notes for the book. About ten minutes later, she was just finishing the outline for the first chapter when she heard the driver cursing.

"What's the matter?" Sarah asked, hoping there wasn't any mechanical trouble or a flat tire.

"I'm being pulled over," he said motioning behind them, as he eased onto the shoulder.

Sarah just assumed the driver had been speeding until she heard a familiar voice.

"We have reason to believe you are transporting a fugitive," the tall figure said to the driver. "You had better go wait in my car while I'll check it out."

The driver dutifully exited the limo and took a seat in the back of the sheriff's car. Then the back door of the limo opened, and the grinning face of Beau Davis peered in.

"So, you thought you could escape the long arm of the law!" he said, getting in and wrapping both of his long arms around her.

"I surrender. You got me," Sarah said.

There was no more speaking for several wonderful minutes. Then promises were made to keep in touch, to meet somewhere soon, to pick up where they reluctantly had to leave off. Of course, they both knew that such plans might never become a reality, but at least it made parting a little easier to take.

"Is everything okay, Ms. Brooks?" the driver asked when he returned to the car. "Are you in any trouble?"

"Oh, yes," she replied smiling. "But for a change, this is good trouble."

Chapter 17

By the time the warm, summer Massachusetts nights succumbed to the cool air of autumn, and the leaves were turning exotic shades of orange and yellow, Sarah Brooks had completed the manuscript of her latest book, *Dead Center: The Haunting of Wegman's Crossing*. Her publisher, Bernie, was practically doing back flips as pre-publication orders were already putting the book on the bestseller list. It had been the most emotional and personal book Sarah had ever written, but it had been a cathartic and healing process that had been necessary if she was to go on with her work.

She had been particularly pleased to write the epilogue, recounting the morning in June when she turned on the TV and watched as Chivington and Fink were being led away in handcuffs. Two weeks before the grand opening, there had been a fight between two of the workers at the center, and one was accidentally knocked over a railing in the atrium and fell to his death. To avoid the unpleasant publicity and legal complications over the death of a mere wandering immigrant, Fink and his uncle had organized a little late night concrete party. At least they thought enough to place a twelve-foot monument on the man's grave.

The concealing of the body of the immigrant also helped to explain why Fink had contacted Sarah in the first place. It wasn't so much the possibility of restless spirits of Civil War soldiers that really bothered him. Riddled with guilt, Fink feared that the ghost of the immigrant was after him, and he had hoped that Sarah would somehow be able to clear the center of all the spirits—without learning about his crime, of course.

Jimmy began his senior year of high school, and already had several colleges courting him. He had published a few articles about his adventures at Wegman's Center, and was now looking forward to a good education, and a career in writing. Of course, he was always on call 24-7 to assist Sarah on her cases.

With the sudden power vacuum, Lela was indeed the right person at the right place at the right time, and the new CEO of Octagon was happy to name her manager of the center. Ten minutes after receiving the good news, Fink's hideous furniture was being carted out of the office.

The four sites in the basement were undergoing a transformation into a new and very unique National Military Park. The Captain Edward Cabot Visitor's Center was also under construction at the entrance to the underground parking lot, and land was being cleared in the west woods for a cemetery, to be dedicated on May 11 of the following year.

Sarah and Beau spoke on the phone, sometimes twice a day, for the first few weeks after she left. Then it was every other day, then once a week. Between their two schedules, it had been impossible for them to get any time together.

One Friday afternoon, she decided to give in to depression, for at least a few hours, and took to lounging in her ratty old sweatpants with Mitty the bear and a box of Belgian chocolates. Then the phone rang.

"Hey, Beau, how are things?"

"I have some good news. Seems I'm hanging up my spurs and moving to Richmond."

"You're not going to be sheriff anymore? What will you be doing?"

"Well, it seems that *someone* had the ear of the Governor back in May, and he heard a lot of really good things about me. Solving the immigrant case didn't hurt my reputation either. So it looks like I'll have a nice cushy office and make a lot of money as one of the Governor's advisors."

"That's wonderful, but what will Brandon County do without its fearless and handsome sheriff?"

"I don't know about the handsome part, but I've persuaded Dan Garrison to run for the job. And people thought *I* was tough on crime!"

"Good for him. He will make a great sheriff. So, when do you make the move?" Sarah asked, not daring to hope he might take some time off.

"In a couple of weeks. I thought I would take a real vacation first…I hear Massachusetts is beautiful this time of year."

"Are you serious?" Sarah asked, practically busting at the seams.

"Absolutely serious. That is, if you Yankees don't mind entertaining someone from south of the Mason-Dixon Line."

"I think you will be quite pleased with our form of entertainment. When do you think you'll be here?"

"Let me check on a few things and I'll call you back."

Five minutes later, the phone rang again.

"Sarah, I'll be there in ten minutes," Beau said with no sign that he was joking.

"Be where? Here? My house? You…you're kidding, right?"

"No, the owner of the gas station in Duxbridge says that the lady ghostbuster's house is only ten minutes away. All the guys here say hello, too, by the way. You know, you're kind of famous around here."

"You son of a bitch! You're in Duxbridge? I haven't seen you in months and you have the nerve to give me just ten minutes before you show up on my doorstep!" Sarah said, horrified that her place was a mess and she looked like a bum.

"Okay, if you want me to turn around and drive back to Virginia-"

"No, no, no! You aren't getting away from me this time."

Sarah scrambled to make herself presentable, throw all the clothes under the bed, and push the piles of clutter into slightly neater piles of clutter. The last thing she did was to go to her website and post a special alert.

Sarah Brooks will not be available for two weeks. Maybe three if she's lucky. If you are experiencing any paranormal phenomena, just tell the dead that they can wait.

Linda Zimmermann is the author of over 20 books, including the popular *Ghost Investigator* series, highlighting her real paranormal investigations.
To explore her ghost hunting cases, go to:

www.ghostinvestigator.com

Join her Facebook Fan Page at:

http://www.facebook.com/pages/Linda-Zimmermann/116636310250

CPSIA information can be obtained
at www.ICGtesting.com
Printed in the USA
BVHW030219221121
622217BV00004B/145

9 780971 232631